CW00496491

THE
WIFE'S
MISTAKE

THE
WIFE'S
MISTAKE

LORNA DOUNAEVA

Bookouture

Published by Bookouture in 2024

An imprint of Storyfire Ltd.
Carmelite House
50 Victoria Embankment
London EC4Y 0DZ

www.bookouture.com

Copyright © Lorna Dounaeva, 2024

Lorna Dounaeva has asserted her right to be identified as the author of this work.

All rights reserved. No part of this publication may be reproduced, stored in any retrieval system, or transmitted, in any form or by any means, electronic, mechanical, photocopying, recording or otherwise, without the prior written permission of the publishers.

ISBN: 978-1-83790-563-8
eBook ISBN: 978-1-83790-562-1

This book is a work of fiction. Names, characters, businesses, organizations, places and events other than those clearly in the public domain, are either the product of the author's imagination or are used fictitiously. Any resemblance to actual persons, living or dead, events or locales is entirely coincidental.

To Denis

PROLOGUE

The wind howled. It sent chills down the police officer's spine as he approached the pool. A cherry-red Ferrari stuck out of the water like it had been dropped out of the sky. He shone his torch down into the vehicle and was met with a gruesome sight. A pale face, head thrown back against the seat; eyes that bulged with terror and mouth contorted in a silent scream. The woman's clothes clung to her body, swollen from the force of the impact, and underneath her puffy eyelids he made out faint bruises in the shape of broken blood vessels.

Her fingers had frozen around her seatbelt in a deathly grip and all around, hundreds of bank notes drifted like snowflakes from the shattered glass house behind.

An eerie sound carried through the air, like maniacal laughter, perhaps the sound of someone howling in the distance. He glanced over his shoulder. He had the feeling someone was watching from the window, even though he couldn't see a soul.

ONE

NATALIE

A rumble of conversation and laughter spilled through the open windows of Daisy's stylish townhouse. The entrance was bathed in an explosion of pink and purple, courtesy of a spectacular balloon arch.

Taking a deep breath, Natalie reached into her handbag and pulled out a tube of raspberry gloss, which she glided across her dry lips. She shook out her brown shoulder-length hair, letting each strand settle into its proper place before turning to look at her husband.

'You look like a dream,' Hayden said with appreciation.

'You too.'

Her gaze traced the outline of his navy blazer as it clung to his sinewy muscles and her eyes clouded with emotion. She forced herself to smile.

He quirked an eyebrow. 'Maybe we should skip the dinner and have our own private party back home?'

'No way. Daisy would kill us.'

The door flew open with a bang, revealing a tall, imposing figure. Ted's broad shoulders seemed to stretch all the way across the frame.

'Natalie! Hayden! So glad you made it!'

Ted welcomed them both with an enthusiastic clap on the back that almost knocked Natalie off her heels.

'Where have you been? The little lady was getting anxious.'

'We had work,' Natalie said pointedly.

They followed him into the hallway and she stopped in awe. On the table sat a glittering mountain of presents, with every colour of wrapping paper, crafted bows, and tags tied with meticulous care. It seemed as if their friends had gone all-out to outdo each other.

'I forgot to pick up the flowers.' She looked at Hayden expectantly, hoping he'd produce a bottle of wine or a box of chocolates from thin air, but he just gave a helpless shrug.

Ted rushed them past.

'Hayden, would you mind giving Daisy a hand in the kitchen? You know where everything is.'

'Er... okay, no problem.'

Natalie slipped into the living room before Ted could find her a job too. There were lots of familiar faces gathered around the long mahogany table. At the far end sat her sister, Liz. Dressed in a colourful jumper decorated with a glittery rabbit motif, she was deep in conversation with Natalie's best friend, Gail. Gail had one arm draped across the back of her chair as she nibbled thoughtfully on a breadstick. Natalie crossed the room and pulled up an extra chair.

'Budge up,' she said.

Liz and Gail moved apart so that Natalie could squeeze into the space between them. She made herself comfortable and then looked around the table expectantly.

'What have I missed?'

'Just the starters,' Liz said. 'We ate yours so Daisy wouldn't throw a fit.'

'How thoughtful of you.'

Natalie edged closer to the table, leaning forward on her

elbows. She could see her reflection in the glossy surface – face slightly pale, lips pressed tightly together.

Gail gave her arm a gentle nudge. 'You alright?'

'Yes, fine.' She managed to keep the waver out of her voice.

They watched as Daisy emerged from the kitchen with a large pan of food, her cheeks flushed as red as her hair from the heat of the oven. Hayden followed close behind, attempting – with great concentration – to balance an equally loaded tray. Meanwhile, Ted buzzed around, topping up everyone's glasses.

'I call this the Daisy Delight,' Ted said as he filled Natalie's glass with ice, then poured an orange liquid from his cocktail shaker. Natalie took a tentative sip.

'Daisy Delight: guaranteed to make you work harder,' Liz muttered under her breath.

'I don't know where she gets her energy,' Natalie said.

'Yeah, well, she's young, isn't she?' Gail replied with a small yawn.

Natalie nodded. It occurred to her she was not entirely sure how old Daisy was. She could be twenty-five. She could be thirty, but she had enough ambition and determination for all of them.

Daisy presided over the table, scooping generous servings of mashed potatoes, roasted vegetables, and her famous fried chicken onto each plate. She smiled benevolently at everyone as they dug in, waving away compliments like a proud matriarch.

'Hey, Daisy,' Ted said and gave a nod towards her left hand. Daisy beamed and extended her arm. Nestled on her third finger was a ring with the largest diamond Natalie had ever seen and Daisy glowed as all her friends huddled round to admire it.

'There's no way that's a genuine diamond,' Liz murmured. 'Ted doesn't make that kind of money.'

Natalie shot her a warning look but Gail was nodding.

'Definitely lab grown,' she agreed. 'But beautiful.'

'Tell them the story of the proposal,' someone said.

Natalie settled back in her chair as Daisy began. She talked twice as loud as a regular person, and often at twice the speed.

'It was a pretty ordinary Saturday afternoon. We were both knackered from work but we didn't want to waste the day, so Ted suggested a picnic in St James's Park. We'd spread out a blanket on the grass and we were eating sandwiches and cheese-cake. Then, out of nowhere, Ted was down on one knee. It took me a minute to clock what he was doing. He was holding out a little velvet box with the ring in it. This ring.'

She wiggled her fingers. 'Of course, I said yes. Then Ted tried to put the ring on my finger, but it was so windy we almost lost it in the breeze.'

'So, I got it on her,' Ted interrupted, 'and then we realised there was this squirrel watching us. It wouldn't take its beady eyes off Daisy. I swear it was after the ring. Or maybe it was just pissed off because I asked her first.'

Daisy looked into Ted's eyes. 'You said something when you proposed.'

All heads in the room turned to him, and a blush crept up his neck as he nodded his head. He cleared his throat and recited: 'I used to think that love was a myth until I found you; now I'm certain that it's real.'

'Aw.' Gail wiped a tear on her sleeve.

Natalie handed her a tissue. Honestly, every little thing set her off these days.

'Except that wasn't how it really happened,' Liz whispered. They leaned in conspiratorially. 'I know for a fact that Daisy picked out the ring she wanted and left the catalogue open on the page for Ted to find. And I bet she was the one who suggested a picnic. Ted strikes me as more of a barbecue in the back garden kind of bloke. As for that thing he said, I'm pretty sure that was from a greetings card.'

Natalie jabbed her in the ribs. 'I don't see anyone proposing to you.'

Daisy tucked herself into Ted's arm and kissed him gently on the cheek. Natalie felt a strange pang in her chest as she watched them. Hayden, who had been hovering in the background, stepped forward and raised his glass, signalling for everyone else to do the same.

'To Daisy and Ted – may they have many years of health and happiness together!'

Daisy shot Hayden a heartfelt smile as the room erupted in cheers. There was a clinking of glasses and an echoing back of Hayden's wish for the couple.

'I bet Daisy put him up to that too,' Liz muttered.

'Good for her,' Natalie said. 'She knows what she wants and she goes after it.'

She looked at Hayden. He looked relieved now he'd said his piece. She beckoned him over and he collapsed into the chair opposite hers. He looked exhausted, she thought. Was he just tired from work, or was it from the weight of the mental load he was carrying?

Everyone turned their attention to the food.

'It's so nice to have someone else take care of dinner for a change,' Gail said with a contented sigh.

Liz nodded. 'Say what you want about Daisy, but the girl can cook.'

The gravy boat was passed down the table. When it reached Natalie, a couple of drops splashed onto the white tablecloth. She covered the stain with her napkin.

'I have another piece of news,' Daisy said, once things had quietened down.

'You don't think she's pregnant, do you?' Gail murmured in Natalie's ear.

Natalie darted a glance at Daisy. 'No! Why?'

'Just seems like they're rushing into it. I mean, I know he's getting on a bit but she's still so young.'

'Well, they're in love.'

The clink of silverware and the clatter of dishes filled the air as Ted moved around the table, refilling everyone's glasses. When Daisy was satisfied everyone was listening, she rose to her feet again.

'So, my other news is that I've been promoted.'

Hayden dropped his fork. 'Again?'

'That's right; I'm now a member of the senior management team.'

Hayden gritted his teeth as he tried to muster a smile. He and Daisy both worked in the hotel industry. They'd been at the same level when they first met, but while Hayden hadn't received a promotion in five years, Daisy kept rising through the ranks.

'Do you get your own office?' Hayden asked.

Daisy nodded.

'I hope you got a nice pay rise too?' Liz probed.

'Fifty per cent,' Daisy said into her knuckles. That caught everyone's interest.

'Fifty per cent! That's fantastic,' Liz said.

'God, what I wouldn't do with a pay rise like that,' Hayden said. 'I'd definitely get a new car.'

'I'd pay off my credit card bills,' Liz said.

'No, you wouldn't,' Natalie cut in. 'You'd spend it all on your cats.'

Gail let out an enormous yawn and covered her mouth with her hand.

Daisy shot her a sharp look. 'Keeping you up?'

'Sorry, I don't get much sleep these days.'

Daisy's expression softened. She leaned in to give Gail a hug.

'Thank you so much for coming,' she murmured in Gail's ear.

Gail turned pink. 'Oh, I wouldn't miss it!'

Natalie wondered if Gail ever regretted having Scarlett; her life was so different now. She must miss the spontaneity of a weekend away, or the ability to duck out to the shops without having to first bundle her baby into the car.

Liz turned her gaze to Hayden.

'How was Manchester?' she asked, her voice low and inquisitive.

Hayden shrugged. 'It was alright.'

Liz continued to watch him, her gaze roving over him like a searchlight.

'My presentation went down well,' he elaborated. 'A couple of people even laughed at my jokes.'

Natalie nudged him. 'Didn't you say someone fell asleep?'

'Yes, that's also true,' he said with a smile.

Liz reached for her drink. 'Sounds a hoot.'

Natalie toyed with her chicken, pushing it around the plate and separating the white and dark meat.

As soon as she set down her fork, the plates were passed up the table and an enormous pavlova appeared – a mountain of glossy meringue, dotted with ripe raspberries. Natalie didn't much care for pavlova but she accepted a plate without a word. All was quiet as everyone dug in, but it was only a matter of time before the singing began. When Daisy had had a few drinks, she always got into the mood for a sing-song.

Natalie nudged Gail. 'You've fallen asleep again.'

Gail jerked her head up. 'What? No, I'm fine.'

'Can I borrow your charger?' Liz asked.

In the time it took Natalie to pluck it out of her handbag and pass it to her, Gail had leaned forward on her elbow and nodded off again.

'Maybe I should drive her home?' Hayden suggested.

'No, she doesn't get out much. She should be having fun,' Natalie said. 'Make her a cup of coffee. That'll do the trick.'

Hayden nodded and headed back down the hall. When he returned with the coffee a few minutes later, they had moved the table against the wall to make more room for people to mingle. Natalie woke Gail who sat up and rubbed her eyes as she tried to focus on what was happening.

Ted reached up and spun the dimmer switch around. Multicoloured spots of light blossomed from the walls, illuminating the room in a kaleidoscope of colour. He put on some music and the bass throbbed through the speakers. It wasn't long before Hayden excused himself again.

'Where did he get to now?' Liz asked.

'I think he's doing the washing up,' Natalie said.

Liz smirked.

'What?' Natalie said.

'He's barely sat down all night. You'd think he was the maid.'

Ted brought out a fresh cocktail, served inside a large pineapple with two straws.

Liz and Natalie moved forward to sample it.

Gail pulled out her phone to capture the moment.

Natalie held the pose, forcing a smile, whilst Liz raised an eyebrow sardonically. Daisy glanced over at that moment and moved into the frame behind them to blow a kiss. Gail put her phone away and Natalie let Liz finish the drink while she watched Daisy and Ted perform a rock 'n' roll dance routine they had obviously prepared. Everybody clapped and cheered, then some of the other guests got up to join the dancing. Natalie wasn't in the mood, but Liz hauled her to her feet.

'This is a party,' she reminded her. 'You should at least pretend you're having fun. Daisy's gone to a lot of effort.'

Natalie felt like she was in a trance as she headed for the middle of the room. Her body swayed to the beat but she wasn't really feeling it. Fortunately, all eyes were on Daisy, who moved with a wild abandon.

Natalie gave up after two songs. Her skin glistened with sweat and she rubbed the back of her neck.

'Let's go outside for a minute,' she suggested to Liz. 'It's way too hot.'

They shuffled their way through the crowd and burst out onto the cool lawn. There were a couple of people smoking by the shed so Natalie and Liz wandered further up the garden.

'Where have you hidden it?' Liz asked in a hushed voice.

Natalie glanced around furtively. 'Not here.'

'Come on, let's just get this over with. If you give it to me, I'll deal with it.'

'No, it's fine. I'll do it. I just need to be sure first.'

Liz pressed her lips together. 'How long is that going to take?'

'I don't know, alright?' She clenched her teeth, frustration radiating from her body. 'I don't want to jump to any conclusions.'

'Sounds to me like you already have.'

They stood in the stillness of the garden while inside, the party buzzed with life.

Liz stared at her for a moment, her expression unreadable in the faint light from the windows, but Natalie would not back down.

The breeze picked up, raising goosebumps on her bare arms. She stood taller and met Liz's gaze unflinchingly. 'I'm going back inside.'

They stopped in the kitchen to refresh their drinks. Liz took a large, purple jug off the counter while Natalie found two glasses. Natalie peered into it. The liquid inside was cloudy and filled with floating grapes and blackberries. She took a whiff but couldn't place the smell. Liz poured and they each lifted a glass to their lips. On the first sip, Natalie felt a wave of heat wash over her. She didn't know what Ted had put in his latest cocktail but it tasted potent.

'Nat, we should get going,' Hayden said when they met him in the hallway. He still had a dishtowel slung over one shoulder.

Daisy shot into the hallway as if she had heard fire crackle at the end of Hayden's sentence. 'Already?'

Hayden nodded and shot her an apologetic look. 'We have to be up early for work tomorrow. You know how it is.'

'You should have swapped shifts with someone.'

'I tried,' Hayden said.

Natalie nodded in agreement, although in her case it wasn't technically true.

'I just need to pop to the loo,' she told Hayden. 'Can you find our coats?'

She slipped into the bathroom and was immediately struck by a familiar splotch of paint on the radiator. Sometimes she forgot that Daisy's house had once been Hayden's too. She could tell he had painted this bathroom. It was the same yellow shade as theirs. He had probably used the same tin of paint. If she looked up, she would probably find another splotch in the shape of a handprint on one of the exposed beams over her head.

She came out to find Gail waiting. 'Can you and Hayden give me a lift?'

'Of course. Do you want to say goodbye to Daisy?'

'No, I think it's easier if I sneak out. That way she can't interrogate me about why I'm leaving or why I gave her such a crap present.'

'At least you remembered the present.'

Hayden had made the mistake of doing the rounds. He thanked Ted profusely for the party and was running the Daisy gauntlet again. Once he returned to the hallway, Natalie grabbed him by the arm. They could all hear Daisy's great booming laugh from the other room.

'Go! Go! Go!' she hissed, as she, Hayden and Gail ran giggling towards the door.

'Wait for me!' yelled a voice behind them.

Natalie turned to see Liz hopping down the steps with one shoe on. This set them all off laughing again.

'What happened to you?'

'She tried to make me sing karaoke!'

'Right then, everyone into the car or we're all for it,' Hayden said.

They all piled in, squeezing in like sardines. The engine grumbled to life once, twice... but refused to start. Hayden cursed and smacked his palm against the dashboard. A cloud of smoke billowed out from the bonnet, making everyone cough and splutter. Hayden seemed unfazed. He restarted the engine, and they peeled off into the night.

Gail's house was first. Natalie gave her an exhausted wave as she climbed out of the car.

Hayden kept the engine running as they watched her totter up the garden path, still giggling as she located her keys and let herself into her house.

Hayden drove round the corner, stopping outside the garages.

'Cheers,' Liz said, rummaging around for her handbag.

Natalie passed it across the back seat to her. Liz took it, then wrapped her arms around her sister in a bone-crushing embrace. Fresh tears pricked Natalie's eyes as she clung to her.

'Let me know if you change your mind,' Liz whispered as they pulled apart.

TWO

NATALIE

Three Weeks Earlier

Natalie hurried up the Thames path towards the Riverside Café. She stopped beside a bucketful of wet umbrellas to throw on her apron and tie the strings behind her back. Already she smelt the intoxicating aroma of coffee, fresh bread and bacon.

She hurried inside, heading behind the counter and slotting into place beside Mason.

'Morning,' she called out cheerfully.

Mason did not reply. He bent over the countertop, eyes focused intently on what he was doing. His movements were robotic as he ground beans, poured milk and sprinkled chocolate shavings.

'What have I missed?' she asked.

'You were supposed to clean the coffee machine. I did it for you.'

'Thanks. I owe you one.'

'And the till keeps rejecting credit cards. Just the ones with the picture of the bear on the front. I think the problem might be with their bank.'

She nodded. Mason's voice was low and indiscernible, but he never spoke louder, no matter how many times he had to repeat himself. Their boss, Jan, made out that he was mysterious, but Natalie simply found him odd.

She got to work, taking orders at the counter.

'Like the tie,' she told one of the regulars.

He looked pleased. 'Thank you, I wasn't sure about the colour.'

'The pink suits you,' she assured him. 'That shade is really in at the moment.'

'Natalie, stop chatting,' Jan hissed in her ear. 'It's bad enough you were late.'

'Slave driver,' Natalie muttered under her breath.

The customers didn't just want a coffee and a sandwich. They came in for a smile and a laugh. A bit of banter. That was what it was all about.

As the morning rush subsided, Jan went off on her break and Natalie ground some of the fancy beans for herself.

'Want some?' she asked Mason. He shook his head furiously, as if she'd suggested they help themselves to the till.

Heat hissed from the spout as she frothed the milk, and she watched golden bubbles rise to the top of her cup. As it was quiet, she carried it over to one of the tables and gazed out the window. The sun had come out now and the rain glittered like silver coins as it fell into the river. She sipped her coffee and allowed herself a moment to indulge in one of her favourite fantasies: owning a café of her own.

She pictured her friends lounging in comfortable armchairs, sipping creamy cappuccinos and lattes, savouring every sip of their free drinks. The Riverside Café would have nothing on 'Natalie's'.

She was saving towards it, although she never managed to accumulate much. But she had faith in her plan. It was meant to be.

She was aware of Mason's dark eyes, boring into her from across the counter. He didn't like it when she broke the rules, but he never snitched to Jan. Just as she'd kept quiet that time he'd dropped a crate full of cups. She'd helped him hide the broken china in the outside bin. They weren't friends, but they kept each other's secrets.

He tapped his watch, signalling that Jan was due back. Natalie scraped back her chair and carried her cup over to the dishwasher. A moment later, Jan walked back in. Her long grey hair had frizzed up in all directions. Jan was probably only ten years or so older than Natalie but every one of those extra years was etched into her face like the rings around a tree.

'Hi, Jan,' Natalie called out to her.

Jan's lips curled in a sneer. She walked through to the store-room but a moment later she came steaming out.

'Natalie, can I have a word?'

Mason shot her a worried look. Jan beckoned her into the kitchen and pulled out one of the cartons Natalie had stocked the fridge with.

'What's this?'

'Er... milk?'

'Look at the date on it.'

Natalie looked and saw that it was two weeks past its best. 'Oh.'

'Do you want to make the customers ill?'

'No, I—'

'How did you let this happen? You're supposed to check and double-check. Tell me, Natalie, are you a halfwit?'

'No. I...'

She had checked. At least, she'd checked the first few cartons. How was she to know the others had a different date on them?

Jan continued to rant, but Natalie tuned her out. She wasn't sure she liked those new coffee beans. They'd left a bitter taste on her tongue.

'Are you even listening to me?'

'Yes, Jan.'

Jan threw up her hands and stormed off, leaving Natalie to dispose of the out-of-date stock. While she was doing so, a stout man in a smart suit stopped just outside the kitchen door. His bald patch gleamed under the light as he peered inside.

'Just wanted to say, that was the best cheese and ham panini I've ever had. The coffee was delicious too.'

Natalie smiled at the praise. 'Thank you. Don't forget to tell all your friends.'

She laid low for the rest of the shift, clearing dishes, and wiping down tables. Time dragged like never before, and all she wanted was to escape home to Hayden. Finally, Jan tapped her on the shoulder.

'Alright, you can go now. If you want to get back in my good books, get here ten minutes early tomorrow, okay?'

Natalie forced a smile and hurried out the door. She made it to the end of the street before she realised she'd forgotten her umbrella. Cars splashed through muddy puddles and she arrived at the bus stop soaked to the skin. Her hair dripped in spirals around her face. To make matters worse, she could see her bus driving away. She would have to wait twenty minutes for the next one.

There was a small newsagent nearby. She trudged towards it and pushed open the door. The bell jingled as she entered, and the man behind the counter smiled. She selected a bar of chocolate.

'Anything else?'

'And a lottery ticket, please.'

His eyes danced with merriment. 'Feeling lucky today, eh?'

She smiled politely and selected her numbers.

He waggled his eyebrows at her. 'If you win, we will run off to Paris together, yes?'

Ugh, in your dreams, she thought but she offered him a tight smile.

An hour later, Natalie's damp coat clung to her body as she stepped off the bus, her shoes squelching through murky puddles that had formed in the grey evening. She shivered violently, her teeth chattering against the cold that had seeped into her very bones.

'Hayden?' she called, as she let herself into their flat.

She was met by silence. With a sinking feeling, she remembered he was on a pub crawl.

She was desperate to take a warm shower to thaw her frozen limbs, but when she turned on the tap, only a trickle of icy water greeted her. Deflated, she changed into some faded grey jogging bottoms and padded into the living room, but there was nowhere to sit. The sofa overflowed with wrinkled laundry.

She grabbed a pile of bedsheets and plugged in the iron, watching it steam softly against the fabric as it moved over each crease and wrinkle. As she stretched and folded the sheets, her eyes flicked to the TV – the lottery numbers were being drawn.

Number seventeen. That was Hayden's birthday. She reached for the smart black skirt she had just changed out of. She only had the one work uniform and she refused to fork out for a second. The next number was thirty-one, her birthday. A tingle ran up her spine, but she ignored it and rammed the iron back and forth over the stiff material. The stubborn crease refused to co-operate, so she tossed it onto the sofa and picked up one of Hayden's T-shirts. She liked the way he looked in this one. It was loose on the neck and tight on the sleeves. Seven, the date of their wedding anniversary. Her grip on the iron tightened. She was pressing down a little too hard. Fourteen, her cousin Oliver's birthday. Twenty-six, her sister's birthday. She wiped the back of her head. Four, the number on their door.

Her throat ran dry, and her heart was pumping out of her chest. Just one more number to go.

'Thirteen,' she rasped. 'Say thirteen.'

The presenter looked directly at her and winked. 'And unlucky for some, number thirteen.'

Her knees knocked together as she released her grip on the iron. With shaking hands, she looked around for her handbag. She tipped the contents out onto the floor and found a hair-brush, a pack of gum and a little book of textile samples. There was the ticket. She inspected it. No, this was last week's. No, no, no, this could not be happening. She shook the bag again, but nothing else came out. How could that be? She checked the inside pocket and found nothing but contraceptive pills. Then, in a flash of inspiration, she rose to her feet and raced over to the coat stand. She grabbed her jacket off the hook and turned out every pocket until at last, she found the little slip of paper. She checked the date, then she checked the numbers. Her chest prickled and her breath became shallow. She had the sensation of being caught in the swirl of a tremendous wave. Nausea swarmed her stomach, then her vision tunnelled as she collided with the floor.

THREE

NATALIE

Her throat felt like she'd been gargling gravel. Her eyes itched and the threadbare carpet irritated her face. A high-pitched whine filled her ears. Her whole body vibrated with the sound. She uncoiled from the unnatural position she was lying in and noticed a dark wispy trail that wound upwards, disappearing into her landlord's ugly orange lampshade.

She caught a whiff of burning polyester and grabbed hold of the sofa to pull herself up. It was hard to think with all that incessant beeping. She forced her eyes to focus. The iron was face down on the ironing board, and smoke was coming from whatever was smouldering underneath. She picked it up and set it back down in its cradle. Her eyes watered as she flicked off the power.

The smoke alarm was still blaring. She grabbed the broom and whacked it until bits of debris fell from the ceiling. One by one, the batteries dropped to the ground and rolled under the sofa. None of the neighbours banged on the door or asked if she was alright. She could set the entire building alight before any of them got off their arses.

Her eyes drifted back to the TV, which was now showing a

documentary about the life cycle of lobsters. Where was the ticket? She looked down and spotted it, discarded on the floor like a piece of rubbish. It must have slipped from her hand when she fell. She picked it up and read the numbers three times then leaned back against the arm of the sofa.

She found the lottery site on her phone. If this was correct, then she'd won twelve and a half million pounds. Twelve and a half million! She pictured Hayden's face when she told him. She hoped he wouldn't have a heart attack. She'd heard of it happening. People got the best news of their life, then collapsed dead on the floor before they even got their hands on the money.

Still a little shaky, she staggered towards the kitchen. She had some cooking wine in the fridge. She found a glass and filled it all the way to the brim. It tasted sour, but she drank it anyway. Her heart fluttered like a bird in her chest. She should go into town and surprise Hayden. She took three steps towards the door before she changed her mind. No way she could drive, not in this state. Instead, she went into the bathroom and splashed some cold water onto her face. As she brought her head up, she glimpsed someone watching her in the mirror. Her stomach dropped and her limbs locked in place. She whirled round and felt an instant flood of relief. She burst out laughing. Hayden had a thing for Megan Fox, so she'd bought him a poster for his birthday. She had forgotten he'd pinned it to the back of the bathroom door.

She returned to the living room and sank into the armchair. Liz answered her call on the second ring. Her face filled the screen, then she zoomed out to show her elderly cat, Marmite, on the sofa beside her, licking his paw.

'Liz, you're never going to believe this!' Natalie paused for dramatic effect. 'I've only gone and won the lottery!'

Liz's face barely flickered. 'I'm having carbonara, wanna see?'

The camera lunged with such speed that Natalie had the sensation of falling face down into her sister's dinner.

'Did you hear what I said? I won the lottery!'

The camera returned to Liz's face.

'How much?'

'Twelve million, according to the web.'

Liz shrieked. Natalie shrieked. Marmite shot off the sofa in alarm.

Liz fell silent for a moment, then she said, 'Let's go to Australia! Or America! We could do a world cruise!'

Her eyes shone with excitement as she considered the possibilities.

'I want to open a coffee shop.'

'You still want to do that?'

'Since I was seven.'

'You won't even have to work anymore.'

'This would be different. I'd be my own boss.'

'What about the Riverside Café?'

'Fuck the Riverside Café,' Natalie said with glee. 'I won't even bother to call. I just won't show up tomorrow.'

'You're wasting a golden opportunity. You get to tell old sour face what you think of her.'

'You're right!' Natalie rubbed her hands together. 'I will go in. I'll enjoy it.'

'What about Hayden? Is he going to resign too?'

'I don't know. You're the first person I've told.'

'I'm honoured. Think of me once in a while when you're living the high life.' Liz stuffed some spaghetti into her mouth.

'You'll be getting your share, don't you worry.'

'When do you actually get the money in the bank?'

'I'm not sure. I haven't called the hotline yet.'

'Are you crazy? I'm going to hang up right now while you call.'

Before Natalie could say another word, Liz was gone.

Natalie stared at her phone, the screen reflecting the anticipation in her eyes. Her finger hovered over the button like a bee
about to dive into the sweet depths of a lily. Then she thought
of Hayden and how much more special the moment would be if
he were there with her. Eventually, she let out an exasperated
sigh and placed her phone back down again, determined to wait
until he could experience it too. A smile crossed her lips – no
matter what happened next, both their lives were about to
change forever.

Three hours later, she sat in the same armchair with a fresh
glass of wine in her hands. Still no champagne, as the occasion
really demanded, but this was the best she could muster from
the local takeaway. She had food too, because her sister's
spaghetti had actually looked rather good, but she hadn't been
able to manage more than a few forkfuls. She found it hard to
keep still. Every so often, she would jump up from her chair and
dance around the room. She had already checked her ticket a
dozen times and still couldn't believe her luck. She had never
won anything before, and yet she'd kept buying tickets, because
she'd always had a feeling, deep in her bones, that she was on
the verge of something amazing.

Setting her glass down, she wiped her sweaty palms on her
shirt. She had her laptop open in front of her as she scoured the
internet for potential sites for her café. It would be a coffee
shop, she'd decided. She wasn't looking for anything too fancy,
just a small cosy building, preferably close to home so all her
friends and family could pop in. Everyone would love her coffee
shop. Not only would she serve the best coffee and cakes in the
whole of London, but she would create a lovely, warm
atmosphere. It would be nothing like the run-of-the-mill places
she saw on every high street. Nothing like the Riverside Café.
Natalie's would be special.

She glanced at the time. Hayden was probably waiting for
the night bus. She wanted to call and tell him to take a taxi, but

he'd think that was too extravagant. They didn't have that kind of money. Not before tonight. She just hoped he hadn't had too much to drink. She could hardly give him life-changing news if he was off his head.

She was surprised to hear a key in the door. Hayden's cheeks were pink from the cold, his dark blond hair a little damp. She rose to her feet and waited as he shook out his umbrella; his cool blue eyes met hers with clear focus.

'Hey, babe! Told you I wouldn't be late.'

He leaned in for a kiss and she unwound the scarf from his neck. She hopped from foot to foot while he kicked off his boots.

'I'll just be a mo,' he said, disappearing into the bathroom.

She fizzed with anticipation as she thought about how she was going to break the news.

'Hayden, you know that Ferrari you've always wanted?'

His phone beeped, then beeped again.

'Could that be work?' she asked. Occasionally, Hayden got calls from the nightshift, when they couldn't figure something out for themselves. She dug into his coat pocket to retrieve the phone. A message popped up on the screen:

Phillip just got on my bus. I'm keeping my head down. Hopefully, he won't see me.

It was from someone called Vivienne.

She glanced down at the next message. It was also from Vivienne:

He's chundered all over some poor old dear. She's screaming at him and clobbering him with her stick. Uh oh, the driver's stopped the bus. This is hilarious. Wish you were here!

Vivienne's third message included a blurred picture. She could make out bus seats and the back of someone's head.

Phillip's been thrown off the bus! I should really get off and see if he's okay, but no thanks. We're in the middle of fuck knows where and I'm not getting stranded with that bellend. He can call himself an Uber. Oh, and Hay, since you were so sweet paying for my drinks, I'm buying the coffees on Monday. It's only fair, babe.

Natalie's skin prickled. Why was she calling her husband 'babe'? And why was he paying for her drinks? She heard the toilet flush, and dropped the phone like it was hot. Her head spun as she bent down to pick it up. Quickly, she marked the messages as 'unread' and shoved it back into his pocket.

She knew who Phillip was. Hayden worked with a Phillip. He was the bellboy, wasn't he? But she'd never heard the name 'Vivienne'. By the sound of these messages, she and Hayden must be close. So why had he never mentioned her?

An unsettling feeling passed through her, like invisible hands around her neck. She leant against the wall, skin tingling as she fought to stay calm. Hayden came out of the bathroom and headed straight to the kitchen. She followed.

'Is there anything to eat?'

'There's spaghetti carbonara.'

She produced the plastic container.

'You ordered takeaway without me?'

He furrowed his brow. Takeaway was an expense they could rarely afford. Natalie opened her mouth to explain but the words caught in her throat. What would he do if she told him they were rich? Would he take her to Paris, like that shop-keeper had suggested, or would he take his half of the money and run off with Vivienne?

'I... was FaceTiming Liz. She was eating carbonara. It looked so delicious I couldn't resist. I saved some for you.'

She picked up the container before he could argue and put it in the microwave.

'Thanks.'

They watched as it spun in circles.

'Had a good night?'

'Can't complain.'

She leaned against the counter. Perhaps that wine hadn't been such a good idea; her head throbbed.

'Who were you out with?'

'Oh, you know, the usual gang.'

'Was Phillip there?'

'Yeah. He follows us around like a bad smell.'

'And what about' – she tried the name out on her tongue – 'Vivienne?'

He kept his eyes on the microwave. 'Yeah, she was there for a bit.'

He hadn't seemed concerned that she'd brought up Vivienne. Perhaps he hadn't realised he'd never mentioned her before.

'Did you go down the Gun?'

'Yeah.'

'The George?'

'No, it was heaving. Why are you so interested?'

Natalie examined her fingernails. 'I might have to organise a pub crawl for my work.'

'Thought you hated them all?'

'I do.'

The microwave pinged. She pulled out the carbonara and gave it a stir. 'Careful, it's hot.'

He put it on a tray and carried it down the hall to the living room where he flopped down on the sofa. A slasher movie was playing on TV.

'What were you watching?'

'I wasn't really paying attention.' She shut her laptop. She didn't want to share the research she'd done on her coffee shop. Not until she knew more about Vivienne.

'Was it fun tonight?' she asked.

'It was alright.'

'Did Phillip get off with anyone?'

He howled with laughter. 'Not bloody likely.'

'What about Vivienne?'

He yawned widely and reached over her for the remote.

'Sorry, I need to catch the football highlights.'

She snatched it away.

He looked at her, startled.

'I haven't seen you all day. We should catch up.'

'Right.' He had that look about him, like he knew he'd done something wrong but didn't know what.

'So, what do you want to talk about?'

She scoured her mind for a way to ask about Vivienne without telling him she'd read his text messages. She came up blank.

'Never mind. I'm going to bed. You watch your football.'

He looked like he thought it was a trick. 'If you're sure?'

'Goodnight, Hayden.'

She rose from the sofa and took a step towards the door.

'Hey, wait!'

She turned and looked at him.

'Aren't you forgetting something?'

'I...'

He lifted a hand and reached out for her. 'Sorry if I'm a bit beery. I do appreciate all you do for me.' He indicated the carbonara. 'You're the best, Nat.'

She blinked and the lottery numbers danced before her eyes.

'See you in bed.'

Upstairs, she wandered into the bathroom and unzipped her washbag. Her make-up felt heavy on her skin and she couldn't wait to scrub it all off. As she pulled out her toner, the doorbell chirped.

She stopped in her tracks. Who would that be at this time of night? Probably one of the neighbours come to complain about where they'd parked the car. Well, they had just as much right to those parking spaces as anyone.

Then her sibling intuition kicked in. Oh God. Liz. She was going to give the game away.

'I'll get it!' she yelled. She raced down the stairs and flung open the door, shoving her sister out into the corridor before she could set off the party popper in her hand.

'Put that away!'

'What?'

Liz still didn't get it. 'Thought I'd help you celebrate!'

'Shush!'

Natalie checked inside, but Hayden was still in the living room. She hoped to God he hadn't heard.

'What's going on?' Liz asked.

Natalie shut the door gently behind her and gestured down the hall towards the communal post rack.

'He had a message on his phone from some woman called Vivienne. They seem very close.'

Liz scratched her neck. 'Could be a mate?'

'Then why has he never mentioned her?'

'So, you haven't told him?'

'And I'm not going to. Not until I know for sure. I'm not funding him to run off with another woman.'

'Okay – so what about the money?'

She sighed. 'According to the website, I've got 180 days to claim it, so I'm going to sit tight for a bit.'

'Are you serious?'

'I really need to know.'

Liz held out her hand. 'Give me the ticket and I'll claim it. If the money's in my bank account, he won't have any claim to it.'

'No, I'll wait. I just need to be sure.'

'Are you out of your mind? If anything happens to that ticket...'

'Don't worry, I've put it somewhere safe.'

'Where?'

She put her fingers to her lips. 'It's safe.'

Liz looked unsatisfied and Natalie felt a twinge of annoyance. 'I am a grown woman. I know what I'm doing.'

Liz's eyes widened. 'Of course you do. I'm just worried about you, that's all. You and Hayden have only been married five minutes. If you think he's already...'

'It's been a year, and I didn't have any cause for concern before tonight.'

'Didn't you? Why did you look at his messages then?'

'I... I don't know.'

'Right, well you'll have to do what you think's best. Just don't leave it too long. If I was you, I'd get it over with. Just ask him, Nat. See what he says.'

'Maybe.'

'Alright, well I'll speak to you tomorrow.'

'Yeah, bye.'

Natalie wasn't really listening. Her mind was still on Hayden and those messages.

She stepped back indoors and closed the door softly behind her. There was a creak as it clicked into place. She turned to see Hayden watching her, curiously.

'Who was at the door?'

'Liz.'

'What did she want?'

She felt herself being sucked into the orbit of his eyes.

'She's been to the theatre. She was in the mood for a chat, but I told her I was tired.'

'What did she see?'

'Uh?'

'At the theatre.'

'Oh, I don't know. She didn't say.'

'Couldn't have been very good then. We going to bed?'

'I thought you were watching the football?'

He moved closer. 'I'll come to bed if you make it worth my while.'

He wrapped his arms around her shoulders. She felt the heat of his body, but she couldn't. Not now.

Go on, say it, she dared herself. *Ask him*. But she couldn't force the words from her lips. *What if he admitted he was in love with her? What the hell was she going to do?*

'Babe, I'm knackered.'

'Are you sure I can't persuade you?'

His hands moved to the nape of her neck. Her body tingled. Was it her he wanted, or was he frustrated after his night out with Vivienne?

'I really have to sleep.'

'Okay then.'

He withdrew a little abruptly, his feet thudding on the floorboards as he backed away. She trudged up the creaking wooden stairs and lay down on the bed. She pulled the winning lottery ticket from her pocket and tucked it under her pillow like an offering to the tooth fairy. No, it didn't feel safe there. She pulled it out and stuck it inside her phone case instead. That would have to do for now. She'd find a better place for it in the morning.

FOUR

NATALIE

She lay awake, long after Hayden came to bed, and stared into the gloom. What else had Vivienne been messaging her husband about? Did he message her with every little thought that came into his head? He used to text Natalie like that all the time, when they first got together. Their communications had dwindled in recent months. She had thought little of it; they both worked such long hours.

Hayden gave a little grunt as she rolled out of bed. She went to his nightstand and unplugged his phone from the charger. He let out a little sigh, then resumed his rhythmic breathing. She crept towards the door and stood there for a moment, watching him. Even in the darkness, she could make out the perfect curve of his lips.

Down in the living room, she switched on his phone. To her disappointment, she found it was locked. He must have been using his phone just before he walked in the door earlier. That's why it had been unlocked. She tried to guess the code but gave up after a few attempts. She resisted the urge to hurl it across the room.

Exasperated, she made herself a cup of coffee and sipped it

while she scoured her husband's social media. She found profiles for several colleagues, including the unfortunate Phillip. She clicked on each one looking for the mysterious Vivienne but there was no sign of her. Perhaps she was new. Or perhaps she was too cool for Facebook.

For all she knew, she was getting her knickers in a twist over a woman old enough to be her grandmother, but she didn't think so. Those messages had a younger vibe.

What on earth was she going to do? She should be on top of the world right now. Instead, she was barely holding it together.

When morning came, she lay back against the pillows while Hayden sang to himself in the shower. He emerged damp and tousled, with droplets of water in his eyelashes. If she looked too deeply into those blue eyes, she would fall for him all over again.

'Are you okay, Nat? You look really spaced.'

'I didn't sleep well,' she told him.

Ask me why, she begged him silently, but he turned and wriggled into his uniform of smart navy trousers and a button-down shirt.

'Hadn't you better get going?' he asked, as he slipped his watch onto his wrist.

'I will, in a minute.'

Wind rattled the windows and the rain left dirty streaks that looked like bony fingers against the glass. She hauled herself out of bed and dressed for work, not caring that she wasn't wearing the regulation skirt, or that her shoes had heels. It wasn't like she planned to put in a full shift. Once Hayden left, she slipped the lottery ticket into an empty baked bean can and hid it at the back of the pantry. It seemed like a safe place. Even if burglars broke in, they wouldn't think to look there.

Hayden had further to travel, so he always took the car, leaving her to the vagaries of public transport.

She walked through the communal hallway and opened the door, stepping out into a raging downpour. The force of the rain was so strong that it bounced off the pavement, creating a fine spray that clung to the streetlamps and illuminated them in a soft glow.

A shudder ran through her body as she searched through her bag for an umbrella, only to find nothing but a few crumpled tissues. She cursed under her breath. She must have left it at work again. She was going to be drenched before she even reached the bus stop.

Perhaps she should call in sick? No, wait. Money was no object, right? She would call an Uber. Smiling to herself, she darted back inside.

The Uber was late, but she didn't sweat it. She felt a jolt of schadenfreude as they passed the sodden queue at the bus stop. One woman had a newspaper over her head to keep the rain off. Another was clutching a soaking wet textbook. Poor suckers. She sat back and thought about what she was going to say to Jan. Whatever she thought of sounded ridiculously cheesy. No matter, she'd find the right words when she got there. She couldn't wait to see the look on Jan's face. Would she scream? Would she stamp her foot like a toddler? Would she lunge at her? She hoped not. Jan could be a little feisty. She'd never dared cross her before. She couldn't afford to.

When they pulled up outside the Riverside Café, she tipped the driver ten pounds. He broke into a big gummy smile.

'Thank you. You have a great day, madam!'

'You too!'

Despite the rain, the pavement tables were crammed with customers sipping frothy coffees and nibbling flaky croissants. The awning snapped in the wind, threatening to blow away and drench the lot of them. Mason came out, carrying a tray of hot sandwiches, which he delivered to one of the tables. He turned to look at her with dead eyes. Was he annoyed she was late? She could never tell with him.

Jan appeared in the doorway. Natalie's heart raced. This was it. The big moment.

'Natalie. Nice of you to show your face at last. Don't think I'm paying you for the first half hour. You can daydream on your own time.'

Natalie took a step towards her, but Jan had already turned back towards the kitchen.

'Jan, I'd like a word please.'

Jan spun around. Natalie met her with what she hoped was a steely look. Jan sensed the change in her demeanour. She looked her up and down.

'What do you want? You better not be bloody pregnant.'

Natalie kept her voice steady. 'No, it's not that. I... I resign.'

Jan's nostrils flared with indignation.

'With immediate effect. So sorry, I won't be working this morning.'

'You have to give a month's notice.'

'No thanks.'

Jan took a step towards her. 'You have to, or I won't give you a reference, you silly girl.'

Natalie forced out a laugh. Was she really doing this? She felt like an actor in a movie. She projected her voice.

'I really couldn't give less of a fuck.'

She felt all eyes on her. Nobody was drinking coffee anymore.

Jan pinched her lips together tightly. 'Come on, we're already understaffed.'

'Then you should have been nicer to me. You're the worst boss I've ever had. You made me work Christmas three years in a row, and you haven't given me a pay rise since you took over. So no, Jan. I won't let you tell me what to do ever again.'

Her voice quivered slightly, but she didn't care. She was doing this.

She waited for the fireworks. Instead, Jan's eyelids grew heavy. Her jaw slackened and her shoulders slumped. She set down the tray she'd been holding and put a hand to her temple.

'If I've been hard on you, it's for your own good. I've had to work all my stinking life. And what do I get for it? Nothing but abuse. If you're serious, then piss off and let everyone else get back to work.'

Natalie swallowed hard, then turned and took a couple of steps towards the street. That was when she heard the rip.

Her head whipped round to see Mason toss his apron onto the ground.

'That goes double for me,' he said.

A nervous laugh erupted from Natalie's throat.

What?

Mason was right behind her now.

'We'd better get out of here. I think she's about to blow.'

He took her by the elbow and steered her out onto the street. She shook him off, disorientated by the way he'd hijacked her grand exit.

She walked fast, swerving in and out of the crowds until her espadrilles rubbed against the back of her heels. She felt a blister forming and stopped to adjust the strap. Mason hovered over her. His breath had a sweet, musty odour. His eyes were large and soulful.

'What's the plan? Do you have another job lined up?'

'No.'

'Right, well, I don't know about you, but I need something for my nerves. Let's get a drink.'

'I just want to go home. You can do the same.'

'I can't face my mum right now...' He looked stricken, as if he had just realised the enormity of what he'd done.

Natalie heaved a sigh. 'Okay, one drink.'

She didn't know if breakfast brandy was an everyday thing for Mason, or if it was just the pressure of the situation, but she paid for his double shot, along with both their coffees. It was the least she could do.

'What would you buy if you won the lottery?' she asked as they settled at a table.

He gazed at her for a moment.

'That's easy.'

'It is?'

'Yeah, I'd use the money to make more money.'

Natalie frowned. 'So, you'd put it in the bank?'

'I'd invest in stocks and shares.'

'You wouldn't go on holiday or buy a new car?'

He shook his head. 'There's no way I'd fritter it away.'

'Then what would be the point of having it?'

'Safety. Security.' He shrugged.

A waitress came over. 'Everything okay here?'

'All good,' Natalie said, taking a sip of her coffee.

'Are there any jobs going?' Mason asked.

She shook her head. 'Sorry, love. They laid off three people last month.'

'But you're still here,' Natalie said brightly.

'Yeah, for now.'

Mason caught Natalie's eye and she forced a smile.

'Would you mind taking a picture of us?' Mason asked.

Natalie furrowed her brow.

'To record the moment,' he explained. 'This is our rock bottom.'

If only he knew.

He huddled closer, and Natalie forced herself to smile. Just one picture. She'd be home soon. She'd never have to see him again.

As soon as the camera flashed, she moved away and

pretended to check her phone. A moment later, she received a text. It was from Mason.

'Sent you a copy.'

She gave him the thumbs up.

'We'll need something with good public transport links,' he said. 'Unless you want to carpool. Where do you live?'

'I'm moving soon,' she blurted. Why stay in the flat when she could have a house? It didn't have to be fancy, something with three or four bedrooms would suit her, and a nice big garden.

Mason looked startled. 'Where to?'

'Don't know yet.'

He let out a sigh. 'I can't wait to get a place of my own, but rent is so expensive.'

She lifted her cup and tried to swallow her coffee, but it felt like grit in her throat. She could employ Mason in her new coffee shop. No, she quickly dismissed the idea. She hadn't chucked in her job just to be stuck with him forever.

'Blue Beans are hiring,' he said, looking at his phone.

'Excellent!'

'But what do we do about references?'

'I'll give you a reference.'

His nose twitched. 'You're not senior to me.'

'They don't have to know that.'

'No, it's lying.' He looked up from his scrolling. 'Are you going to apply?'

'I'll think about it. I want to weigh up all my options before I decide.'

He sniffed. 'Thinking won't pay the rent.'

She opened her wallet. 'Look, I can lend you some money. Just till you've got a new job.'

He shook his head. 'I don't take handouts. Besides, we're in the same boat, aren't we?'

His eyes met hers and she shifted in her chair and fiddled

with the clasp of her handbag while she tried to think of a polite way to tell him to mind his own business. For all he knew, she was going to let Hayden support her. Or perhaps she was going to college.

'I really think you should talk to your mum.'

'Do you think?'

'Best to get things out in the open.'

Take it from me.

She excused herself and went to the toilet. She took her time reapplying her make-up, but when she came out, he was right outside. They walked in silence to the tube station. She sped up as she reached the escalators, but he was right behind her as she headed for the Docklands Light Railway.

'Looks like we're going the same way,' he said.

The train was waiting at the platform. They hopped on and sat side by side. Mason found a newspaper on the next seat and flicked through it, presumably looking for jobs. Natalie concentrated on her phone, but when she looked up, he was watching her. She averted her gaze, and studied the tube map, trying to pick the perfect location to move to. With twelve and a half million, she could afford any neighbourhood in London. She could start again in style. She just hoped it would be with Hayden.

'This is my stop,' she announced with relief.

Mason discarded his newspaper. 'I'll get off here too. I need a walk.'

A primal scream erupted in her head. She stepped onto the platform and out onto the shiny grey pavement, dodging puddles. He trotted along beside her, quiet and thoughtful now as the reality of what they had done sank in. A group of teenagers barged past, forcing her to step into the road. Hayden would have said something, but Mason didn't seem to notice. He seemed more interested in the contents of his pockets.

'I've got liquorice. You want some?' He dangled a long piece in front of her like a rat's tail.

'No thanks.'

They were almost at her place now. She stopped outside the communal garden.

'This is me.'

She waited a moment, hoping he'd leave, but he stayed with her as she walked up the path.

'I'd better go,' she said and punched in the code to the building.

There was a click and the door opened. His hand shot out and he held it open for her.

'Thanks.'

She walked down the dimly lit corridor. A fleeting glance over her shoulder confirmed he was still lurking in the open doorway as she stepped inside her flat and closed the door behind her.

FIVE

NATALIE

She went straight to the kitchen and checked on her lottery ticket. There it was in the empty baked bean can at the back of the pantry. Satisfied, she drifted from room to room, trying to decide what to do with the rest of her day. It would be hours until Hayden came home. She itched to call her best friend, but Gail would want to know why she wasn't at work. She didn't feel like filling her in yet. Not until she knew more about the mysterious Vivienne. Instead, she texted her sister:

Can you meet me for lunch?

Liz didn't respond right away. She'd be busy wrangling toddlers at the nursery where she worked, so Natalie settled in front of the TV with a bowl of popcorn. An hour later, her phone buzzed.

I'm not free till two. Why don't we drive over to Barley Hill? Have a picnic?

I'm really not in the mood for a picnic. Can you just
meet me for lunch?

There was a slight pause.

Okay then. Where do you want to go?

I'll find somewhere and send you a link.

Okay. See you later.

After a few minutes browsing the web, she got up to go to the loo. As she walked out into the hallway, she stopped dead. The front door wasn't shut properly. She peered out into the corridor. There was no one about. The wind rattled the front door to the building. That was open too. She scurried out and pulled it shut, waiting until she heard it click into place. Now no one could enter without first putting in the code.

The lottery ticket! Her heart pounded as she scurried into the kitchen and opened the door to the pantry. Where was it? She messed all the tins up in her panic, but then she found the hollow baked bean can. She peered inside. The ticket was still there. Still safe.

Light-headed with relief, she put it all back and shut the pantry door. She'd better get ready if she was going to be on time to meet Liz.

As she walked through the doors of Leone's, Natalie immediately felt out of place in her jeans and T-shirt. The waiter escorted her to a private booth tucked away in the back corner. A small vase filled with fresh flowers sat on an intricately carved wooden table. Cautiously, she opened the menu and scanned the list of dishes – truffle-stuffed ravioli, porcini risotto, ribeye steak with béarnaise sauce. Her heart skipped a beat as she eyed the prices. She was fighting the urge to turn and run when Liz slid into the seat opposite. There was a splash of red paint on her glasses and she had blue glitter in her hair.

'Busy day?' Natalie asked.

'Pretty average. So, what are we doing here?'

'Just thought it would make a change.'

Liz peered out the window, her gaze lingering on the towering skyscraper across the water. 'You're spying on Hayden, aren't you?'

Natalie's shoulders slumped. 'Is it that obvious?'

Liz turned to look at her, her forehead creased in concern. 'What dirt have you dug up on Vivienne?'

'Not a lot, really. Do you think I'm overreacting?'

'I don't know. It sounds like something and nothing.'

'What does that mean?'

'On the one hand, it's probably nothing. You get close to people at work. It's a matter of survival. You form allegiances and draw battle lines.'

'I thought you liked your work?'

'I do, but every workplace has politics. People you can trust versus people who are trying to shaft you. Friends and bastards. That's life.'

'I suppose.'

'So, maybe Hayden's just formed an allegiance with this woman. But on the other hand, we don't know what she looks like, do we? She might be smoking hot.'

'Liz!'

'Just giving you my honest opinion. You need to get a look at her. If she looks like the back end of a bus, then you've got nothing to worry about.'

'You don't think Hayden can resist an attractive woman?'

'Well, it's a lot easier to resist an unattractive woman than an attractive one. Plus, this Vivienne might also be married.'

'She didn't sound very married, the way she was wittering on to him.'

'Maybe she feels unappreciated.'

The waiter brought over the bottle of champagne Natalie had requested.

'Are you ready to order?' he asked as he filled their glasses.

Natalie scoured the menu, wanting to try something exotic.

'I'll have the caviar and oysters, please.'

Liz stifled a laugh and the waiter cleared his throat expectantly.

She rearranged her features. 'Just a bowl of chips for me; thank you.'

Natalie adjusted her posture as she looked around the opulent restaurant. The wealthy patrons were mainly women with expensive nails, who clinked crystal glasses and chattered about their horses, or their holidays, between bites of their lavish meals. She couldn't quite picture herself ever feeling comfortable in such a place, but maybe one day it would all feel routine – just like grabbing a salad at her local restaurant.

When their food arrived, Natalie's jaw dropped at the presentation. The caviar came on a silver platter. It looked like a pile of tiny black pearls, and the oysters quivered horribly on their bed of ice.

Liz reached for one of her chips and dipped it in garlic sauce. The crunch echoed throughout the room, and Natalie's stomach rumbled hungrily in response.

'Do you want to try an oyster?' she asked as she picked one up.

'Not in this lifetime!' Liz replied with a smirk. Taking a deep breath, Natalie raised the slimy creature to her lips. It was like swallowing a sea slug, but she forced it down with half a glass of champagne.

Undeterred, she scooped some caviar onto one of the thin pieces of toast and bit into it.

'Well?' Liz said.

Natalie smiled bravely.

'It's okay but I'd prefer jam.'

Liz pushed her chips into the middle, and Natalie took a handful.

'So what's the plan? Are we going to Hayden's work?'

Natalie nodded. 'I need you to distract him. Get him outside if you can.'

'How am I going to do that?'

'Say you want to plan my birthday or something.'

'Your birthday's not for ages.'

'Okay, well you'll think of something. All you have to do is keep him busy for five minutes. Once you've got him out of the way, I'll ask reception to put out an urgent call for Vivienne. She'll come out and I'll finally get a look at her.'

'Then what? You're not going to start a fight are you?'

Natalie stared down at her oysters, their slimy exteriors glistening under the restaurant lights.

'I won't know for sure until I talk to her.'

SIX

NATALIE

The Canary Grand Hotel was an imposing building, twenty storeys high. Natalie got neck ache just looking at it. She waited outside while Liz went in and took a look.

'He's working on the front desk,' she reported back. 'We'll have to wait a few minutes because there's a queue.'

'Okay,' Natalie said unhappily. She didn't want to wait. She wanted to get this over and done with.

'Any sign of Vivienne?'

'There were no women on the front desk. I went into the restaurant and checked a few name badges but no luck. She might not even be on shift today. Has that occurred to you?'

'Or maybe she's a chambermaid.'

Natalie pictured the mysterious Vivienne, wearing a flimsy little outfit and turning down the bedcovers.

She shuddered as she thought of all the rooms Vivienne would have access to. If she and Hayden wanted to fool around, it wouldn't be hard to arrange. Or perhaps Vivienne was one of the managers, someone more senior than Hayden. Was that why he hadn't told her to get lost?

They waited a few minutes and Liz peered into the lobby again.

'It's quieter now,' she said.

'Okay, go on in.'

As Liz walked inside, Natalie hurried around to the side of the building, hoping that no one would spot her. She located the door she was looking for and stepped into the restaurant. There were only a handful of guests there, talking and sipping coffee. Taking a deep breath, she hunched her shoulders and wove her way between the tables until she reached the hallway that led towards the front of the building. When she reached the lobby, she blended into a doorway and watched her husband at the desk. Hayden spoke to a colleague before following Liz across the lobby and out onto the veranda. As soon as they were outside, Natalie slid over to the desk.

'I need to speak to Vivienne,' she said.

'Vivienne?'

'She works here,' Natalie said a little louder. 'Can you hurry please? It's a family emergency.'

She waited impatiently as he picked up the phone and made a call.

'She's just coming.' His eyes were filled with concern. 'Can I get you anything? Glass of water?'

'No, thank you.'

She glanced behind her. Hayden and Liz were standing in front of the hotel. He had his back to her, but if he were to turn round, he would see her right away. She shifted her weight from one foot to the other, willing Vivienne to hurry.

'Ah, here she is now.'

Natalie heard the sound of heels on marble and turned to see a tall, graceful woman walking towards her. Her stomach dropped as she took in her smoky eyes and glossy black hair. She was a dead ringer for Megan Fox.

'Sorry, wrong Vivienne,' she told the man at the desk.

Before he could answer, she scurried across the lobby. Liz saw her coming and distracted Hayden by pointing at something in the sky.

Natalie dashed past them, her breath coming in ragged bursts. People jumped out of her way as she threaded through the crowd, but she kept running until she stumbled upon a pocket-sized park, like an oasis in the concrete jungle. Exhausted, she collapsed onto a bench and covered her face with her hands, tears streaming down her cheeks. Vivienne already had her claws into Hayden. There was no question she would lose him. It was just a matter of time.

'You should have seen her,' she sobbed, when Liz caught up with her. 'She's his perfect woman.'

Liz looked at her doubtfully. 'But you and Hayden are so perfect together.'

'I know.' She wiped a hot tear from her eye.

Was she being ridiculous? Natalie really didn't know anymore. She was losing all perspective.

'What do you think I should do?'

Liz handed her a tissue and rubbed her arm. 'I think you need to claim that goddamned lottery money. It's giving me hives.'

'I know.'

'You don't have to torture yourself like this. Let me claim it for you.'

'What if I'm just being paranoid? Hayden might not have done anything wrong.'

'Seriously, your flat could catch fire. You could lose it all.'

Natalie wrestled with her conscience. She could open a secret bank account for the money, but if Hayden left her, he would still be entitled to half of it. She could get in a lot of trouble later. On the other hand, if she let Liz pretend it was her win, Hayden would have no claim to it. It would still mean lying to Hayden in the short term, but she had to protect herself. If he was going to leave her for Vivienne, she wasn't about to support their lifestyle.

She remained in the park a while after Liz left. On her way home, she drifted into one of the designer shops in the mall. Shopping had always cheered her up in the past. She tried on a pair of jeans that cupped her butt and made her legs look like she was six feet tall.

She checked the price tag and swallowed. They cost more than a week's salary at the Riverside Café.

'Any good?' asked the saleswoman.

'I'll take them,' Natalie said, handing over her credit card.

As she walked out of the shop, an estate agent's window caught her eye. They had a handful of commercial properties for sale. None of them looked quite right for her, but maybe they knew of somewhere suitable for her shop. Choking back tears, she pushed open the door and stepped inside.

Hayden was disarmingly normal when he got home that night. He set his keys on the side and walked over to Natalie to kiss that perfect spot right behind her ear. She closed her eyes as she felt his arms wind around her. She unravelled like a shoelace and for a moment there was nothing but the two of them.

'How was work?' he asked when they pulled apart. 'Did Jan give you grief for leaving early?'

She squinted at him, unsure what he meant.

'One of the neighbours saw you at the tube station.'

'Nosy git! Which one?'

'The old bloke.'

Avoiding his question, she headed into the kitchen and rifled through the freezer, searching for something for dinner. He trailed after her.

'Why did you leave early?'

'I had toothache.'

She found a cottage pie and placed it in the oven. Her posh lunch had left her unsatisfied.

'How is it now?'

'Not too bad.'

'Are you going to the dentist?'

'I'll wait and see.'

'You can't piss about with toothache. I know you hate going but...'

That floored her. She didn't hate the dentist. He must be thinking of Daisy. Or Vivienne?

'Leave it. I'm fine.'

He threw his hands up. 'Just trying to help.'

She stayed in the kitchen, stacking the dishes they had left out that morning. When the cottage pie was ready, she carried it out to the living room and they ate in silence in front of the TV. She couldn't tell if he was sulking or merely absorbed in the series they were watching.

Hayden's phone beeped and she looked at him sharply. He didn't check it, even though it was sitting on the arm of the chair beside him. It beeped again, but he still seemed engrossed.

'What if it's work?' she said.

'It can wait.'

Her own phone buzzed.

What are you going to do about the ticket?

She switched it off. She knew Liz meant well, but all her nagging wasn't helping.

Hayden slipped an arm around her and pulled her close. After a while, her shoulder started to ache, but she didn't change positions. She wanted to stay in his arms for as long as she could.

SEVEN

NATALIE

'Here you go, sleepyhead!'

Natalie blinked as Hayden placed a cup of coffee on her nightstand.

'Thanks,' she said, rubbing her eyes.

He ripped back the curtains. 'Look outside. It's a beautiful day!'

Natalie propped herself up on one elbow. She saw nothing but the drab walls of the building opposite. Not for long, she promised herself. Soon she would have a beautiful house with a view. She watched as Hayden slapped a generous dab of cologne onto his neck and messed with his hair in front of the mirror.

'You really should get a wriggle on.' He didn't take his eyes off his own reflection. 'You don't want to be late for work.'

Natalie pretended to stir. For the past week, she had gone through the same charade, pretending to get ready, then crawling back into bed the minute he left for work. She didn't even enjoy her secret lie-ins. Her mind flipped between euphoria about the lottery win and foreboding about Vivienne.

She remained vigilant, waiting for her chance, but she still hadn't managed to get access to Hayden's phone.

'Natalie?' Hayden said.

Natalie opened one eye. Hayden would be out the door any minute now and she'd be able to relax. She rolled onto her side and let sleep wash over her. She had thrashed about all night, but at last her tired body was ready to give in.

A cold rush of air hit her as Hayden peeled the duvet from her drowsy body and tossed it across the room.

Natalie jumped. He might as well have poured a bucket of ice over her head.

'What did you do that for?' she yelled as she retrieved the duvet.

'You're going to be late!' He tapped his watch.

She stomped off to the bathroom and stood under the shower for as long as she could bear. The lukewarm water gave her goose pimples. When she walked back into the bedroom, he was still there, looking at his phone.

'It's a good thing I've got staff training today. I don't have to be in till nine, so I can give you a lift.'

Her eyes widened. 'That's alright. You go ahead. Jan won't care if I'm a few minutes late.'

'Course she will. Go on, get ready. You can't afford to piss off the boss.'

He watched as she found a clean T-shirt and pulled on her hated work skirt. Good job she hadn't set fire to it yet. She ran a brush through her damp hair and dabbed her face with moisturiser.

'We really should go.' There was a touch of impatience in his voice.

She repressed a sigh. 'I can still catch the seven fifteen bus. There's really no need to drive me.'

'That bus takes ages,' he said. 'Come on, you can do your make-up in the car.'

He placed a hand on her back and gently steered her towards the door. She scrambled for a fresh excuse, but he was checking his reflection in the window. Checking he looked good for Vivienne.

With a deep breath, she climbed into the car, her handbag on her lap. Hayden was looking at his phone as he got in. A deep frown formed on his face.

'Our rent payment bounced!'

'Oh.'

She waited while he logged into their joint bank account. 'Natalie, we are massively overdrawn! Look at all these charges!'

She leaned over his shoulder and saw what he was talking about. There was the money for her lunch with Liz, her Uber fares and her various other charges she hadn't expected to go through so quickly.

'Leave it with me,' she said. 'I'll call the bank from work and sort it all out.'

He looked at her curiously. 'I don't know how you can be so calm. I'm absolutely seething. Someone must have skimmed one of our cards.'

She placed a hand on his shoulder. 'Don't worry. It will all be fine.'

He drove in silence. Probably still worrying about the rent. She felt bad about that. Maybe she should tell him about the lottery. But then she pictured Vivienne and that smug look on her face. She'd looked like a woman who got what she wanted. The question was, did Hayden love Natalie enough to resist?

Hayden glanced at her. 'You look knackered, Nat.'

'I didn't sleep well.'

'Why not?'

She ran a hand through her hair. 'Just work stuff.'

His frown deepened. 'You really need to quit that job. It's not worth the stress. I think you should leave as soon as possible.'

She darted a look at him. 'Seriously?'

'Well, as soon as you've got another job lined up. We still have to pay the rent.'

She nodded. 'Sounds like a plan.'

'Let me know when you've squared things with the bank, won't you? I want to buy a new suitcase. Our old one's totally knackered.'

'Why do we need a suitcase?'

'I've got that conference next week, haven't I?'

She shot him a blank look. 'What conference?'

'The annual hoteliers' meet. It's up in Manchester this year. I did say.'

Did he? She was pretty sure she'd have remembered. Who would go to this conference? An entire group of them or was it just a ruse to spend the weekend with Vivienne?

'How long will you be away?'

'I leave Sunday, back Tuesday.'

'I'll miss you.'

He glanced at her. 'It's only for a couple of days.'

'I know.' She dropped her head. They were right outside the Riverside Café now.

'Do you want me to come in with you? Jan will go easier on you if I'm there.'

'No, it's fine.'

She climbed out of the car and gave him a wave. He lingered, waiting for her to go in. One of her former colleagues was outside, wiping down the tables. She could walk up and say hello, pretend she was just passing. Then head off down the street.

She spotted Jan through the window.

Oh hell. She'd seen her.

Jan's face lit up. She didn't smile often, possibly because all her teeth were either crooked or broken. Or maybe just because she had little to smile at, but she was smiling now. A wide, unpleasant smile that made her lips crack. She met Natalie on the path.

'Come crawling back, have you?'

Natalie would have left, but Hayden was still there, waiting for a gap in the traffic.

'Er, not exactly.'

'Then why are you wearing your uniform?'

'It's laundry day. I had nothing else to wear.'

Jan's eyebrows drew lower. 'If you've come back to gloat, you can sod off right now.'

Natalie stood her ground. 'You still owe me my last pay packet.'

'Are you kidding me? You left me short-staffed, I had to close early.' She took a step towards her. 'Now I'll tell you what I told Mason. You ain't getting your job back. Get that through your thick skull.'

Natalie tilted her head. 'Mason asked for his job back?'

'Yup. You know he only quit to impress you?'

Natalie folded her arms. Mason wasn't her problem. Another glance towards the road confirmed that Hayden had finally driven off.

'You're not even listening, are you? Daydreaming as always. That's why I never gave you a pay rise. You spend half your life on another planet.'

The words stung, but Natalie told herself she didn't care. She walked off and didn't look back until she was safely on the other side of the street. Her mind turned to Hayden's conference. Her skin crawled at the prospect of him and Vivienne spending the weekend in some fancy hotel. She rang Liz to ask her advice.

'He doesn't even have to go to the conference,' Liz said. 'Just tell him you've won the lottery. Then he can quit his job and he'll have no reason to go. He won't have to see Vivienne ever again, let alone shag her.'

'But what if he's already shagging her?'

Liz was quiet for a moment. 'So let Hayden go to the conference. You go too.'

Natalie sidestepped a street busker. 'I can't just tag along!'

'Don't tell him. Wear a wig. Get some glasses. Hell, you can have my old ones. Buy some clothes from a charity shop. Something you would never usually wear. He won't recognise you.'

* * *

Natalie watched as the sun glinted off the broad expanse of the Thames and in the distance she could make out the masts of the *Cutty Sark* outlined by seagulls wheeling around its bow. A pleasant breeze rustled her hair as she met with Ethan, her estate agent.

'I've got the perfect shop for you,' he had insisted over the phone. He had said this three times already, and each time he had been wide of the mark. Still, she was willing to oblige.

'The shop I'm going to show you has a small flat above it which will be handy if you want to live there,' he told her. 'And if not, you could make some extra income renting it out.'

Natalie nodded thoughtfully, as if she was in the habit of owning spare flats.

They turned onto a side road and stopped halfway down. The shop was a garish green and had a strong odour of rotting fruit.

'It used to be a juice shack,' Ethan said. 'A professional clean would sort out the smell.'

He unlocked the door and led her inside. The space seemed dingy at first glance. Then he flicked a switch and the whole place lit up. Natalie noted the beautiful brickwork and pictured little wooden tables positioned in twos or fours. She'd put in a little breakfast bar at the window, she mused, so her customers could people-watch as they drank their coffee.

She walked over to the counter. She'd have no trouble fitting the coffee machines, a fridge and a large display case to show off the cakes.

'It's a little pricey for what it is,' he advised, 'but you should be able to knock the owner down a bit if you're interested?'

Natalie circled the shop, taking in all the little details. The upstairs flat was built into the attic. There was a space for a bed, a small kitchen, bathroom and living room. She pictured herself spending her breaks up there, looking down on the street below. She came back down and took another look around, slower this time, taking in every detail.

'So, what's the verdict?'

'I'll think it over.'

She didn't want to sound too keen, but she had a good feeling about the place.

Ethan offered to drop her back home, but she was in the mood for a walk, so she strolled through the foot tunnel. She wanted to make an offer on the shop, but she needed to talk to Hayden first. She was tired of sneaking around. She didn't want to wait for Manchester. Better to sit down with him and ask him outright about Vivienne. She would know if he was lying. This was Hayden. She knew him like the back of her hand.

The sun was shining on the water as she crossed the bridge. The Canary Grand lay just ahead, its vast tower disappearing up into the sky. She spotted Hayden outside, smoking a cigarette. She stared, unable to believe what she was seeing. Because the Hayden she knew didn't smoke.

She backed away slowly. She'd never noticed the smell of smoke on his breath, but now she thought about it, he'd been chewing a lot of gum lately. And breath mints. He always had them in the car. She'd liked that he always smelled so minty fresh, but now she understood why. He had started smoking, and he didn't want her to know.

It was disconcerting to say the least. She wasn't a fan of cigarettes, but she hated the lying more. When had it started? And why for the love of God hadn't he told her?

EIGHT

NATALIE

Natalie watched as Hayden lugged his suitcase down the stairs. It looked heavy, considering he was only supposed to be away for a couple of days. With a jolt, it occurred to her that this might be it. He might be leaving her for Vivienne. But if that was the case, he'd have to tell her at some point, wouldn't he?

Hayden, we've won the lottery.

She looked at him, taking in the beauty of his eyelashes. Such long, dark eyelashes. Liz said they were wasted on a man. She reached out and squeezed his hand. He squeezed it back.

'When's your appointment with the bank manager?' he asked.

'This afternoon,' she reassured him. 'They said it would all be fine. It just might take a few days for the money to come back into the account, but we should be fully refunded.'

'That's a relief. Please ring me if there are any problems.'

'I will do. Are you off then?'

'Not just yet. I think I'll pop out and get some petrol first. That'll be one less thing to worry about once I hit the road.'

She nodded and he was out the door, leaving the suitcase at the foot of the stairs. She unzipped it and examined the contents. There were no condoms in the side pockets, but he could be buying them right now. Or was it cigarettes he needed? Did Vivienne smoke too? She rifled through his clothes and stopped when she found his underwear. He'd packed the red boxers she'd bought him for Valentine's Day. The knot in her stomach tightened. He almost never wore them for her.

The front door opened abruptly.

'Forgot my wallet.'

Natalie froze. She couldn't come up with a reasonable explanation for what she was doing.

He stared at her for a moment, clearly wondering why she was going through his suitcase.

'You forgot to pack your swimming trunks!' she blurted.

'There won't be a pool.'

'Oh. That's a shame.'

They maintained eye contact for a fraction longer than was comfortable.

'Make sure you put it all back.'

'Don't worry. I will.'

She waited for him to leave, then she closed her eyes and exhaled.

What in the world was she doing?

She headed upstairs to pack her own bag. She'd borrowed a couple of maternity dresses from Gail. Natalie had told her they were for a friend, but Gail had grown so misty eyed she had almost thrown them back at her. Liz had lent her the glasses and she'd bought the wig. It was grey and silky and made her look significantly older.

'You still look hot,' Liz had said with an eye roll. 'Is there anything you don't look good in?'

Natalie had stared at her own reflection. 'I look like Mum.'

'Yeah, you really do.'

Her mother had been just a few months older than she was

now when she'd died. Perhaps that was why Natalie didn't want to do anything for her upcoming fortieth birthday.

She heard the car outside and shoved her bag under the bed. Her stomach fluttered as she heard Hayden on the stairs.

'Gotta love you and leave you,' he said, swooping in to give her a kiss. His breath was minty as always, but now she was looking for it, she tasted tobacco. She ran her hand up his back. He had always loved that. 'Do you have time to say goodbye properly?' she asked.

'You know I'd love to, Nat, but I've got a long drive ahead of me. I really should hit the road.'

She considered throwing herself at his feet and begging him not to go, but his attention had already strayed. He grabbed his watch from the nightstand.

'Can't forget this,' he said with a smile. And with that, he was out the door.

She followed him out onto the street and waved goodbye, feeling pathetic as a tear rolled down her cheek.

'You'd better not disappoint me, Hayden,' she whispered. 'Or you won't know what's hit you.'

Five hours later, she sat in the first-class carriage on the train to Manchester. She'd always wondered what it was like to travel in style, and she was a little disappointed it wasn't fancier. There was more space and fewer people but she had half imagined the tables would be made of gold and there would be pillows and blankets. The reality was rather bleak and she scarfed down her complimentary sandwiches without really tasting them.

The countryside passed in a blur, and she thought about the life she would live once she claimed her money. Her friends and family had always smiled politely when she'd talked about owning her own café. She'd never got the impression they thought she would actually do it. She wiped an angry tear from her face. She couldn't wait to show them all.

When the train finally screeched to a halt, she had the urge to head across the platform and board the next train back to London, but she took hold of herself. She had to see first-hand what Hayden was getting up to.

The hotel was one of the larger ones in the city centre, so she shouldn't have much trouble blending in. She was already wearing the voluminous dress and she had put on her wig and glasses in the station toilets. Fortunately, she was able to check in on her phone and head straight for her room, thus bypassing reception.

She kept her eyes peeled as she walked through the lobby, checking all around for Hayden, but there was no sign of him or Vivienne. As she walked past the bar, she heard a raucous laugh. Without thinking, she swung round to see a familiar figure holding a pint of beer and banging the table at something that had apparently amused her. Natalie was rooted to the spot. What the hell was Daisy doing here?

She ducked behind a display case. She didn't recognise any of the other people at the table, but that was definitely Daisy. There was no mistaking that voice, nor those vibrant red curls. Keeping her head down, she found the stairs and heaved her bag up to the third floor. The floral carpet muffled her footsteps as she searched for her room among the row of identical doors. She spotted it at the end of the hall and rushed up to it, waving her keycard frantically over the electronic lock until the light flashed green and the door clicked open.

She fell inside, throwing down her bag and shedding her wig and glasses. Her mind was spinning, trying to make sense of Daisy's unexpected presence. Hayden and Daisy had once worked together, that was how they had met, and he had moved in with her after just a month. Largely, he admitted to Natalie, because he couldn't afford the rent on his own.

Somewhat predictably, their relationship had only lasted a few months but when they had split, Daisy had declared it was time for a fresh start, so she'd transferred to another hotel.

She must be here with her own work colleagues. It made sense, now Natalie thought about it. The conference was for people who worked in the industry. Daisy had not mentioned she would be here. Did Hayden know she was coming, or would he be as surprised as she was?

Overcome with tiredness, Natalie lay down on the bed and her mind drifted, as it often did, to the night she'd met Hayden.

She'd been waiting on tables at the Riverside Café. Jan was doing one of her special late-night events to cash in on the Christmas festivities. A large corporate group was booked in that evening, and they had occupied a long table at the back. Natalie's heels had ached from being on her feet all day, and the low hum of conversation had become a steady roar. She could barely keep up with the orders.

The corporate group had already gone through several rounds of drinks when she had placed a tall pink lemonade in front of a blue-eyed, blond-haired hunk.

'Hey, look at Hayden's drink!' one of the others had shouted.

Everyone had turned to stare. The hunk had looked down at his drink and kept his expression straight.

'Yes, this is exactly what I ordered,' he'd said.

He'd twirled the glass around to get a better look at it. The pink lemonade had bubbled to the surface and threatened to fizz over the edge. It contained a purple parasol, and a wedge of grapefruit was perched delicately on its rim, speared through the middle with a plastic flamingo on a stick. He'd leaned forward and taken a dainty sip. His workmates had erupted with laughter and Natalie realised she'd given him the wrong drink.

'I'm sorry. Yours was the beer, wasn't it?' she'd said.

'No, please. I want this drink.'

When their eyes met, an unmistakable spark of electricity had shot through her; it had felt like they had been magnetically fused together and neither one of them wanted to break the connection.

He had hung back after the rest of his party left and offered to walk her home. His features were gentle and unassuming so she hadn't hesitated to say yes.

'He'll murder you on the way home. We'll find you in a ditch,' Jan had warned when she went to get her coat, but Natalie hadn't worried. There was something about this man. It sounded cheesy as hell, but she had known he was the one.

Her phone buzzed, and she jumped up to get it. It was Hayden. She was about to answer when she realised it was a FaceTime call. Shit. She couldn't do that. He'd see she was in the hotel. She waited a few minutes then sent him a text:

Sorry can't talk. Working overtime. All okay?

He replied immediately: *Knackered from the drive. Might have an early night.*

He hadn't mentioned Daisy. Perhaps he hadn't run into her yet.

Hope you're not on the first floor with all the party people?

No, I'm up on the third floor. I've just found a connecting door that leads through to Phillip's room.

Ugh! I hope you locked it!

Of course. Not going to let that freak watch me sleep. Going to have a snooze now. Speak tomorrow.

Except instead of tomorrow, he'd used a tomato emoji.

Natalie rested for a few minutes, then put the wig and glasses back on and made her way down to the bar. If he was meeting Vivienne, she would catch him red-handed. She spotted Daisy and her colleagues straight away. Daisy was talking loudly, as usual. Natalie found a quiet table and kept her head down. Daisy stayed all night but Natalie didn't catch sight of Hayden or anyone else she knew. She hoped that meant he really had gone to bed. After a few hours, she'd had enough. Daisy was arguing with a colleague. It started out as a friendly debate but was growing increasingly fractious. If she weren't supposed to be hiding, Natalie would be tempted to steer Daisy upstairs to her room before she made a complete fool of herself.

Back in her room, Natalie tried to watch a film but she found it hard to relax. Guilt nagged at her. Tired as she was, her veins were filled with adrenaline and she struggled to follow the plot.

She was about to give up for the night when she heard a loud, screeching voice. Daisy.

It had to be. Daisy was singing. Loudly. She stumbled along the corridor, listing from one side to the other like a passenger on a sinking ship.

Natalie ran to the door and peered through the peephole. It would be helpful to pinpoint Daisy's room so she could avoid her. All at once, an eye appeared in the glass. The hairs on Natalie's arms stood up on end. The iris appeared bloodshot and rimmed with red veins. Natalie stared back, horrified. The peephole only worked one way, didn't it? Yet there was something disturbing about the way Daisy stared without blinking. It had to be because she was inebriated, but it felt as though she was staring right at her.

Then the door handle moved. No! She couldn't get in, could she? The door was locked.

She heard Daisy screech: 'My keycard won't work!'

Daisy pounded on the door. She was unnaturally strong, and the door shuddered with each bang. Natalie felt the walls and ceiling shake. What was she doing? It sounded like she was battering the door with something heavy. A fire extinguisher perhaps?

She hurried over to the nightstand and picked up the phone to dial reception. She would get them to send someone up before Daisy broke down the door. The phone rang and rang. No one was answering.

Bang. Bang. Bang.

The door shuddered so hard she thought it would come off its hinges.

Then she heard a man's voice. 'No, Daisy, this one's your room, you silly mare.'

The banging stopped and Daisy laughed. There was a click and she heard her disappear into the room next door.

With a huge sigh of relief, Natalie went into the bathroom and washed the make-up off her face. She caught her reflection in the mirror and cracked a smile. Her eyes were wide and her nerves were jangled but at least now she could get some sleep.

A metallic sound jolted her out of her reverie. Her room must be connected to Daisy's, like Hayden's was to Phillip's, and now she could hear Daisy in the bathroom. What a nightmare. Daisy was so drunk!

Daisy thumped about for several minutes until she finally went quiet.

Natalie crept into bed and laid in the darkness. Her mind whirred with unhappy thoughts as she wondered how she had come to be here. Was this complete and utter madness, spying on her husband like this? Just a few months ago, she couldn't imagine doing such a thing. Couldn't imagine Hayden would ever be unfaithful. And yet here she was, alone in a hotel room with the sound of Daisy's snores coming through the walls.

NINE

NATALIE

Daisy didn't do anything quietly. Natalie heard her singing to herself in the shower and it made her wonder if Hayden had picked up the habit from her. Then she heard her out in the corridor, talking loudly about what time the restaurant opened for breakfast. Even her footsteps were noisy as she strolled down to the lifts.

She dialled Hayden's number, feeling a tightness in her chest. He sounded groggy when he answered. She wished she could FaceTime him, but then he'd expect to see her too.

'Hey, I just wanted to wish you luck with your presentation today. Are you ready?'

He hesitated for a moment before responding, 'Yeah, I think so. I miss you, Nat. I wish you were here with me.'

His words were a balm for her frazzled nerves. 'Me too. Did you sleep okay?'

'Not great. The walls are paper thin.'

Didn't she know it!

'Listen, Nat, can you do me a favour? I need you to take a picture of the meter.'

'The... meter?'

'The gas meter. It's under the sink. I need to check our last bill was correct.'

'I'd better do it later. I have to catch my bus.'

'Okay. Don't forget. I love you.'

'Don't forget I love you too. And don't worry. You're going to smash that presentation.'

'See you tomato.'

'Yeah. Text me when you know what time you'll be back.'

She hung up and stared at the wall. He'd sounded so normal, so natural. If Vivienne were in his room, he would be in a rush to get Natalie off the phone. Maybe she was wrong about this whole thing. Maybe she was just a crazy, paranoid wife.

She dressed in another of Gail's maternity outfits and resumed her vigil at the door. Soon enough, she was rewarded by the sight of Phillip strolling out of his room. He knocked on the door next to his and waited a few minutes. When the door opened, Natalie opened her own door to get a good look. Yes, there was Hayden. She sucked in her breath. Hayden looked delicious in his smart suit. He ran a hand through his hair and checked his watch, too preoccupied to notice her watching. Phillip mumbled something and Hayden slapped him on the back, his face crinkling into a huge grin. Then he grabbed Phillip by the shoulder and steered him towards the stairs. Natalie stood still. From the way Hayden talked about him, she had assumed he didn't like Phillip, yet here they were, laughing like old friends. Was this some guy code that she was unaware of? She shook her head. At least there was no sign of Vivienne, which meant Hayden must have spent the night alone.

She waited half an hour before she dared go down to the restaurant. By that time, most people had finished. She loaded her plate quickly and took a place in the corner. As she bit into her toast, she noticed a schedule on the wall. She felt a tingle of pride when she spotted Hayden's name. His presentation was at nine thirty in Conference Room One.

As she was finishing her coffee, Vivienne emerged from the bank of lifts. She looked stunning in a white T-shirt and a tight pencil skirt.

Natalie rose from her seat. Vivienne's heels clacked loudly as she headed past reception. Natalie darted after her, keeping her head down. When they reached the conference rooms, most of the attendees were already inside. Vivienne glanced briefly over her shoulder and Natalie wondered if she had clocked her, but then she disappeared inside.

Natalie hesitated. Nobody appeared to be checking tickets and there was a smattering of empty seats, so she took one right at the back.

Daisy was a few rows in front of her but she couldn't spot Hayden, or Phillip for that matter. The first speaker came on stage and she suppressed a yawn. The dull drone of his voice made her sleepy. She looked around but everyone else appeared to be enthralled. The speech finally came to an end and then Hayden was up. He stood at the lectern and her heart swelled.

He looked confident, but Natalie saw the way he tapped his feet and fidgeted with his microphone. He clicked on his first slide. It was upside down. There was a pause and then Vivienne leapt up onto the stage to adjust the projector. Hayden rewarded her with such a big smile that Natalie felt like she'd been punched in the gut. His topic was dull and uninteresting, but his voice was low and steady and captivated everyone in the room. She had been worried he might spot her, but his eyes kept returning to Vivienne, who seemed entranced by his every word.

When she couldn't take it any longer, she got to her feet and crept out through the door. She felt so wretched she was tempted to go back to bed but instead, she dragged herself out into the cold city air.

The streets were alive with people, music and laughter. Her eyes glazed over as she passed the world-renowned galleries and museums. She felt numb, uninterested in anything until she caught a whiff of freshly ground coffee. She followed her nose to a charming little coffee shop, tucked away amongst a row of weathered buildings.

She peered inside and saw cosy old armchairs and little round tables. She went in and approached the counter.

'A cappuccino and a macchiato please,' she said to the barista. Her gaze shifted to the glass display case filled with treats. She settled on a thick slab of creamy pistachio cheesecake.

She paid and carried her tray to a little alcove where she settled in a leather armchair. Instantly, the tension left her shoulders. She took notes of everything: the price, the taste, even the cups. As she held the last forkful of pistachio cake in mid-air she was startled by the shrill ringing of her mobile. Glancing around sheepishly, she fished her phone from her pocket.

'Hello? This is Natalie,' she murmured. She could see from the display that it was Ethan, her estate agent.

'Natalie, someone has made an offer on the juice bar. It's a great opportunity, but if you don't act soon, you'll miss your chance.'

Natalie bit her lip. She'd never bought a shop or any sort of property before and had no idea how much she should offer.

'I'd like a few more days to consider but I am interested. Can you pass that message along to the owner?'

'I'm afraid if you hesitate, the property will be gone.'

Natalie ran a finger along the rim of her mug. For all she knew this interested party could be made up, but she couldn't lose her café.

'Alright then. Tell the owner I'd like to make an offer.'

'How much?' Ethan kept his voice level, as if they were discussing the purchase of a new sofa, not a life-changing amount of money.

'Tell them I'm willing to go five grand above the asking price,' she said. 'That will be my only offer.'

She put down the phone and felt good about it. If the owner declined her offer, it wasn't meant to be.

She finished her cheesecake and stepped out into the sun, feeling its warmth upon her skin. She headed to the bank and applied for a new credit card. She needed to get the money to pay the rent from somewhere, and hopefully she could use it to pay off some of her other expenses. It was exhausting, keeping up this charade.

She filled the rest of the day with shopping and a trip to the cinema but by the time she returned to the hotel, darkness had taken over the city and the sense of loneliness returned.

She walked through the lobby, quickly spotting Hayden in the bar with his colleagues. A tightness formed in her chest as she watched him say something to Vivienne, who smiled and giggled like a schoolgirl. Checking her wig was on straight, she walked past them and ordered a dry white wine. Then she found a quiet corner so she could sit and observe.

There was no sign of Daisy. Perhaps she had gone out on the town. A few of Hayden's party were heading back to their rooms. She watched as Phillip went to get more drinks, leaving Hayden alone with Vivienne. She saw Vivienne's lips move ever so slightly as she spoke in a low voice. Hayden nodded in agreement. It was torture, watching the two of them alone. What were they talking about? She wished she could hear. Hayden mumbled something and scrambled to his feet. She watched as he headed outside to the patio, presumably to smoke. Her eyes shifted to Vivienne and she seethed with silent rage. Vivienne looked serene and confident. She had restyled her hair for the evening, so it fell in waves around her face. Natalie fought the urge to yank a strand out of her head. Couldn't Vivienne get her own man? Why did she have to go after hers?

When Hayden returned, he headed to the bar and offered Phillip a hand with the drinks. Then the three of them sat together at the table, but it was clear Vivienne only had eyes for Hayden. Hayden's body language was less obvious. Once again, she noticed that he and Phillip seemed to be quite matey.

Hayden finished his drink then rose to his feet. This time, Natalie heard him clearly.

'Right, I'm going to hit the hay. I'll see you all bright and early in the morning!'

'Oh, come on, the night's only just begun!' Phillip complained.

'Maybe, but we've got another day of this tomorrow and I need my beauty sleep.'

Vivienne said something Natalie couldn't make out, but Hayden brushed her off with a wave of his hand. As he headed off towards the lifts, Natalie wanted to punch the air with glee. Hayden had passed the test.

She waited until he got into the lift, then she headed that way herself. Should she surprise him? she wondered. She could knock on his door and tell him she'd just found out they'd won the lottery; they could celebrate in style. Her lift arrived. Before she could step inside, Vivienne got in. Natalie hesitated for a moment, then followed. Vivienne's perfume filled the lift like a personal storm cloud. Vivienne pressed the button for the third floor and kept her eyes focused on the door. Natalie couldn't help but watch her. It felt so strange to be alone with this woman, who had been keeping her awake at night. Her resemblance to Megan Fox really was uncanny.

When the lift arrived at the third floor, Vivienne got out quickly. Natalie followed at a distance. It took her a moment to realise she was going the wrong way. The room numbers were going down instead of up. Vivienne spun around on her heel. Her eyes bored into Natalie's.

'Stop following me.'

'I... I wasn't.'

Vivienne gave her a long hard stare. 'You were in the bar earlier. You've been watching me all night. You give me the creeps.'

'I... I'm sorry.'

She knew she should explain, but she was too embarrassed. Instead, she turned and scurried off towards her own room. She hesitated as she passed Hayden's door. It would feel so good to be with him, but her run-in with Vivienne had put a damper on her mood. She didn't really feel like being sociable now. She just wanted to get an early night and head back home. She would decide what to do about the lottery when Hayden got home.

* * *

As soon as her taxi dropped her off, Natalie unlocked the door to the flat and rushed inside, intent on opening the windows so the rooms wouldn't smell stale. But as she entered the living room, she paused. Had she really left the cushions strewn across the sofa like that? She could have sworn she'd tidied before she left for Manchester. She looked around, but everything else was in its place. She must be imagining it.

She went into the kitchen and threw open the door to the pantry. She pulled out all the tins, her hands scrabbling madly for the empty bean can. Where was it? She burst out laughing as she closed her hands around it. There it was, and there inside was her winning lottery ticket.

It's here. It's fine.

She drew a deep breath and walked over to the mirror, practising her surprised expression. She'd tell Hayden there was a possibility they'd won and then she'd get him to check the numbers. She wanted him to feel a part of it, after all, they were in this together.

Her phone buzzed and she glanced at the display. It was Gail. She felt instantly guilty. Gail had called a couple of times recently and she hadn't got round to ringing her back. She flopped down on the sofa and settled in for a chat.

'Hi, Natalie, how are you?'

'I'm fine,' she said brightly.

'What have you been up to?'

Natalie glanced down at her nails. 'Just been... you know, busy with work.'

'What about Hayden?'

'What about him?'

'Well... I just saw him drive by.'

'Did you? He's on his way back from a conference.'

'I'm probably making a mountain out of a molehill, but he had a woman in the car with him. I expect she was just a colleague then?'

Natalie's heart stopped. 'What did she look like?'

'Oh, you know. Young-looking. Long, dark hair.'

It was Vivienne. It had to be.

'Sorry, I'm going to have to call you back,' she told Gail.

'Oh God, I shouldn't have told you, should I? Don't do anything rash. It's probably perfectly—'

'It's fine. I'll see you at Daisy's party, okay?'

She ran to the window. Hayden was parking outside. He was alone, no sign of Vivienne. He looked rather serious as he wheeled his suitcase down the driveway. As if he was composing himself for an interrogation.

'How was your drive?' she asked as he walked through the door.

'Long,' he said, setting down the suitcase. She stepped forward to hold him, desperate to feel his arms around her, but he gave her a brief squeeze and pushed past her.

'Sorry, Nat, I really have to pee.'

He rushed to the bathroom and she stood in the hallway,

waiting. She checked his coat pocket, but his phone wasn't in there. He must have it on him.

He came out and slumped down on the sofa. He started telling her about his presentation.

'What about the evenings? Did you have a lot to drink?'

He shook his head. 'Not really. I was too tired. Oh, and guess who I ran into?'

'I don't know. The pope?'

'Daisy! Her presentation was really funny. You should have seen it.'

Natalie forced a smile. If he started talking about bloody presentations again, she was going to scream.

She leaned closer. 'Any gossip?'

'Like what?'

'I don't know. You tell me.'

She glanced at the suitcase, wishing he would just volunteer the information she wanted. If there was nothing between him and Vivienne, why did he never mention her?

'Did you give Daisy a lift home?'

'I would have done but she'd already left.'

She looked at him expectantly. *Come on, Hayden, tell me. Say you gave Vivienne a lift. It's cool, just as long as you're honest.*

But he simply closed his eyes and leant back against the sofa.

Natalie trudged upstairs and rang her sister.

'Well?' said Liz. 'What's the verdict?'

Natalie faltered. 'I'm still not sure. I didn't catch him in the act. I mean, the conference was real and it didn't seem like they were up to anything but then he gave Vivienne a lift home and didn't tell me.'

'So you still don't have proof then, either way?' she asked quietly.

'No.' Natalie's voice barely reached a whisper.

'Which way are you leaning?'

Natalie swallowed hard. 'I need more time. I don't know if he's cheating. They might just be friends.'

They both fell silent for a moment before Liz spoke up again, this time with an urgency that hadn't been there moments before. 'That's enough,' she said firmly. 'It's time to claim the money.'

TEN

NATALIE

If it wasn't for the loud incessant ringing of her phone, Natalie might have slept through the whole of the next day. There seemed little point in getting up, but the damn phone kept ringing. It felt like someone was drilling a hole in her head. She unplugged it from the charger and held it to her ear.

'Hello?'

'Natalie! I'm delighted to tell you that the owner has accepted your offer. The juice bar is yours.'

The room swirled around her.

'That's... wow! Thank you.'

'Natalie, I'm going to need more information from you. I'll send you over the paperwork. We'll need to see proof that you have the money to pay for the transaction, and you'll need to hire a solicitor. I can recommend one if you like?'

'Yes please.'

'Great. The sooner you return all of that, the sooner we can go ahead with arranging a survey and we'll get the memorandum of sale over to you later today.'

Her head was spinning. So, it was happening. She was going to have her own coffee shop. She went into the kitchen and poured herself a large glass of water. Her throat was so dry, she drank it down in one go. Then her phone beeped and she saw a message from Hayden.

The dry cleaners called. You forgot to collect your coat.

She stared at it numbly, then it buzzed again. *PS I love you.*

She smiled involuntarily. Did he? Then why wouldn't he tell her about Vivienne? She glanced up at the clock. She'd better take a shower; she had made plans to meet Liz at CeCe's.

The cocktail bar was down by the water. The walls were a vibrant pink and there were bottles of every colour lined up along the sleek granite bar, reflecting the hypnotic blue light of their signature neon shots.

'What are you going to have?' Natalie asked, passing Liz the cocktail menu. The dull hum of conversation and the clinking of glassware filled the room.

'I'll just have a lemonade.'

'Oh come on, that's so boring.'

Liz shoved the menu back at her.

'You're no fun.'

The waitress approached their table, pen and pad at the ready. 'What will it be, ladies?'

'I'll have a Mai Tai please,' Natalie said.

'And I'll have a lemonade. With two cherries.'

Natalie made a face. 'So, what am I going to do?' she asked as the waitress scurried off.

'I say you just do it,' Liz said. 'I'll come back to your place and we'll phone it in. If I made the claim, then all the money will go into my bank account. He won't get a penny unless he deserves it. And you can start enjoying life.'

'Won't he know when I start buying stuff?'

'He'll just think you have an incredibly generous sister, which you have, by the way.'

Natalie sighed. She still wasn't comfortable with the idea. 'I'm still not sure he is messing me around but if I confront him, he's bound to lie. And if I'm wrong, I don't want him to know I ever suspected.'

The waitress arrived with their drinks. Natalie removed the sprig of mint from her Mai Tai and they clinked glasses. Liz swirled her lemonade with a straw. Two plump maraschino cherries bobbed in the effervescence.

'Perhaps I should make the call at my house,' Liz said. 'We can't have him walking in while I'm on the phone.'

'I want to be there!' Natalie objected. 'It's a big moment. Besides, the ticket's at my house. I suppose we could pick it up and then go to yours?'

'Yeah, that'll work.'

'Hey, did you notice him over there?' Natalie tilted her head to analyse a man sitting alone, lips pursed in concentration as he read a thick dog-eared novel. His hair was dark and unruly, as though he'd been running his fingers through it. 'He looks just your type.'

'Meh.' Liz barely gave him a second glance.

Natalie shook her head. 'Being single is wasted on you.'

Liz met her eyes. 'I'm not interested in picking up a man in a bar, okay?'

'But look at that book he's reading. I've seen it on your shelves.'

Liz sighed and pushed back her chair. Natalie watched transfixed as she strode confidently towards him. This was unbelievable. Was she actually taking her advice?

Liz approached with a warm smile. The man set aside his book and looked up at her. He said something that made her laugh and although Natalie was too far away to make out his words, she caught her sister's delighted expression.

When Liz returned to their table, Natalie grabbed her hand. 'So! Did you get his number?'

'Hardly.'

She watched as the man rose from his chair and shoved the book into a worn leather bag. He crossed the room without a word and jerked the door open with a jolt that rattled its hinges.

'He wasn't really reading,' Liz explained.

'I saw him turn a page.'

Liz blinked at her. 'He didn't even know what it was about. I'm not convinced he can read at all.'

'But why...'

'People are not always who they seem, Natalie. The book was a ploy, to make him look approachable when in fact he's just some lazy twat who thinks he knows how to impress women.'

Natalie reached for her drink with a grimace of disgust and chugged the last few sips.

'For goodness' sake. Where have all the good men gone?'

Liz took an even sip of her lemonade and shrugged.

'You want another?'

'Not for me thanks. What time does Hayden finish work?'

'Not for another hour.'

'Great. Let's get going.'

Natalie asked for the bill and ordered a bottle of champagne to take away. But when she tried to pay, the waitress shook her head.

'I'm sorry, madam, but your card has been declined.'

She looked at her sister, silently pleading for help.

Liz crossed her arms and stared at Natalie for a moment then she fished out her wallet and swiped her card through the reader.

'Sorry,' Natalie murmured. 'You know I'm good for it.'

Liz shrugged and looked at the time. 'Come on, we can catch the five fifteen if we hurry.'

'I've got a better idea; let's get an Uber.'

'I could get used to this,' Liz said as they relaxed in the back of the car. Natalie nodded and closed her eyes. She shouldn't have drunk her Mai Tai so fast. The world was spinning.

When the Uber pulled up outside Natalie's, they hurried into the building.

'Hayden?' she called as she unlocked the flat.

There was no reply. Natalie went to the pantry and rifled among the tins. She found the hollow one and pulled it out. It was empty.

'I don't understand.'

Desperately, she pulled all the tins out. Then she shone her phone around the empty cupboard, searching every inch. It was no use. The ticket was gone.

Liz stared at her with her arms crossed. 'What have you done with it?'

'I'm telling you, this is where I left it,' Natalie insisted. She ran a hand through her hair, feeling more and more frantic. 'It was here, I swear!'

She twisted a lock of hair so tight it hurt. Her mind conjured up all sorts of scenarios. Burglars lurking in the shadows, nosy neighbours trying their luck. Mason, that day he'd walked her home. A chill ran up her spine.

'Mason. It could have been Mason.'

'Why? Did you tell him about the win?'

'Of course not. I haven't told anyone.'

'Then it's much more likely that you hid it somewhere else.'

Her eyes moved to the table. She picked up an empty wine bottle.

'Did you drink this last night?'

Natalie stared at it. 'I had a glass after Hayden went to bed.'

'Looks like you had more than a glass.'

As Liz spoke, a brief flash of the night before sparked in Natalie's mind. She recalled lying back on the worn leather sofa, with an empty glass of wine cradled in her hand as tears coursed down her cheeks.

'I think you're right. I think I got drunk last night.'

'So, you got drunk, you took out the ticket and hid it somewhere else,' Liz said calmly. 'Think hard, where did you put it?'

Natalie's fingers dug into her scalp as she paced the room, her body tense and alert. Anxiety buzzed in her ears. She'd been feeling paranoid, worried the ticket wasn't safe. Her eyes darted from wall to wall like a trapped animal searching for an escape route. She could feel sweat dripping down her forehead as she ran her hands along every surface, desperate to find the ticket.

'This is what it feels like to lose your mind,' she told Liz, her voice thick with despair.

Liz pulled her close. 'We'll find it,' she promised her. 'It's going to be alright.'

They were in the bedroom by the time Hayden arrived home. He watched them with a curious expression, observing their frenzied movements.

'What are you doing?'

Natalie glanced up at him. 'I'm having a clear out.'

She threw clothes out of the wardrobe and piled shoeboxes in the middle of the room. She intended to search through each and every one of them. Their boxes of Christmas decorations too. She couldn't imagine hiding the ticket in any of these places but she was running out of ideas. They had searched every single room in the house. Even the bathroom.

'I'd better get back home,' Liz said, defeated. 'The cats need their dinner.'

Natalie barely heard her. She continued her frenzied search until exhaustion took over.

* * *

With each passing day, Natalie's dreams floated further out of reach. Without the ticket, she had no way to pay the deposit on her café. Ethan rang her daily, hounded her for proof of funds. Worse still, she had maxed out all her credit cards in order to pay the rent. With no job and no money, the situation was getting desperate. Saturday came and Gail invited her around for lunch. She agreed but she wasn't really in the mood. Until she found that ticket, her life was in limbo.

ELEVEN

NATALIE

Natalie stepped over a mess of colourful plastic toys. Baby Scarlett lay on an animal-printed floor mat, babbling and giggling to herself. Gail's boyfriend, Andy, was on his knees in the corner of the room, hammering at the wall and her dad, Damon, stood nearby, overseeing the work.

Natalie found Gail at the stove, stirring a pan of sauce. She hadn't been much of a cook before she'd had Scarlett, but she seemed to have developed a knack for it. She loved feeding people, whipping up pasta dishes and rich indulgent puddings like the ones her mum made when they were kids.

'Can I give you a hand with anything?' Natalie asked.

Gail smiled. 'You can take this out if you like.'

She handed her a large bowl filled with freshly cut lettuce and tomatoes. Natalie took it to the dining room table and placed it in the centre. She took a seat and smiled politely as Andy poured the wine. He had little to say for himself and she wondered again why Gail had settled for someone with so little personality. Gail served the lasagne and Damon winked at Natalie as he piled her plate high with steaming vegetables.

'Oh, I'll never eat that many.'

'Nonsense. You're a growing girl.'

'I'm nearly forty, Damon.'

'You are not!' He looked horrified.

Natalie looked down at her plate of food, ready to dig in when Damon said: 'Perhaps Natalie would like to say grace?'

Natalie bit her lip. 'I don't really do that any more.'

Everyone was silent for a minute.

'Well then, let's just eat, shall we?' Damon turned his attention to Scarlett, who was dropping spoonfuls of food on the ground and giggling hysterically.

'How's Hayden?' Andy asked.

Natalie felt a flush of colour creeping over her cheeks.

How was Hayden? She had no idea. They had been increasingly distant since the conference. She found it hard to even look at him. She forced a smile.

'He's fine. Busy with work. That's where he is today, actually.'

As if sensing her discomfort, Damon cracked one of his terrible jokes and Natalie laughed louder than it really warranted.

'When are you planning to go back to work?' she asked Gail, as she wiped her mouth with a napkin.

Gail looked down at her plate. 'I'm not sure. My boss is offering me four days a week if I want to stay in my current role, or I can take a demotion and go back three days.'

Natalie frowned. 'That doesn't sound very fair.'

Gail shrugged. 'Beggars can't be choosers.' She gave a tight smile and speared a piece of broccoli.

Natalie glanced over at Andy, but he didn't have anything to say on the subject. She bet he wasn't making any compromises with his career.

When they'd all finished eating, Natalie stacked the plates and brought them to the sink.

Gail opened the dishwasher. 'You're still brooding about that woman, aren't you?'

Natalie hesitated. 'It's probably nothing,' she said. 'I wouldn't mind if he gave a colleague a lift, but why hide it? I asked him about his journey and he never mentioned her.'

'Why don't you just have it out with him?'

'Because I'm scared.'

'You can't go on like this. It's driving you barmy. Besides, it might be nothing.'

'I know. I just... It's never the right moment. He's so tired when he gets in from work and he's been going in early.'

Gail shot her a look.

'I know,' Natalie said. 'The longer I leave it, the worse it gets.'

She opened the drawer and found some clingfilm to wrap the leftover bread with.

'That's enough about me. How have you been?'

'Tired. Scarlett's not sleeping well, I think she's teething.'

Natalie nodded and tried to listen but her mind drifted the way it always did whenever Gail talked about Scarlett. She stayed a little longer, drinking coffee at the table while Gail rocked Scarlett off to sleep. She hugged her friend tightly before she left.

'Thanks for the food – and the chat.'

'Talk to him,' Gail said, as she stepped out onto the street. Natalie nodded. She was not looking forward to an evening alone with Hayden but she couldn't avoid him forever.

The communal garden was full of clutter as Natalie crossed the grass to her building. She entered quickly, pulling the keys from her bag as she hurried down the hall. As she stood outside her door, muffled chatter floated to her ears. She paused, straining to hear who was inside with Hayden. She unlocked the door and headed for the kitchen to find him with his phone pressed tightly to his ear. He looked up at Natalie and beamed, excitement radiating from every pore.

'You're not gonna believe this,' he said, eyes wide.

'Believe what?'

'Babe, I think we've won the lottery.'

TWELVE

NATALIE

Natalie threw her arms around him in disbelief, tears streaming down her face.

'What? Are you serious?'

Hayden nodded. 'I went to Borough Market on the way home from work. Picked up a packet of orange pekoe tea. I came back home and took the teapot down from the shelf and found a lottery ticket from a few weeks back. Why on earth did you put it in there?'

Natalie shifted her gaze around the room, avoiding eye contact. She licked her lips nervously and tried to find the right words. 'I... I really don't remember,' she finally said. 'I must have had one too many wines.' Her voice was barely above a whisper.

Hayden narrowed his eyes and let out a gruff snort as he shook his head.

'I almost threw it away when I saw the date. Still, I thought I might as well check it before I chucked it out. I looked online and we matched all the bloody numbers.'

Natalie laughed hysterically. Neither of them were big tea drinkers so the teapot was mostly ceremonial, brought out when they had guests. It was an unusual place to hide the ticket. She would never have thought to look there.

Hayden was looking at her anxiously. 'I know I should have waited until you got home. It was your ticket, after all. Please don't be angry with me, I just got carried away in the moment.'

Natalie waved his concerns away. 'So, the lottery people agree we've won?'

'Yes, they just have to verify it, but when they do, we'll be rich.'

'How rich?'

'Twelve and a half million,' Hayden said. 'Can you believe it?'

Natalie sank into a chair and sat there, shaking. It was for the best, she told herself. No more secrets, no more deceptions.

'They're going to send a rep out to see us tomorrow. Can you get the afternoon off work?'

Natalie laughed. 'No need to go in. We'll just quit.'

'No.' He shook his head. 'The money's not ours until it's in the bank. We should go to work as normal. The appointment's not until three. And I think we should keep this between us until we know for sure.'

'I agree. What do they need to know?'

'They just need to make sure the ticket is legit. I expect they get a lot of people faking it.'

Natalie nodded. 'Ours is real,' she said with confidence.

'Of course it is. This is it, baby. We're going to be millionaires.'

They brainstormed ideas for things they wanted to spend the money on.

'We should buy a house,' he said. 'That's priority number one.'

'Yes, something by the river. I want a view.'

'I need a tennis court.'

'I want a walk-in wardrobe.'

'And new cars. Brand new from a showroom. And what about a big party for your fortieth? We could celebrate in style.'

Natalie shook her head. 'No, I really don't want to draw attention to it.'

'But why not? It's a big birthday.'

'I really don't want to think about getting old.'

'Don't worry – you don't look a day over thirty.'

'All the same...'

She leaned back in her chair, listening with one ear. She wanted to tell him about the coffee shop but that would have to wait until they had the money.

Hayden clapped his hands together. 'Right, we need to celebrate properly. I'm going to go out and get us some champagne.'

Natalie squinted. 'I thought you wanted to wait until we had the money in the bank?'

'Sure, but I think we can stretch to a bottle of bubbly.' He grabbed his keys.

'Wait! Where's the lottery ticket?' she asked. She couldn't bear to let it out of her sight.

'Don't worry, I've got it somewhere safe.'

She watched a little nervously as he headed out the door.

He took a long time to buy the champagne and she regretted not going with him. She pictured him wandering up and down the aisle, unable to decide. They'd never bought real champagne before, not even for their wedding. How would he know which one to choose?

Or perhaps he'd stopped off to break the news to Vivienne. She pictured him surprising her at home, telling her he was about to become rich. Would that change anything between them? Would it mean that they could be together?

When Hayden finally returned, he held a bottle of champagne in one hand and a box of chocolate truffles in the other.

'That took a while,' she commented. Her voice sounded strange and high pitched, but Hayden didn't seem to notice as he popped the cork. He poured out two glasses and held one up.

'To my fabulously rich trophy wife.'

She picked up the other glass. 'To my fabulously rich trophy husband.'

They clinked glasses and each took a gulp. The champagne was crisp and dry with tiny bubbles that burst on her tongue.

'Where did you put the ticket?' she asked, trying to keep her tone casual.

He shot her a killer smile. 'It's all good, babe.'

'But where is it?'

He leaned close and their lips met in a soft kiss. She felt warmth spread throughout her body.

'Don't worry,' he told her. 'It's in the safest place possible.'

She clenched her teeth, maddened at his refusal to answer, but given that she had already lost the ticket once, she decided to let it go.

When she awoke the following morning, Hayden was getting dressed in his smart work trousers and crisp white shirt.

'Come on, Natalie, you'll be late!'

'Right behind you.'

She was ashamed of the lie, but it wouldn't be for much longer. The man from the lottery was coming at three. She was counting down the hours.

As soon as Hayden left for work, she had a nose around the flat. Wherever he had hidden the ticket, it was well concealed. She hoped he hadn't taken it with him to work. The thought of losing it to a pickpocket was more than she could bear.

She used her nervous energy to clean the flat, attacking every corner with her feather duster and wiping down surfaces with a damp cloth until everything looked squeaky clean. She fluffed the cushions and sprayed lemon-scented cleaner. Then she churned some coffee beans and set out a plate of Jammie Dodgers. It was impossible to sit still for long, knowing everything hinged on this meeting.

Hayden arrived home with minutes to spare and ate three of the Jammie Dodgers, one after another.

'Leave some for our guest,' Natalie said.

'Sorry, I'm just nervous, I suppose.'

'You'd better get the ticket,' she said, with an anxious glance at the clock.

'Don't worry, I've got it.'

Her heart threatened to burst out of her chest when the doorbell rang. Hayden quickly brushed his hands on his trousers and opened the door to welcome a balding middle-aged man with glasses and a briefcase.

'Hi, I'm William, the senior winnings advisor.'

He showed them some ID and shook both their hands firmly. Natalie led him through to the living room.

'Can I get you a cup of tea or coffee?'

He politely declined with a wave of his hand.

'I'm going to take a look at your ticket and validate your claim,' he told them once they were seated. 'I'll need to see some proof of identity from each of you. Have you filled out the claim form?'

'Yes,' said Hayden.

'Okay then. Let's have a look at the ticket.'

Hayden went to the bookshelf and pulled out the DVD of their wedding. A lump formed in Natalie's throat as he opened the case and produced the ticket.

Everyone was silent as William examined it. He didn't say anything for what felt like an eternity. Natalie glanced at Hayden for reassurance. She saw the fear in his eyes. Then William looked up and smiled.

'This all looks correct. Once everything has been confirmed, the money will appear in your bank account.'

'How long should that take?' Hayden asked.

'It should go through within the next forty-eight hours.'

He went through every aspect of what winning such an amount would involve. Natalie tried hard to listen but her mind wandered as he went on about tax implications and investing wisely.

Hayden nudged her with his foot and she sat up a little straighter.

'Now, it's completely up to you if you want to go public. Living in London, people might not notice your win as obviously as if you lived out in the sticks, but it will be hard to hide if you decide to buy a fancy car or house. If you do decide to go public, you can then control the media. We can organise a press conference to get your story out there. After that, interest should wane and you can both get on with your lives. If, on the other hand, you don't choose to go public, then you'll need to be careful who you tell because these things have a habit of getting out.'

'You think our friends and family would give us away?' Hayden asked.

'It happens more often than you would think. Anyway, I'm sure I've talked long enough but don't worry, I'll be in touch in a few days to see how you're getting on.'

He rose from his chair, gathering up his papers and closing his briefcase with a distinct click. He gave a parting nod and out he went, letting the door ease shut behind him.

Hayden walked over to the cabinet and opened it to retrieve two glasses.

'Champagne?'

Natalie nodded. They sat back down on the sofa and tried to relax.

The hardest part is over, Natalie consoled herself. Now she just had to wait.

THIRTEEN

NATALIE

The following morning, Natalie's phone buzzed with a call from an unknown number.

'Hello?'

'Hi, my name's Sibel Sherlock,' said the voice on the other end of the phone. 'William asked me to give you a ring. You see, I won the lottery five years ago.'

Natalie smiled. She had agreed William could pass on her number to a previous winner but she hadn't expected to hear from anyone so soon.

'Yes, I think I remember seeing you on the news, actually.'

She recalled the dazed look on Sibel's face as she was handed a giant cheque. She'd worked at Tesco, hadn't she?

Sibel let out a low chuckle. 'I wanted to ask if you'd like to come round for a cuppa? I've been where you are now, and it might help to chat.'

'Thank you,' Natalie said. 'That would be lovely.'

'Do you want to come?' she asked Hayden as she waited for Sibel to text her address.

'What for?' he asked, sitting in front of the TV with his phone. 'What can she tell us that we don't already know?'

Natalie's eyes sparkled with anticipation. 'We're about to live the good life and she's already living it. I want to know what it's really like, so we don't make the same mistakes.'

Hayden barked out a laugh. 'Don't worry. We'll find our own ways to screw this up.'

A few hours later, Natalie pulled into the driveway of a large house with white stone walls and an eye-catching red roof that reflected the bright sunlight. Tall trees with pink blossoms arched over the cobblestone path, leading up to a large bubbling fountain.

Natalie took a deep breath. She had never visited a place like this before, let alone been invited to walk through the doors as a guest.

Sibel herself opened the door. Natalie had half expected a servant. She wore a tailored suit, paired with a pale pink T-shirt, her sleeves rolled up to reveal her slim wrists.

'Welcome,' she said warmly. 'It's nice to meet you.'

'Thank you so much for inviting me.'

She stepped inside. An opulent hallway greeted her, with marble floors and velvet wallpaper.

'I hope you don't mind dogs?' Sibel asked, as three cocker spaniels descended the stairs and raced about in a flurry of fur and paws. The smallest one made a beeline for Natalie and jumped up at her.

'Rochefort! Down! Sorry about that.'

Natalie was not used to dogs, but she smiled as Sibel shut them in the kitchen and led her into the living room.

Tall windows overlooked a meticulously manicured garden and soft piano music wafted through the speakers. Sibel gestured for Natalie to sit on one of the sofas. Then she lifted the porcelain teapot, pouring out fragrant Earl Grey tea. 'Do help yourself,' she said with a gracious smile before waving her hand towards the table. Natalie marvelled at the selection of finger sandwiches filled with crunchy cucumber, and buttery scones dripping with raspberry jam. As they sipped their tea, Sibel told Natalie a bit about herself:

'This house was the first thing I bought. I paid for it outright, so I knew I would always have a roof over my head. So many people fritter away their winnings. I was determined I would not be one of them.'

Natalie nodded. 'It amazes me how people can blow through so much money,' she said.

Sibel shot her a sideways glance. 'Oh, you'd be surprised. When you have a lot of money, it's easy to think you'll never run out. So, I invested heavily in stocks and shares, which have provided me with enough income that I don't have to worry. I only splash out on the things I really want. I could afford to hire a housemaid but I don't love the idea of strangers wandering around my house. It would make me feel uncomfortable.'

Natalie nodded. She couldn't agree more.

'I'm not much of a party person these days. Animals are my passion. I couldn't have pets in my rented flat. Now I have an aviary for homeless birds, plus my three dogs and a dozen rabbits. I have all the time in the world to take care of them. I live the life I want to live.'

'So, you live alone?' Natalie asked, polishing off one of the delicious sandwiches.

Sibel looked at her for a moment, as if considering whether to confide.

'I was married when I won. Things were fine for a while. We did a world cruise, that was a lot of fun. But Henry bored easily. He ditched me for a younger model, and when that relationship didn't last, he moved on to the next one.'

Natalie peered down into her teacup.

'Do you... think you'd still be together if you hadn't won the money?'

Sibel considered. 'I don't think money changes the person you are. It boosted his ego a bit, gave him the confidence to move on, but I think that says something about him. Me, I'm pretty much the same as I always was, and to be honest I'm far happier with my animals than I ever was with him.'

She set down her teacup. 'Keep your head, Natalie, and enjoy the life you've been given. We really are the fortunate few.'

Hayden was on the internet, looking at cars, when she got home.

'I've narrowed it down to two,' he told Natalie. 'I can't decide between them. I think I might get both.'

Natalie smiled. 'Let's not get carried away. The money's not even in the bank yet.'

'I know, but I have to pass the time somehow. The waiting is driving me crazy.'

'Me too.'

She longed to tell him how long she had been waiting for this money, how scared she was about what would happen once they got it. Instead, she moved into his arms and stayed there as long as she could.

The phone rang. It was William. Hayden put him on speakerphone.

'I'm happy to tell you that your claim has been accepted. I'll give you a ring to let you know when you can expect the money. It shouldn't be more than a couple of days.'

'That's amazing!' squealed Natalie.

Her heart pounded and a smile spread across her face. She threw her arms around Hayden, tears welling up in her eyes. They celebrated with cheap Buck's Fizz from the corner shop because all their cards were maxed out.

* * *

'Mr and Mrs Peel? Please step this way.'

A smiling bank employee ushered Natalie and Hayden into a private room with swish curtains and leather chairs.

'In the old days we used to have champagne for our VIP customers,' she said apologetically, 'but I'm afraid we aren't allowed to do that anymore.'

Natalie shrank back in her chair as the bank manager strolled in.

'Mr and Mrs Peel? I am satisfied that everything is in order. I can now confirm that the amount of twelve and a half million has been transferred to your joint bank account.'

Natalie bit down on her bottom lip to quell the noise that threatened to burst from her mouth.

They remained in the office for a few minutes, but Natalie didn't take in a word anyone said. It was only when she and Hayden stepped outside again that the enormity of the situation began to sink in. She turned and looked at him.

'What now?'

'I've got something I want to say,' he told her.

She swallowed, dreading his next words.

He shuffled his feet and worked his hands nervously in his pockets, avoiding her eyes. She braced herself for what he was about to say. He leaned in and spoke in a low voice, his eyes darting about as if someone might be lurking in the shadows.

'Let's keep this between us, okay? We don't have to let the entire world know. I mean, we'll have to tell our family, but we don't have to broadcast it.'

Natalie's eyes flickered from his face to the ground, her fingers twisting and untwisting at her side. She chewed on her bottom lip, debating whether now was the time to speak up. It would be so much easier, so much more comfortable to remain silent, but now that they had the money, she had to know.

'What about Vivienne?'

He tilted his head. 'What about Vivienne?'

She forced herself to look at him. 'I know about you two.'

Hayden's eyes widened. 'What are you talking about? She's just a colleague.'

'Gail saw a woman with you in your car when you came back from Manchester. You clearly gave her a lift home but when I asked you about your journey you didn't mention her.'

'God, Natalie, that was nothing. I'm sorry I didn't say anything. I just didn't want you to think I was trying to get off with her. I just... wanted to make sure she got home alright. I know I should have said but I was worried you might take it the wrong way. Seems like I was right.'

Natalie swallowed hard. 'Don't put this on me. You're the one who lied.'

His nostrils flared. 'I did not lie! I can call her if you want. You can ask her what happened. She was supposed to take the train, actually. She already had her ticket.'

'So why didn't she take the bloody train?'

'There was a creepy woman at the hotel. At first she was just staring at Vivienne, but then she tried to follow her to her room. Vivienne was scared she would follow her home. I'd have felt responsible if anything had happened to her, so yes, I gave her a lift, but I was just trying to protect her from her stalker.'

Natalie felt a wave of shame wash over her. She had been the one who had made Vivienne feel uncomfortable and scared. She was the stalker.

FOURTEEN

HAYDEN

Three Weeks Earlier

Hayden strode into the Canary Grand. He sat down at the front desk and logged onto his terminal. His manager, Ivan, would be in late that morning so Hayden needed to stay on the ball and keep everything running until he got there.

He was hardly in his seat for three minutes before Vivienne strutted in. Her long white beautician's coat hung past her knees, the top three buttons purposely left undone. She had an unnatural sheen and her forehead looked like a porcelain doll's – Hayden suspected she'd been having extra Botox.

'Morning, Hayden,' she said, leaning against the counter as if she owned it. Her bright red lips curved into a mischievous smirk. She stepped closer to him, one hand reaching out to touch his arm. Her perfume stung his nose.

'Don't forget you owe me a coffee,' he reminded her. He was still a bit hacked off about that stunt she'd pulled at the pub. The classic, 'Oh, no! I forgot my wallet!'

He didn't believe her for an instant, but what could he do?

She'd already ordered the round for their table. Someone had to pay and he was the only one at the bar.

'Yeah, course,' Vivienne said, staring at her nails. 'Don't worry. I'm good for it.'

Yeah, sure she was.

'You're looking good today,' she said.

She stood behind him and ran her long fingernails up and down his desk.

'Stop it,' he muttered through gritted teeth, but she just smiled a small, knowing smile before turning around and heading off towards the treatment rooms. There was a provocative sway to her hips as she moved. When would she get it into her vain little head that he wasn't interested?

He wished he could tell Ivan but he'd just get laughed at. Vivienne could get away with murder and she'd still have a job.

He worked diligently all morning, helping customers, answering questions, and checking people in and out. For lunch, he ate a sandwich from home. He would have preferred a hot meal from the restaurant, but they hadn't paid their rent yet and he was worried about going overdrawn.

A woman stepped up to the counter, and his heart skipped a beat. For a moment he thought it was Natalie but then he realised it was her sister. Liz's shoulders were slumped, and she wore an oversized jumper that had seen better days. It was a shame she didn't make more of herself, because Liz would be very attractive if she made a bit of effort.

'Liz! What are you doing here?'

'I've been to the chiropractor. It's just down the street.'

'Oh.'

She shifted her weight and tucked a lock of hair behind her ear. 'Anyway, since I was passing, I thought I'd pop in and see you.' She leaned closer, her tone conspiratorial. 'I could use some advice actually.'

She'd piqued his interest. 'What about?'

'It's er... kind of personal. Can we step outside?'

'Liz, I can't. I'm working.'

Ivan gave him a sideways glance. 'I can hold the fort for a few minutes if you want to catch up with your lady friend.'

'She's my wife's sister, actually.'

Ivan raised an eyebrow. 'Is that right? Well, go on then. While it's quiet.'

Hayden stepped out from behind the desk. He felt a twinge of curiosity about what Liz wanted. Liz had always been a bit weird. He'd tried to set her up with a friend once – a friend who'd been most enthusiastic when he saw her picture. But he had returned from the date deflated.

'My best lines bounced off her like bullets off Superman's chest,' he'd complained.

Hayden had been embarrassed. 'What can I say? She's an acquired taste.'

Hayden followed her across the lobby, out into the sunshine. Greenwich sparkled in the afternoon light, its sleek modern office blocks reaching up to the sky. Stylish couples posed and took selfies while young professionals in crisp suits hurried along the riverfront or sipped draught beer at the trendy bars. The enticing smell of seafood drifted through the air.

'I'm thinking of doing something inadvisably, incomprehensibly stupid and I want you to talk me out of it,' Liz said.

His eyebrows shot up. 'Why are you asking me? Why not Natalie?'

'Because I want a totally unbiased opinion.'

He leaned forward, feeling slightly suspicious. Was this some kind of joke? Liz had never given the impression she valued his opinion. 'So what is it?'

She fiddled with her handbag. 'There's someone I like. Have liked for a long time, and I've never said anything because, well, it's complicated...'

'Is it someone I know?'

Her shoulders moved up and down in a way he took to mean yes. He tried not to gape. This was intriguing. It was news to him that Liz even had a heart, let alone had lost it to someone.

'That's the thing...' Her gaze trailed off towards the Thames. Hayden bit back his impatience.

'Come on, you can tell me.'

'The trouble is, this person has a lot to lose if they admit they have feelings for me. I think they'd rather settle for a mundane life than take a leap and be happy.'

'Who is it?' he asked again.

She shook her head. 'This is embarrassing enough as it is. But I just thought... you're good at talking to people, without making yourself look like a complete tit. So, what should I do? Should I lay it on the line and risk losing a good friend or should I be a good girl and keep it zipped?'

He bit down on his lip. 'This is all very intriguing, Liz. But honestly, it would really help if I knew who it was. Then I could tailor my advice.'

'No, it's too embarrassing.'

He twirled the ring on his left hand. Oh God, she couldn't mean him, could she? He'd certainly never sensed any interest there. As far as he was concerned, there had never been any sort of spark between them. In fact, any time their eyes met, her response had seemed more like icy disapproval than a blaze of affection. But how could you tell with a woman like Liz?

'I think it might be best to keep it to yourself for now. Why don't you wait it out a bit? See if those feelings grow stronger, or disappear? That way you won't have to risk anything.'

Liz seemed satisfied. 'Thank you, Hayden. That's actually good advice.'

'So, you're really not going to tell me who this is?'

'Nope.'

'And can I tell...'

'You breathe one word to Nat and you're dead.'

'Okay then. Good to talk.'

His mind raced with confusion and curiosity, but he managed to keep a neutral expression on his face as he headed back inside.

* * *

Hayden's car rolled to a halt outside the flats that evening and he drew a breath, glad to have made it home. There were only a couple of months left until it was due for an MOT and there was no way it was going to pass. Given the state of their finances, he would probably be consigned to the bus.

He spotted Daisy walking by with her little Scottie dog, Presley.

'Hi, Daisy,' he called.

She turned and nodded. Presley wrinkled his little black nose and sniffed at a pile of rubbish. Scraps of sausage roll and banana peel had spilled onto the grass, and a cloud of flies hovered around the mess.

Daisy glanced up at the flat. 'Natalie's home early.'

'Is she?'

'Yeah, I saw her earlier. She...'

'You got any cigarettes?'

'You told me to stop giving you them.'

'I know, but I really need one. Otherwise, I'll have to go and buy a whole pack.'

She fumbled in her pocket. 'Go on then.'

'Thanks, Daze.'

He stuck it in his mouth and she handed him a lighter. He'd given up when he met Natalie. She didn't like cigarette smoke, so he'd told her he was a non-smoker. For the most part, he had stuck with it, but he still had the occasional one, when he needed it. Daisy didn't light one for herself. She just stood there watching.

'Good day at work?' she asked.

'Someone left an inflatable sheep in one of the rooms. We shoved it in Phillip's locker.'

She giggled. 'Wish I could have seen that.'

'As it happens...'

He pulled out his phone and let her watch the clip, laughing with her as Phillip leapt up in fright.

He handed her back the lighter. 'Wouldn't do to be caught with this.'

'I've got gum.'

'Ta.'

'Hayden, I just thought you should know... When I walked past your place this morning, I saw Natalie. She had a bloke with her.'

His stomach contracted. 'What bloke?'

'He walked up to the door with her but he didn't go in.'

'Did they...' He could barely bring himself to say it. 'Did they kiss?'

'Oh no, nothing like that. He was just... there.'

But why the hell was she home in the middle of the day? And who was this bloke?

'Did he look like a delivery guy?'

'No, she definitely knew him. I saw them walking up the road together, from the tube.'

He tilted his head. 'What did he look like?'

'Very ordinary.' She stole a glance at his feet. 'He had naff trainers.'

He knelt down and stroked Presley's silky ears, trying to ignore the unease that bubbled up inside him. He knew Natalie wasn't the type to play around but he couldn't shake the fear.

He went inside, eyes darting around the room for any sign of another man's presence. He crossed the living room to kiss Natalie, inhaling deeply, but all he could smell was her scent –

the same familiar blend of peaches and vanilla that had always been hers.

He looked into her eyes.

'How was work?' He studied the subtle changes in her expression. 'Did Jan give you shit for leaving early?'

Her lips tightened and her hand moved to her forehead.

'One of the neighbours saw you at the tube station,' he told her.

Her face twisted into an expression of indignation.

'Nosy git! Which one?'

'The old bloke.'

She walked off to the kitchen and he followed, questioning her about why she'd left early. She told him she had a toothache and he offered to book her a dental appointment, knowing how she hated the dentist, but this seemed to put her on edge.

He should have known better than to give Natalie a suggestion. She was as stubborn as a mule. He headed to the bathroom and spat out his gum, then chugged a capful of mouthwash. He let it swirl around in his mouth for as long as he could bear. He reached for his towel and found himself looking into the accusing eyes of Megan Fox.

It wasn't a bad poster but it didn't do anything for him. Natalie had walked in on him one day when he was viewing an adult film on his computer. He'd closed the tab quickly, but in his haste, he had inadvertently opened a news article about Megan Fox. Natalie had homed in on that article, the way women did.

'Do you have a thing for Megan Fox?' she'd asked.

'Er... yeah.'

He hadn't known who Megan Fox was, let alone had the chance to formulate an opinion about her. But Natalie had got carried away. So now he had to live with this poster of her on his bathroom door when he'd much prefer Taylor Swift.

He walked through to the living room and sank into the

well-worn sofa, soft cushions swallowing him up. His phone beeped. Daisy had sent him a rude joke. He clicked on the link and burst out laughing. Then he deleted it, knowing Natalie wouldn't approve.

The oven timer beeped, and the smell of melted cheese and mince wafted through the room. Natalie emerged with two plates cradled in her arms. He watched as she balanced them effortlessly, her movements smooth and precise.

They ate in silence, eyes glued to the TV as an action movie blared. He was nervous about the man Daisy had seen. Perhaps he was just a neighbour. The trouble was, Natalie didn't realise how attractive she was, or how many men would kill for one night with her. She'd told him once that she'd been approached by a modelling agency when she was seventeen. He couldn't understand why she hadn't gone for it. He would have leapt at the chance. But Natalie wanted different things out of life. All she'd ever wanted was a coffee shop of her own.

His phone beeped and the screen lit up. Natalie stared at him expectantly, but he didn't check it in case it was Daisy with another one of her inappropriate jokes.

'What if it's work?' she said.

'It can wait.'

Then Natalie's phone beeped.

Was some man texting her?

He fought the urge to wrestle it from her hand. He wasn't a caveman. Instead, he slipped an arm around her and leaned closer to see who it was from. Relief flooded his body when he saw the message was from Liz. Nevertheless, he kept his free arm firmly locked around her to remind her that she was his.

FIFTEEN

HAYDEN

Now

Hayden and Natalie walked in a daze, both still processing the fact that they had their money. As they walked, Hayden's phone chimed.

'It's William,' he said, when he saw the name on the screen. He put the phone to his ear.

'Hello, William.' There was a moment of silence before the enthusiastic voice on the other end congratulated them.

'So, you're sure you want to keep the win quiet?' William asked. Hayden exchanged a glance with Natalie.

'Yes,' he confirmed.

'Okay, that's entirely up to you but if you change your minds, give me a call.'

William wished them luck and hung up. Hayden pocketed the phone and intertwined his fingers with Natalie's. The sky darkened as they headed back. They quickened their pace, their feet pounding the pavement.

They reached the car just in time and scrambled inside, slamming the doors shut. The sky opened up, unleashing a flurry of icy stones onto the asphalt. The dense hailstones whirled in savage circles around the car, rattling against the windows as if they were trying to break in.

Natalie laughed. 'That was close.'

Hayden eyed the relentless avalanche of hail.

'Tell me about it. I felt like we were being hunted.'

'Hayden, I'm really sorry about accusing you. I just... I don't know what I was thinking.'

He pulled her close. 'It's okay, let's forget about it, shall we?'

He relaxed his arms and she moved back into her own seat.

'Hey, I was thinking, maybe we should take the publicity after all?' he said. 'I mean, how can we possibly keep it hidden? We're going to buy a new house, not to mention new cars. And you're going to open your own coffee shop. How do you explain that without revealing our secret?'

'I could say I got a loan from the bank.'

'Maybe, but people are going to notice after a while, aren't they?'

Natalie frowned. 'We don't have to decide just yet, do we? Let's keep it to the family. Give them a chance to take it in, and then we'll think about who else we want to tell. I really don't fancy having the whole world know. It feels personal, you know?'

Hayden nodded. 'Okay, just the family for now. As long as we're on the same page...'

Back home, they flopped down on the sofa. It was time to ring round the family and share the news.

'Who do you want to call first?' Natalie asked.

'My parents,' he said. 'I know they'll be over the moon!'

He dialled his parents' number, heart thumping in anticipation. He held his breath as he waited for his mum to answer, already picturing the look of disbelief on her face when he announced their big news.

'Oh, hello, darling. I was just saying to Dad that we haven't spoken to you in ages. We thought you were getting too busy to speak to us oldies.'

He ignored her attempt to guilt him. He could ring three times a day and his mum would still say it wasn't enough.

'Mum,' he began hesitantly, 'we have some incredible news. Please make sure Dad's got his hearing aid in, it's important. And turn the TV down. I don't know how you can hear anything over that.'

'He's watching *Dad's Army*.'

'Can he pause it? We've got something big to tell you.'

'Oh,' she said, her voice rising in pitch. 'They have something to tell us!' Her words echoed through the flat and Hayden had to hold his phone away from his ear. He waited impatiently for his dad to come to the phone.

'Right then, lad, what is it?'

'We've won the lottery, Dad. Twelve and a half million quid.'

He imagined the relief on his parents' faces as they heard the news – no more worrying about money or bills.

'Oh, I thought you were going to say Natalie's pregnant,' his mum said. 'We're still waiting for a grandchild, you know.'

Hayden raised his voice slightly. 'Mum, did you hear what I just said? We've won twelve and a half million!'

There was a loud clapping sound.

'Bloody marvellous!' said Hayden's dad. 'Now you can finally get on the housing ladder.'

'We intend to.'

'And you can replace that rust bucket of a car.'

'Yes, I'm just deciding what to get.'

Natalie came closer to the phone. 'And I'm going to open my own coffee shop.'

'Well, that sounds lovely!'

Hayden's mum's voice lifted. 'I'll come and have a coffee when it opens. Will you be serving walnut cake?'

Natalie smiled. 'I certainly will.'

'Have you ever made walnut cake?' Hayden whispered in her ear.

Natalie shook her head from side to side. He grinned and squeezed her shoulder.

'How are you going to manage all that money?' his dad asked.

'We're going to meet with a financial planner to help us set up a plan,' Hayden assured him. 'They'll advise us on what to invest in and how much to keep in our bank account.'

'Very sensible,' his dad agreed.

'You hear of so many lottery winners blowing through their money,' his mum added. 'They call it the lottery winner's curse.'

'Well not us,' Hayden assured them. 'We're going to do this right.'

He ended the phone call with a firm reminder to keep the lottery winnings a secret.

The room was still, the only sound coming from the clock ticking on the wall. Hayden broke the silence. 'It's funny what my mum said.'

Natalie rolled her eyes. 'Yeah, it was like our wedding all over again. I'm so sick of people speculating about whether or not we're going to have a baby. That will be one advantage of getting older, I suppose. At some point people will stop asking.'

'Are you completely sure that's still want you want?'

She looked at him. 'Of course it is. I don't want children. I told you that on our very first date.'

'Oh, I know. I just wanted to make sure. I mean, things are different now. We could afford an army of nannies if we wanted.'

'I don't want,' she said firmly. She narrowed her eyes. 'Do you?'

He hesitated for a fraction of a second. 'Not if you don't. It's your body.'

She chewed her lip. 'But if it was down to you?'

'I'm happy with things as they are,' he said, seeing he'd struck a nerve. 'I just don't want you to have any regrets, that's all.'

'No regrets here.' Her eyes settled on the grimy window. 'I can't imagine anything worse than the pressure of having full responsibility for a tiny human being.'

'But it wouldn't just be you. I'd be there with you all the way.'

Her gaze was distant and her eyes seemed to search for something, far away from him. Her lips thinned into a faint frown, and he frowned back. He found it confusing, her lack of maternal desire. She was a kind, loving woman. It just didn't quite fit somehow, but if she said she didn't want children, he wasn't going to push it.

'You look worried,' he said.

'I'm just scared of losing it all,' she admitted, her voice barely above a whisper. 'What if there's a run on the bank or something? I think we should buy a house as soon as possible. And I'm going to buy my coffee shop; I know just the place.'

He nodded solemnly and managed a small smile. 'I agree with all of that, but first things first. I think it's time we did a little shopping.'

Hayden spent the afternoon visiting car showrooms while Natalie shopped at Harrods. He chose two Ferraris, one in red and one in silver for himself, and a brand-new Audi for Natalie. The cars would take a couple of weeks to ship, which meant he would have to drive his old rust bucket for a little longer.

'Just as well,' said Natalie as they drove back home. 'I mean where the hell are we going to put them?'

She was right. If he left a fancy new car outside their building it would either get stolen or torn apart for scrap. Nobody wanted anyone else to be better than them.

'We could ask Daisy and Ted if they have any room in their garage,' Hayden suggested.

'And what are you going to tell them?' Natalie asked. 'I thought we were supposed to be keeping the win a secret?'

'It's just Daisy and Ted.'

'I know, but I haven't even told Gail. It wouldn't be fair to tell them and not her, and then she'd tell Andy. They tell each other everything.'

'Maybe we should tell them,' he said. 'They are our friends.'

They got out of the car and walked through the communal garden. He punched the code into the keypad and they entered the building. The hallway was dark. The only source of light came from their flat. Natalie walked with her head down, pulling her keys from her handbag. Hayden grabbed her wrist.

'Wait!' His gaze was fixed on their front door. He saw a shadow shift under the doorframe. 'Someone's in our flat.'

SIXTEEN

HAYDEN

Hayden nudged the door. His heart was beating out of his chest but he had to maintain a façade of bravery since Natalie was right behind him. A creak reverberated throughout the room as the door swung open. Someone was sitting on the sofa, feet resting on the coffee table, toes pointing up at the ceiling. A cup of coffee sat steaming on the edge of the table.

Natalie pushed past him, no longer afraid. She leaned down and threw her arms around the intruder.

'Alright, Goldilocks! How the hell did you get in here?'

'Your neighbour let me into the building, and when I knocked on the door, I realised it was open.'

The voice was familiar but Hayden couldn't place it. It was only when he walked around to stand next to Natalie that he realised it was her younger cousin, Oliver. He hadn't seen him since their wedding.

'You're saying the door was open?'

Hayden looked at Natalie. He recalled rushing out the door, but surely they'd locked it properly? He sat down on the sofa and took a long hard look at Oliver. He had the same chestnut hair as Liz and Natalie, though a single curl at the nape of his neck gave him a mischievous air. 'So, what gives?' he asked. 'I thought you were travelling Europe?'

'I was. The weather was boiling in Spain. It was getting to me, so I thought I'd come and see you guys. It's okay if I stay for a couple of days, isn't it?'

'Of course,' Natalie said.

Oliver talked a mile-a-minute, pulling up pictures from his phone to show them. His gaze flitted across the room in search of something, occasionally stopping on Hayden with a raised eyebrow, before returning to Natalie. Hayden knew Natalie was fond of her cousin but Hayden didn't trust him an inch. Oliver could be a little impulsive. Natalie put this down to the fact that he was dropped on his head as a baby. The whole family doted on him because he was the youngest, but the man was approaching thirty now. He was hardly a child.

'Do you want another coffee?' Natalie asked.

'Not for me thanks. Unless you've got something stronger?'

Natalie rushed off to the kitchen and brought back a beer. His beer. Hayden knew it was silly to mind about stuff like that, but he was still suspicious about the way Oliver had entered the house. Not to mention his timing. He must have jumped on a plane the minute he heard their news. Natalie had told Liz to keep it to herself, but she must have let it slip.

Oliver perched on the arm of the worn-out sofa, gesturing wildly as he expounded on wild and fantastical ideas for what they should do with their lottery winnings. Natalie listened with rapt attention, her chin resting in her hands.

'I've already decided to open a coffee shop,' she told him, with pride in her voice.

Oliver's face lit up. 'Why stop at one when you could have a chain of coffee shops?'

Hayden squirmed, uncomfortable at Oliver's suggestion. Although Natalie had worked at the Riverside Café for years, she had never run her own business before. And now that they had money, Natalie didn't need to work her fingers to the bone. He understood that the café was her dream but what Oliver was suggesting was ludicrous.

He opened his mouth to disagree but realised that it wouldn't do any good. Instead, he dug out a pair of headphones, hoping to drown out Oliver's voice. Had he always been this annoying? He honestly didn't know.

He sat down at the kitchen table and scoured the internet for a new house. One in particular took his fancy. He rang the number listed to arrange a viewing.

'That particular property has only just come on the market,' the estate agent said. 'I can fit you in at nine o'clock tomorrow morning if you like?'

'Yes please.'

'Marvellous. You'll be the first to see it.'

Hayden smiled to himself. The house looked amazing. Who knew, maybe it would turn out to be their dream home?

Natalie and Oliver stayed up, drinking wine and talking late into the night. Hayden trudged up the stairs to their bedroom, frustration boiling beneath his skin. As he lay down on the bed, he heard their muffled laughter through the thin walls. He clenched his jaw at the sound of Oliver's voice and pulled the duvet over his head, trying to shut out the noise.

The early morning light filtered through the curtains. Hayden carefully placed his hand on Natalie's shoulder, gently shaking her awake. She grumbled in response and rolled away from him, using her pillow as a barrier.

'Come on, Nat!'

He watched as she stirred from her slumber, groggy and disoriented. She padded over to her dressing table and took a brush from the drawer to smooth out her tangled hair. She scrutinised her reflection, poking at her dark circles under her eyes.

'Do I need make-up?'

He shook his head. 'No. You're already beautiful. We need to get going.'

They went downstairs and tiptoed through the living room. Snoring vibrated through the flat. The front door rattled as he pulled it open, letting in a sliver of light that illuminated Oliver sprawled on the couch, clutching an empty beer can. Crumpled fast food wrappers littered the floor around him.

'How long is he staying?' he asked Natalie, as they walked out to the car.

'I'm not sure,' she said, slipping her hand into his. 'He said he might move back to London permanently. Isn't that great? It's about time he settled down.'

'Just as long as he's not going to sleep on our sofa forever,' Hayden muttered.

He parked outside the estate agent's office and they went inside. A beaming woman strode forward to greet them. The tailored fit of her chocolate brown trousers contrasted with the soft lambskin jacket that draped from her shoulders. She stretched out a hand to shake.

'Hi, I'm Christie. Pleased to meet you. Think of me as your own personal shopper for houses.'

Christie spoke with the confidence of someone who knew what she was doing.

'Where did you park?' she asked as they walked outside the office. Hayden pointed. She cast a dubious look at his old banger.

'Let's take my car, shall we?'

She led them over to a blue Volvo and they climbed inside. She drove them through their old familiar neighbourhood and kept going until the city melted away behind them.

Drab grey buildings gave way to open green spaces and

tree-lined roads. The spindly branches seemed to reach for each other, meeting above the roof of the car. Christie took them down a private road until they reached a plot with a manicured lawn and a beautiful glass dome that sparkled in the sunlight.

Natalie gasped. 'Is this the house?'

'It certainly is,' Christie said, bringing the car to a stop.

They hopped out and walked up to the Glass House. Christie used her phone to unlock it and the front door swung open. Hayden's eyes widened. The domed ceiling of the atrium towered above, crafted from glass panels that let in a cascade of light. He admired the intricate pattern of the panes, mesmerised by the way they sparkled in the sun.

'Note how the glass panels flood the interior with light, offering an expansive view of the Thames,' Christie said, as they moved inside.

Hayden squinted at the river. He saw kayakers and motor-boats gliding past, far too close for his comfort. 'It doesn't feel very private.'

Christie smiled. 'Everything is controlled through your phone. With the click of a button, the windows can be tinted for complete privacy. You have a fantastic view of the river to the front and expansive grounds that reach out on either side. You can have as much isolation as you need. Perfect peace of mind.'

The city's hum had grown distant, fading into nothingness, and he felt his shoulders relax.

Natalie was transfixed by the magnificent glass staircase that spiralled around the room.

'That's mostly for show,' Christie said. 'There's also a lift.'

She pointed to a door in the centre of the room. The keypad was illuminated by a faint blue light. She used her phone to unlock it and there was a gentle hiss as the door slid open.

They all stepped inside and the door closed softly behind them. The lift jostled slightly as they travelled up to the next floor.

The focal point of the kitchen was a large island, the size of a small car. The countertop was a solid block of white quartz and there were comfy blue barstools set around it. Perfect for entertaining, Hayden thought.

'As I mentioned earlier, this is a smart house so you can control everything from your phones,' Christie was saying. 'And I mean everything, from the lighting to the temperature control and even the door locks.'

They moved through the living room and Hayden admired the massive flat-screen television built into the wall. Natalie was eager to explore further, peering into the cosy guest rooms.

'Do you want to see the master bedroom?' Christie asked.

They took the lift up to the top floor. There was space for a queen-sized bed and the walk-in wardrobe was a shopper's paradise, while the bathroom boasted a jacuzzi and a shower with multiple jets. Hayden walked over to the balcony. The sprawling city stretched out before him, the Thames weaving through it all like a shimmering black spool of ribbon. He turned and caught Natalie's eye.

'I love it!' she whispered.

'Shh! We still have to negotiate the price. But I love it too.'

Christie cleared her throat. 'If you've finished in here, I'll show you the grounds.'

They took the lift back down and walked outside. As they made their way around the building, they stopped to marvel at the immaculate tennis court in front and then moved on towards the private patio shrouded by trees at the back. There was a fully stocked bar and sunloungers placed around what Christie referred to as a Grecian pool. It was shaped like a rectangle but with the corners cut to give it an added elegance.

Hayden caught Natalie's eye. He couldn't believe this was happening. She'd always joked they'd win the lottery, but he'd never thought it would actually happen, and now here they were standing in what he hoped was about to become their dream home.

He walked over to the railings and let the breeze ruffle his hair. He stayed perfectly still, mesmerised by the river and its never-ending movement. The water was almost black in the shadows, but glimmered emerald where it caught the light. It was perfect, absolutely perfect. His heart ached with a frightening premonition that this would be the last time he would ever be truly happy.

SEVENTEEN

HAYDEN

When Hayden's alarm went off, he got up as quietly as he could, leaving Natalie curled up on her side of the bed. He headed for the bathroom and lifted the toilet seat. He was mid pee when he heard a snuffling sound. Glancing to his right he saw Oliver, fast asleep in the bathtub. For goodness' sake! He peed as fast as he could, fury burning within him. It was a bit much when a man couldn't even be alone in his own bathroom.

He dressed quickly and stomped down the stairs, slamming the door on his way out. The path was littered with bright pink silly string that stuck to his shoes and there were discarded beer bottles in the grass. He would not miss the boxy flat, or the communal garden. He wouldn't miss Oliver either.

The Canary Grand was bustling with activity. Normally, he would have tensed up at the sight of the long queue, snaking its way around the lobby, but today he relished the challenge.

Phillip was wheeling a trolley load of suitcases towards the lift.

'Alright, Hayden? Do anything nice at the weekend?'

Phillip loved cars, so Hayden almost told him about his new purchases but stopped himself in time.

He strode towards the reception desk, where Ivan was tapping away on his computer. With a nod of acknowledgement, he logged onto his own terminal and began helping with the backlog.

Later, when it was quiet, Ivan told him he could take his break.

'That was good work this morning, dealing with that awkward customer. You did well to keep your cool.'

Hayden basked in the praise. He knew he was good at his job but it was nice to hear it. Even if it made what he was about to do all the more painful. He took the letter from his pocket and handed it to Ivan, who raised a brow.

'What's this? You inviting me to a party?'

Hayden forced a laugh. 'No, I've decided it's time for me to move on so this is my letter of resignation.'

Ivan went silent. He looked down at the letter as if he couldn't believe his eyes.

'Why, where are you off to?'

Hayden didn't know what to tell him.

'You got another job?'

'Not yet. Just... looking for a change.'

Ivan regarded him oddly. 'You know you're in line for a promotion if you stay on.'

'Am I?'

Hayden's heart lifted, then plunked back down with a thump. He liked it here but there was no need to go on working. He wanted to spend more time with Natalie. That was what really mattered.

The smell of garlic and tomato sauce wafted from the kitchen as Hayden stepped through the front door that evening. Natalie, Liz and Oliver sat around the table with pints of beer and cans of

Coke. The Monopoly board was spread out in the centre. There were neat little stacks of paper money and plastic buildings were dotted around the board. Liz was studying her properties closely as Oliver rolled the dice and Natalie counted out money.

'What's all this then?' he asked.

'We're nearly finished,' Natalie said. 'Then we're going clubbing.'

He fought the urge to laugh. 'Seriously? Clubbing?'

'Yep.'

Natalie landed on Park Lane and Oliver's face lit up with glee.

'That's it, you win,' she said, pushing away from the table.

Oliver chuckled. 'We should play with real money.'

Liz shook her head. 'You wish.'

Natalie looked at Hayden. 'There's pizza in the oven if you want some. I'm going to get ready.'

She headed for the bedroom and Hayden followed. 'Are you seriously going clubbing?' he asked as she flicked through the hangers in her wardrobe.

'Yeah, why not?'

'Because you're nearly forty?'

She turned and looked at him. 'You should come. It's been ages since we did something like this.'

He shook his head. 'I'd feel ridiculous.'

He walked back down to the living room and found Oliver on Natalie's laptop. He peered over his shoulder. Oliver was looking at flats on Rightmove.

'Looking for a place to rent?' he asked.

'No, I want to buy.'

'In London?'

As far as he knew, the only work experience Oliver had was working behind a bar. There was no way he could afford a mortgage.

Natalie appeared in the doorway. Oliver shot her a look and she pressed her lips together.

'What have you promised him?' Hayden asked.

'Nothing,' Natalie said.

Hayden leaned over and snapped the laptop shut. 'Right. We need to talk about money.'

Natalie stiffened beside him but she nodded. Liz slipped silently onto the sofa.

'So, Natalie and I have been talking,' he continued. 'And we've worked out how much money we can afford to give away. We're giving each of you one hundred thousand.'

'That's very generous,' Liz said with a smile. 'Thank you.'

Oliver clenched his jaw, barely containing his anger. 'You've won twelve and a half million. You're set for life.'

'How much did you expect to get?' Natalie asked.

Oliver's mouth was set in a grim line and his eyes had a hard light.

'I don't know. Enough to buy myself a house and jack in my job.'

Natalie looked like she was wavering, so Hayden spoke up.

'Listen, Oliver, we want to help you out. Of course we do. But the money has to last us. If we give too much away, too soon, we'll end up broke. It happens all too often. So, we're giving you a hundred thousand for now and we can reassess it in a few years.'

'A few years?'

Oliver's face was red, and his eyes burned with rage. His fists were clenched at his sides, and he was trembling with anger. He gathered up all of his belongings with swift jerky motions, throwing his rucksack over his shoulder. With a loud bang, the door flew open then shut as he stomped out of the flat. Natalie rushed after him, her voice frantic. 'Where are you going?'

'Don't worry about me. I'll stay at the Travelodge!'

Hayden's face was pinched with irritation and he shook his head in disbelief.

He was angry at Oliver for upsetting Natalie, but his latest tantrum confirmed that his visit was all about getting his hands on their money. He was nothing but an entitled gold-digger. He placed an arm around Natalie's shoulder.

'Let him have his strop. If he wants his money, he'll be back.'

EIGHTEEN

HAYDEN

Natalie stared at the steam rising from her mug of hot chocolate. 'Are you sure we're doing the right thing? I mean, maybe Oliver has a point. Maybe we should be more generous.'

Hayden worked his jaw. 'I think we've been pretty generous. Sure, that money won't buy him a house in London but it's more than enough for a deposit.'

Natalie stirred her hot chocolate with a spoon. 'Yeah, I guess you're right... but maybe I could offer him a job at my coffee shop?'

Hayden shook his head sadly. 'I don't think he'll go for it.'

He was impressed by how quickly Natalie had found premises for her coffee shop. She had always talked about owning a café, but it had been in vague, dreamy terms. He'd never expected her vision to come to fruition. Following through on a plan had never been her strong point, up to now.

'Do you think I should ring him, see if he's alright?' Natalie asked as she finished her drink.

Hayden squeezed his eyes shut, trying to suppress his frustration with Oliver.

'No, leave him for now. Let him stew a bit.'

. . .

In the bedroom, they peeled off their clothes. Natalie's body shone in the moonlight as she stepped out of her jeans. He moved to the bed, slipped between the cool sheets and closed his eyes. Natalie climbed in beside him but proceeded to thrash around, her breathing uneven and restless. She pulled at the duvet, then flopped over to the other side of the bed. She let out a mumbled apology as he clenched his jaw. With a sigh of resignation, he rolled over and closed his eyes, eventually succumbing to sleep.

Hayden was the first to wake in the morning. He reached for his phone and found a bunch of calls and messages he'd missed the night before:

Ted: *Alright mate? Are you coming or what?*

He wracked his brains. Coming where?

Then one from Daisy, around midnight: *Gail's too nice to say anything but where the hell are you? You'd better both be in hospital or something.*

What?

Then another from Daisy at around 2 a.m.: *You're not in hospital are you?*

He furrowed his brow as he looked over at the calendar on the wall. He located yesterday's date. Something was scribbled in Natalie's flowery handwriting: *Andy's birthday drinks, 9 p.m. at the Dog and Drake.*

Damn. They'd both completely forgotten. Never mind, they would buy Andy an expensive present to make up for it.

He poured himself a steaming cup of coffee and slumped on the sofa, wincing as he sat on the broken spring.

His phone buzzed, and he swiped to answer it.

'Hello?'

'You're on the cover of the *Chronicle!*' His mother's voice boomed with excitement through the speaker.

'What? Mum, I have no idea what you're talking about.' The mug in his hand trembled, splashing hot coffee on his lap.

'It's a lovely picture of you and Natalie. Here, I'll read it out to you. It says, "Local Couple Wins Lottery Jackpot!"'

'Oh my God, are you serious?'

'I most certainly am. Your dad bought all the copies in the newsagent!'

'It's in the other paper too,' he heard his dad say. 'Not on the front cover, but near the back. They used the same picture.'

This was not good. Not good at all.

'You didn't tell anyone, did you?' he asked.

'Of course not,' his mum said, indignantly. 'You asked us to keep it quiet and we did.'

'Thanks, Mum.'

There was only one person he could think of who would spill their secret.

He barged through to the bedroom and pushed the door open. Natalie was still fast asleep, her chest gently rising and falling with each breath. He marched across the room and reached out to shake her awake.

'Oliver has blabbed to the press!'

Natalie stirred from her sleep and blinked, confusion and disorientation lingering in her eyes. 'What's that?'

'It's all over the papers.'

Natalie twisted around in the sheets. 'No one reads the papers anymore.'

'My mum saw it. And it'll be in the online editions too. Word gets around.'

She rubbed her tired eyes. 'Do you really think Oliver did this?'

'Who else?'

She swallowed. 'I really don't think he'd blab.'

'I think that's exactly what he's done and now everyone will know, including all our friends. We'd better call everyone this morning and tell them before the news gets out.'

She nodded. 'Yes, let's do that.'

'Oh and heads up. It seems we missed Andy's birthday drinks last night.'

'Shit!'

'Shit indeed.'

On the bright side, telling their friends they'd won the lottery seemed to absolve them from missing Andy's party. Ted laughed uproariously like it was the funniest thing he'd ever heard.

'This isn't a joke,' Hayden told him. 'We really have won the lottery.'

'I know, I believe you,' he said. 'I don't know why I can't stop laughing.'

A shriek sounded in the background.

'Is Daisy alright?'

'She's fine, she's just swinging from the curtains,' Ted said. 'Daisy get down from there. You're going to hurt yourself.'

Hayden smiled. 'Think you're going to need a tranquilliser dart, mate.'

'Don't think I can catch her.'

'Give her some brandy then. That'll calm her down.'

Across the room, Natalie was talking to Gail on loud-speaker. Gail clapped so loudly it sounded like a gun going off, prompting Scarlett to howl. Natalie held the phone away from her ear. Gail had apparently handed the phone to Andy.

'Sorry about missing your birthday,' Natalie said.

'Never mind that,' Andy said. 'This is great news. You know, I always thought they rigged the lottery. I never thought it was possible to win.'

When they'd rung just about everyone they could think of, Natalie stretched her arms towards the ceiling with a yawn. 'Since we're both up, why don't we go out for breakfast?'

He smiled in agreement, and they quickly threw on some clothes before heading out the front door. The morning air was crisp, and Natalie insisted they stop at the newsagent to pick up a paper. 'For posterity,' she said with a grin.

They stared hard at the picture, taken on their honeymoon in Blackpool, the twinkling illuminations of the famous seafront lighting up the background.

'They must have got it from my Facebook,' Natalie said.

He nodded tightly. 'We'll have to change our privacy settings straight away. I don't like the idea of people snooping into our lives.'

They headed to a greasy spoon café along the main road near Limehouse station. The simple interior comprised Formica tables and vinyl flooring. It would not win any design awards but Hayden and Natalie liked the simplicity and the food. They both ordered full English breakfasts and large mugs of coffee.

Natalie's eyes lit up as she talked, gesturing widely with her hands. 'After this, I'm going to show you my coffee shop,' she told him. 'The decorators are coming Monday and they reckon it will take about a week to transform it from a juice bar into a coffee shop. I hope to have it all ready to open within a couple of months. I've agreed with the owners that I can rent the space first so I can get it ready while the sale goes through.'

'Wow!' Hayden said, a little in awe of her enthusiasm. He hadn't thought about what he wanted to do yet. He'd work that out once he had completed his last few shifts at the Canary Grand.

'You'll be employing staff, right? You can't run it all yourself.'

Her focus snapped back to him. 'I'm thinking of asking Gail. We'd work really well together and it would be a laugh.'

He nodded his approval. Gail's level-headedness was exactly what was needed to ensure the new café wasn't a failure. They both dug into their breakfasts, eating with relish.

When he had finished, he sat back and patted his stomach, satisfied with the meal. When the waitress returned with the bill, he gave her a generous tip to show his appreciation.

They returned to their car and he jammed the key into the ignition. Nothing happened. He turned the key again. After a few grunts of frustration, the engine finally coughed to life. Thick grey smoke billowed out of the tailpipe as the car clattered down the street. It was as if the car knew its time was up.

'I can't wait to get the new cars,' he said, as they pulled up outside the flat.

He barely registered the people standing about on the pavement until the blinding flashes of light filled his vision. A chorus of cheering and clapping erupted from a group of reporters. They shouted questions and pushed microphones close to their faces.

'What's it like to become millionaires overnight?'

'Don't talk to them,' Hayden hissed in Natalie's ear.

Natalie's eyes were wide as they sprinted across the communal garden. They could hear the thunder of camera shutters behind them. Yellowed curtains fluttered as the neighbours leaned out for a better look.

Frantically, Hayden punched numbers into the keypad until it beeped twice and the deadbolt clicked. He yanked the heavy door open, shoved Natalie inside and slammed it shut just as the mob of paparazzi reached them.

They tore through the hallway. Hayden's fingers shook as he fumbled with his keys. He opened the door to their flat and they burst inside, slamming it shut. The deadbolt clanged into place like a prison gate closing behind them.

NINETEEN

HAYDEN

They shut themselves in the flat for the weekend, keeping away from the world.

'I'm going to try out some recipes,' Natalie said.

Hayden followed her into the kitchen, where she put on her apron and began mixing up batches of dough. He sat at the table and played games on his iPad while she creamed together butter, sugar and eggs. She carefully measured and folded in the dry ingredients, scooping out perfect spoonfuls of chocolate chips and nuts. Soon, trays of delicious treats were lined up in the kitchen – chocolate chip cookies, fudgy brownies, lemon bars, and more. It all smelt, and tasted, amazing but once the baking frenzy was over, boredom set in.

Under normal circumstances, there was nothing he liked more than spending quality time with Natalie, but he sensed she was not in the mood for intimacy. As the hours passed, isolation crept in like a cold sweat and Natalie decided to reach out to the one person who might know what they were going through. Hayden perched on the arm of the sofa, his body leaning in as they waited for the call to connect. Natalie pressed the speaker button on her phone and placed it on the coffee table between them so Hayden could hear their conversation.

'I remember it well,' Sibel said. Hayden could hear the grimace in her voice. 'There's nothing worse than the feeling of being hounded by reporters, but don't worry, the lottery folks will handle it for you. People will recognise you in the street now. That can be daunting, but it will die down. It's your friends and family you need to think about.'

'We've told our friends and family.'

'That's good, but be ready for the letters.'

'Letters?' Natalie asked.

'Letters, emails, phone messages. You will be deluged with them in the coming days. Once people hear you've got money, they will want it. Some will just be trying their luck. Others will want you to donate to their charity.'

Natalie and Hayden exchanged a glance. He squeezed her hand. Sibel was still talking.

'They'll probably offer you a press conference. That's what they did for me. They use that to make an official announcement about your win. You smile for the cameras and then it all goes away.'

'Do you really think that's the best way to go?' Natalie asked. 'I really don't like the thought of all that fuss.'

'Believe me, it's better to get it over and done with, otherwise you're constantly living on edge.'

Natalie thanked Sibel for her advice and hung up the phone.

'What do you think?' she asked Hayden. 'Shall we tell William we want a press conference after all?'

Hayden chewed his lip. 'Maybe we should.'

A loud knock sounded at the door. Natalie's eyes darted around the room. 'Have they got inside the building?'

Hayden sprang to his feet. 'Don't worry. I'll get rid of them.'

He walked to the door and shouted, 'Who's there?'

'It's Rod from number three,' came the tense reply. 'I spent forever looking for a parking space with all the press vans out front! Just come out and speak to them, will you?'

'No can do,' Hayden said firmly. 'We've been advised not to.'

'We didn't invite them here,' Natalie added.

Rod grumbled angrily before storming off.

Hayden turned back to Natalie. 'It's not our fault.'

She nodded. 'This is exactly what we wanted to avoid.'

Hayden's phone vibrated.

'Who's that?' Natalie asked, her voice tinged with apprehension.

'I don't know. It says number withheld.'

'Don't answer it.'

Hayden's hand reached for the phone. Natalie watched with anxious disapproval as he pressed the green button and lifted it to his ear.

The woman on the other end introduced herself and a grin spread across his face. He looked at Natalie. 'It's someone from the lottery,' he whispered. 'Put it on loudspeaker.'

Natalie's shoulders relaxed as the woman explained that if they wanted, they could have a press conference set up for Monday afternoon.

'What would that involve?' Natalie asked.

'We'd do most of the talking. You would just have to sit, smile, and let the photographers take pictures.'

'That doesn't sound too bad, does it?' Hayden said once he put down the phone.

'No, it doesn't,' Natalie agreed.

They practised in front of the mirror.

'We need to sound thankful,' Hayden said. 'And we should mention that we've already allocated our charities. That might help cut down the begging letters.'

'We'll get them anyway.'

'I know. And of course we'll be helping out our favourite causes, but we need to deter gold-diggers.'

He peered at his reflection.

'Don't smile so much. It makes you look smug,' Natalie told him.

'Well, you should smile more. You don't want people to think you're ungrateful.'

She burst out laughing. 'We're screwed whatever we do.'

He nodded. 'You're probably right.'

* * *

On the day of the press conference, Natalie wore a new black leather skirt that hugged her curves in all the right places. Hayden pulled her in for a kiss. Her lips were soft against his and she tasted like spearmint. She pulled away first.

'We'd better get going.'

'It's not like they're going to start without us.'

As they entered the town hall, heads turned in their direction. They strode to the front and took their places on two chairs placed side by side.

'We'll need an extra chair for my sister,' Natalie told the organiser.

Hayden narrowed his eyes. 'I didn't know Liz was coming.'

'She said she'd be here, for moral support.'

There were around twenty people packed into the small room, and it was filled with the sounds of buzzing, coughing and the clicking of cameras.

When Liz arrived, Hayden was glad to see she was not wearing one of her garish jumpers. She had come straight from work so she still had on a sensible blue sweatshirt with the nursery's logo. All the same, she had dark circles under her eyes and her hair was limp and tangled. He felt a pinch of frustration, concerned that she would ruin their photo op.

'Sorry I'm late,' she said as she slid into the empty chair next to Natalie.

'What's wrong with her?' he whispered.

'Her oldest cat, Marmite, died,' Natalie whispered back.

'How awful.' Hayden had never really understood Liz's obsession with her cats but he knew they meant the world to her.

The lottery official scanned the crowd, adjusting his glasses. 'Right, I think we're about ready to begin.'

Hayden flexed his fingers as he looked into the cameras. Would people be pleased for him or jealous of his good luck? His stomach gurgled as the questions began.

'What do you plan to do with the money?'

He forced himself to smile. 'I'm going to get a new car. My old one's had it.'

Natalie flitted a glance at him. 'I'm going to start my own business,' she said into the microphone. 'And of course, we've already allocated some money for our favourite charities.'

'What about your family? Are you going to treat them?'

'Yes, our family mean the world to us. They'll all be getting gifts.'

He glanced over at Liz, expecting her to say something but she just gazed off into the distance.

'Hayden, is it true you're still working?'

'Just for a little longer.'

'Are you finding it hard to let go of your old life?'

He let out a soft laugh. 'No, not really. I just want to finish up before I move on to the next thing.'

'And what is the next thing for you?' Another reporter shouted from the crowd.

'I'm not really sure yet,' Hayden said with a shrug.

He glanced at Natalie. 'I just want to enjoy life and spend time with my family.'

As cameras clicked and flashed around him, Hayden

couldn't wait for this to be over so he could retreat back into obscurity.

After the press conference, they made their way to the car dealership. They posed for photographs holding the keys to cars similar to the ones they had already agreed to purchase. As the cameras flashed, he looked over at Natalie and realised again how lucky he was.

'You did great,' the lottery rep said, when it was all over. 'Hopefully all the interest will die down now and you can get on with your fabulous new lives.'

'I hope so,' said Natalie.

They took a taxi back home. Natalie rested on Hayden's shoulder and he leaned his head against the cool window as they drove through the city, catching glimpses of their reflections in shop windows. He asked the taxi driver to stop at a takeaway and bought some pizza for dinner. He handed over his credit card, barely even noticing how much it cost. When they reached their neighbourhood, he was relieved to see all the media vans had left their street so they could slip quietly into their building.

'Anywhere here is fine,' he told the driver.

He'd already paid on the app, but he fumbled in his wallet and fished out a fiver as a tip. The driver gave him a polite nod in return.

Hayden climbed out of the taxi and held the door open for Natalie and they walked across the lawn, carrying the pizza. The smell of mozzarella wafted through the hallway as they made their way to their flat. The door was wide open.

'Oliver?' Natalie stood on the threshold, peering through the darkness.

There was no reply.

'Wait here,' Hayden said. He passed her the pizza box and made a move towards the doorway. She grabbed his arm, her fingers digging into his skin.

'Hayden! Don't. There might be someone in there!'

'Don't worry, I'll be careful.'

She released his arm and he stepped inside, shoes squeaking as he crept into the darkness and felt along the wall for the switch. He flipped it on, flooding the room with light.

The flat was a mess; the furniture had been overturned, books tossed onto the floor, and ornaments, shoes and DVD cases everywhere. He winced as he carefully navigated around the broken pieces of glass that crunched beneath his shoes and made his way up the stairs to their bedroom. As soon as he crossed the threshold, his eyes fell on the shattered remains of his old tennis trophy. Its mahogany base was broken into fragments, the golden cup dented and barely recognisable. He stepped closer, his eyes widening as he saw what lay beneath.

TWENTY

HAYDEN

'Hayden?' Natalie called up the stairs. 'Hayden, are you alright?'

The words caught in his throat. He reached forward and pulled the piece of paper out from under his ruined trophy. He picked it up, trying to understand the words written there in large bold letters:

You don't deserve the money.

He flipped it over. There were just two words on the back.

I do.

'Hayden?'

Natalie's voice was louder now, more panicky.

'It's... it's alright,' he called back.

The piece of paper felt hot in his hand. He shouldn't have touched it, he realised. His fingerprints would be all over it. All the same, he'd better show it to Natalie, see what she thought.

When he came back downstairs, Natalie was on her phone,

pacing up and down as she waited to speak to someone at their local police station. She stopped abruptly when he presented her with the note. Her eyebrows furrowed in confusion and then rose higher as her eyes skimmed over the paper. Disbelief clouded her face before turning into rage.

'Do you think Oliver could have done this?' he asked. 'I mean... he was pretty angry.'

She shook her head firmly, her lower lip trembling. 'No, he was just having a tantrum. This is malicious.'

She exhaled sharply and he reached out to embrace her, wishing there was something more he could do.

She clung to him for a moment before gently pushing away, steadying herself on shaky legs.

They stepped out into the hallway and Natalie finally got through to the police.

As soon as they answered, her voice became confident and firm.

'They said they'll come and take a look,' she said when she hung up. Slipping her phone into her pocket, she exhaled as if she had just finished a marathon.

'So, we just leave it like this?'

She shrugged before sinking onto the stairs. Her eyes were red-rimmed, though she blinked frantically to keep the tears from spilling over. Her lips quivered as she tried to smile.

'This is ridiculous,' she said, her voice wavering. 'We've won the lottery. What have I got to cry about?'

'I know,' he said softly, stroking her hair. She leaned in for a moment as if drawing strength from him.

'The mess bothers me,' she admitted after a long pause. 'And I don't like the thought that someone's been in there.'

'I don't like it either,' he said grimly, clenching his jaw. He couldn't bear the thought that someone hated them so much. The way they'd broken his tennis trophy and that note. It felt personal. This wasn't just some hacked off neighbour. Someone was genuinely angry that he and Natalie had won all that money and they hadn't.

They nibbled at the pizza then stared at their phones for a while. The minutes ticked by.

'It's been ages,' Natalie said.

'Yeah.'

'Why don't we get a hotel for the night?'

'The police said they'd come.'

'Alright then. We'll wait a bit longer, but let's go back into the flat. I'm getting a stiff back sitting here.'

They carefully manoeuvred their way over the scattered glass, broken picture frames, and other debris that littered the living room and sat down on the worn sofa. Hayden glanced up at the large wooden cabinet in the corner to see that Natalie's Virgin Mary figurine remained intact despite the destruction all around them. Its eyes remained watchful as ever, and heavy with disapproval.

Whilst Natalie distracted herself with the TV, all Hayden could think about was the Glass House. He had hired a top-notch property lawyer to ensure that the process went as quickly as possible, but it would still be several weeks until it was theirs. It was so frustrating, waiting for their new life to begin.

The police did finally swing by. They drank Hayden's orange tea and jotted down details in their notebooks.

'We're sorry that this happened,' one of them said. 'But there's not much that can be done just now. I'd advise you to keep your doors and windows locked and remain vigilant.'

Hayden nodded. That was about what he'd expected.

After the police left, they sat in the flat staring at the mess of their belongings.

'It doesn't feel like home anymore, does it?' Natalie said.

'No,' Hayden agreed. They already knew they were moving, but now he couldn't wait to get away. Just knowing someone had been there sent a shiver down his back. He could put the bolt on the door, but what about the windows? He didn't feel safe anymore. The flat felt too vulnerable.

'Let's go and stay in a hotel, shall we?'

Natalie nodded. 'At least then we'll get some sleep.'

She went and packed a bag while he went online and searched for somewhere. They could have stayed at the Canary Grand, but somehow he didn't fancy it, so he booked them into a smaller hotel where no one would know them.

In the morning, they took a taxi to Southampton, where they managed to get a last-minute suite on a luxury cruise ship.

'Oh my God, look at the size of that thing!' Natalie squealed as they arrived.

Hayden gazed at the colossal ship, craning his neck to take in the full view.

They spent the next six weeks living among other wealthy people, sailing from port to port, visiting Bilbao, St Tropez and Rome. Onboard, no one cared that they ordered extravagant bottles of wine with their dinner or that Hayden had purchased Natalie an elegant bottle of perfume at the on-board boutique. Yet despite all the luxury, worry still lingered in Hayden's mind; who had broken into their home and left them that eerie note? That same unknown person would still be waiting for them when they returned.

The night they came home, Natalie went to Liz's while Hayden met his work colleagues for leaving drinks. There was a good turnout but he couldn't help wondering, had all these people come to see him, or were they there for the free drinks?

Everybody had an opinion on how he should spend his millions. He tried to change the subject, but it was all anyone wanted to talk about.

'You need to invest in cryptocurrency,' Phillip advised. 'If you leave all your money in the bank, it's vulnerable.'

'What do you mean?' he asked.

'Didn't you hear about that bank going bust the other day? Yours could be next.'

Hayden didn't know the first thing about crypto, let alone how to buy it.

'I've got a financial advisor to deal with all that. She's been really helpful, advising us what to do with our pensions and investments.'

Phillip nodded slowly. 'Just be careful not to put all your eggs in one basket. That's where crypto comes in. The government can't touch it.'

Hayden frowned. He had already decided that as soon as they moved into the new house, he would draw out a chunk of their winnings to keep at home in a safe. But converting another chunk to crypto seemed like a good idea too. That way, if the bank did collapse, they wouldn't lose the lot.

'Oi, Hayden! Are you getting the drinks in or what?'

He turned to see Vivienne at the bar. She had a cheek. She never had paid him back what she owed him, but he could hardly quibble now that he was a millionaire.

Someone demanded tequila and they ended up ordering several rounds of shots in addition to the usual beers. At the end of the night, he was shocked to see the bill was over £800. He paid without a fuss, but promised himself he was going to be more careful. The last thing he wanted was to squander his millions. Still, it had been a fun night, especially when Vivienne tripped over her own feet and pulled some poor unsuspecting man down with her.

The fluorescent glow of the lights cast a warm orange hue on Phillip's sharp cheekbones as they travelled home. Hayden had planned to take a taxi, but then he was gripped by a wave of nostalgia for the night bus so he had got on with Phillip. Vivienne sat at the front, ignoring both of them. She was still pissed off because they had laughed so hard at her mishap.

When the bus lurched to a stop, Hayden said his goodbyes and hurried across the road. He let himself into the building, and then into the flat, checking that he'd put the bolt firmly over the door, and moved softly towards the bedroom. He snuggled in next to Natalie, enjoying the warmth of her body.

A little while later, she shook him awake.

'Hayden! Wake up. You're having a nightmare.'

He sat up straight, soaked with sweat. His dream came back to him in an instant. He had been chasing coins that rolled away down a drain.

'The money...'

'The money's fine,' she said. 'Go back to sleep.'

Natalie was right. There was really no need to panic. Even so, he pulled out his phone and checked. He couldn't rest until he saw the huge number in their bank account. Only then could he fall back to sleep.

TWENTY-ONE

HAYDEN

'Happy housewarming!'

Daisy stood on the doorstep in a vibrant pink and green crochet dress. She held out a tin of home-made flapjacks, smothered in marshmallows and chocolate.

'Where's Ted?' Hayden asked.

'He's got a migraine,' she said, stepping past him into the house. Her eyes widened as they swept across the room, taking in the glittering glass prisms.

'Wow. That looks awesome.'

'Wait till you see the pool!'

He led her through the house to the patio.

'Look at that!' she said with delight. The sun shimmered off the water, glimmering aquamarine.

She hugged him with excitement and they both gazed out at the pool. It had rained all night but now the sun burned as brightly as if this were the South of France. He shook his head, still unable to believe that this beautiful oasis was his.

'So, are you going to pour me a drink or do I have to die of thirst?' Daisy asked.

'Yes of course!' He walked over to the bar and showed her the selection of bottles.

'I've died and gone to heaven!' she said, selecting a bright green liqueur and mixing it with lemonade.

Hayden wondered how it must feel to be the ex-partner of a millionaire. He wasn't sure he would be so gracious in Daisy's shoes.

'So, what have you been up to?' she asked.

'Unpacking, mostly,' he replied.

In fact, Natalie had been so busy setting up her coffee shop, he'd had to do most of the unpacking by himself. He had envisioned himself spending his days practising his serve on the tennis court, or going for long drives in the country but instead he'd spent his first week lugging boxes around, arranging and rearranging their belongings until his back ached and his arms were sore.

Natalie wandered out in a new pink bikini. She had just returned from a high-end beauty salon and got herself a spray tan. The effect was stunning. With her glowing skin, and the sun's rays dancing on the water, he could easily believe they'd moved to some tropical climate. They just needed a few palm trees to complete the effect.

'Hi, Daisy,' she said, as she walked to the edge of the pool and dipped a toe in. She shot him a warning look.

'Don't push me!'

'Wouldn't dream of it.'

She sat at the edge of the water, bathing her feet.

'Why doesn't the pool smell?' she asked. 'The pool cleaner said he'd added chlorine.'

'Chlorine doesn't actually smell,' Daisy said.

Hayden laughed. 'I'm pretty sure chlorine smells.'

Daisy shook her head. 'Only if someone pees in it.'

'You're making that up!'

'Google it.'

Daisy walked over to the sound system. 'Mind if I put on some tunes?'

'Go ahead,' Hayden said.

'Hey, Natalie, you're going to love this,' she said as she put on some music. She wiggled her hips experimentally, and Natalie smiled. It was nice to see them getting along so well. There had been a little awkwardness early on in their relationship because Natalie was convinced Daisy would hate her but Daisy wasn't like that. She got on with everybody.

Gail arrived next with Andy in tow. She was pushing a buggy while he carried Scarlett in a sling. Hayden forced a smile. Gail was very easy-going, he could see why Natalie was so fond of her, but he'd never got used to Andy. How did a person manage to be both dull and intense at the same time? He wished he'd been the one to stay home with a migraine instead of Ted.

Andy accepted a beer and settled with Scarlett on his lap. Liz and Oliver walked in together. Natalie surged forward with a bright smile and hugged them both. Hayden clenched his jaw as he watched.

Was he supposed to pretend Oliver's tantrum had never happened?

Whilst Liz and Daisy cooed over Scarlett, Oliver stripped down to his trunks. There was a loud splash as he dived in.

Hayden watched as he sliced through the water, arms moving rapidly up and down as he swam back and forth like a shark in a fish tank.

A loud honking sound told him the lads from work had arrived. Hayden almost fell on them with relief. Although he knew he could count on Phillip, he'd heard nothing since he posted the invite in the work WhatsApp group so he'd had no idea how many were coming.

They hadn't taken him seriously when he'd said it was a pool party – none of them had bothered to come in swimwear.

They were all dressed smartly in pressed shirts and jeans. He led them to the garage to show them his new Ferraris. He took Phillip out in the silver one for a few laps around the property while the others clapped and cheered.

'Do you want me to order a delivery?' Phillip asked as they returned the car to the garage. 'Something to get the party started?'

Hayden frowned. 'What sort of something?'

Phillip dipped his head. 'I don't know – maybe you'd like some hash or coke?'

'No thanks, I'm good with a beer.'

They went to join the rest of their work friends, who were now clustered around the bar, sipping colourful drinks and laughing.

Liz whipped off her ugly fuchsia-and-black leopard-print wrap and tossed it aside, revealing a lithe, toned body. Her skin glowed in the sunlight. Hayden's gaze lingered a moment too long and their eyes met. A smirk tugged at the corners of her lips before she turned away. He redirected his gaze at the bird-house behind her. It wouldn't surprise him if Liz could read minds.

Laughter echoed from the other side of the pool. Oliver was telling a story and the other guests were falling about laughing. Probably at him, rather than with him, Hayden thought. Still, he was pleased so many of his former colleagues had come, and doubly pleased Vivienne hadn't tried to tag along. He didn't need any drama with Natalie. He still couldn't believe she thought he'd have gone for her.

As the afternoon wore on, Scarlett dozed peacefully in her buggy, shielded by a parasol. The quiet rhythm of her breathing contrasted with the loud laughter of their guests.

'Gail, why don't you come for a swim?' Natalie said. 'The pool's lovely and warm.'

Gail looked at Andy. 'Shall we?'

He glanced fleetingly at Liz. 'Can you watch Scarlett for us?'

Liz smiled, her eyes crinkling at the corners. 'Of course, take your time.'

Gail and Andy peeled off their shorts and T-shirts, revealing swimwear underneath.

Hand in hand they jumped into the glistening blue water. Natalie jumped in after them but got out after a couple of lengths and flopped down on a sunlounger next to Daisy. Hayden watched as they leaned into each other and strained to hear what they were saying but their voices were too soft. Were they talking about him? Exchanging notes? He wished Ted had come. The party felt a little out of kilter without him. Ted was so good at entertaining. He knew exactly how to put everyone at their ease whereas Hayden always felt like he was playing a part.

He walked over to the bar and took inventory of the bottles. There was still lots of ice, he was pleased to see. Phillip came over to join him.

'Do you want a drink? There's plenty of everything. Vodka, gin, beer or wine?' He quirked an eyebrow.

Phillip shook his head with regret. 'Thanks for the party, mate, but we've got to head off.'

'Already?'

Phillip glanced at the floor. 'Yeah, we've got tickets for a new club that's just opened. We'd better head off now if we're gonna make it down to Rochester in time.'

Hayden nodded sadly and watched as all his work friends downed their drinks and trooped out.

'Thanks for coming,' he called after them.

His face felt taut with the effort of smiling. No one had mentioned the club to him. But why should they? He didn't work with them anymore. It was hardly surprising he was out of the loop.

Natalie appeared at his side, her fingertips lightly tracing the contours of his back. She gazed up into his eyes, her lips curved in a faint smile.

'I think now would be a good time. Daisy's been dropping some savage hints.'

He nodded and went inside to the kitchen. Through the open windows, he heard voices from the garden. Was that Andy or Oliver? Their voices carried on the wind, followed by a female voice saying:

'Come on, they can afford it.'

His eyes landed on Natalie's hideous figurine of the Virgin Mary. He'd hoped the ugly yellowing porcelain might get smashed in the move, but here she was, still glaring at him with thinly veiled contempt. Next to her lay the two envelopes he'd left on the windowsill, the edges curling in the afternoon heat. With an unsteady hand, he grabbed them both and walked back outside.

Daisy and Oliver were back in the pool, racing up and down.

'Daisy?' he called. 'Can you come here for a minute?'

Daisy hoisted herself out and shook off the excess water. Hayden handed her a towel and gestured for her to sit next to Gail.

'What's all this about?' Daisy asked as she lowered herself into the chair. Her eyes were wide and expectant, hands squeezing each other in her lap.

'You are our best friends and we want to give you a little something,' Hayden said.

He held out the two envelopes they'd prepared earlier. Each one contained a cheque for 100k. He and Natalie had considered the amount carefully. They wanted to be generous whilst still leaving themselves enough money for the future.

Daisy opened hers and threw her arms around Hayden and

Natalie. 'Thank you so much. This will really help us out, especially with the wedding coming up.'

Gail opened hers and looked uncomfortable. She looked over at Andy and Hayden got the sense that they'd already discussed this between them.

'Thank you both, but we don't want your money,' she said.

Hayden glanced at their sleeping baby. 'What about Scarlett? You could put it away for a college fund.'

Gail looked at Andy once more. 'We don't know if Scarlett will even go to uni but if she does, she'll pay her own way like we did.'

Her words sounded uncharacteristically harsh and he sensed that these were Andy's opinions Gail was parroting. Natalie looked upset.

Gail's face softened. 'We appreciate the thought, we really do. But we really wouldn't be comfortable. Everything we have, we've earnt ourselves. We want to keep it that way. And we really wouldn't want the money to come between us as friends.'

Daisy slipped her envelope into her handbag. 'Well, I have no conscience. Ted and I are happy to accept.'

Her words were spoken with humour, but Hayden couldn't help think the joy had been sucked out of the moment by Gail's refusal. He glanced over at Andy. This was coming from him, he was sure of it. Gail never used to be so precious about these things.

Daisy reached for a bottle of tequila. 'Who wants a shot?'

Hayden and Natalie drank with her but Gail and Andy declined. They stayed a while longer, and watched in silence as the setting sun glinted off the river. Its orange light danced across the pool's surface and the evergreen trees cast long shadows over the garden. The cool evening air brought a welcome breeze. 'Well, it's been a great party but we ought to get going,' Gail said, clambering to her feet.

'Yeah, we'd better get Scarlett home,' Andy agreed.

Hayden glanced at the baby. Scarlett was still sleeping contentedly in her buggy.

'Daisy, we can give you a lift,' Gail said as she gathered up her things. 'You're in no fit state to drive.'

'I'm fine!' Daisy insisted, but Gail was right. She was slurring her words.

Poor Daisy. She never could hold her drink. He escorted her to Gail's car and waved them all off, feeling a little deflated.

When he returned to what was left of the party, Natalie, Oliver and Liz were chatting quietly among themselves. He sniffed the air. Something was different. What was that? He stepped a little closer to the pool. Yes, there was a distinctive smell of chlorine. He looked around, doing a mental calculation in his head. Only a few people had been in that water, besides himself and Natalie, and they would never dream of peeing in their own pool. He didn't think Liz would either.

That left only Gail, Andy, Daisy and Oliver. He couldn't imagine any one of them behaving that way. As he sat there, thinking these thoughts, Oliver strolled over to him and patted him on the back.

'Great party, Hayden. I really like this place, especially the pool. Thanks for inviting me today, I appreciate it after the way we left things. No hard feelings, hey?'

Hayden forced a smile. *I'm on to you*, he thought, as Oliver fetched them both a beer.

The party continued, just the four of them. Hayden changed the music to something more atmospheric and switched on the night lights. Liz brought out a pack of cards and they played blackjack until she won for the fourth time and no one wanted to play any more. Natalie fetched them all fresh drinks while Liz and Oliver argued loudly about politics. Hayden stretched out on a sunlounger and Natalie took the one next to him. He tapped her lightly with his foot and she smiled, shifting her weight closer to him. They sipped their drinks and listened to the mellow rhythm of the music.

By the time Liz and Oliver headed off, Natalie couldn't stop yawning.

'I'm going up to bed,' she said, clearing away a few of the glasses.

'I'll be up soon,' Hayden promised. 'I just want to finish my beer.'

He sat back in his sunlounger, wondering what to do about Oliver. As he lay there, beer in hand, his eyelids grew heavy. He really ought to go up to bed, he thought, as he drifted off to sleep.

Hayden stirred and opened his eyes, immediately regretting it as the morning sun seemed to intensify the pounding in his head. He squinted at the party remnants scattered around him: plates, cans, and a shard of green glass with the rest of the broken bottle lying to the right of his chair.

He realised with a sour stomach that there was an expanding pool of brown liquid seeping towards the edge of the patio and trickling into the pool below. He slipped his feet into his flip-flops and stepped across the warm deck, feeling the crunch of glass beneath his feet.

As he peered into the depths, a chill shot down his spine. Under the shimmery water, he saw a pale form against the greeny-blue hues of the pool. A tiny motionless body lay at the bottom.

TWENTY-TWO

NATALIE

Natalie jolted awake.

What was that? The wild, blood-curdling scream sounded like it came from a wounded animal but instinctively, she knew it was Hayden.

She sprinted into the lift and reached the ground floor in time to see Hayden dive into the pool, hitting the water with a whack.

'Hayden, what are you...?'

She looked down and saw for herself the pale form on the bottom of the pool.

'Oh God!'

She dived in, kicking her legs until she reached down to the bottom. Her lungs felt like they would burst but Hayden already had hold of the tiny child and was swimming up to the surface.

The baby didn't move as Hayden laid her on the side of the pool. Her limbs barely shifted, eyelashes fluttered slightly. Natalie felt for a vein but there was no pulse.

'She's not... She's not breathing.'

Hayden grabbed his phone from the table. He was already

dialling 999 as Natalie tried to recall what little first aid training she'd had. She had to open the airways. She tilted the baby's chin, looked inside her mouth and then...

'Hayden, stop!'

There was heat and confusion in her cheeks.

'It's a doll. Just a doll.'

He swung round and stared.

Welts were already forming on his stomach where he'd smacked the water.

'What do you mean?'

The eyes were so realistic. The hair, the veins. Even the tiny wrinkles on her face.

'It's a doll,' she confirmed. 'Really lifelike, but just a doll.'

Hayden cancelled the call and they sank down onto the sunloungers.

'So, this was what, a prank?'

'Looks like it.'

'Not a very funny one.'

'No.'

Her heart was still pumping as she considered the implications. Someone had snuck onto their property last night and deposited this very realistic little human into their pool.

'Those dolls aren't cheap,' she said.

'Expensive prank?'

'It's disgusting.'

Her limbs shook and she reached for a towel that had been left out the night before.

For a moment, neither of them spoke.

'Do you think we should go to the police?' Hayden asked.

'I don't know. I mean what's the point?'

He nodded along. 'I suppose you're right, I mean, what are they going to do?'

They both looked up at the Glass House, and all the luxury they were living in. It was hardly going to elicit sympathy.

Natalie popped a couple of aspirin. Her hands were still shaking. The guilt she had felt when she saw the doll was immense. She felt as though the entire world was closing in, and even though it had turned out to be a fake, she couldn't get the image out of her mind.

'I'm going to my sister's,' she announced.

Hayden gave a small nod. 'Why don't you take one of the Ferraris?'

Natalie shook her head. She was so much more comfortable in her nice sensible Audi.

Half an hour later, she was at Liz's house. There were tufts of fur caught under kitchen cabinet doors and scratches dotting the tile countertop where the cats had climbed up. The curtains had claw marks down them and a marmalade-coloured cat had pulled an extension cable loose and was now pawing and chewing at it.

Liz didn't seem to notice any of this. She flitted around the kitchen, reaching out to pet the cats before remembering that she was supposed to be making coffee.

Natalie hovered in the living room. Two mugs sat together on the windowsill.

'Did Oliver stay over?' she asked.

'No, he's staying at a hostel,' Liz said. 'He likes it there. There are lots of young people for him to party with.'

Natalie settled onto the sofa and was immediately greeted by an orange tabby. His fur was so frazzled, he looked like he'd been through a spin cycle. He leaned into her palm and purred loudly, then jumped off her lap and ran for cover, as if spooked by an unseen force.

She turned her attention to her sister. There was definitely something different about her but she couldn't figure out what.

Liz placed the steaming mugs of coffee on the table. Natalie told her about the awful prank with the doll.

Liz squinted at her. 'What, like a blow-up doll?'

'No, a baby doll,' Natalie said in exasperation. 'It looked like a real baby, one of those really realistic ones. For a minute, I thought it was Scarlett.'

Liz exhaled. 'That's pretty messed up, Nat.'

'I know, I mean, why would someone do something like that?'

Natalie felt the weight of her gaze, pinning her to the spot. For one weird moment she considered that Liz could have done it, though she couldn't imagine why she would. Liz continued to look at her. Her voice dropped, as if she didn't want her cats to hear. 'I have one thought.'

'Well?'

'Could it have been your daughter?'

TWENTY-THREE

NATALIE

Her words struck like stones.

'No! Of course not. She isn't even... I've had nothing to do with her.'

Liz watched her patiently. 'Think about it, Nat. With all the publicity, she might have figured out who you are. She'd be fully grown by now. It must have entered her head that you're out there somewhere. Don't you think it's possible she's tried to find you?'

Natalie's throat clenched. 'She did find me.'

Liz's eyes widened. The air seemed to freeze around them. 'What did you just say?'

Natalie swallowed, feeling like she was about to plunge into icy waters.

'A couple of years ago, the adoption agency forwarded me a letter from her. In the letter, she said she had requested her original birth certificate, so she knew who I was, and she wanted to meet me. She signed it "Heather".'

Liz stared at her. 'She kept the name you chose?'

'It seems so. The letter ate away at me so I wrote back via

the agency, and told her I wished her well but I didn't want to meet her. She has her life and I have mine.'

Tears stung her eyes, but she bit her lip and refused to let them fall. She didn't want Liz to see how much this was affecting her. She had worked so hard to put this part of her life behind her.

Liz's sympathetic nod cut through her like a knife.

'It could well be her then.'

Natalie twisted her hands in her lap. 'If it is her, then what do I do about it? I don't want to get her in trouble.'

'How about you actually meet with her? See what kind of person she's turned into.'

Natalie gripped the arms of her chair. 'No! It's too late for me to do anything about it now.'

Liz tilted her head. 'Is it really? You're a grown woman. Don't you think it's time to take responsibility for your past? You're not still letting Robin call the shots?'

'Oh no. He's long gone.'

'Well then. What's stopping you?'

Natalie wiped her forehead with the back of her hand, leaving a damp streak on her skin.

'It wasn't easy for me, giving her up.' She closed her eyes and shook her head, trying to block out the memory.

'It can't have been easy for her either.'

'No, I know.'

Liz leaned forward. 'You are being given a second chance here, Nat. You could meet her, put things right. You don't have to do it alone. I'll be with you.'

Natalie shook her head again. Liz still didn't get it. 'There's also Hayden...'

Liz's mouth opened and closed. 'He doesn't know?'

Natalie shook her head. 'And I'd like to keep it that way.'

TWENTY-FOUR

NATALIE

Twenty-Two Years Earlier

Natalie couldn't keep her eyes off Robin as she admired his sun-kissed skin and the copper curls that hung just above his fore-head. As he smiled down at her, the strength melted from her muscles and a warm, gooey feeling flooded her body. She was used to attention from childish schoolboys, but Robin was older and wiser – every ounce of him dripped with maturity and sexiness. He was everything she wanted in a man... everything she wanted in a future husband.

He had been there through those dark days when her mum was ill. Her mum's cancer had robbed Natalie of her innocence and left her broken inside. It was a kind of pain that only Robin could soothe. He would put his strong arms around her, steadying her, grounding her, and she knew as long as he was with her, she would be okay.

She glanced at her watch. 'I have to get home,' she said with regret. 'Dad wants me to make dinner tonight.'

'Can't Liz do it?'

Natalie wavered. She'd been calling in a lot of favours

lately. If Liz did her chores one more time she'd probably owe her a kidney.

But one look in Robin's eyes and she knew she couldn't resist.

'Give me a minute, I'll call her.'

She hopped out of the van and walked across the road to the telephone box.

Liz was not happy.

'You said you were going to help me with my history homework,' she complained.

'I'll do your homework,' Natalie countered. 'If you make dinner.'

There was a pause. Liz was thinking about it.

'Hurry,' Natalie urged. 'My money's going to run out.'

'Oh, all right then,' Liz said, 'but you better get me at least a B.'

'I'll get you an A,' Natalie promised.

She looked back at the van, its blue paint dulled by years of wear and dirt. Robin's fingers tapped a steady beat on the dashboard as the radio played softly in the background. She scanned up and down the street to check no one was around. There was no way anyone could find out about her and Robin – especially not her dad.

'So, you can stay a bit longer?' Robin asked when she climbed back into the van.

'Just one hour.'

'One hour is all we need.'

His eyes twinkled as he pulled her close.

Robin dropped her off round the corner. She walked up to the house to find her father waiting on the doorstep. His face was so red it looked like he might burst.

'You're late.'

Natalie hurried inside and set down her backpack.

The kitchen smelled of roast beef and cumin, Liz's favourite dish. Plates had been set out on the crisp white tablecloth, but Natalie knew that would not satisfy her father. He hovered over her.

'When are you going to get serious? You've got opportunities I never dreamed of.'

Natalie was tired of his life story. He was an intelligent man, but his lack of qualifications forced him into work that he felt was beneath him. He stood in the shadow of his younger superiors, who strutted around with a sense of entitlement. He wanted better for his daughters. Which meant Natalie had to buckle down and study. He thought she should go to university, but Natalie wasn't sure what she wanted. All she knew was that university would rip her away from Robin, unless she could convince him to come with her.

One month later, Natalie perched on the edge of the bath at Robin's house. The house was silent and empty; everyone had gone out for the day, leaving them alone at last.

Natalie stared down at the pregnancy test in her hand, anxiety bubbling up within her as she waited for Robin's response. His face trembled with emotion but he said nothing, leaving her to guess what exactly he was feeling: happiness? Anger? Fear? She couldn't tell.

The air in the room seemed to thicken like a fog. It wrapped around her as he slowly raised his head. His gaze pierced her, and he spoke with a low, cold voice. 'You have to get rid of it.'

Her stomach churned at the thought of what he was asking; having a baby was supposed to bring them closer together, instead it had done the opposite. She dug her nails into her palms, feeling the hot tears welling up in her eyes, determined not to let him see her cry.

'We could run away,' she said, desperation creeping into her voice. 'Start a new life somewhere else.'

Robin shook his head sadly. 'I can't just leave everything and everyone behind.'

He reached out and gently touched her cheek with his hand. 'And you have so much potential, Nat. You should go to university and make something of yourself.'

Natalie felt a flash of anger at his words. Wasn't having a family making something of herself? But she held back the retort, biting down hard on her tongue.

Robin reached out for her arm and squeezed it reassuringly. 'I'll support you through this, I promise.'

Natalie turned away from him, her mind racing with conflicting emotions. Part of her wanted to stay and fight for their unborn baby, but another part knew Robin was right. She wasn't ready to be a mum.

'I really think you should stay in school. Get your A levels. You've worked too hard to throw it all away.'

'You sound like my dad,' she muttered under her breath before walking out of the room.

Robin closed his eyes and took a deep breath. 'I just want what's best for you.'

Getting pregnant was her first mistake. Telling Liz was her second. Liz was too good. Too serious. She went straight to their dad and told him.

'I'm sorry,' Liz mouthed.

Natalie shot daggers at her with blazing eyes, filled with contempt and fury. She cursed herself for ever believing that a fourteen-year-old could be trusted to keep such an important secret.

Turning towards her father, she braced herself for the

inevitable eruption of anger. But instead of flying into a rage, he spoke in a quiet, tremulous voice.

'I want to meet this boy.'

Natalie swallowed a sob. 'No,' she said. 'He won't meet you.'

She watched her father as he paced the room, fists clenched tight. His face was a mask of rage and grief – his eyes narrowed, lips pressed together in a thin line.

'Then he's a coward. You shouldn't have to deal with this alone.'

Natalie felt a twinge of pain in her chest, but she kept silent. His words felt like acid on her skin.

'Maybe he'd talk on the phone,' she suggested.

The phone call between Robin and her dad was short. Her dad asked him direct questions. She didn't hear Robin's answers.

'What are your intentions towards my daughter?'

His tone softened slightly, the subtle hint of desperation clear in his words.

'Do you intend to support the child?'

After a tense silence, he sighed, 'I see. I thought as much.'

He turned and looked at her.

'You're not keeping that baby,' he told her.

'I don't want it!' she shot back.

His shoulders relaxed. 'Then it's agreed. You'll stay in school till the end of term, and then you'll go and stay with your gran.'

Natalie was confused. 'But why?'

'You'll finish your coursework and exams, and when the time comes, you'll have the baby and give it up for adoption. No one will ever know.'

'Why can't I have an abortion?'

He stood up from his chair and loomed over her.

'Because your mother would roll in her grave,' he said in a low rumble.

Natalie thought of her mother and the delicate silver cross she had worn around her neck.

'I don't want to go through with the pregnancy.'

'You should have thought of that before you started messing around with that boy.'

She was screaming inside, but she knew that no matter how much she pleaded and begged, the matter was settled.

TWENTY-FIVE

NATALIE

Now

Natalie rang from the coffee shop so Robin wouldn't know who was calling.

'Hi, it's me,' she said urgently.

'Natalie? What are you doing, calling me at home?' His voice sounded a little breathless, like she'd caught him off guard.

'Someone left a baby doll in my swimming pool.'

'Slow down. You're not making any sense.'

'It was freaky, really lifelike. I think it might have been our daughter. I just wanted to warn you.'

Robin was silent for a moment. 'You never told anyone about me, did you?'

'No, of course not.'

'You're sure?'

'Of course, I'm sure.'

'Well then...'

She clutched the phone in her hand, waiting for his voice to fill the silence. She closed her eyes and visualised him, full of remorse for how wrong things had gone between them. But as she opened her eyes, she was met with an empty dial tone. She let out a sigh. Robin would never be the man she wanted him to be. It didn't matter. She had Hayden now. She smiled as she realised that this was a different kind of love. It was stronger, more mature, and more fulfilling.

She checked the clock on the wall and felt her blood pressure rise. She had already gone through two gruelling interviews, one with a teenage boy with poor hygiene, and another with a young woman who couldn't figure out how to work a basic coffee machine. To make matters worse, the woman had then proclaimed that she could not stand the smell of coffee and said it smelled like wet soil. Sighing, Natalie shifted in her chair and crossed her fingers for better luck with this next one.

The next applicant arrived five minutes early, immediately giving Natalie a favourable impression. Her auburn hair was pulled back in a sensible ponytail, and she wore fashionable but sensible clothes – black trousers with a grey top and a fitted jacket.

'Hi, I'm Amy Kipling, like the cake,' she said with a warm smile.

'Thanks for coming in,' Natalie said. 'I'd like to start by getting you to make yourself a cup of coffee, but don't worry. I'm going to talk you through it.'

They headed over to the machine and Amy had no problems with the task. Her movements were confident and efficient as she heated the milk and spooned coffee grounds into the machine.

Once she had made her coffee, they went and sat down at one of the tables.

'Can I ask how you heard about the job?' Natalie asked.

'Someone mentioned it at Sainsbury's,' Amy said. 'That's my current job. I work there afternoons and evenings but lately I'm not getting enough hours.'

'So, what made you want to work here?'

'I won't lie, I was hoping for free coffee! But I'm also really excited about the idea of working here, getting to know all the customers and being part of something new. It sounds like a lot of fun.'

Natalie smiled. She liked Amy already. She had a feeling they would work well together.

After Amy left, Daisy and Gail arrived for a tour of the coffee shop. Natalie was pleased to see that Gail was without Scarlett for once. Perhaps they could get a glass of wine after.

'This place is amazing,' Gail said as they walked around. 'My dad was saying he used to bring us here when it was a juice bar.'

'Did he? Maybe that's why it feels so familiar.'

'It's looking good,' Daisy said. 'Still a bit of a whiff but I'm sure that'll be gone once you start brewing coffee in here.'

Natalie nodded. 'Yes, it's a lot better than it was. I'm really pleased with how it's turned out.'

The walls were a creamy brown, with cake and coffee cup stencils dotted here and there.

'I can't believe how quickly you've put all this together,' Daisy said.

'Nor can I,' Natalie admitted.

Luckily for her, Hayden had not questioned the speed with which she'd acquired the coffee shop. He didn't even notice she had paid her solicitor on the very day the lottery funds went into their account. But why would he? They were rich now. They didn't have to keep checking their bank balance the way they did when they were broke.

She was counting the days now until the big launch.

'What are you going to call the place?' Gail asked.

'I was just going to go with Natalie's.'

Daisy narrowed her brows. 'Original. But isn't Hayden going to run it with you?'

'Nah, it's not really his thing.'

Daisy considered. 'You're probably right. It's a bad idea to work together. You'd have to thank him every time he loaded the dishwasher.'

Gail giggled. 'You'd have to remind him to take his feet off the tables.'

'Okay, he is actually housetrained,' Natalie said, as she concluded her tour. 'Do you have time for a glass of wine?'

Both women nodded enthusiastically and they stepped out into the cool evening air.

The pub down the street was heaving. They fought their way through the crowd and Daisy ordered a bottle of champagne.

Natalie was a little taken aback as she normally just had beer.

'I'll get that,' she offered.

'Oh, no. This is on me,' Daisy said. 'I insist.'

They found an empty table outside on the cobblestone pavement and settled in for a chat. Daisy dominated as usual, entertaining them with outrageous stories about the hotel she worked at.

'I'm going to look for a new job,' Gail confessed.

Natalie looked at her. 'Really?'

'Yeah, I'm not willing to accept what my current boss is offering me. I want to go back on my own terms.'

Natalie's eyes lit up. 'Why don't you come and work for me? It'll be fun and flexible, I promise. You could do anything from managing the shop to just a few shifts serving the coffees. As much or as little as you wanted. We'd have so much fun.'

She had expected Gail to be excited but she barely met Natalie's eye.

'I don't think it would be right for me, thanks all the same.'

Natalie opened her mouth in dismay. She didn't understand Gail's reluctance. Hadn't they always dreamed of working together?

'I like working in the building sector,' Gail explained. 'It's where my talents lie. I'm not looking for a career change. Just better hours.'

Natalie looked down into her glass. 'Oh, I see.'

'I did have a thought though.'

Natalie raised a brow.

'I don't think your job would be right for me, but it sounds perfect for my mum.'

'Your mum?'

Natalie pictured Marian Goodwin. Late fifties but looked and acted much older, as if life had worn her down.

'She's always been good to you,' Gail reminded her. Natalie knew this only too well. When her own mother was dying, Natalie had often taken refuge at Gail's house, enjoying the home-cooked dinners she didn't have to make herself. She'd enjoyed the normalcy that was sadly lacking in her own home.

She owed the woman, it was true, but she wasn't sure she would be comfortable working with her. Besides, she wanted her coffee shop to be hip and trendy.

'Let me think about it,' she said. 'I did have one other person in mind.'

That one other person was still awake when Natalie rang her doorbell on the way home. She answered the door dressed in striped pyjamas, and held it open just enough to allow Natalie inside without her army of cats getting out.

'It's after curfew, is it?' Natalie asked.

Liz nodded. Years ago, one of her tabbies had got run over in the dark. The cat in question only lost his tail but after that, Liz stopped letting the cats out at night, shutting down her flat every evening after dinner.

Natalie could see that Liz was tired so she sat down and got straight to the point.

'Liz, I was wondering if you would like to work with me at

the coffee shop? We could make it a partnership, and split the profits fifty-fifty. What do you say? It would be so much fun!'

Liz listened carefully but her face did not light up as Natalie had hoped.

'I already have a career, Nat.'

'Oh, I know you love the nursery, but this would be even better. You'd be your own boss. We'd be partners.'

'Thanks for thinking of me, but it wouldn't work. I don't like people.'

'Don't you have to deal with people at the nursery?'

'Children are different. They say what they mean. There's no small talk.'

'You would only have to work part-time. You could be at home more for your cats.'

'It's just... not for me.'

Natalie nodded sadly. She knew better than to try and twist Liz's arm. Once her sister's mind was made up, there was no reasoning with her.

Liz shifted in her seat. 'Have you thought any more about what we talked about? I really think we should reach out to your daughter.'

'What about the weirdness with the doll?'

The more she thought about it, the more concerned Natalie was.

'She's probably hurt that you rejected her,' Liz said. 'I'm guessing the doll stunt was to get your attention. And it worked, didn't it?'

'What does she want from me? Do you think she's after my money?'

'If she is, that's a pretty weird way to go about it. I reckon she probably just wants to remind you she exists.'

As if she'd ever forget.

After leaving Liz's, Natalie headed back home. She had tried so hard to bury the past but bits of it kept bobbing up to the surface. She recalled her father telling her about an older couple who longed for a child but were unable to conceive. They had sounded like worthy people, very involved in their community. Natalie's father had placed his hands on her shoulders and looked into her eyes. 'What you're doing for these people is a gift. Your mistake will be their blessing. You're giving this baby a wonderful home with parents who can provide for her. Keep your head up, Natalie, and know that you're doing something good.'

She pulled up at the traffic lights and tried to shut out the memories, but it was all flooding back. The nurses had been kind to her, offering words of encouragement as she rode the wave of unbearable pain. She had pushed and pushed until the baby had finally emerged from her trembling body.

The midwife had cleaned the baby up, then handed her over. That was the first and only time Natalie ever cradled her daughter in her arms.

She had gazed down at the precious little bundle and kissed her gently on the cheek. She and Robin had created this little miracle. She didn't know how long she held her. Every inch of her body screamed not to let go.

'Can I get you anything?' the nurse had asked, as the baby was whisked away.

'Please can I use the phone? I... I need to speak to my boyfriend.'

The nurse handed her the phone and stepped back, leaving Natalie to make the call. Her hands had trembled so much she could barely press the buttons. When Robin answered, his voice was a little flat.

'Natalie?' he'd said.

She'd taken a deep breath and told him about their daughter. Silence had stretched out on the other end of the line before he'd murmured a response. 'Well done.' His voice was hollow and distant. The words had felt like an icy slap against her skin.

Despite the warmth of the delivery room, Natalie had shivered as she realised that it was over.

The years since then had been an internal tug-of-war between hating her father for forcing her to go through with the pregnancy, and the knowledge that her daughter was better off without her. She never did go to university. The twenty-odd years she spent working dead-end jobs felt like atonement for her sins.

TWENTY-SIX

NATALIE

The Glass House loomed in the distance. It never failed to snatch her breath, the way it rose like that over the horizon, its glass dome lit up by the sprinkling of stars. As she pulled into the driveway, she was struck by a sudden thought. On the night of the party, Gail and Andy had given Daisy a lift home. So where was Daisy's car? She hadn't left it in the driveway. And it wasn't like Daisy to splash out on a taxi. Not before they gave her the money, at least.

She looked up at the house and a realisation came to her. The house had security cameras. The one at the front was obvious, but she had also discovered a discreet one out on the patio, disguised as a birdhouse. All she had to do was play back the footage for the night of the party, and she would know exactly what had taken place that night, creepy doll and all.

Without getting out of her car, she logged into the app and played back the footage from the night of the party. It was motion activated, so the first thing she saw was a car arriving for the party. They'd left the gates open that day, so she wouldn't have to keep getting up to let people in. She peered closer. The footage was a little grainy but she was certain that was Daisy's car, and it looked like she was with Ted.

Why hadn't he come to the party? Daisy had said something about a migraine, hadn't she? She watched as they both got out of the car. They were standing in front of the house and Daisy was gesticulating wildly. Then Ted threw his arms up in the air. It looked like they were arguing. She watched as Ted returned to the car and slid into the driver's seat. A moment later, he sped off, leaving Daisy standing all alone.

Daisy reached into her handbag and pulled out a cigarette. She cupped her hands around the flame, drew in a deep breath, and watched the smoke curl up through the thin evening air. Natalie guessed she was cooling off before she rang the bell.

She rubbed her temples. Daisy must have come up with that story about Ted to cover up their argument. Well, that was between them, she supposed. She cast her mind back. Daisy had seemed her usual self that evening, talking and giggling like normal. She'd been wearing her engagement ring and she'd even mentioned the wedding. You would never have guessed she'd just had a big row with her fiancé.

She sped up the recording, and watched the blurry figures come and go. She could make out Hayden, waving as his colleagues left. Daisy, Gail and Andy followed shortly after. Then Liz and Oliver. She remembered returning to the patio with Hayden, drinking late into the night. At some point, she had suggested they go up to bed. Hayden had stayed to finish his beer, but he never did come up.

With a deep breath, she moved onto the next bit of the recording. She saw Hayden alone on the sunlounger, the beer bottle dropping from his hand. He was clearly asleep.

'Come on, show yourself,' she muttered. Her heart was beating in her chest, waiting to see what happened next.

She let out a gasp as a hooded figure emerged from the shadows. Hayden was right there, fast asleep on his sunlounger. The hooded figure stood motionless, studying him as he slept.

Why hadn't the alarms gone off? That was right, they'd been too drunk to set them.

The figure seemed to shimmer as it moved towards the pool, bending down to touch the water. Natalie watched with fascination as the doll floated on its surface. At first it drifted peacefully, then it went under, sinking down into the depths. The intruder didn't leave right away but stood there and watched for a while, before going to the patio doors and gazing into the living room. Natalie sucked in her breath as she watched the creepy figure disappear inside the house.

TWENTY-SEVEN

NATALIE

She stared at the grainy black and white footage, her heart pounding madly. The figure, who moved with a strange, graceful gait, had gone out of frame. Fear squeezed her chest tight as she swallowed hard, her mind conjuring up an impossible thought: what if they had never left?

She shivered, despite the warm day. Taking a deep breath to steady her nerves, she went inside and checked each room, one by one. Every window was closed, she could control that from her phone. Every external door locked.

How did they get out?

She sank down on a sunlounger and watched the footage again. This time she left it running long enough to see Hayden jump into the pool. She saw herself run out of the house. She almost missed the shadowy face at the kitchen window, watching as they plunged into the pool and tried to resuscitate the doll. As she and Hayden had flopped down in the sunloungers, the hooded figure walked out of the house and stood behind them for a while before disappearing out of sight.

Natalie froze as Hayden walked towards her. Should she tell him there had been an intruder in the house? Her heart raced as she weighed her options, fear and uncertainty washing over her. If they went to the police, they might discover that the intruder was her own daughter and then what? If she was ever going to tell him, that time was over a year ago, before they got married. Silently, she slipped her phone into her pocket.

Hayden cleared his throat. 'I was thinking I might set up a charity.'

Natalie leaned forward. 'Really?'

'We're getting so many requests for help. I'd like to go through them all and see where we could really make a difference. Maybe I could get into fundraising too. It would feel good to give back.'

Natalie's heart swelled with pride as she looked at her husband. He had seemed a little restless since leaving his job, but now he was brimming with energy and purpose. This was exactly what he needed.

'That sounds like a wonderful idea. We can turn the study into your office.'

He beamed. 'That would be great.'

He headed indoors and she turned her attention back to the CCTV. The footage chilled her to the bone. She really ought to do something. At the very least, she should warn Hayden. Cheeks flushing with shame, she clicked delete.

TWENTY-EIGHT

NATALIE

Natalie was expecting a consignment of plump purple leather sofas at the coffee shop, so when she heard thudding at the door, she leapt up to answer it. But this was no delivery driver. Standing in front of her, pointy facial hair springing from his face and neck like needles, was her old colleague, Mason.

'I came about the job,' he said, his gaze drawn to the shiny new espresso machine.

Natalie waited.

It took him a moment to clock who she was.

'The barista job,' he stated. He looked at her accusingly. 'Did you already get it?'

She'd advertised both online and on noticeboards in the local area. She'd given out the coffee shop's phone number, but she hadn't expected anyone to just show up, least of all Mason.

'You haven't heard then?' she ventured.

'Heard what?'

She drew in a breath. 'This is my café.'

Mason blinked. 'You're the manager?'

'I own it.'

The corners of his mouth crinkled and he let out a painful laugh.

'So seriously, I want to get in first and apply for the barista position. Who do I speak to about that?'

'That would be me.'

He looked behind her, still expecting someone to step out from her shadow.

Natalie steeled herself. There was no way she was giving him the job. Might as well put him out of his misery.

'I'm really sorry but you're too late. The position has already been filled.'

His face drooped. 'Will you give them a copy of my CV?'

He extracted a sheaf of paper from his laptop bag and peeled off a sheet. Natalie glanced at it. The only job listed was the one he'd had at the Riverside Café. That was his entire career.

'Haven't you had any other experience?' she asked.

He grimaced. 'I did a few days at Blue Beans but it didn't work out.'

'Oh, I'm sorry to hear that.'

'Yeah, well if anything comes up, just give me a call.'

He backed out the door, almost tripping over his own feet.

'Take it easy!' she called after him.

She shut the door behind him and sighed. Now she felt bad. It was like stepping on a wounded puppy. But she couldn't work with him again, she just couldn't.

She went over to the computer and scrolled through her list of online job postings, checking for suitable applicants.

Amy was going to be working part-time, but she still needed a right-hand person who knew what they were doing. Someone who would have her back, especially while she was still finding her feet.

After an hour of scrolling through the applications, she

pushed the laptop away with a sigh. She picked up her phone and rang Gail.

'Okay, tell your mum the job's hers if she wants it.'

There was a pause.

'Why don't you tell her yourself?' Gail said. 'And can you make it sound more like a request, like she'd be doing you a favour, which she will, by the way, because she doesn't want to be anybody's charity case.'

There was a harshness to Gail's tone that she had rarely heard before. Was she annoyed that Natalie had taken so long to reach this decision?

'Right. Will do. Thanks.'

She dialled Marian's home number.

'Hi, this is Natalie.'

'Hello, what can I do for you?' There was a quality in Marian's voice she couldn't make out. Was it pleasure? Or annoyance? Natalie wasn't sure. Her palms were sweaty as she rushed through her proposal, expecting any moment that Marian would interject. There was an uncomfortable silence before Marian spoke.

'That sounds interesting. Let's talk later in the week.'

Relief washed over Natalie. 'That would be great! When can you come in?'

'Let's say Thursday evening, around seven. Or is that too late?'

'Seven's fine.'

It was only once she'd hung up that she realised Marian hadn't actually accepted the job. It was still down to Natalie to convince her she wanted the position.

Natalie worked tirelessly for the next few days, getting the shop ready. She spent hours in the kitchen, measuring, mixing, folding and gently stirring until all of her recipes were perfect. She settled on a combination of breakfast pastries, cupcakes, sponges and cookies, all to be arranged in colourful displays that would entice people into her shop.

She brushed her hands on her sunflower-patterned apron and surveyed the flour she had scattered over the floor during her baking frenzy. As she reached for the broom, she heard a soft thud behind her. She jumped and turned to see a figure watching her from the doorway.

The figure took a step towards her. Natalie instinctively shot a glance at the knife block.

'Sorry, we're closed.'

'It's just me, love.'

Relief flooded through her veins when she saw it was Marian.

'Sorry, didn't mean to startle you. We did say seven o'clock, didn't we?'

'Yes. Yes, we did. Please, come on in, I'll be right with you.'

Natalie swept the spilled flour into a pile. Marian was quite right, she had said seven. How could she have forgotten?

While Natalie was sweeping, Marian circled the café with a critical eye, taking in the renovations. 'You must be thrilled?' She trailed her calloused palm over the glossy tiles, fingers resting on the intricate stonework. 'Who would've thought this was possible? I remember when you were just a scrawny kid, messing around with Gail in the paddling pool. And now look at you!'

Natalie smiled.

'How's your dad doing?'

'About the same.'

'You should visit him.'

Natalie remained silent. She didn't want to think about her dad; she wanted to talk about the coffee shop. Her hands moved quickly, yanking hard on the blinds until they released a flood of golden light into the room.

'Let me show you the coffee machine.'

She filled a glass carafe with tap water, listening to it gurgle as she poured it into the top of the machine. She then removed the paper filter and spooned in coarsely ground coffee until it was level with the top of the filter. Finally, Natalie flicked her wrist to remove any extra grounds and placed her finger on the power button. The machine whirred and steamed as Natalie led Marian through each step, pressing buttons and turning knobs, until the carafe filled with the perfect blend.

Marian took a sip of the steaming coffee and nodded with appreciation. 'Thank you, Natalie,' she said.

Natalie paused as she tried to think how to best explain herself. Marian was a highly renowned caterer with years of experience under her belt. She had even catered Natalie's wedding. She had to make her pitch perfect if she wanted Marian's help.

Natalie took a deep breath before speaking. 'Marian, I need someone who knows what they're doing to help make this café a success. I've got all these ideas and I just need someone to help me bring them to life.'

Marian nodded with interest as Natalie spoke, leaning in slightly. 'I can definitely see the potential here.'

Natalie's heart swelled.

'I make one mean cheesecake and can work a room like no other,' Marian said, tucking her hair behind her ear. 'But I'm also here to help you in any way, Natalie. I can do whatever you need to get the place up and running. I can sort out the food hygiene and fire safety certificates and all that jazz. You name it, I can do it, and best of all, you know me. You know you can trust me.'

Natalie laughed. That was half the problem. It felt weird giving instructions to someone who had been like a second mother to her. She had spent way too much time at Gail's growing up, especially when her own mum was bedridden. She wasn't proud of the way she had avoided her mother in those final days but it had been her way of coping.

'So look, Natalie. If I were you I would take me on a trial basis. If we work together well, then we'll make it permanent. And if we don't, there'll be no hard feelings.'

'That sounds very fair,' Natalie acknowledged.

She felt a little of the tension leaving her shoulders.

'You know, I helped run the finance side at the bakery so I can cash up for you if needed, and I'm up for dealing with ordering and purchasing.'

'That would be a great help.'

She smiled at Marian, glad that she had plucked up the courage to ask for her help. She was clearly the right person for the job.

Marian ran her fingers over the newly lacquered counter.

'About your dad – you should go and see him. Tell him about this place. He'll be really proud. Your mum would be too.'

Natalie looked down at her lap. Even all these years later, she found it hard to talk about her mum.

'I believe in you,' Marian added, giving Natalie a reassuring smile before standing up from her chair. 'We're going to make a great team.'

Natalie was aware they hadn't discussed terms and conditions, but that was okay. She would let Marian name her price.

'When can you start?' she asked.

'Tomorrow if you like?' Marian said.

Natalie broke into a huge grin. 'That's great because the grand opening is just a few weeks away and I'm really going to need you onboard.'

TWENTY-NINE

NATALIE

Natalie twisted her hair into a tight bun. She was wearing a light blue, vintage-style apron with large pockets. She'd bought two others, in pastel pink and yellow, for Marian and Amy who were busy cooking with her in the kitchen.

The front of the shop had been repainted. The yellowing brickwork was now a crisp white with brown window ledges and purple shutters. She had a beautiful sign that said 'Natalie's'. She worried it was a little self-indulgent naming the shop after herself, but this was her dream and she loved it.

The coffee shop was small, but cosy. Everything was just as she had envisaged it.

'Aren't you worried people will just come in here to use the toilets?' Liz asked, inspecting the place with a critical eye.

Natalie shrugged. 'They'll stay for the coffee.'

'I guess that's the joy of being rich. You don't have to sweat the small things.'

Natalie raised a brow. 'I am planning to make a profit.'

'That's good,' said Liz, eyes fixed on the espresso machine. Natalie studied her sister's posture; her dark hair was pulled back in a low ponytail, her lips downturned in a frown. Natalie felt a little frustrated by her lack of enthusiasm. Weeks of hard work had all led up to this moment, yet she could still sense the cloud that had hung around Liz since Marmite passed away. She crossed her fingers that this night would be enough to help pull her sister out of her funk.

She pushed her worries to the back of her mind. There had been no more sightings of the creepy hooded figure. She had checked the CCTV regularly, just to be sure. But it still niggled. She wished she could know for sure if it was her daughter.

She walked around the café one last time, checking everything was in place. She had the coffee machine ready to dispense little shots of espresso and hot chocolate, and hundreds of small cakes and pastries for customers to try. She had a couple of teenagers handing out flyers all around the centre of Greenwich so she was hoping for a good crowd. Everyone loved free samples.

She glanced at the clock on the wall and gave Marian a nod. She stepped forward and unlocked the door. Her lips curved into a smile as she surveyed the crowd. There was Gail, bright-eyed and fresh-faced in her floral dress and sandals, arm linked with Andy. Daisy and Ted were weaving their way through, their hands clasped tightly, but there was no sign of Hayden.

A length of festive ribbon had been strung across the threshold and a bubbly young actress stood at the entrance with scissors in her hand, ready to cut it. She was not someone Natalie had heard of, but she had a popular following on Instagram and she had told all her followers there would be freebies.

She stepped inside, pushing the door open wide with a flourish. Her legs trembled underneath her as she struggled to contain her excitement, but her smile never faltered. 'Welcome, everyone!' she said, gesturing to her establishment with arms outstretched. 'Welcome to Natalie's!'

The air was filled with a tantalising smell of freshly brewed coffee as Marian began dispensing the coffee shots.

Natalie picked up a tray from the counter, pleased with the turnout. As she handed out samples of warm cupcakes and freshly brewed coffee shots, she recognised her science teacher among the throngs of people. He still wore his old brown tweed suit, albeit a bit tattered from years of use, and his face was now creased with wrinkles and worry lines. She directed him towards the cupcakes and moved along. No doubt he was here to ask for a donation to his school science club.

She turned to face a reporter, dressed in a crisp grey suit and leather shoes, notebook tucked under one arm. Before he could introduce himself, Natalie pressed an espresso cup into his hand. The steam curled around her fingers as she spoke. 'It's from Brazil. Finest beans I've ever tasted, ground to perfection.' She forced a smile onto her lips and gestured for him to take a sip. The man cleared his throat. 'Natalie, if you don't mind me asking – what was it like when you found out about your lottery win?'

Natalie's jaw clenched. She took a deep breath and forced herself to relax. 'Today isn't about my win,' she said calmly. 'I would have opened this café eventually anyway. I've been working hard to save up for it all my life.'

At that moment, Gail walked over. 'Best coffee I've ever had,' she declared, eyeing the reporter. 'Have you tried the lemon cake? It's delicious – like heaven in your mouth!'

Natalie smiled and tried not to squirm at Gail's enthusiasm.

'Do you need any help?' Daisy asked as she and Ted approached.

'I think it's all under control thanks,' Natalie said.

Marian seemed to be everywhere, silently gathering up discarded napkins and cups, giving Natalie time to chat with the customers.

She moved through the crowd, encouraging people to try the coffee and tell their friends.

'You've actually done a pretty good job on this place,' said a familiar voice.

Natalie turned to look at Jan. She expected to see a sneer on her face, but her former boss looked serious.

'Do you think so?'

Jan leaned closer. 'Hopefully all those years of training didn't go to waste? You'll do alright, as long as you don't let your mind wander.'

Natalie swallowed her pride. 'Thanks. I... I appreciate you coming along tonight.'

'Where's Hayden?' Daisy interrupted.

'I don't know,' Natalie admitted. She checked her phone but there were no missed calls.

'He's probably stuck in traffic,' Ted guessed.

Natalie nodded. 'Please excuse me, I'd better mingle.'

She made her way to the counter and surveyed the selections. A fragrant almond cake was displayed prominently on a white plate with a delicate border of pink icing. She picked up a knife and cut it into small squares, so everyone could try it. While she was doing so, she overheard a remark from someone in the crowd.

'I give this place six months.' It was the reporter she'd spoken to earlier.

His companion cackled into her coffee. Natalie clenched her fists. She stared at them with determination. She was about to prove them both wrong. She shifted her gaze and her stomach clenched as her eyes connected with Robin's.

THIRTY

NATALIE

Natalie watched as Robin rolled his white shirt sleeves up to his elbows, and the light fabric floated around his slim shoulders. His jeans were artfully ripped at the knees, and his shoes were a perfect shade of pale brown suede, with scuff marks that seemed intentional. He ran his fingers through his thinning hair, carefully arranging it over his forehead.

She walked over to him and thrust a shot of coffee into his hand.

'You finally did it then,' he said.

'Yes. Yes, I did.'

She was a little unnerved he'd come. His eyes were a little too wide. As if he knew any minute everything could come crashing down on top of him.

'Have you heard anything more from Heather?' he asked.

'No.'

'If she contacts you, I need you to promise you won't tell her who I am.'

'I've never told anyone. I'm not going to out you now.'

She was annoyed he'd even suggested it.

He held up his hands in surrender, but the irritation remained etched on Natalie's face.

'Oh, come on, Natalie, don't be like that. You know I have a lot to lose.'

'We both have,' she reminded him. 'Believe me, I don't need this any more than you do.'

'Hayden doesn't know?' he guessed.

'Hayden doesn't need to know. How can I possibly explain the fact that I've lied to him all these years?'

'Wow.' He whistled. 'I just assumed you'd have said something. I mean you two are married and all...'

'I thought it was better this way. I didn't think it would come up.'

Robin's eyes flicked to Marian, who stood in the kitchen doorway with a wicker basket of pastries.

'If it is Heather, you could pay her off.'

She bit her lip. He made her sound like a nuisance, an inconvenience. Did he have no guilt at all?

'If it is Heather, I'll talk to her. Try to make her understand.'

His eyes remained wide. She could read the fear.

'Please, Nat. Just get rid of her.'

She winced. She'd never realised before how cowardly he was. How scared of being discovered.

'I'll let you know,' she promised.

He set down his cup without taking a single sip. 'Right. I should be going. This is your big night after all. Take care, Nat.'

'You too.'

He scurried off a little too fast, walking straight out the door. Oliver slid into his space.

'What did he want?' he asked.

'Nothing.'

'I've always thought he was a bit of a worm.'

'Yeah? Well takes one to know one.'

Oliver refused to take offence. 'Nice set-up you've got here.

The loos are super deluxe. You might want to charge for the bog roll.'

Natalie suppressed a smile. 'I want my customers to feel comfy.'

'I'm sure they will.'

'So, what can I do for you?'

'Nothing. I'm just here to support you.'

'That's very big of you.'

There was still no sign of Hayden.

Across the room, Liz was talking to Gail and Andy. She looked like she was having a good time. So did the customers for that matter. Everyone was drinking the espresso and the cakes were going fast.

Oliver cleared his throat. 'Just for the record, it wasn't me who shopped you to the press, you know.'

Natalie arched an eyebrow. 'Is that right?'

'I mean, I thought about it, but I didn't do it. I'm not a rat.' He shifted from one foot to the other. 'You know, I wouldn't be surprised if Liz did it.'

Natalie burst out laughing. 'That's low, even for you.'

'She said your daughter contacted you.'

Natalie took a step back, stunned.

'You knew about her?' she asked incredulously. Her eyes shifted to the floor, her voice barely above a whisper.

'Chill, Nat. I've always known. I was around often enough to hear your dad rant about your lowlife boyfriend. Don't worry, I'm not going to blab. I can be very discreet.'

'Wait, what exactly did Liz say?'

'Liz worries about you. She's always worried you'd regret giving up your daughter.'

'So, she contacted the papers?'

'I don't know. It makes it easier for your daughter to find you, doesn't it?'

'Shh!' She glanced around to check no one had heard.

'You're talking nonsense,' she told him. 'Liz wouldn't do that.'

'How can you be so sure?'

Natalie fumbled for an answer. The air in the room seemed to thicken and she fanned her face with a napkin.

Just at that moment, Liz walked towards them. Her gaze travelled from Natalie to Oliver before settling on Natalie's face.

'Am I interrupting something?'

'No,' Natalie said, holding her gaze a little too long.

THIRTY-ONE

NATALIE

Natalie leaned against the grimy, wood-panelled bar. Her skirt stuck to her legs in the humid air as she clinked shot glasses with her friends. They had moved from the coffee shop to the bar across the street. She was glad the launch had gone well but she was getting frantic about Hayden. Why wasn't he answering his phone? She couldn't believe he had missed the launch.

Her phone vibrated. Finally.

'Is that Hayden?' Daisy asked, peering over her shoulder.

Natalie nodded, scanning his message. 'He got stopped by the police for speeding. They kept him for ages. He reckons they thought he was a car thief or something. They've only just let him go.'

She let out a breath, relieved. She'd started to think something awful had happened.

Daisy laughed. 'The police were probably jealous of his flashy car.'

Natalie shot off a sympathetic reply. Poor Hayden. He didn't like to get in trouble. He was a good boy at heart.

She leaned back against the bar, finally able to relax. The evening had given her a lot to think about but she didn't want to focus on any of that just now. She wanted to blow off some steam.

They huddled together like a pack of wolves on the prowl, their laughter echoing off the peeling walls. Daisy danced up to the bar and looked the barman dead in the eye. 'Another round!' she bellowed, her voice strong yet jovial. Natalie felt her cheeks grow warm. If she had said something like that, she would have appeared rude, but Daisy had a way of being both commanding and funny at the same time.

Her curls bounced energetically as she twirled around and flashed Natalie a smile. The glint in her eyes warned her it was going to be a wild night.

Daisy staggered back to the table with a wooden plank holding dozens of shot glasses in green, blue and red. She set it on the table and flashed a mischievous grin at Natalie.

'Who wants to play a drinking game? It goes like this: Drink if you've ever used someone else's toothbrush.'

Natalie pulled a face and took a shot.

'I have too,' Daisy admitted.

'Then why are you not drinking?' Gail asked.

'I asked the question. Your turn, Liz.'

'Drink if you've ever stolen underwear off a washing line,' Liz said.

Gail giggled but no one moved.

'Drink if you've ever asked to speak to the manager,' Gail said.

Daisy drank.

'Your turn, Nat.'

Natalie thought for a moment. 'Drink if you've ever peed in a pool.'

No one drank. Nat shrugged. Who was going to admit it anyway?

'Drink if you've ever returned a present,' Daisy said.

Liz and Gail both drank.

'Gail?'

'Drink if you've ever messed around with someone else's man.'

The room grew cold. Natalie hesitated for a fraction of a second, but Gail didn't notice. She was focused on the other two. Nobody drank.

'Drink if you've ever lied to a friend,' Liz said.

Natalie felt her cheeks grow hot. No one moved but everyone was looking intently at the drinks. Boy, this was getting uncomfortable.

Liz let out a deep, tired sigh and retrieved her phone from her pocket.

'I think I've been social long enough,' she said, opening up the Uber app.

'Can I get in on that?' Gail asked.

Natalie clenched her jaw. She couldn't believe they were leaving already. They were just getting started.

'Drink if you want to stay out all night,' Daisy said.

Natalie threw back her next shot and felt a warm sensation bubble in her chest. She felt a deep sense of camaraderie with Daisy.

The opening chords of a new song boomed from the speakers and Daisy launched herself towards the dance floor. Natalie reached for the remaining shot and necked that too. She waved goodbye to the two party poopers and scrambled after Daisy.

There was no room on the dance floor until Daisy shouted: 'Coming through!' and the crowd parted to let them through.

Daisy grabbed Natalie's hand and they stumbled through the tightly packed crowd, pushing aside elbows and avoiding spilled drinks. Natalie's face was flushed. Even in the dim light of the club, she felt eyes on her, as they squeezed through the gap towards the space in front of the DJ box.

They began to dance. Daisy's movements were wild and

unchained and her curls bounced up and down as if they were trying to keep up with her feet. The air was thick with heat and sweat as Natalie tried to match her. The effort was both exhausting and exhilarating.

By the time they left the dance floor, they were both dripping with sweat. Daisy steered her over to the bar and they ordered double shots that burned a trail down their throats.

As Daisy urged her back to the dance floor, Natalie couldn't help but sense that there was a hidden competition between the two of them.

'Jeez, I haven't got this bladdered since the hoteliers' conference in Manchester.' Daisy let out a raucous laugh, her mouth open so wide Natalie could see all the way down to her molars.

'Oh, was it good?' Natalie asked.

'It was a blast. You should have been there.' Daisy fixed her with an intense gaze for a moment, then winked and turned away.

THIRTY-TWO

NATALIE

Natalie was jolted awake by the shrill sound of her alarm. She groaned. How was it morning already? She sent a frantic text to Marian, asking if she could manage the early morning shift on her own.

Marian rang her straight back. 'How was last night? Gail said it was a late one.' Her voice hovered between curiosity and concern.

Natalie hesitated for a moment, debating whether or not to be truthful. 'It was... a bit too much,' she admitted, pressing a hand to her temple where a headache was forming.

'What you need is a greasy bacon sandwich and a nice cup of ginger tea,' Marian advised.

Natalie shuddered. 'I might just have some Lucozade.'

'Well don't worry about Natalie's. I can cover for you just fine. Come in when you're ready.'

'Thanks, Marian. You're the best.'

Natalie closed her eyes again, promising herself it was just for a few more minutes.

She awoke to the sound of a distant church bell. She reached for her phone and saw that she had slept later than she'd intended. A dull ache started in her temple. There was no way she was driving today. She ordered a taxi and staggered into the shower. The water was scalding hot but it felt good against her skin. She stood there for an age, letting the steam fill the room and clear her head.

'Nat? Your taxi's here,' Hayden called.

Natalie's eyes flew open. Cursing under her breath, she shut off the water and leapt out of the shower. In the bedroom, she threw on the first clothes she could find. She hurried into the lift and Hayden watched with a bemused smile as she slid into her shoes on her way out the door.

'Sorry! Bye!' she shouted over her shoulder before rushing off.

She sank into the back seat of the taxi, her eyes unfocused as memories of the night before replayed in her mind. She clenched her fists around the straps of her handbag and tapped her right foot impatiently as she thought about what Oliver had said. How could he have known about Heather all these years? And why hadn't he ever told her? She shook her head and stared out the window as she remembered what else he had said. She didn't believe for a moment that Liz had been the one to spill her lottery win to the press but something was going on with her sister. As for Daisy, she was certain she knew Natalie had been in Manchester. What she didn't understand was why she hadn't blabbed.

Hayden texted her, full of apologies once again for missing her big launch.

I'm sure you will make it up to me, she messaged him back. He didn't reply. Perhaps he was feeling embarrassed. She leaned back against the seats and fell back to sleep, waking with a jolt when the taxi pulled up.

'Just here, love?'

'Er, yes thanks.'

Natalie hopped out and joined the stream of people

walking along the busy street. She turned onto Button Lane and took a few steps forward before a strange noise erupted from her throat. She gazed up at her newly painted sign. It had been perfect just the day before, but now it looked wonky.

With dismay, she realised that the second 'a' in her name was missing, along with the all-important apostrophe. Instead of Natalie's, it now read 'Nat Lies'.

Her heart dropped to the pit of her stomach. She could not take her eyes off the ruined sign. *Nat Lies*. The statement seemed to scream down at passers-by. Her throat constricted as she recognised the calculated cruelty of this act. Someone had done this. Someone wanted to hurt her.

Everywhere she looked, faces darted away, avoiding her questioning gaze. Her mouth dried up and her breath became shallow. What had she ever done to deserve this? She struggled to hold back her tears as she stepped into the café. The place was empty except for a couple of customers sipping their coffee at a table. The warmth of the oven and the sweet scent of freshly baked cake filled the air, but Natalie couldn't appreciate either.

Marian stood at the food prep area, turning out a cake.

'Natalie?' she called. 'Are you okay?'

Natalie shook her head slowly, feeling like she might break down at any moment. 'Have you seen the sign?' she asked through quivering lips.

'Yes. I saw it this morning.'

'What time was that?'

'About six.'

So, whoever vandalised the sign must have done so in the early hours, after Natalie left the bar across the street.

Marian put a hand on Natalie's shoulder. 'It's going to be okay.'

Natalie couldn't find the words to reply. Tears streamed

down her cheeks. Marian guided her up the stairs to the flat. She opened the door and gestured for Natalie to go inside.

'It really will be okay,' she said, giving Natalie a hug. 'I've asked Damon to come and fix it after work.'

Natalie wiped her cheeks. 'Today?'

'Yes, so don't take it to heart. It's just mindless vandalism; nothing that can't be fixed. You've worked too hard to let them bring you down like this. Now dry those eyes, and let's get back to business – it's just plain jealousy, you'll see.'

Natalie looked down at her hands. She hoped fervently that it really was some random, who resented her for winning the lottery. But deep down, she didn't believe it.

Marian gave her a tiny smile and left the room, leaving Natalie to pull herself together. She let out an anxious breath, still processing Marian's pep talk when her phone buzzed in her pocket. She pulled it out and saw a text from Hayden:

Hope all's good at the coffee shop? Let me know if you need me to come in.

Her thumb hovered over the response button but she didn't feel like unloading on Hayden. Besides, she would have to be careful what she said to him in case the culprit was Heather. Thoughtfully, she tucked the phone back in her pocket.

She worked steadily through the morning. She was pleased to see a lot of office workers coming in for hot sandwiches and coffees. Word was getting around, despite her ruined sign.

'I'm just going to take a quick break,' she said, once Amy arrived.

She went upstairs and curled up on the sofa. She had only intended to sleep for a few minutes, but the next thing she knew, it had gone three in the afternoon.

'Natalie!' Amy's voice floated up the stairs. 'There's a delivery for you.'

'Can you sign for it?' Natalie called back, rubbing the sleep from her eyes.

'It's something personal,' Amy said.

Natalie tensed. What now?

She descended the stairs. Amy smiled and held out a huge bouquet of flowers in the same shades of white, brown and purple Natalie had used for her branding.

'Who are they from?' Amy wanted to know.

Natalie reached for the flowers, caressing their petals with her fingertips as she searched for a note.

Marian put her hand to her forehead and pretended to swoon. 'Oh, young love!'

Natalie smiled politely, but her stomach was in knots. What if they weren't from Hayden? What if they were from Heather?

'Better put them in water,' Marian said. Natalie nodded and headed towards one of the decorative vases she had on the shelf. She took out the flowers and a piece of paper fluttered to the floor. She bent down to pick it up and read the handwritten words:

Roses are red,

Coffee can burn,

You've had your fun,

Now it's my turn.

With trembling fingers, she flipped the note over, examining the looping and curling ink of the unknown handwriting. She was sure it was a woman who had written it; she couldn't think of any man with such precise penmanship. She wished she could inspect it further, but it was getting busy and she needed to focus on serving the customers. Instead, she stuffed it into the pocket of her apron. Pasting a smile on her face, she headed back to work.

It was late in the afternoon when Damon arrived. He walked in with a big cheesy grin on his face.

'I hear you need my help.'

Natalie shot him a grateful smile. His overalls were caked in dust, and an odour of sawdust pervaded the air around him as he set his heavy wooden toolbox on the floor.

He glanced over at Amy.

'Hi, I'm Damon.'

'Amy Kipling, like the cake,' she said, ready with her go-to introduction. 'Can I get you a coffee?'

'Maybe after, thanks, love.'

'I'll start cashing up, shall I?' Marian offered.

She nodded. 'That would be great.'

Natalie hovered as Damon set out his work tools.

'I didn't know you did this sort of work?'

'Well, Marian said you were desperate. Looks like a fairly basic job. I found the missing letters in the alley. A little bit of elbow grease and we'll have them looking like new again. It's no trouble – just glad to help out.'

'Thank you. I truly appreciate it.'

'So, what happened? Pissed off the wrong bloke, did you?'

'What makes you think it was a bloke?'

'Oh, I dunno. Women don't like climbing ladders. Don't want to break their nails or something.'

Putting his everyday sexism to one side, Natalie wondered if he had a point, but she didn't think so. Any able-bodied person could have done it.

'Why don't you call it a night, love?' Marian said. 'I'll wait until Damon's finished, and make sure everything is locked up.'

Natalie nodded, wondering now why she had hesitated before taking Marian on.

'Thank you,' she said. 'I'll be a bit more with it in the morning.' She collected her handbag and gave Damon a wave, grateful to be done for the day.

The street was alive with people bustling and jostling, carrying shopping bags or hurrying home from work. A young woman with silver earrings glanced at her curiously.

Could you be Heather? Natalie wondered.

She realised she was staring and quickly averted her eyes.

The truth was, she didn't even know who she was looking for. She wouldn't know Heather if they stood side by side on the tube. It was driving her nuts. Natalie shoved her hands deep in her pockets and balled them into tight fists. She could no longer avoid it. She had to talk to Heather. At least then she'd know who she was up against.

THIRTY-THREE

NATALIE

'Tell Damon I owe him,' Natalie said to Marian the following morning. The sign outside the café looked good as new. You'd never know it had been damaged.

Marian chuckled. 'I would but it would only go to his head.'

Natalie made the coffee while Marian worked the dough. Her fingers were thick and strong from years of labour.

Gail pushed the door open with her foot, the baby carrier strapped to her chest cradling Scarlett. Natalie poured a stream of rich black coffee into a large paper cup and secured a plastic lid on top. Gail smiled, leaned forward, and gratefully accepted it.

'Are you coming to Liz's party?' she asked. 'Dad said he'll have Scarlett for the evening.'

Natalie's eyebrows shot up to her forehead. 'Since when is Liz having a party?'

'Oh. She didn't tell you? She invited us this morning, over Messenger.'

Natalie pulled out her phone, but there were no messages from Liz. Curious.

Gail went on her merry way and Natalie tried to get back to

work. So what if Liz was having a party? She had far more pressing things to think about anyway, like how to find Heather. She wished she'd kept the letter the adoption agency sent her. For a while, she had kept it at the bottom of her underwear drawer but its presence had brought her so much guilt that it had been a relief to throw it out when she moved in with Hayden. It hadn't occurred to her that one day she might need it.

Natalie popped round to Liz's house on the way home from work. When Liz opened the door, a pair of cats stormed out, weaving between her legs. She stepped into the living room, where two more cats were playing with each other on top of a bookcase – one pouncing onto the shelf and sending a book tumbling down. She spotted another cat in the kitchen, curled up on one of the rickety wooden chairs.

'Did you always have this many cats?' she asked.

Liz shrugged. 'People bring me strays.'

'You don't think it's getting a bit much? I mean, there must be rules about how many cats you can keep in your flat.'

'They need me,' Liz said firmly. 'I'm not going to turn them away.'

'Please tell me you're at least trying to rehome them? You're starting to look like a hoarder!'

Liz barked out a laugh then shook her head. 'Don't worry. It's fine. I take good care of each and every one of them.'

Natalie studied her sister's face and saw a mask of grief. It was there in the sudden tightening of her lips and the narrowing of her eyes. Marmite's death must have hit her harder than she'd realised.

'So, tell me about the party.'

'It's no big deal, I just thought I'd have a few people round for pizza on Friday night.'

'Why didn't you ask me?'

'I was going to.'

Natalie sat back, mollified. 'So, what's the occasion?'

'There isn't one.'

Natalie didn't believe her. Liz was such a private person. There had to be a motive behind her decision to invite people in. Perhaps she was going to persuade them all to adopt strays. That sounded like something she would do.

'There was something else I wanted to talk to you about,' she said, accepting a cup of coffee.

Liz raised a brow. 'Oh?'

'Someone sent me some flowers with a weird poem attached to them.'

'You think it was Heather?'

'Do you?'

'I wish I knew.'

Liz tilted her head. 'What sort of a poem?'

Natalie glanced up at the ceiling. 'To be honest, it was kind of creepy. I think I'm going to have to meet her. It's the only way to put a stop to all this.'

Liz stepped forward and hugged her tight.

'Careful – my coffee.'

'The trouble is, I don't know where to start. I don't even remember the name of the adoption agency. I was wondering... do you think there's any chance Dad might remember? He was the one who arranged it all.'

Liz pursed her lips and looked away, her eyes flickering across the room.

'You haven't spoken to Dad in a long time. You don't know what he's like now.'

'What is he like?'

'Vague. Forgetful. Sometimes he knows who I am, sometimes he thinks I'm a member of staff. The chances of him remembering are pretty slim.'

'He might though.'

'I can ask him if you want.'

'No, I think I'd better ask him myself.'

'You haven't visited him in years.'

Natalie looked down at her hands. 'All the same.'

'Oh for goodness' sake!' Liz gulped down her coffee and slammed the mug down on the table, startling the cats. 'If you really want to go, I'll come with you.'

'What – now?'

'No time like the present. He'll be having his tea around this time. If we leave now, you can catch him before he goes to bed.'

Natalie glanced at the clock. 'Isn't it a bit late for visitors?'

Liz shook her head. 'The staff are pretty easy-going. I can usually talk them round.'

Natalie set down her own mug and followed Liz out of the flat.

She watched as Liz unlocked the door of her aging hatchback, its paint was faded and there was rust creeping up the sides. Natalie didn't understand why she didn't get something new. She didn't appear to have done much at all with the money she'd given her.

She clutched her seatbelt as Liz sped through the busy streets, her stomach tied in knots. She dreaded facing her father and reopening old wounds – but what scared her most was the possibility that he would remember, despite Liz's high expectations to the contrary. It wouldn't be the first time her sister had been wrong.

The white building looked serene, with a short green manicured lawn and potted plants in vibrant reds, blues and yellows adorning the front entrance. As they stepped through the revolving doors, Natalie noticed several people bustling about in neat blue uniforms. An elderly woman shuffled past them, her frame creaking as she moved, and with each laboured breath she exhaled, a low, gurgling moan that reverberated off the white walls.

Liz spoke to the receptionist and scrawled their names in the visitors' book.

'You know where you're going?' the receptionist asked.

Liz nodded. Natalie's shoes seemed to stick to the floor as they walked down the corridor, but when they reached his room, her father beamed from ear to ear. He greeted them both with open arms, as if it were only yesterday that he had last seen Natalie.

'Tell me, are you still working in that café?' he asked.

'No, I've opened my own,' she told him proudly.

His eyebrows twitched. 'That's my girl! What about that young man of yours? When are you getting hitched?'

'We're already married, Dad.'

His smile faltered and his eyes clouded and he looked down at his lap.

'I should have been there to give you away.'

'Liz gave me away.'

He shook his head, like what she was saying was too strange.

'You were ill, Dad, remember?'

The wrinkles around his mouth deepened. 'He wouldn't even come round and meet me. What sort of man is he?'

Natalie exchanged a glance with Liz.

'Dad, you're thinking of Robin. I married Hayden. You like him, remember? He brought you whisky.'

Liz cleared her throat. 'Dad, we were wondering if you could help us with something? Natalie has decided she wants to find her daughter. Do you remember the name of the adoption agency you used?'

Their father's eyes flickered from Liz to Natalie and back again. He shifted in his armchair and rubbed his hands together.

'You'd have to ask your mother about that.'

Natalie's eyes scanned the room in desperation, her teeth digging into her lower lip. If she corrected him, she would shatter the old man's spirit.

He opened his mouth with a force that seemed to reverberate throughout the room, stretching his jaw so wide that his eyes disappeared under heavy lids. She glanced at Liz. 'It's getting late,' she said, her voice low. 'I think we should get going. We can come another time.'

Rising, Natalie slowly embraced her father. At first, he seemed stiff, but then his arms tightened around her as if they could never be separated again. He still smelt like musty wool and aftershave. She inhaled sharply as a flood of emotion threatened to overwhelm her.

'I've missed you so much,' he whispered in her ear. Tears slipped down Natalie's face as she clung to him tightly, feeling an unexpected rush of love.

Finally, she stepped back, wiping the wetness from her cheeks. Liz stepped forward to hug him too. As she did so, he said something.

'What was that?' Liz asked.

He was looking at Natalie again.

'The people who adopted your daughter. Their last name was Kipling, like the cake.'

THIRTY-FOUR

NATALIE

Natalie felt the floor tilt. Her knees went weak and she stumbled, feeling the carpet slip beneath her feet. Her mind scrambled to make sense of what she had heard. Liz put a hand on her shoulder, offering support.

'What's wrong?' she asked. 'You look like you've seen a ghost.'

Natalie's mouth went dry and she struggled to form words. 'The girl who works for me. Her name is Amy Kipling.'

They walked back through the building. Liz waved to the receptionist and signed them out before they pushed through the double doors.

'It's probably a coincidence,' Liz said, after giving it some thought.

'It's not a common name though, is it?' Natalie said, her forehead creasing in concentration. 'I've never met anyone else with that name.'

Liz stopped abruptly, her eyes narrowing as she studied Natalie's face.

'When did you hire her? Was it before or after you were in the papers?'

Natalie shifted uneasily. 'After.'

'Maybe it is her,' Liz said thoughtfully. 'Maybe she was so desperate to meet you she applied for the job.'

'But what about the doll?'

'I don't know,' Liz said, shaking her head.

It was hard to imagine Amy doing anything like that, let alone sneaking into her house. And then there were the flowers. Amy had told her there was a delivery van outside, but she never actually saw it. What if Amy had bought the flowers herself?

A chill ran through her entire body as if an icy wind had blown across her skin.

'So, what do I do now?'

They stopped at Natalie's on the way home. The bar opposite was pumping out music, and people hung around outside, talking and smoking cigarettes.

'What is it you're looking for?' Liz asked, as Natalie sat down at the computer.

'Amy's HR records,' Natalie said. 'Her date of birth will be on there.'

Liz busied herself making two cups of coffee with extra froth, while Natalie searched. Marian did most of her admin, so it took her a while to find what she was looking for.

'Amy Kipling, no middle name. Her date of birth is not the same as Heather's but it's only six months out.'

She squeezed her eyes shut.

'She might have used her date of adoption instead,' Liz said. 'These things take time to go through.'

Natalie looked up. 'That's a thought. But why would she go by Amy? When she wrote to me, she signed herself "Heather".'

Liz gave her a sidelong glance.

'She's a grown woman. She can call herself whatever the

hell she wants. Maybe she feels more like an Amy? Have you tried looking her up on social media?'

'No, let's do that!'

She typed Amy's name into Google, but Liz was faster.

'There's a bunch of Amy Kiplings on Facebook. I guess the name's not as unusual as we thought.'

'Try Heather Kipling,' Natalie said.

'Same,' Liz said. 'I don't think any of these could be her.'

They searched a while longer, but neither of them found anything relevant.

'Oh, God this is excruciating,' Natalie said. 'I've half a mind to just ring her and put myself out of my misery.'

'You could do that,' Liz said, 'but I can think of a better idea.'

THIRTY-FIVE

HAYDEN

Two Days Earlier

Hayden stepped into his office, the thick carpet muffling his steps as he made his way to the safe. He spun the combination and opened it, so that he could check on his stash of banknotes. He'd got into the habit of withdrawing wads of cash every time he went out and bringing it home. It made him feel safer, knowing it wasn't all in one place.

His hands gently ran over the crisp bundles as he spread them out on the mahogany table. The Scottish one-hundred-pound notes were particularly special. He'd never even seen one before they'd won the lottery. Now he collected them like other people collected stamps.

He picked up a bundle and flipped through it, resisting the urge to throw it up in the air so it could rain down on him. The feeling of having this much money was something he would never take for granted.

He looked around the room – noticing how the sunlight reflected off the glass walls and ceiling – and tried to enjoy his freedom. He wanted to get Daisy and Ted over to play tennis, but Ted kept wimping out, saying his back hurt, and everyone else he knew was at work. He'd tried joining the tennis club but the judgemental looks from the regulars made him feel uncomfortable.

Never mind, he would sort through the mail, then he'd feel like he'd achieved something today. Natalie's big launch was tonight and he needed to be there to support her. He'd only been to the coffee shop once or twice so far. Mainly because he found Marian rather intimidating, disapproving even, as if she knew what he was going to do before he even did it.

Settling into the chair, he sifted through the backlog of their post. Most of it was begging letters, with a few household bills mixed in. He might as well make a start on it. He pulled out neatly folded papers – bills from the electricity supplier and an overdue rent notice from their old flat. They'd already paid that in full. He balled it up and tossed it into the bin.

He picked up an official-looking letter addressed to Natalie and decided to open it. Goodness only knew when Natalie might get round to it and it could be important. He pulled out a sheet of paper – it was Natalie's P45. He scanned the document quickly. Natalie's pay and tax information was neatly listed but something caught his eye: the date of her last day of work didn't match up with what he knew. According to this document, she'd stopped working for the Riverside Café almost a month before the lottery money came through. How could this be?

He logged onto their joint bank account and checked when Natalie had last been paid. The date matched up with what it said on her P45. He narrowed his eyes and reviewed their purchases from when they'd gone overdrawn. Sure, he'd bought a few pairs of trainers but Natalie had withdrawn £500 over a few days. What had she needed that sort of cash for? She'd spent on other things too: such as taxis and takeaway food. It was almost as if she'd known they were going to win the lottery.

They *had* already won, he realised with a jolt.

He recalled the day he'd found the ticket. He'd come home from Borough Market with a bag of orange pekoe tea but when he took down the teapot, he'd found a neatly folded square of paper inside. At the time he had found it endearing that Natalie had left it in such an odd place but now it seemed strangely intentional. She wasn't just scatty or drunk. She was hiding it from him.

The only part he couldn't understand was why she hadn't claimed it herself. Had she planned to take the money and run? Or was she still weighing up her options, deciding what to do?

He tried to stay calm, but his heart raced and his palms grew sweaty. Should he confront her? What if he was right? He didn't think he could stand it. He took a deep breath and pushed away from the desk. He had to get out of the house before he went nuts.

He headed outside and ran his hands lovingly over his cherry-red Ferrari. A few minutes with the top down and the wind in his hair was usually enough to lift his mood.

He felt an intense pressure inside him, so he kept driving, all the way down to the coast. He got out of the car and trudged towards the shoreline. The strong wind whipped his face as he watched the waves break against the shore. He rolled up his jeans and slipped out of his trainers, wading into the cold water. He imagined himself up to his waist, his chest, his neck. He could keep going, until it swallowed him entirely. Then she would be sorry.

The sound of children laughing erupted behind him. There was a group of them, chasing one another as they raced down the path to the sea. He closed his eyes and sighed, relishing the saltwater spray on his skin. But the moment was gone. Reluctantly, he stepped out of the surf and trudged through the sand to collect his shoes.

He barely remembered the drive back home. He just knew that he wasn't ready to face Natalie, so he turned into the car park of the Ship, a small pub that never seemed to have many customers. He would just have the one, he decided, as he pushed open the heavy wooden door.

He sat on a barstool, his back rigid against the wooden chair. The barman gave him a curt nod before pouring his whisky into a tumbler. The amber liquid danced in the glass and the smoky aroma tickled his nose. He pulled out his phone and tapped on an image of himself and Natalie, taken during their honeymoon. His thumb paused on the glowing screen as they smiled at each other, her arms looped around his waist. He shook his head in disbelief and took a long swig from the glass, feeling the whisky burn the back of his throat. Then he raised two fingers to the barman for another.

He nursed his drink and watched the barman's cloth as it moved across the counter in a practised rhythm. He took another sip, this time letting the whisky linger on his tongue before swallowing. Warmth spread through his body, numbing his pain.

Doubt crept into his mind. Maybe he had misunderstood Natalie's intentions. Had she wanted to surprise him? But if that was true, why hadn't she said anything when he claimed the prize? He remembered how her face had contorted slightly when he'd told her about the win. He'd assumed it was from the shock of the moment, but now he wondered if there was some-thing else brewing beneath the surface. A wave of anxiety washed over him and his heart rate climbed.

'Hey, you got a cigarette?'

He shifted his gaze towards the young woman who'd just approached the bar, taking in the University of Greenwich sweatshirt that hung past her waist. She wore baggy jeans that puddled around her ankles like spilt ink and her reddish-brown hair was pulled back Princess Leia style, in neat buns on either side of her head.

He plucked his only cigarette from his pocket and handed it over without a word.

'Thanks.'

He watched her long fingers wrap around it, then she headed outside.

He finished his drink and was about to leave when she reappeared and flashed the barman a shy smile.

'I'll have a whisky, please. Single malt.'

She placed a hand on the back of his chair and looked at him. Her cheeks were spattered with freckles.

'What will you have? Single malt?'

He nodded, feeling uneasy as the barman automatically poured him another.

Should he object? It seemed rude. It was just a drink, after all. It didn't mean anything, and he couldn't remember the last time anyone had offered. In fact, since he'd won the lottery, he'd been forking out for everything. This made a pleasant change.

The barman pushed the whisky towards him. He gripped it and toasted the woman.

'Thank you,' he said, clinking glasses. He held her gaze a little longer than intended.

'Lexi,' she said with a smile.

'Hayden.'

He stole another glance at her. She had a cute little snub of a nose offset by cool intelligent eyes.

They sipped their drinks in silence for a few moments.

'Second year psychology,' she said. 'What about you?'

He glanced at her sweatshirt. Did she think he was a student? No, obviously he was too old. Even if he looked good for his age.

'I hope you don't mind if I psychoanalyse you?' she went on.

'Analyse away.'

'Good, because I'm conducting an experiment.'

He leaned forward and gave her his full attention. 'Tell me more.'

'It involves talking to strangers.' There was a glint in her eye that sent a tingle down his spine.

'Well, you know that can be dangerous.' He leaned in close enough to feel the heat of her breath on his skin.

Her voice dropped. 'Are you dangerous?'

He stifled a laugh. 'Deadly.'

She smiled. 'I like that,' she said, scribbling a few lines in her jotter.

'What are you writing?'

'Sorry, that's confidential.'

'Isn't it about me?'

'Do you want it to be about you?'

They went on in this manner for a few minutes. It was harmless, Hayden decided. Just a bit of joshing to lift his mood.

When Lexi excused herself to go to the toilet, he picked up his phone and thought about what he was going to say to Natalie. If he left now, he could still make her grand opening, but he was still upset about her lying. Maybe it would be better to talk to her after, in private. He could hardly bring that up in the middle of her launch.

She'd wonder where he was though. He'd better come up with something good. Whilst he was pondering what to write, two uniformed police officers walked in to have a word with the barman.

'Is that your Ferrari outside?' the barman asked Hayden.

'Yes,' he admitted.

The police both looked at him. 'How can you afford a car like that?'

He glanced around, not wanting everyone to hear.

'I won the lottery. You can google me if you want. Here.'

He pulled his driving licence from his wallet and they looked at it.

'All right then. Sorry for bothering you. Mind you don't drink and drive.'

As they headed back out the door, Lexi appeared at his side.

'What you been up to?' she whispered in his ear.

He gave her a lopsided grin. 'Told you I was dangerous.'

He turned back to his phone and shot off a quick text to Natalie. He said he'd been pulled over by the police for speeding. It was entirely plausible. The police had been tailing him a lot lately. His new car attracted them like wasps to a hog roast.

'What are you typing?' Lexi asked.

He shifted and held the phone close to his chest. 'Sorry, that's confidential.'

She raised an eyebrow. 'Haven't you got a mouth on you?'

'If you like that, you should see the rest of me.'

Jesus, what was he doing? His pulse quickened as a familiar sensation of adrenaline surged through his veins. He hadn't flirted like this in ages. But it didn't mean anything. He just needed something to keep his mind off Natalie's betrayal. If that was even what it was.

He checked the time. He'd finish his drink, then he'd get a taxi and catch the end of Natalie's soirée. He'd buy everyone drinks and everyone would forget he'd missed the main event.

Lexi studied him intently, tapping her pen against her notepad. 'Let me guess. You're an only child?'

He chuckled in response, and she smiled knowingly.

'How can you tell?' he asked.

Without answering him, Lexi shifted her focus to the notepad in front of her and started scribbling down notes.

'How was your childhood?'

He let out a laugh. 'How long have you got?'

He barely noticed when she nodded to the barman to refill their glasses.

'Did your mum cook big Sunday roasts?'

'Still does.'

She leaned in. 'You strike me as the kind of guy who doesn't like to let people down.'

'Yeah?'

'I can tell you're kind. Considerate. You think about other people, but you keep your opinions to yourself. You don't want anyone to think you're a try hard.'

The barman looked over at them.

'We're closing soon. One more for the road?'

Hayden glanced down at his empty glass. What time was it?

He consulted his watch. Damn, Natalie's event would be over. He might as well stay and have one more.

'These are on me,' he insisted.

The barman poured them two more. They clinked their glasses together before necking them.

'So, you going to walk me home or what?' Her voice was soft and hopeful.

'Okay then.'

He'd had too much to drink, so he left the Ferrari in the car park.

They headed along the riverfront, talking and laughing. She kept stealing glances at him – shy yet meaningful. The air felt electric and he leaned closer to her as if pulled by an invisible force.

'This is me,' she said, showing him an old building close to the university. 'You should come in for coffee. Get yourself sobered up a bit before you go home.'

She didn't wait for his reply.

They climbed the creaking wooden steps of the run-down building. Everything around them was dingy and broken, but Lexi's door shone brightly in contrast. It was painted turquoise with a shiny door knocker that glinted in the dim light.

He bit his lower lip, imagining how she might react if she

knew about his grand glass house with its sprawling gardens. Well, she didn't need to know. It wasn't as if he was going to invite her over anytime soon.

They stepped inside. She closed the door behind them and made her way to the kitchen. He followed, wanting to be closer. He stood by the counter watching as she moved around the room with ease, humming a soft melody under her breath as she worked.

The aroma of freshly brewed coffee filled the air. He breathed it in and tried not to think of Natalie. She placed two steaming mugs of coffee on the counter before taking a seat next to him, their legs touching ever so slightly. He chose the mug with 'The Regent Hotel' written on it. She chose the Snoopy one. They drank in silence for what felt like an eternity before Hayden finally spoke.

'Lexi, I had a good time with you tonight, but this can't—' Before he could finish what he was saying, she leaned towards him until their lips were just inches apart...

His phone buzzed in his pocket. He ignored it and gazed at her. His heart pounded as he closed the gap between them and kissed her. Excitement pulsed through his body as she melted into him, her arms trailing around his neck as she deepened the kiss further. A tingle of electricity spread through his body and he let go of all his doubts as he brushed his fingertips along her soft cheek. The warmth of her breath on his face sent a shiver down his spine, and when he pulled away, her eyes were heavy with desire.

She took him by the hand and led him to the bedroom. With trembling hands, she undid the buttons on his shirt. She ran her hands over his chest and he sucked in his stomach.

He traced the zipper of her hoodie down with his fingertips and eased her jeans off her hips, revealing lacy pink underwear. He placed her delicately in the centre of the bed and explored the velvety softness of her body. Her breasts were smaller than

Natalie's, but just as tender. She moaned loudly at the slightest touch, a sound that seemed to reverberate through his body. Then she traced her nails along his skin until he reached the brink of insanity. There was no going back from this point; he had to have her. The passion between them ignited like a wildfire, leaving nothing but smouldering ashes in its wake.

It was dark when he awoke, and the rusty taste of whisky lingered on his tongue. Lexi lay beside him, her body curled up like a cat. The fug of sweat and sex lingered in the air. He pulled the sheets over her. He was in the horrors now, as his fermented mind played back images of his drunken escapades. He tumbled out of bed and staggered to right himself.

His feet were cold, as if slabs of ice had been glued to his soles. He shivered and squinted into the darkness. His hands stretched out in search of clothing. He pulled on his jeans, careful not to rustle the fabric too loudly.

Lexi's light came on as he bounded down the stairs, but he didn't look back. He pulled his phone out of his pocket. Natalie was not home yet. She had sent him a flurry of drunken texts, providing him with updates on her journey home. He quickened his pace, arms pumping with determination as he spotted the entrance to a tube station up ahead.

His footsteps slowed as he saw the gate was closed. There was not a single taxi in sight and it was too late for the night bus. Panic set in as he realised he was running out of time. He flew down the street, feet pounding against the asphalt. Sweat rolled down his forehead as he raced back to the pub. His car was still in the car park, parked next to a tatty white Fiesta.

He knew he was well over the limit as he got behind the wheel. It would be just his luck if the police stopped him, but he had to get back home before Natalie. He didn't feel like he had a choice.

Luckily for him, the roads were deserted. He took the corners a little too wide, and twice he hit the kerb. It was a relief when he saw the canopy of trees in the distance, marking the winding road that led towards home. He was grateful, too, that he had left the gates open. His headlights barely illuminated the Glass House. He pulled to a stop, admiring the way the transparent panels reflected silver light from the moon.

The house held its breath as he unlocked the door and made straight for the lift. He pressed the button and leaned heavily against the wall. It spat him out at the top and he stumbled to the bed.

A split second later, he heard a thump that announced Natalie was home. She called out his name, but he couldn't muster up the energy to answer her. He felt the vibration of the lift and then she slipped into the covers beside him. Her warm skin contrasted with his ice-cold body. He slipped his arms around her and held her tight.

'Sorry I missed your big night,' he murmured.

'That's okay.' She sounded tipsy. 'It went really well.'

'I'm glad.'

His stomach twisted, dreading her reaction if she were to find out what he'd done. It was a mistake, a stupid mistake. Could she ever find it in her heart to forgive him?

THIRTY-SIX

HAYDEN

Despite his late night, Hayden woke before Natalie and went downstairs to stare into a cup of coffee. He wished he could erase the previous day from history. Finding that P45. Meeting that girl in the pub. She wasn't even that hot. Ugh, when he thought about it now, it made him shudder. He heard a car outside.

'Nat? Your taxi's here!'

A few minutes later, she came down in the lift.

He watched as she pulled her shoes on. Her hair was still damp from the shower. He longed to run his hands through it but she was clearly in a hurry.

'Sorry! Bye!' she shouted as she rushed out the door.

'I'm sorry too,' he said quietly.

After Natalie left, he dragged himself into the shower and stood there for a few moments. With trembling hands, he reached for the tap and turned the hot water on full blast – almost to the point of scalding. He lathered up with an abrasive loofah, scrubbing his skin raw as if he could wipe off his bad choices. Then he turned it right down and let the water cascade over his body until he ached from the cold.

He grabbed his towel. Dampness clung to his skin and a fresh chill crept up his spine. His wedding ring was not on his finger. His jeans lay crumpled on the floor. He grabbed them and turned out the pockets but he found nothing inside but air. Fear climbed up his legs. He checked the bedroom, then took the lift down to the living room and searched beneath the sofas. His hands frantically scoured the carpet, but the ring was not there. His chest ached as reality sank in. There was nothing for it. He would have to go back to Lexi's.

He threw on some clothes and headed outside. The sun glinted off the curves of his Ferrari as he stepped out onto the driveway but he knew driving it to Lexi's was a bad idea. A car like that would be easily spotted outside the run-down student accommodation. Best to leave it at the pub, in full view of the main road. He'd better check there anyway. He recalled twisting it around as he sat at the bar. With any luck it was there and not at Lexi's.

Memories flooded back as he walked inside, blinking as his eyes adjusted to the dim light. He approached the bar and explained his plight to the barmaid; her cold grey eyes were indifferent.

He said a silent prayer as she bent down to search through a box of lost property but she emerged empty-handed, her face blank.

'No, no one's handed it in. If it were in here, our cleaners would have found it.'

Or kept it, he thought to himself with a sour taste in his mouth.

Despite his thirst, he couldn't bear to wait a minute longer in the pub. He turned around and set off along the Thames path towards Lexi's. The river was so still, the water reminded him of the glass panels on his house. He half expected it to shatter to pieces from the ripple of his breath.

He turned the corner, no longer sure if he was going the

right way. He cursed himself for not asking her for a phone number. Eventually, he found himself standing outside the tube station he'd passed the night before. He studied the streets and buildings around him, trying to remember which way to go next. He sighed in frustration and wished he had paid more attention.

The piercing sound of screeching brakes filled the air as a bike hurtled towards him. He leapt out of the way, narrowly avoiding a collision. Daisy spun around in front of him, her helmet slipping off her head as she came to a halt.

'God, Daisy. Are you trying to kill me?'

He slumped against the wall, his breath coming in shallow gasps. Daisy pulled a packet of sweets out of her pocket.

'Wine gum?'

He waved it away with a shake of his head, not trusting himself to speak.

'I had a good time with your missus last night. She tells me you've been a naughty boy.'

His stomach dropped. 'What do you mean?'

'You got a speeding fine,' she reminded him.

Bloody hell. He was forgetting his own lies.

She tilted her head slightly and gave him an amused yet stern look. 'How much was the fine?'

'Two... two hundred?'

The corner of her mouth twitched upwards ever so slightly. What was that? Didn't she believe him?

She rocked back and forth, causing her back wheel to squeak.

'Where are you heading?' she asked.

'Going to see a mate.'

'What mate?'

'No one you know.'

Daisy raised an eyebrow. 'Sounds mysterious...'

She trailed off and he felt strangely exposed. He scrabbled

for an explanation, but it was too late – Daisy was already pushing away on her bike.

'Well, I'll let you go. Ted needs his bacon!'

He gritted his teeth and tried to push Daisy from his mind as he followed the river, navigating its curves until a narrow road lined with grey tower blocks came into view. They looked identical. He thought Lexi's was the one on the left but he wasn't positive. He tried the door to the building and discovered it was unlocked, or rather the lock was broken. Someone had jammed something inside. As he climbed the worn stairs, patches of discoloured paint peeled off the walls like dried skin. The smell of urine hung thick in the air like an invisible fog, and his chest tightened with each passing step. Had it been this bad the night before, or had he been so drunk he hadn't noticed? He felt a wave of relief when he reached the third floor and saw the turquoise door. He rang the bell.

Lexi peered out with guarded eyes.

'Hi... er, think I might have left my ring here?'

She mustered a thin smile.

'I'm sorry. I haven't seen any rings, but you're welcome to come in and look if you like.'

He stepped inside the cramped living room and surveyed the messy scene before him. A bowl of cereal lay cold and untouched on the coffee table. Crushed beer cans littered the floor. He hadn't noticed those last night. He began his search, lifting cushions and checking under the sofas and the coffee table.

'You want a cup of tea while you're here?'

'Thanks, but I've got to get back.'

'To your wife, right?'

A pit formed in his stomach as he reluctantly nodded. God, he felt like a shit.

More unwanted memories flashed through his mind as he entered the bedroom. Shaking them away, he yanked back the curtain and saw there were multiple stains on the bedspread. He wondered how often she changed the sheets.

Holding his breath, he gingerly shook it out and peered under the mattress's edge then got down on all fours and swept his hands through the pile of clothes and dust under the bed. His fingers grazed something cold and metallic, and he reached out to grab it but it turned out to be a penny.

Lexi filled the doorway.

'I'm going to run the hoover around later. Leave me your number. I'll call you if I find it.'

'Yeah, cheers.'

She watched him with sad eyes as he scribbled it down on a notepad. He kept his head low, not daring to meet her eye as he left.

As he traipsed back to the pub, inspiration struck. He returned to his car and typed 'Hatton Garden' into the satnav. The area was famous for its jewellery shops, Daisy had told him so repeatedly when they were together.

He was still feeling a little rough, but the idea seemed like a good one. He drove through the narrow city streets, dodging cars and vans. A little while later, he pulled up outside a row of shops adorned with bright neon signs. He walked into the first jewellers he saw.

The display counter was filled with rings. Their gemstones glinted in the fluorescent light. He cleared his throat. 'I want to see your most beautiful wedding rings,' he said, a little breathless from his journey.

The shopkeeper's eyebrows shot up in surprise. 'Certainly, sir.'

He grabbed a set of keys from a cupboard behind him. Hayden licked his lips. If he got this right, Natalie would be blown away by his romantic gesture and would never realise his old ring was missing.

'What size is the bride?'

'I don't know – average?'

'I suggest you go for a medium. If it doesn't fit, we can resize it for you. Do you want them engraved?'

'No. I need them today.'

This drew a set of raised eyebrows.

'I see, in that case we have a more limited range of options. These are platinum, or would you prefer rose gold?'

He didn't know. He didn't have a clue.

'Which ones are most popular?'

The shopkeeper gestured toward a glass case that showcased rings of every size and cut. Hayden's eyes darted across the velvet lining, entranced by the shimmering diamonds. A bead of sweat formed on his forehead as he tried to work out what Natalie would like.

'When's the big day?' The shopkeeper asked.

Hayden cleared his throat and glanced at the floor, cheeks flushing pink. 'Tomorrow.'

He didn't know why he'd said that. He must have panicked. Now, everybody in the shop was looking at him. Everyone wanted to wish him well. He hoped to God no one recognised him. The last thing he needed was to read about his supposed wedding in the news.

'Natalie?' he called when he arrived home.

Good, she was still at work. He pulled the two new rings from his pocket and laid them on the bed. The stones sparkled and glimmered in the sunlight, and although the one he'd bought himself was slightly too small for his finger, he didn't care if it got him off the hook. He slipped them into his pocket and went downstairs to set the scene.

By the time Natalie came home from work, the scent of garlic and rosemary filled the air.

'Something smells amazing,' she said in awe.

'I've got lamb and potatoes in the oven,' he told her. 'Should be ready in fifteen minutes.'

'Lovely. That gives me time to get changed.'

She looked fine to him. More than fine, in fact. He loved the way her skin looked after a day in a warm kitchen. She headed upstairs and he turned his attention to the gravy.

By the time she came back down, he'd draped a red table-cloth over the dining table and placed a row of evenly spaced candles along the centre. The flickering flames cast an orange glow around the room, casting shadows on the walls like outstretched fingers. He uncorked a bottle of red wine and poured a glass for each of them before setting it back down on the table. They both took small sips, neither of them wanting to drink too much after the excesses of the previous evening.

'So, tell me about the launch,' he said with a smile. 'Was it a hit?'

Natalie nodded. 'There was a good turnout and everyone seemed to like the coffee. Now tell me more about what happened to you. Daisy's been blowing up my phone wanting details.'

He shrugged it off, embarrassed at his lie. Why couldn't he have said he had a migraine?

'It was nothing really. You know how they keep stopping me? Well, this time I was going a bit too fast.'

'A bit?'

'Okay, maybe a lot.'

She frowned. 'You need to be careful. You're not invincible, you know.'

'I know.'

He took a gulp of his wine. The fiery liquid coursed through his veins like an inferno. He pushed the glass away.

'Did you ever think our lives would be like this?' she asked, gazing at him from across the table.

'What do you mean?'

'It's not just the stuff, is it? It's like people expect different things from us. We can't be the same people we were before.'

He gazed back at her, finding her words rather profound.

Maybe this was why she had put off collecting the lottery winnings; maybe she'd had a sense of it, how all that money would change their lives. He leaned back in his chair, hands gripping the edge of the wooden table.

'Nat, there's something I want to—'

He was interrupted by the chime of the doorbell.

Natalie looked at him quizzically. 'You expecting anyone?'

He shook his head. 'I'll get it.'

He went to the door but there was no one out there. He blinked in confusion. They had a long driveway. Whoever had rung the bell must be there somewhere. He took a few steps forward.

'Who's there?'

He saw a flicker of movement in the trees. The sound of pounding feet, racing away. He clenched his jaw and spun abruptly towards the house. Something was draped across the doormat. His heart leapt into his throat as he saw what it was. He was looking at a pair of pink knickers with lacy trim.

THIRTY-SEVEN

HAYDEN

The air left his lungs; had Lexi been here? But that was impossible. She didn't know where he lived. Or did she? He realised now that he'd told her his real name and it wasn't exactly a common one. It wouldn't have taken much for her to google him and discover he'd won the lottery. It was entirely plausible some newspaper or web article had given away his location, after all, how many people lived in glass houses?

Fear choked him. No, this couldn't be happening.

He knelt down on the cold, hard ground and grimaced as his hand wrapped around the undies. He didn't want to touch them, but he could hardly leave them out in the open like this so he stuffed them into his pocket.

He glanced up at the security camera and frowned. Suddenly it didn't seem like such a great idea to have a camera up there. He pulled up the app on his phone and deleted the last twenty-four hours of footage. Just to be on the safe side, he left it switched off.

His phone vibrated in his other pocket. He pulled it out and saw a message from an unknown number. There was no text, just a series of numbers. What was that supposed to mean?

The phone beeped again.

Transfer fifty thousand pounds. I've sent you the details.

The phone beeped a third time. *Pay up or I'll tell your wife.*

The words made his stomach clench. He looked at the first text again. A muscle quivered in his jaw. That scheming little bitch. Okay, he probably should have mentioned he was married, but this was blackmail.

'Who was it?' Natalie asked when he returned to the table.

He ran a hand through his hair. 'Someone collecting for Alzheimer's,' he said. 'I told them to send me the details and we'll see what we can do.'

She beamed at him, her eyes full of admiration. 'I love that you're so passionate about your charity work.'

She rose from her seat and reached for his plate to take out to the kitchen.

'Let me take care of this,' he offered. 'You've had a long day.'

Her smile faltered as she rubbed her temples. 'I am shattered. Thanks.'

She picked up her phone and headed through to the living room.

Hayden let out a long breath. He understood Lexi was angry. He'd said nothing about being married. Perhaps she'd wanted more than a one-night stand. Perhaps she'd imagined she had a real chance with him. What was it they said: hell hath no fury like a woman scorned?

He pictured her sneaking up to the house and flinging her knickers on the doormat like a bomb. Good job he'd got there before they detonated. If Natalie had found them, it would have been hard to explain. But the price Lexi was asking was about more than money. It was her pride. She'd got carried away. Fifty thousand was a fair chunk of their winnings. It was hardly fair. He would come back to her with a counter-offer, he decided.

He could afford to splash out on a gift for her. Despite her generosity in the pub, her flat had been a dump so it ought to be easy enough to buy her off.

A Lexus for Lexi, that had a ring to it. Surely she'd be happy with a brand-new car? He crammed the plates into the dishwasher and texted her back, but there was no response. Fine. She probably needed to think about it. He disposed of her knickers at the bottom of the kitchen bin then joined Natalie on the sofa. He felt a pang of remorse as he watched her. She was breathtakingly beautiful despite the dark circles under her eyes. Her long, tan legs were stretched out on the coffee table, and her hands were behind her head in an almost casual display of elegance. How could he have risked everything for one night of reckless fun?

He took her hands in his own and looked into her eyes.

'I think it's time we upgraded. Don't you?'

He held out the velvet box, opening it slowly to reveal the new ring. Natalie gasped and ran her fingers over the intricately detailed gold.

'Oh Hayden, you shouldn't have!'

'But I did. Let's see it on you!'

He carefully removed her simple gold ring and replaced it with the new one. The band was delicate and sparkled in the light, a perfect fit on her slender finger. She studied it for a moment, her gaze fixed on the intricate diamond pattern inscribed around the edges. He slid his own matching band onto his finger and held them side by side. 'See, we match?'

He pulled her close, inhaling the smell of her hair and skin. He loved her so much that he could barely contain himself. His phone buzzed in his pocket. He fought the temptation to check it as Natalie moved away from him towards the fridge, where a bottle of champagne was waiting.

He held his breath as he looked down at the screen, desperately hoping for a response. Lexi's words made him instantly nauseous.

The price has just doubled. Transfer one hundred thousand pounds into my bank account or I'll tell your wife.

His stomach dropped and a wave of panic washed over him. He blinked hard, trying to compose himself as a new message popped up on the screen.

You have until midnight.

He stared straight ahead, hands gripping the armrests of the sofa as Natalie handed him a glass of champagne.

He forced a grin on his face. 'Cheers!'

They clinked glasses and he tried to relax as Natalie scrolled through Netflix for something to watch. She drank her champagne and settled on a series and cuddled up close to him. He felt her body relax in his arms. He held her until she fell asleep.

He glanced at the clock and the red LED numbers glared back. Nine p.m. Lexi's demand hung in his mind like a noose tightening around his neck.

He trudged into his office and slumped in the chair behind his massive desk. He slid his phone out of his pocket and dialled Phillip's number, tapping the eraser end of a pencil as he waited for an answer. Phillip was the ultimate nerd but he might just be able to help.

His voice cracked as he spoke. 'Hi, it's Hayden. I need your help. I need to know how to access the dark web.'

There was a long pause. 'If you need weed, I know a bloke.'

'No, I need something else. I don't want to talk about it over the phone.'

Phillip chuckled and Hayden wanted to reach through the line and strangle him.

'What do you need, a hitman?'

Hayden didn't answer right away, his mind racing through the possibilities.

'Are you doing anything right now?' he asked.

'I'm at work. Working the front desk.'

Hayden raised his eyebrows. 'Since when do you work on the front desk?'

'I got promoted. They've stuck me with the nightshift but I quite like it. It's quiet a lot of the time so I get to do my own thing.'

'Alright. I'm on my way.'

Hayden moved like a ghost through the living room, careful not to wake Natalie, who was still sound asleep on the sofa.

He ran his fingers along the coffee table until he felt the cold metal of his car keys. He gripped them tightly in his fist and took a deep breath before carefully opening the front door. He heard her stir as he opened it. He waited a moment, but she went right back to sleep. He scribbled her a note just in case she woke up. As soon as the door shut behind him, he raced towards his car, hoping Phillip would provide the solution he was looking for.

He started the car, drawing comfort from the hum of the engine. He was so deep in thought, he paid little attention to his surroundings until he saw the bright lights of Greenwich ahead, the dome of the O2 arena, sparkling like a crown against the starless night sky. He pulled into the hotel car park and grabbed his parking pass from the glove compartment, hoping it still worked. If it didn't, what were they going to do, fine him? He let out a bitter laugh that quickly dissipated in the night air.

He stepped across the threshold and felt a pang of nostalgia as his shoes squeaked against the glossy marble floor. It felt strange to see Phillip hunched behind the desk, typing away.

'Phillip?'

Each click of the keys seemed to carry through the empty room. Whatever Phillip was doing, Hayden was sure it wasn't work.

He grabbed Ivan's chair and dragged it over.

'So,' Phillip said seriously. 'What are we doing here?'

Hayden hesitated. 'I need to frighten someone,' he confided. 'I don't want to kill her or anything drastic. I just need her to back off.'

Phillip smirked. 'Is it Vivienne?'

'No. It's someone you don't know. She's blackmailing me and I'm on a deadline. I need someone fast. Like tonight.'

'That's a tall order.'

'I know.'

'You'll have to pay more for a rush job.'

'I know!'

'It's going to cost you.'

'I get it.'

He waited as Phillip took out his phone and logged onto a site he'd never seen before. He navigated through layers of security protocols.

'Is this the dark web?' Hayden asked, as he scoured through a message board.

'Shh!' Phillip glanced behind them, as if he expected the police to appear. He was even more of a nerd than Hayden had thought.

'It's really important it can't be traced back to me,' Hayden said.

'No kidding!'

Hayden felt himself shutting down as his anxiety took over – maybe he should just pay Lexi the money she had asked for. Then he wouldn't have to do anything illegal. But it was so much money. How could he possibly get that past Natalie?

'Right, got someone,' Phillip announced. 'This bloke is ex-army, built like a tank. He says he'll go to her home and have a word with her. Is that what you want?'

'Yes please!'

'Alright then. Hand me your credit card.'

He hesitated for just a moment before placing it in Phillip's waiting palm.

'Is he going to hurt her?'

'Do you want him to?'

'No, I just need her to back off.'

'Alright, text me her address.'

Hayden pulled out his phone and sent over the info.

'I don't actually know her last name,' he admitted. 'It's just Lexi.'

'That'll have to do.'

He waited for Phillip to send the information across. It only took a few minutes. A ding signalled the arrival of an email, and relief flooded through him.

'Congratulations, the deal is done.'

He wanted to celebrate, but a nagging fear lingered in the back of his mind.

'What if he doesn't do it?'

'Can't control that, I'm afraid. We'd leave him a negative review though.'

Hayden let out an explosive laugh that rang around the lobby. 'I wouldn't dare leave him a negative review. What if he comes looking for me?'

Phillip nodded in agreement as he put his phone back into his pocket. 'Anything else I can do for you?'

Hayden shook his head. A swell of emotion rose inside him and he fought to keep his composure. 'No, you've done more than enough. If ever you need something from me, don't hesitate to ask.'

Phillip's eyes shone with appreciation and he clenched his jaw tight. 'It's all good, mate, I got your back.'

Hayden stood clumsily and shuffled out the door.

He should have gone straight home. Instead, he drove through Lexi's neighbourhood, taking in the boarded-up windows of abandoned buildings and the faded graffiti that adorned the brick walls. His headlights illuminated the cracked and pitted pavement in front of him. The street was silent apart from the occasional sounds of teenagers yelling and laughing in the distance. He pulled into a space, shut off the engine. Then he sat, watching the building.

Fifteen minutes later, a battered car drove up. It was a rusty old vehicle with dents and scrapes along the fenders. He sat up straight. Was this the thug? The man who stepped out of the car was large and built like a boxer. His heavy boots were silent as he approached the building, his eyes hidden by shades. He crept inside and the door clicked softly as it shut behind him.

Hayden gnawed on a fingernail as he waited for the light to go on in Lexi's window. With a deep breath, he rolled down the window and listened for any signs of commotion. Would there be shouting? A scuffle? He had no clue how these things worked. All he knew was that Lexi shouldn't have tried to black-mail him. She had brought this on herself. As he waited, he noticed a light flicker on the top floor before fading back into darkness. He narrowed his eyes at the now dark building. If he didn't know better, he'd say the bloke he'd been watching had gone up to bed. So not the thug then?

He messaged Phillip.

Has he been yet?

A few minutes passed before Phillip replied.

The status has changed to: could not deliver. She must have been out. Do you want him to try again tomorrow?

Sourness crawled up his throat and his mouth flooded with a rancid liquid that tasted like metal and spoiled meat. He gagged, desperately trying to keep down the contents of his stomach.

No, he texted back. Tomorrow was too late – today had been his only chance.

Okay. He'll want to keep the payment though.

Hayden's jaw tensed. He got out of the car and walked towards the building. His steps quickened as he stomped up the stairwell to Lexi's flat. He raised a clenched fist, ready to bang on the turquoise door, when an elderly woman appeared behind him.

She stood in the shadows of the stairwell, her petite frame almost hidden by the yellowed walls. Her wire-rimmed glasses were perched on her nose as she squinted up at him. 'No one lives there,' she said, her voice heavy with concern. He ignored her and banged his fist against the door. 'It's been standing empty for months,' she insisted. 'The door doesn't even lock.'

He reached for the doorknob. She was right. It wasn't locked. He stepped inside and looked around, the realisation slowly dawning on him that he'd been duped. This wasn't even Lexi's flat – she'd probably been squatting in it. His memory flashed back to her choice of clothing: that university-branded jumper had been deceiving. She probably didn't even go to the university. All that psychology talk was just a ploy to get him to talk to her.

An icy breeze brushed across the nape of his neck. He looked around. Her clothes were cleared out of the wardrobe, her books and magazines from the living room shelves, even the kettle was gone from the kitchen – she had left no trace of herself behind.

He returned to the car and glared at the glowing digital

clock on its dashboard. Eleven forty-five – he was almost out of time. He banged his fist against the steering wheel in frustration, feeling the sting on his skin.

If Lexi turned up on his doorstep, he could tell Natalie he'd never met her before. He'd claim she was just some woman who had found his ring and wanted to extort money from him. But what if she didn't believe him? She'd ask her sister, and Liz could always see through him. If it came to it, he was screwed. There was no other option; he had to transfer Lexi the money. But how would he ever explain it to Natalie? He could hardly say he'd spent it on the horses.

He pulled out his phone, fingers trembling as he opened his banking app and tried to transfer the money. He realised his bank had set a lower limit, so he could only transfer fifty thousand at a time. He growled in frustration. What were the chances she would be satisfied with that? A warning message popped up, asking if he was sure. He clicked the 'yes' button and his vision blurred.

His request triggered a phone call from the bank, and he had to verify his information.

'Yes, that's all correct,' he said, even though the words stuck in his throat. He ended the call and exhaled heavily as the money left his account. His head fell back against the seat and he let out a primal scream that echoed off the dashboard and filled the air around him.

On the stroke of midnight, his phone pinged with a new message. He sucked in his breath. Maybe it had all been a test. Maybe she was returning the money, now he had learnt his lesson. He leaned forward hopefully.

Where's the rest?

Hating himself intensely, he messaged her to explain the delay. He lifted a hand to wipe away the sweat that had beaded on his forehead. What was she going to do? Would she wait patiently for the rest of the money? Or would she go ahead with her threat and tell Natalie?

Exhaustion coursed through his body as he longed for the comfort of his bed. Taking one last deep breath, he started the car. The leather upholstery creaked as he clenched and unclenched the wheel.

His head spun as he headed out onto the main road. He took a few deep, laboured breaths and then veered off to the side of the road. He threw open the door, barely scrambling out in time. His vision blurred as he stumbled into the nearby bushes and vomited until there was nothing left. Cold sweat soaked through his clothes as his muscles trembled uncontrollably.

When he turned to get back into the car, a police car pulled in behind him. Two officers stepped out, adjusting their hats as they walked towards him. They exchanged amused glances.

'Evening, sir. Have you had anything to drink this evening?'

'Only a glass of wine at dinner. I'm not drunk. I just wasn't feeling very well.'

Oh, the irony. The night before he had told Natalie he had been stopped by the police and now here he was. It was as if all his lies were coming true.

'Would you mind taking a breathalyser?'

'No problem.'

Sweat slicked his palms and he rubbed them on his jeans. Even though he knew he wasn't drunk he felt nervous, still reeling from the loss of his money. He wanted to tell them what had happened. Maybe they could help.

He brought the breathalyser up to his lips and exhaled into it. His breath came in ragged bursts and his hands shook badly. He clamped his eyes shut, still trying to quell the nausea in his stomach.

The police exchanged a few low words, eyes narrowed with

disdain. He clenched his jaw, willing himself to stay composed. They seemed disappointed when he passed. One of them checked his driving licence and registration plate. Finding nothing at fault, they finally let him go.

'You look like death warmed up. Go home and get some rest.'

He nodded and climbed back into his car where he sat behind the wheel for a moment, gathering his composure. The police were the least of his troubles. He didn't know how Lexi was going to respond to his slow method of payment. For all he knew, she was on her way to his house right now to tell Natalie.

He didn't think so though; if he were her, he'd wait it out. After all, there was a lot of money at stake. But even if Lexi kept quiet, how was he going to explain the money he'd squandered to Natalie? It wasn't like he could have spent so much money in a single night and he had nothing to show for it.

The answer came to him as he started the engine. He would tell Natalie he had transferred the funds into a new account specifically for charity work. He would say he was using it to distribute money to good causes. She was unlikely to object. She would think he was kind and generous when, in reality, he was simply paying for his horrendous mistake.

THIRTY-EIGHT

NATALIE

Robin's van was bigger than the one he'd had when Natalie was seventeen. Still, it felt weird to be back here, parked opposite the old phone box that now housed a defibrillator. She glanced at him sideways, trying to remember what it had felt like to be in love with him. All she saw now was a selfish man who should have been there for her but wasn't.

'It has to be her, doesn't it? I mean, how many Kiplings do you know? It's too strange to be a coincidence.'

'Why don't you just ask her?' Robin said.

'What if she says no? Then it's going to be really weird working with her. And what if she tells someone?'

He sighed. 'For what it's worth, I'm sorry I didn't support you back then. I was a selfish git, and I feel bad about it now.'

She nodded slowly, her brow furrowed with the years of hurt that lingered in her heart. 'You were,' she agreed.

The corner of her mouth twitched as she noticed the way he tucked his chin into his neck, just like he used to when they were together. She felt a flicker of something in her chest, a reminder of what it used to be like between them.

'I'm going to get proof,' she warned him. 'I need to know for sure.'

He bowed his head. 'Just be careful, Nat. If this gets out, we've both got a lot to lose.'

'Aren't you curious about her?'

'Of course I am, but it's much too late for me to be her dad. I don't deserve to be a part of her life. I made that decision a long time ago.'

And nor do you, the implication stung.

She headed into work and was surprised to see the queue that stretched out of the door and halfway down the road. She hurried inside and ducked behind the counter, working double-time to keep up with the orders.

'Tall latte!' Marian called out. 'Caramel macchiato!' Natalie nodded, swiftly heating the milk and swirling it into a heart-shaped pattern on top of the coffee.

Amy was cleaning down tables and carrying dirty crockery over to the sink. Natalie studied the young woman's face carefully. Were those Robin's eyes? she wondered. They had a certain sparkle to them. And she was a good listener. Amusing, but softly spoken. Did she get those traits from him? It was impossible to say.

As the morning rush dissipated, a peaceful silence descended on the coffee shop. She smiled at the young woman, who was absorbed in her phone. 'Amy, what kind of coffee do you want?'

Amy's blue eyes shifted up from her screen inquisitively. 'Frappuccino please.'

Natalie grabbed two ceramic mugs and made the drinks. With no customers waiting to be served, she invited Amy to take a seat at the counter.

'Doing anything nice for the weekend?' she asked.

'I'm working,' Amy said.

Natalie nodded. She knew that she had a second job at Sainsbury's.

'That sucks. Do you live locally?'

Amy gave a throaty laugh. 'As if! Have you seen the price of rents around here?'

'Fair point,' Natalie said, lips pressed together. 'So where did you grow up?'

'Not far from here.' Amy's face hardened slightly. 'I lived in a council house. Renting is different.'

'So do your mum and dad still live around here?'

'My parents are divorced,'

Natalie bit her tongue, feeling awkward and intrusive. She couldn't keep bombarding Amy with questions like this; the next one had to count.

She sipped her coffee, her brown eyes fixated on Amy. 'Kipling is such an unusual name. I don't think I've known any other Kiplings.'

'Haven't you?' Amy gave her a small smile. She leaned back in the chair and crossed one leg over the other. Her long skirt rustled as she moved.

'I don't think I've known any other Peels,' she said.

'Ah, well Peel is my married name,' Natalie replied with a small shrug. 'I still think of myself as a Butler.'

Amy seemed unruffled. Maybe it really was a coincidence. There was only one way she would know for sure. When Amy finished her coffee, Natalie plucked the cup off the table and stashed it in a clear plastic bag.

She asked Marian to watch the shop and headed quickly upstairs. Liz was right. The DNA test only took a few minutes to perform. As soon as it was done, she sealed the envelope and walked down to the post office. The DNA testing company had promised she should have the results back within two weeks. Anxiety coursed through her veins as she returned to work, dizzy with anticipation. She didn't know how she was supposed to wait that long.

THIRTY-NINE

NATALIE

Twenty-Two Years Earlier

'I've changed my mind,' she sobbed down the phone. 'I don't think I can do it.'

'Don't worry, Nat,' Robin told her. 'It's a natural process. That baby will be out of you in no time.'

'No, I'm not talking about the birth. I'm talking about afterwards.' She kept her voice low, not wanting to alert her elderly grandmother who was snoring softly in her armchair. 'I don't think I can hand her over.'

Robin was silent for a moment. He cleared his throat. 'You can't change your mind.' His voice echoed down the line, leaving no room for argument. 'You've already signed the papers. Everything's been finalised.'

The lump in her throat grew until it felt like a boulder. Her breath hitched in her chest. She hunched forward, clutching at her stomach.

'It'll be okay, Nat. Your dad's right. It's for the best. You just have to get through this. You've got your whole life ahead of you. You can go to university. You can do anything. You're much too young to be a mum.'

She crumpled to the floor, her body shaking with sobs. The walls of the room closed in around her, absorbing the sound of her pain. After holding her baby for those brief moments, she felt an unbearable sorrow because Heather was not hers to keep. She thought of those tiny pink lips, the wispy hair, and wrinkled forehead, memorising every detail as the tears streamed down her face. Her baby belonged to someone else now. An older, more deserving, better qualified mother

'Nat? Natalie, wake up. You're having a nightmare.'

Natalie blinked. Hayden was bending over her, a worried expression on his face.

Natalie rolled over. Her pillow was wet through. She heard him shift beside her.

'What were you dreaming about?' His tone was gentle but curious.

She shook her head. Hayden was still watching her, waiting for an answer.

'I don't remember.'

A thought flashed through Natalie's mind, like a salmon breaching the surface.

Esme.

Esme Kipling.

Was she remembering a name, or had her subconscious concocted it? Was that what they had named Heather, the people who had adopted her? She wished she could remember but she had been so numb at the time that it was difficult to differentiate between dreams and reality.

'Where are you going?' Hayden asked as she leapt out of bed.

'Can't sleep,' she murmured. 'I'm going to make coffee.'

His gaze burned her back as she shot out of the room. It was a rare day that she was up before him, but that didn't matter right now. She charged down the stairs and started the coffee machine. Then she reached for her laptop. Her fingers trembled as she typed *Esme Kipling* into the search bar.

There were five hits, but they all appeared to be about the same person. She clicked on an article that had appeared in the *Bristol Evening News*. Apparently, Esme Kipling was the head-teacher of a school in Bristol. There was a picture too. She appeared to be an older woman with grey hairs sprinkled through ebony locks. Her eyes were a crystalline blue, and her lips curved slightly upwards, creasing the corners of her mouth. She was way too old to be Heather, but could this be the woman who had adopted her?

Her hands shook with anticipation as she grabbed a pen from the drawer and jotted down the number for the school. She had almost pressed the dial button when it hit her that no one would be there over the weekend. With a heavy sigh, she leaned back into her chair. She would just have to wait until Monday to speak to Esme. It was a long shot, but if she didn't call her, she'd never know.

* * *

'Why is your sister throwing her party on a Sunday night?' Hayden asked the following day. 'I mean, why not have it on a Saturday? Most people have to work on a Monday morning.'

Natalie shrugged. 'I don't really understand why she's throwing one at all. The last time Liz had a party, she was thirteen years old and she made jelly with vodka. Liz didn't even like vodka. She just thought it would be funny to get everyone drunk.'

'Thanks for the warning. I'll know not to touch her jelly.'

Natalie frowned. 'You know what? I think it might be a good idea if I go early and lend a hand – you know, check out what she's planning to serve.'

Hayden nodded in agreement. 'I've got some charity work to do, then I'll come over later. What time did she say?'

'About eight.'

'Okay, so I'll see you around then.'

The moment Natalie stumbled into Liz's flat, she was hit by the smell of cat litter. Liz was still dressed in her pyjamas and the place was covered in cat hair. You would never know she was due to host a party in just over an hour.

Natalie put her hands on her hips. 'Okay, let's get to work. We need to herd all these cats outdoors and run the vacuum round – there's enough fur for an entire rug!'

'Magnus and Cookie are indoor cats,' Liz objected.

'Okay, how about you shut them in your bedroom for now and get the rest outside? You really can't have people over with the place looking like this.'

Liz shrugged like it didn't bother her and Natalie wished she'd thought to hire a cleaner. It was going to be tough to tackle all this in the time they had.

'How many people are coming?'

'Just a few,' Liz said. 'It's not a big deal.'

But it was a big deal to Natalie. Her antisocial sister was having a party. She needed it to go well.

While Liz hoovered, Natalie wiped down counters, polished surfaces and scrubbed the bathroom. She searched for the source of the lingering smell and found a half-empty can of cat food trapped behind the kitchen bin. She took it outside, then lit the vanilla candles she had given her sister for Christmas.

She sent Liz off to get ready, while she fluffed the cushions and draped string lights across the mantel, giving the room a warm, inviting glow.

Liz reappeared with her dark brown hair neatly brushed

and styled. She wore a dress Natalie had given her – a soft navy wool fabric that hugged her figure in all the right places, accentuating her curves far better than the loose, shapeless jumpers she usually favoured.

Hayden arrived with two bottles of champagne tucked under his arm. 'Looking good, Liz,' he said as he handed over the bottles. 'Here, get these straight in the fridge.'

Natalie stepped forward. 'The fridge is full of cat food.'

Hayden shot her a look before turning his attention back to Liz. 'Alright, we'll stick them in the bath with some cold water then.'

'Don't suppose you brought any glasses?' Natalie asked.

Hayden stared at Liz. 'What? Don't you have any?'

Liz sighed and ran a hand through her hair. 'I've got plenty of mugs.'

Hayden pulled a face but there were voices out in the corridor. Daisy and Ted brought another bottle of wine, then Gail and Andy arrived with fragrant roses. All the better for masking the smell of cat pee.

Natalie set to work pouring drinks for everyone. She was surprised that none of Liz's colleagues had shown up. She felt sorry for her sister and couldn't help but wonder why she didn't have more friends. Or a boyfriend. She looked so nice tonight. What a shame there was no one special there to appreciate it.

When she had finished serving everyone, Natalie looked around for Hayden. He sat in the corner, nursing his drink and keeping mostly to himself.

'You okay?' she asked.

'Yeah, I'm fine,' he said with a frown. He'd been quiet lately. She thought it might be the shock of winning all that money. She still had to shake herself some days too, but she'd had longer to take it in.

Daisy was in the middle of telling a long elaborate story. Daisy's stories were always incredible, outrageous even. With each sentence, Natalie became more and more sceptical, but the rest of the room was enthralled. Daisy had a way of spinning tales that drew people in and made them believe whatever she said.

Natalie noticed the snack bowl was empty and got up to refill it. As she walked towards the kitchen, she saw Liz and Andy huddled together. His face was lit up with a laugh while her eyes were locked on him as if he was the most fascinating creature on the planet. Natalie cleared her throat, causing them to break apart.

'Can I have a word, Liz? Outside?' She gestured to the door.

Liz's face shifted from surprise to annoyance.

'Can it wait, Nat? I was in the middle of a very interesting conversation.' Andy glanced away, like none of this concerned him.

Natalie forced a tight smile. 'It really can't wait.' She reached out a hand and grabbed Liz's arm and pulled her out into the hallway.

'What's this about?' Liz asked darkly.

'Stop it,' Natalie hissed. 'You'll break Gail's heart.'

'We were just talking, Nat.'

Natalie's eyes narrowed. 'You like him, don't you?'

Liz hesitated, her cheeks flushing pink. 'I'm not going to act on it. I'm not like you, Nat.' The words stung Natalie like a slap to the face.

'I'd never cheat on Hayden.'

'No, but Robin was married, wasn't he? That's why he never came to the house.'

Natalie swallowed. 'That was a long time ago. You should know better. Gail has been a good friend to you. Do you really want to risk that?'

Liz shook her head, her lips drawn in a thin line. 'I mean what I said. I'm not doing anything wrong. Andy and I just have so much in common. Why is it so scandalous for a man and woman to be friends?'

Natalie sighed and crossed her arms over her chest. 'It isn't, but I really think you need to back off a bit.'

'You need to keep your own house in order. Hayden's giving out really weird vibes tonight. I mean weirder than normal.'

'Hayden's fine.'

'You think?'

Guilt crept into her mind. It was true she'd been neglecting him lately, too caught up in her own drama.

They stepped back into the flat and Liz fiddled with the ancient stereo until a slow, dreamlike sound filled the air. As the music echoed through the room, one of the cats leapt onto the windowsill, its long, dark figure stretching against the light.

Andy was sitting with Gail now but the spark was gone from his eyes. Daisy perched on Ted's lap, her arms entwined around his neck like ivy.

Hayden handed Natalie a glass of wine.

'You okay?' she asked, gently placing a hand on his shoulder.

'I'm fine.'

An unsettling feeling lingered in the air between them. His eyes were hollow and distant, and she knew Liz had been right.

Liz shuffled off to her bedroom, closing the door behind her. Natalie wondered if she should go after her, but sometimes her sister needed to be alone. A few minutes later, she re-emerged wearing soft cotton pyjamas with polar bears printed on them and a fuzzy white pair of slippers that made her feet look like two little clouds.

'Looks like the party's over,' Hayden said.

'I suppose so.'

Gail hugged everyone goodbye, while Daisy rolled her eyes. 'It's only half past nine,' she said in exasperation. 'My dog stays up later than this. Who's coming to CeCe's?'

'It's Sunday,' Natalie reminded her. 'Everywhere will be closed. Besides, we've got work in the morning.'

'He hasn't,' Daisy said looking at Hayden. 'Why don't you come back to ours?'

Hayden sighed, his body slumped with exhaustion; Natalie could see the fatigue in his eyes.

'Thanks, but I'm knackered.'

Daisy's face contorted into a scowl, and her eyes twitched as Natalie saw the unmistakable signs of an impending Oliver-style meltdown. She tugged Hayden's arm. 'Let's go.'

They headed back to the car. Hayden put the radio on and they listened in silence.

'What's that?' Natalie asked, as they pulled into the drive-way. She peered through the glass into their living room. The soft light of the moon illuminated an ominous deep red puddle that crept across their pristine cream carpet.

Hayden threw open the car door and sprinted towards the house, his phone in his hand. He fumbled with the screen, unlocking the door. He held up a hand and whispered, 'Wait here,' as he stepped inside.

He disappeared indoors, his footsteps swallowed by silence. Natalie paced in circles on the porch, until she couldn't stand it any longer, then she followed him.

The living room looked shockingly normal. The carpet that had appeared to be stained with blood was now pristine.

'It must have been a trick of the light,' she said with relief.

'But how?' Hayden asked.

Natalie fiddled with the settings on her phone until the deep red shadow appeared again. Not only that, but there was the shadow of a large pumpkin on the wall and a ghost floated on the ceiling.

She burst out laughing. 'That had me going for a minute there. One of us must have changed it by accident. I guess this is the Hallowe'en setting.'

She looked at Hayden but he didn't laugh with her. In fact, he'd turned rather pale.

'You okay?' she asked.

'Yeah, I'm fine.' He managed a smile. 'I just thought... I mean it looked as though someone had spilled their guts in here, you know? It's the stuff of nightmares.'

FORTY

NATALIE

Natalie tapped the steering wheel, her eyes scanning the road for a break in the Monday morning traffic. She had been on the phone to Bristol Academy for ten minutes and was still yet to be connected.

'Hello?' a garbled voice finally answered.

'Yes, hi! I'm trying to reach Esme?'

The silence on the other end was punctured by the clatter of car engines and horns blaring in the background.

'I'm afraid Esme's in a meeting right now. She won't be out until twelve.'

Natalie's shoulders fell with resignation. 'Okay, I'll call back then.'

She drove the last couple of miles to the coffee shop and parked in her designated space. She spotted Marian through the big storefront windows, laughing and talking with customers as they enjoyed their cappuccinos and lattes. She pushed open the door and Amy's infectious laughter spilled out. Natalie smiled proudly. The way her team interacted with people was so warm and genuine you'd never know the coffee shop was brand new.

She gave them both a wave, then pushed through the

swinging door to the storeroom. She pictured Jan watching her as she checked the dates on the milk, and shuddered. She wouldn't be making that mistake again.

Her phone rang. She answered it, trying to keep her voice steady.

'Hello? This is Natalie?'

'Good morning. This is Trish at the Mulberry.'

For a moment, her mind went blank, then it came to her. Her father's care home.

'Your father's fine but he is asking to see you again. He really enjoyed your visit.'

'That's nice,' Natalie said, absently. 'Tell him I'll come in when I can. Probably later in the week.'

She wasn't sure how she felt about her father. It had been a shock to see quite how elderly he was now. It had never really occurred to her that he might need her.

She finished in the storeroom and went back out into the café.

'I've just told Amy she can go on her break,' Marian said.

Natalie glanced at the clock and nodded. She went to the coffee machines and began making the orders.

'One vegan cappuccino with soy milk,' Marian called out.

Natalie steamed the milk until it frothed up like snow. She poured it into a cup and added coffee before she passed it to Marian.

'Wait, what milk did you use?'

'The... soy,' she pointed to the carton.

'No, no, no. That's the non-fat. You need the other one.'

Natalie bit her lip. 'Thank you,' she murmured as she started again. She couldn't believe she'd made such a basic mistake. Thank goodness she had Marian to catch these things.

'Looks like business is booming,' said Gail, appearing at the counter.

Natalie nodded and began making up Gail's order.

'Liz's party was fun.'

'Yeah,' Natalie agreed. 'I'm not sure she'll be having another one though. I think she just wanted to prove she could.'

'It was a little odd,' Gail conceded. 'I've never drunk champagne from a plastic beaker before and when I went to get our coats from the bedroom, there was a pile of cats sitting on them.'

'That sounds about right.'

'Andy was saying we should host next time. We haven't had a party since Scarlett was born.'

'That would be nice,' Natalie agreed, but she couldn't help but wonder at Andy's motivation. He was no more the party type than Liz was. Was he holding one purely as an excuse to spend time with Liz? Personally, Natalie couldn't understand why one woman would be interested in him, let alone two.

At twelve o'clock, Natalie went upstairs to call Esme. It wasn't the best timing. She'd left Amy refilling the napkin tray before heading off for her shift at Sainsbury's – leaving Marian to cope with the lunchtime rush by herself. She felt bad but it couldn't be helped. Natalie needed to speak to Esme Kipling. Her stomach squirmed with anticipation – what would Esme have to say?

She held her breath as the ringing echoed in her ear. It took a few minutes for the person on the other end to locate Esme, and Natalie was so nervous she accidentally bit her tongue. She was wiping the blood from her mouth when Esme came on the line. Her voice was crisp and clear.

'Good afternoon, Esme Kipling speaking.'

'I... Hello. My name is Natalie Butler.'

She deliberately used her maiden name. It didn't matter that she was married now. That wasn't part of the conversation.

She swallowed hard. What on earth was she supposed to say?

'Hello? Are you still there?'

'Yes, sorry. It's a... it's a personal matter, actually. Something quite sensitive.'

'Okay, I'm listening.'

'I... I'm calling because I'm looking for someone and she has the same last name as you. Twenty-two years ago, I gave a baby girl up for adoption and now I'm trying to find out what happened to her.'

The only response was a hollow silence.

'H-hello? Can you hear me?' Natalie said.

She listened intently. There was a faint buzzing in her ear, followed by a small click as the call was disconnected.

FORTY-ONE

NATALIE

For a moment, Natalie was too shocked to react. Esme had hung up on her! She stared at her phone. Should she try again? Perhaps it was too much for her, Natalie ringing out of the blue like this. But she was so close. She had to speak to her. She had to find out about her daughter.

Before she could overthink it, she dialled again, expecting to be fobbed off by a receptionist. She did not expect Esme herself to answer.

'I'm so glad you called back! I'm so sorry about that. I'm afraid I dropped the phone. You did give me a bit of a shock.'

Natalie settled back in her chair. 'I'm sorry for startling you. I just really wanted to speak to you.'

Esme grew silent again for a moment. 'You said your name was Natalie?'

'Natalie Butler, yes.'

'I don't quite know what to say.'

'Did you... do you know what happened to my daughter?' There was a long pause. 'I'm... I'm sorry for calling out of the blue like this.'

'That's okay. I always knew you'd call one day. I hope life has been kind?'

She hadn't heard about the lottery win then. That was good. People acted weird when they knew. Natalie didn't want to deal with that right now.

'I've been fine,' she said. 'Giving up my baby was the right decision for me, even if it was a hard one. I wasn't planning to contact you but...'

'Curiosity got the better of you?'

'Something like that.' Tears pricked her eyes. 'I wanted to ask you how she is and what she's doing now?'

Esme let out a pained sigh. 'I have to be honest with you, Natalie. I don't know. Heather was never the easiest of children. She took against my husband from a young age. She would scream and throw herself across the floor in fits of jealous rage whenever I gave him any of my attention. We split when she was eight but even after the marriage ended, she punished those who got too close to me – leaving malicious notes for them or keying their cars.' Esme's voice shook. 'She was determined that I was hers and no one else would have me.'

Natalie studied her fingers and wondered where all this was leading.

'I met someone a few years ago, a wonderful man called Kyle. We took it slowly, but it was serious between us from the beginning. By then, Heather had grown into an independent young woman and I thought she would accept him. Things seemed to be going smoothly, so I invited him to move in and then... well, let's just say they didn't get along. One day, I came home from work to find Heather had moved out. I thought she'd be back once she'd calmed down but there was nothing but the note she left. I haven't heard from her in over a year now. I'm so sorry. I wish I had better news.'

Natalie sniffed. 'Have you... have you reported her missing?'

'Yes, the police did some preliminary investigating but she's an adult and it looks clear she doesn't want to be found. So, I'm afraid I can't tell you where she is, Natalie. But if you find her, I'd be incredibly grateful if you'd call me, just to let me know she's safe.'

'Yes. Yes, of course.'

Natalie left Esme her mobile number and said goodbye. Then she slid her phone into the pocket of her apron. When she returned to work, Marian was dealing with an ever-growing queue.

'It's been murder down here,' she grumbled.

'I'm so sorry,' Natalie muttered. 'It was an important call. Let's get this queue down a bit, then you can take a long lunch.'

It took a while for the queue to whittle down and by the time the shop was quiet again, both Marian and Natalie were exhausted.

'You look like you need a break yourself,' Marian said as she slung her coat over her arm.

Natalie laughed wearily, rubbing her forehead 'I'm fine. It's just been one of those days.'

Towards the end of the shift, Liz dropped in, carrying a sleek red briefcase.

'What's with the bag?' Natalie asked, as she prepared her sister's coffee.

'It was a gift from my boss,' Liz said. 'You wouldn't believe how much paperwork I get now I'm in charge of the baby room. It's ridiculous.' She let out a weary sigh.

Natalie frowned. 'I hope they're paying you overtime if you're taking work home with you.'

Liz shook her head. 'I wish!' She looked around the room.

'Hey, which one is Amy?' she asked in a hushed voice.

'She's not here right now.'

'Oh.' Liz looked disappointed, and Natalie had the sense that she'd only come in to get a peek.

'I've sent off for a DNA test,' she confided. 'Amy doesn't

know anything about it, and if I'm wrong, she doesn't need to know.'

'How are you going to explain it if it is her?' Liz asked. 'I mean, it's a staggering invasion of her privacy, don't you think?'

Natalie tuned out her sister's criticism.

'Hey, it was your idea, remember? I've also tracked down Heather's adopted mother,' she said, looking directly at Liz.

'You have?'

She took satisfaction from her sister's shocked expression.

'Yeah, she seems nice but she said she hasn't seen Heather in a while. Sounds like they don't get along.'

Liz tapped her index finger against the side of her mug. 'Why don't you ask her to send you a picture? That way you don't have to wait for the DNA test?'

Natalie's mouth fell open. 'Why didn't I think of that?'

Liz swallowed down the last of her coffee and placed the mug back on the counter. 'That's what I'm here for. Listen, I've got to get back to work but keep me updated. If Amy turns out to be Heather, I want to be the first to meet her.'

'You will be,' Natalie promised.

She glanced at the queue, which had grown again.

'Better get back to it,' she murmured as she slipped back behind the counter.

Twelve cappuccinos, a flat white and an espresso later, the door of the café burst open. Natalie glanced up from the coffee machine to find two policemen in her shop. She waved them to the front of the queue, but it wasn't her coffees they were interested in.

'Marian Goodwin?' The policeman's gruff voice echoed through the café.

Marian let out a shuddering breath, her gaze darting towards Natalie in terror before returning to the police.

'I'm Marian. What is it?'

'Mrs Goodwin, we have something very difficult to tell you. Please can you step outside with us?'

'You can go up to the flat if you need somewhere quiet,' Natalie offered.

The officers escorted her towards the stairs, and before she disappeared from view, Marian looked back at Natalie with an expression that was equal parts sadness and fear. The heavy clomping of their shoes echoed in Natalie's head, amplifying each beat of her heart against her ribcage.

FORTY-TWO

HAYDEN

Natalie kissed Hayden goodbye and grabbed her keys. She was heading to the coffee shop again. It seemed to him she was always there these days. She worked longer hours than she ever had at the Riverside Café. He wanted to be happy for her. Running her own coffee shop had always been her dream, but at the same time, he missed her. He'd thought winning the lottery would mean they had more time together but in reality, he barely saw her.

'Why don't you go and help her with the café?' his mum asked, when he rang.

'I used to work with Daisy,' he reminded her. 'And look how that turned out.'

His mum laughed. 'She was a little firebrand, wasn't she? But your Natalie's not like that. She wouldn't boss you around.'

'No,' he conceded. 'I just feel like I want to find my own thing.'

He headed into his office and went automatically to the safe to check his stash of money. He leafed through the wads of notes then locked it all away again and settled in his chair, admiring the view.

The walls were comprised of panoramic windows that seemed to invite the outside world in. The view was amazing, there was no disputing that, but he felt exposed, convinced that barge passengers could see every move he made.

He spun in circles in his computer chair, wheels squeaking on the floor. A million pounds was now gone from his account. He checked the time – he'd have to transfer the next chunk of money to Lexi before midnight. Every time he sent her money, she came back with a new demand. He was beginning to think it was never going to end. He'd scoured the internet but he couldn't figure out a way of tracing the money he'd sent. The bank transfers were too slow, so they'd switched to crypto, on Phillip's advice. But once it went into Lexi's crypto wallet, that was it. Gone. He sighed in frustration.

Another ten thousand pounds had been spent on the hired thug. Yet, according to his statement, it had gone straight into Phillip's bank account. He could see Phillip's name clearly in the transaction. That didn't make sense. He hadn't questioned it at the time, but why hadn't it gone directly to the thug? He could have used his own crypto wallet. Phillip knew that. His stomach lurched as he realised he'd been taken in. There probably never was a thug. Phillip had seen a chance to make money out of him and he'd taken it.

Betrayal seared through him like a hot iron. Tears pricked his eyes and his throat felt tight as he stumbled out of the room. He was so angry he could have smashed a hole in the wall, but instead he dug his keys out of his pocket and stalked outside.

He slid into the driver's seat of his red Ferrari. The roar of the engine vibrated through him like electric shock therapy. He flipped the switch for the roof to go down then cranked up the radio until the music rattled his bones. The warm wind whipped past him, like a balm on his raw emotions. He drove recklessly, heading for anywhere that wasn't here, until eventually he found himself back at the Canary Grand.

Ivan was manning the front desk by himself. He gave him a wave but there was no sign of Phillip. He should have listened to Vivienne. She had warned him Phillip was a cockroach. It made perfect sense he had taken a job working nights. He pictured his thin, spindly frame cocooned in bed sheets, with the stolen money tucked under his pillow.

Hayden walked through to the lounge where he ordered a shot of whisky, and found a chair by the window. He watched the river pass by in a steady current, its surface sparkling in the afternoon light. It was a bit sad, this need of his to return to his former work place. He'd felt untethered since he'd given it up. He was discovering that he didn't like his own company as much as he thought he did. In fact, he didn't really like himself at all.

He nursed his whisky, knowing he could only have the one since he was driving. No doubt the police would be hot on his tail on the way home.

His phone buzzed. Another message from Lexi.

Where is the rest of my money?

Her money? She had a cheek. He'd been paying her off as fast as his bank allowed. He gripped his tumbler tightly, tension radiating throughout his body. She was never going to leave him alone, was she? She wouldn't be happy until she'd taken it all. She said she wanted two million, but he didn't believe she was going to stop there, so what was he supposed to do?

He considered going to the police. Maybe they didn't have to tell Natalie. Then he thought about the officers who had breathalysed him. Remembered how they'd snickered at him. No, the only alternative was to deal with Lexi himself. He wouldn't try to hire someone to threaten her this time. The only problem was he didn't have a clue where to find her.

He thought back, trying to remember everything she'd told

him. She'd said she was a Greenwich student but he had no reason to believe that now. Her flat was fake, so she might not have anything to do with the university. She could have picked up that hoodie at a charity shop. In fact, she had looked a bit like a vagrant, now he thought about it: underfed, ill-fitting clothes. At a guess, she was either destitute or on drugs. Maybe both. She been drinking whisky with him all night. At the time, he'd thought that was cool. Now it seemed like a glaring red flag.

She had clocked him, the minute she'd walked into the pub. Had she recognised him from the papers or had someone tipped her off that he was there? Potentially, one of the bar staff could have recognised him and rung her to come and try her luck. Maybe she had given them a cut.

Perhaps she had been following him around for a while. His Ferrari was like a cherry-red beacon. She'd told him she didn't drive, but what if she'd lied about that too? She could have left her car in the pub car park like he'd done and come back for it the following day. With a jolt, he recalled seeing a tatty white Fiesta when he collected his car from the pub. All the staff would have gone home by then. Chances were, that was Lexi's car. If only he'd taken down the licence plate.

Think, Hayden. How could he find her? He recalled his search of the flat. She'd had a microwave meal on the table. He'd seen a Tesco carrier bag. An empty bottle of vodka. What about the coffee she'd made him? Something had been written on the mug. What was it? He shook his head, unable to remember.

He finished his drink and walked back through the lobby. As he stepped outside Vivienne waved a pack of cigarettes under his nose. Feeling like a toad, he accepted one and lit it. Smoke drifted from between his lips like a butterfly, twisting and turning silently as it disappeared into the sky. They chatted for a few minutes before she flicked her cigarette butt away and turned to go back inside.

As he stood there, deep in thought, he became aware of a

movement above him, something heavy in the air. He jerked his gaze skywards and saw a person plummeting towards him, arms outstretched, eyes wide with terror. Before he had time to react, someone grabbed his arm and yanked him out of the way. The body hit the ground in front of him with a sickening crack and split open like an overripe melon, spilling crimson blood and glistening entrails.

FORTY-THREE

HAYDEN

His vision blurred then came back into focus, zooming in on the lifeless body splayed out in front of him. The skull had cracked open like a soft eggshell, brains spilling out onto the pavement. The eyes were wide open yet unseeing, as if he was staring deep into his soul. Hayden's hand flew to his mouth. He knew this man. He was Gail Goodwin's dad, Damon.

Everything was happening in slow motion. It felt like he had wool in his ears, his legs were heavy, his heart too fast. He had a perverse desire to look at the body again, but he couldn't make himself do it.

'Are you alright?'

He turned and saw Vivienne. Her eyes were wide with concern, as if she expected him to keel over. He realised it was her who had dragged him out of the way. She'd saved his life, but he couldn't find the words to thank her.

All around him, people were looking up at the rooftop terrace, as if expecting more bodies. Hayden looked that way too, raising a hand to shield his eyes from the sun. He could make out the silhouettes of people clustered around the railing and an icy chill ran down his spine. Had Damon fallen from up there? Or had he jumped?

He heard a woman on the phone with emergency services, but even she didn't venture any closer.

Vivienne put a hand on his arm. 'You're as white as a sheet. Why don't you come back inside? Get something to drink.'

He shook his head. 'I c-can't.'

She looked even more worried. 'Do you want me to call someone?'

He thought of Natalie, there was nothing he'd like more than to feel her loving arms around him, but it would take time for her to get there.

'D-Daisy,' he said, handing her his phone. 'She works just over there.'

He zoned out while Vivienne made the call. He heard the sound again, the sickening crack of the body hitting the ground, as if someone had thrown down a sack of heavy clay pans. He looked around, startled, but no one else seemed to hear it.

'She's coming now,' Vivienne told him. He looked up and saw Daisy across the water.

'Thanks.'

He took his phone back and walked slowly towards Daisy, taking care not to look at the body. He reached the bridge and started across it. Then a helicopter flew over, pushing air down towards the ground as its blades beat like thunder. Everything around him trembled in its wake, and his legs went weak. He gritted his teeth and clung to the railings, consumed with a deep sense of helplessness as he stared down into the murky water below. Was this how Damon had felt? So vulnerable and alone? He wanted to move forward but his feet felt like they had been encased in cement. Out of the corner of his eye he saw Daisy walking towards him from the other side. As she drew nearer, she reached out her hand.

'It's alright,' she murmured, pulling him into her arms. 'I'm here now.'

Together they shuffled, edging towards the end of the bridge. He felt relieved as he reached the other side. His heart rate dropped and he felt his breathing returning to normal.

'It must have been a terrible shock,' Daisy said. 'Did you see the bo—'

He waved his hand in front of her. 'No, please. I really don't want to think about it. I feel sick.'

'Okay,' she agreed. That must have been an effort for her, because Daisy loved a story, but he wasn't ready to share this one just yet. He wasn't sure he'd ever be ready.

She kept hold of his arm as they walked towards her place of work. The four white columns of the Regent Hotel towered over the bustling street below. Ornately carved balconies hung from every floor, and large windows winked in the sun. It was only half the size of the Canary Grand, but almost a century older and infinitely more stylish. He felt an unexpected jolt of recollection. The Regent Hotel, that was it. That was what it had said on Lexi's mug.

Daisy guided him into her office, its walls lined with prestigious awards. She gestured for him to take a seat and pushed a box of tissues towards him.

'Sit with your head between your knees,' she said, her voice soothing. 'I'll get you a whisky.'

He shook his head, fighting the wave of nausea that threatened to overtake him.

'Okay, well then you sit quietly for a bit while I finish what I was doing. There's a bottle of water on the table.'

He took slow, measured breaths, trying to ground himself in the office's warmth. The desk clock ticked softly in the background as Daisy clacked away at her keyboard. His vision cleared as he concentrated on the sound of her typing.

'Daisy, I need you to do something for me.'

She looked up.

'Your wish is my command.'

'I need you to look up a guest for me.'

'Who?'

'There's this woman. She's been blackmailing me.'

She stopped dead and looked at him.

'Exactly how much mess have you got yourself into?'

He hesitated. He didn't want to give her the full details.

'I need to know if she's been staying here,' he said, sidestepping the question. 'Her name is Lexi.'

'Does she have a second name?'

'I'm afraid I don't know it.'

'Well okay, I'll run it through, but don't get your hopes up. You know I'm not supposed to do this?'

'Oh, I know. I really appreciate it.'

She typed in a query and the computer immediately froze.

'It does that.' She clicked something and started the process all over again. It seemed to take forever.

'No hits,' she announced when it had finished. 'You sure you don't know a last name?'

Hayden thought hard, but nothing came to mind.

'What's Lexi short for?'

'I don't know. Alex? Alexa? Alexandra?'

Daisy typed all of those in and they waited.

'The computer's very pedantic,' she explained. 'You have to get the spelling exactly right.'

'What a pain.'

'Tell me about it. We're supposed to be upgrading to a new system but it's really expensive and the management keep getting cold feet.'

'Right, well, thanks anyway.'

'Alexis,' Daisy suggested. He stared down at his feet while she typed the name in. Tried not to think about the body.

'Here we go – room 407! An Alexis Briggs has been staying there all week.'

Hayden nodded slowly. 'Might be her. Is there any more information? Is she a young woman, in her twenties?'

'If the date of birth she's given is correct, then yes. It's still a long shot.'

'Only one way to find out.'

They walked down the hall to the lift and got in. Daisy was calm and collected – a stark contrast to his own tense body. He had no plan of action if the guest in room 407 really turned out to be Lexi.

Daisy knew the corridors like the back of her hand. Her short legs marched briskly, leaving Hayden struggling to keep up. Moments later, they stood outside room 407.

'Stand to one side,' she said. 'That way she'll only see me. We don't want to frighten her off.'

He nodded, fists clenched ready.

'Housekeeping!' Daisy called, knocking loudly.

There was no reply.

She pulled a master key from her pocket. 'Right then, we're going in.'

He followed Daisy into the empty room. There was little to indicate anyone was staying there apart from a pair of shoes sticking out from under the bed. They were nothing like the scruffy trainers Lexi had been wearing the night he'd met her. These were fancy red heels, more the kind of thing Natalie would wear.

'Search for clues,' Daisy said. She wasted no time rifling through the drawers. Hayden found a wallet. He pulled it out and searched its contents. There were no credit cards, just a wad of notes. He had a mind to take it but it didn't feel right. What if this wasn't Lexi's room after all? What if it belonged to some innocent woman with a similar name?

He noticed something on top of the wardrobe. He reached

up and pulled it down. It was a copy of his slide deck from the presentation he had given in Manchester.

'How could she possibly have this?' he asked as he flipped through it. 'I hadn't even met her then. It doesn't make sense.'

Memories of Manchester came flooding back. He remembered the unforgiving hardwood chairs and how his back had ached from the long hours spent sitting in them.

He and Daisy had waved to each other across the room, but she had stayed with her group and he had stayed with his. It wasn't until he popped back to his room during the lunch break that she had come knocking on his door.

'My minibar is empty,' she'd told him, walking straight in. 'So, I thought I'd raid yours.'

She'd breezed past him and opened the door of his minibar, revealing a handful of bottles and cans. She'd grabbed a bottle of gin and a small can of tonic water.

'Thanks,' she'd said, taking a sip from the gin and then a little from the tonic.

'Would you like a glass?' he'd asked, amused.

'No, I'm fine.'

She'd flopped onto the bed, wriggling out of her shoes with a sigh of relief. 'My feet are killing me,' she'd groaned, toes curling into the navy sheets.

'Why don't you wear flats?' he'd asked.

Daisy had fixed him with a hard stare. 'I'm already the shortest person at the conference, and probably the youngest too. Wearing heels helps me fit in.'

'I think you're doing just fine,' he'd said, and he'd meant it. Daisy had been promoted twice in the short time since she'd left the Canary Grand. He had an uncomfortable feeling he had been holding her back.

'I bet you'll be running the Regent one day.'

Daisy had grinned in response. 'That's the plan. Of course, ideally, I'd like to own it too.'

Hayden had selected a miniature bottle of Jack Daniel's from the mini bar and poured it into a tumbler.

'What time is the next presentation?'

'Two, but I'm skipping it. It's going to be this rambling jobsworth from my accounts team. He talks in a droning monotone that's guaranteed to put everyone to sleep.'

'I suppose I'll skip it too then,' he'd said, taking a slow sip of whisky. Maybe it was wrong, but it had felt like an illicit thrill. 'This is fun. I feel like we're skiving school.'

Daisy had smiled, her eyes crinkling at the corners as she nodded in agreement. 'It's been too long since we spent time together, just the two of us.'

He'd taken another sip. 'So, tell me about your life, Daisy.'

She'd let out a contented sigh. 'I'm so happy with Ted. I can't wait for our wedding.'

'I'm glad.'

'I'm glad we've stayed friends. I've always wished we'd had a chance to say goodbye properly though. One last night together. That would have been nice, wouldn't it?'

She'd gazed up at him with a mixture of sadness and longing in her eyes.

He'd swirled the whisky around in his glass and brought it to his lips.

'I'm not sure we should go there. It would just make things more complicated than they need to be.'

Daisy had swallowed hard and looked away. 'Sometimes complicated can be good,' she murmured, almost too low for him to hear.

She reached up with both hands and pulled at the elastic band which held her long, red hair in a tight bun. She shook it out, curls cascading down her shoulders. Her hair had always been his favourite feature. All those wild curls matched her untamed spirit.

'You know, it took a bit of convincing, but Ted and I have come to a special agreement.'

He'd raised his eyebrow inquisitively.

'We've agreed to one fling each year,' she'd explained. 'But there are rules: no talking about it and no sharing details with our friends. Just one night of freedom that we don't have to answer for. That's the secret to keeping a marriage alive, don't you think?'

Her eyes had drilled into his, waiting for a reaction.

'I think you're playing with fire,' he'd said, but when she'd reached out for his zipper, he hadn't complained.

He snapped back to the present. 'This isn't Lexi's room, is it?'

Daisy remained silent, refusing to meet his eyes. She had opened a couple of buttons on her blouse, he realised. He could see the frilly edge of her bra.

'You know what I think? I think this is your room – or at least one you escape to when you want to have a little fun. Dammit, Daisy, how much fun are you having, exactly? Scratch that, it doesn't matter. I don't have time for this.' His voice grew louder as desperation crept through his veins. 'I told you, I'm being blackmailed!'

'Let me help you,' she pleaded, reaching out her hand, but he had had enough. He marched out of the room before she could stop him, even more determined to find Lexi and prevent her from ruining his life.

His heart felt like a lead weight as he stomped into the lift. He jabbed the button for the ground floor and watched as the doors closed on him. He raised a hand to steady himself and squeezed his eyes shut, half expecting the floor to disappear beneath him.

The lift pinged and he rushed out of the building, relieved to feel the cool air on his cheeks. He drew a deep breath and retraced his steps across the bridge. The emergency services were still buzzing around the Canary Grand and he fought the urge to vomit.

His hands trembled as he reached his car and he crawled inside, sinking into the driver's seat. He started the engine and stared blindly at the dashboard, his mind whirring. Tonight he would have to transfer another quarter of a million to Lexi and he had no idea when this torture was going to end.

FORTY-FOUR

NATALIE

Natalie tried to concentrate on her customers, but she couldn't shut out the strangled sobs coming from the flat above. Marian had been up there a long time. What had the police told her? It must have been something truly terrible to take this long. She tried to stay calm, but it was agony not knowing. Had something happened to Gail?

She bustled behind the counter, making drinks and toasted sandwiches. Her apron was damp with sweat and her shoulder muscles burned from lifting heavy trays.

Marian finally emerged some twenty minutes later.

'She's had a shock,' the police told her. 'She'll need to go home.'

Natalie nodded. 'Of course.' She looked at Marian, whose eyes were blood red, her face deathly pale.

'Oh, Marian! What is it?'

Marian shook her head in bewilderment. 'It's Damon. He fell from a balcony. He's gone.'

Natalie felt like the wind had been knocked out of her. Her arms and legs went limp as she tried to take in the news. Marian and Gail must be devastated. A million questions raced through her mind but now wasn't the time. Swallowing hard, she blinked away the tears that pricked the back of her eyes and gritted her teeth.

As soon as Marian left, she flipped the sign on the door from 'open' to 'closed', then she drifted around, picking up stray napkins and putting chairs back in their proper places until the last of her customers left.

Her phone buzzed. She was surprised to see a text from Andy. His message brought tears to her eyes:

Have you heard about Damon? Gail is broken hearted. Can you come over?

She sucked in a breath. Calling in on Gail was the last thing she felt like but her friend needed her. She texted him back, promising to drop in on her way home.

She cleaned the coffee machine and swept the floor, then she went upstairs to collect her bag and coat from the flat. She was about to come back down when she heard a noise.

'Is someone there?' she called out. 'I'm sorry but we're closing early.'

She took three steps down the stairs before she spotted Mason at the counter. His lips were set in a thin line and his eyes glinted as he gave her a slow nod.

'This is no way to run a business, Natalie.'

His voice was sharp and authoritative, and he took a step closer towards her with each word. Her heart pounded in her chest as she looked around for an escape route.

'How did you get in?'

'The door wasn't locked properly. You should be more careful.'

'What do you want?'

'I came down to see how you were doing. Why are you so pale?'

'I've just received some bad news, if you must know. Now if you don't mind, I need to get going.'

Her hand instinctively went to her pocket for her phone, but it wasn't there. Panic bubbled up inside her as she scanned the counter and saw it sitting on a pile of receipts.

'I see you fixed the sign.' His fingers nervously picked at the threads of his faded T-shirt.

Her eyes widened with a sudden realisation. 'That was you, wasn't it?'

'I've no idea what you're talking about.' He wasn't a good liar.

'And the flowers?'

His cheeks flushed. 'Did you like the colours? I chose them especially for you.'

'What about the note?'

She couldn't picture him writing poetry. He didn't have the imagination.

'That was Mum. She's still pretty bitter.'

Natalie stared at him. 'What? I've never even met your mum!'

He kept looking at her, his intense gaze forcing her to take in his springy hair and the sharp cleft of his chin. Oh God! Why had she never seen it before?

'You're Jan's son, aren't you?'

'She didn't think we should tell people. She didn't want to show any favouritism at work.'

'Favouritism? I thought she hated you! But why the hell did you walk out on her?'

'Because of what you said. She never gave me a pay rise, and she was always having a go at me.'

'But she's your mum!'

He shrugged. 'I actually came down here to tell you I got a new job, at the Cod and Tackle.'

'Well, good for you but why did you wreck my sign?'

'Because it wasn't fair, you getting all that money. People like you always land on their feet, while people like me suffer. The least you could have done was given me a job.'

'It sounds like you've done alright for yourself.'

'Look, I'm sorry about the sign. Mum thought it would be funny, messing with the spelling. We didn't mean to damage it. That was an accident.'

She took a deep breath and spoke with measured calmness.

'Right, well, thank you for your honesty, now if you don't mind, I'm going to lock up.'

He seemed to shrink before her gaze and she couldn't decide if he was really a creep or just a sad little man.

'I can walk you to the station if you want?'

'No thanks. I've got my car.'

'Maybe you could drop me off then?'

'I don't think so.'

She stood with her arms crossed, and waited for him to back down. To her relief, he turned and walked towards the door. As soon as he left, she locked it behind him. She would wait a few more minutes, just to be on the safe side.

She should have known it was Jan messing with her. She'd seen it in her face at the launch. She'd been too cheerful, too friendly. Of course Jan wasn't happy for her. It was a relief, though, to discover who had been behind it. Most of all, she was glad it wasn't Heather.

When she was absolutely certain that Mason was gone, she walked out to her car and climbed in, locking the door behind her. She wished she could head straight home and take a long bath but she still needed to call in at Gail's. The prospect filled her with dread. She had never been much good in these situations, and Damon's death was so sudden, so unexpected. She hadn't had time to process it herself yet.

. . .

Gail's terrace house was in Natalie's old neighbourhood, sandwiched between a crumbling council building and some fancy new executive flats. She rang the bell and Andy let her in without a word. She followed him through to the living room. The TV was on, blaring a noisy children's programme, and a selection of mugs of lukewarm tea stood on the table, ranging from full to empty.

Gail's eyes were red and puffy, her cheeks streaked with tears of disbelief. 'Oh Natalie, I can't believe it!'

Natalie shook her head. 'I can't believe it either.'

Natalie stepped forward and hugged both Gail and Scarlett who was in her arms. They might have stayed like that if Scarlett hadn't started to squirm. Natalie drew back but then she didn't know what to do with herself, whether to sit or stand. Her hands hung awkwardly at her sides.

'Do you want some tea?' Gail asked.

'Not for me,' Natalie replied.

'I'm making it anyway. I need to keep busy.'

'Well, okay then.'

She handed Scarlett to Natalie. Natalie fought the wave of panic she always felt when someone asked her to mind a baby. She settled on the sofa and Scarlett shifted in her arms, standing up on her lap and pushing against her jeans with her feet as if she was trying to break free. Natalie smiled down at her and brushed a finger along the small girl's cheek, taking in every detail from the bright blue of her eyes to the little blond curls that sprouted from the back of her head.

Andy drifted towards her. 'What made him jump, do you think?' he asked. 'I mean, he had everything to live for. Don't you think?'

Natalie met his gaze. She understood he was hurt and confused but what could she possibly say to that?

'I mean, how could he leave Scarlett? She's his only grand-child. He adored her.'

'Maybe he fell?' she said quietly. She prayed he fell. It would be a lot easier on the family.

He nodded grimly. 'He wasn't even supposed to be in Greenwich. He was meant to be collecting timber from Lewisham.'

Natalie raised an eyebrow, but said no more as Gail had returned, carrying fresh mugs of tea. She set them on the table with the others.

Natalie held out Scarlett, who was getting wriggly.

'Just pop her on the play mat,' Gail said. She leaned forward and held her head in her hands.

'It must be quite a shock,' Natalie said, setting Scarlett down. She wasn't quite mobile yet, but she did a good impression of swimming through air.

'It was the Canary Grand, you know,' Andy said. 'The garden terrace.'

Natalie's mouth fell open. 'The Canary Grand?' Yes, of course she was familiar with the garden terrace. Hayden had taken her up there. It was quite secluded, the kind of place couples went to be alone, but the kind of place you'd go to kill yourself? She could think of gentler, less public, methods.

She stayed a while, sitting in silence while she drank the tea. When she had finished, she rose to her feet.

'I'd better get going now,' she said softly. 'If you need anything, just call, okay?'

Gail nodded and followed her to the door.

'How's your mum doing?' Natalie asked as she stood on the doorstep.

Gail shrugged. 'She's a mess. I tried to talk to her but she just wants to be alone right now.'

'Understandable, I suppose.'

'You know he was ten years older than her? We always thought he'd be the one to go first...'

Natalie wrapped her friend in a hug. There were no words

that would take away the pain. A lump had formed in her own throat, and it was all she could do to get back to her car. It wouldn't do to cry in front of Gail. This was Gail's father. Gail's grief. Natalie had no right to it.

It was raining by the time she got home and Hayden's car was not in the driveway. She stood in the rain for a few minutes, taking comfort from the coolness, and let the tears run freely down her face.

A moment later, Liz's car rumbled through the open gates. Natalie turned to greet her sister, but it was Oliver at the wheel.

She brushed the tears from her eyes and walked over to him.

'Oliver! What are you doing here?'

He climbed out of the car. 'I thought you might need someone.'

She squinted at him curiously. 'Why?'

'You know.'

She swiped her phone against the door lock and it clicked open. A chill descended upon her as she stepped inside, so she adjusted the thermostat, and the air instantly warmed.

'I heard about Damon,' he said.

She glanced up at him. 'I didn't know you even knew him.'

'I remember him,' he said, watching her intently. 'He was Robin, wasn't he?'

Natalie swallowed. 'What are you talking about?'

'Oh, come on, Nat. It wasn't so hard to figure out. He was married to Marian, as in Maid Marian. So, you called him Robin, like Robin Hood. It was a code, wasn't it? That's why he wouldn't leave his family. Why you couldn't keep the baby.'

She felt herself start to shake. 'You were just a little kid. How did you...?'

'People always underestimated me. No one thought I understood anything. All those secretive phone calls. All that nipping out to the shops or to Gail's. I knew what you were up to, even if no one else did.'

'Have you... told anyone?'

'Just you.'

'Then please, Oliver, keep it that way. I never told anyone, least of all Gail. I can't lose my best friend. Especially not now.'

FORTY-FIVE

NATALIE

Oliver looked offended. 'I've kept the secret this long, Nat. I'm not about to blab. What do you take me for?'

She laid her head on his shoulder. 'I'm sorry. It's all been too much.'

He wrapped his arms around her waist, and she felt the solid warmth of his embrace. Her mind drifted back to when he had been a toddler, jumping onto her lap and cuddling close. He was so big now, so grown up. She was proud of the man he had become. She blinked away the tears that pooled in her eyes, marvelling at how their roles had changed.

She heard the roar of Hayden's Ferrari outside. She and Oliver stared at each other for a moment, then they each took a step back.

Hayden stumbled into the house, his face pale and drawn. His lips moved like he was trying to form words, but Natalie couldn't make out what he was saying.

Oliver tilted his head. 'I take it you heard what happened to Damon?'

'I was there,' Hayden said. 'He landed right in front of me. I've never seen anything like it.'

Natalie rushed over to him and threw her arms around him. Fresh tears brimmed at the corners of her eyes. 'I'm so sorry you had to go through that,' she whispered, her voice trembling.

Oliver hovered awkwardly in the background. 'That must have been really rough, mate. You take it easy, okay?'

He lingered for a moment longer before making his way towards the door. Natalie watched, and nodded gratefully but Hayden was a mess. He needed her.

'Let me get you a drink,' she said, helping him into a chair.

She poured them both generous measures of brandy. She didn't normally like the stuff, but she needed something for the shock.

'If you could go back in time, would you buy that winning lottery ticket again?' Hayden asked, as he sipped his drink.

Natalie stared at him. 'What do you mean? Of course I would. This bad luck, this has nothing to do with our win. It's not our fault, Hayden, these things just happen.'

He nodded shakily, but she could see he wasn't convinced.

'Look at our beautiful house,' she said, waving her arm around. 'Aren't you happy to live here? And you don't have to work anymore. That's nice, isn't it? And I have my coffee shop...'

He nodded, but she could see there was something else going on in his head. Something he wasn't about to share.

The following morning, she left Hayden sound asleep and set off early to open the coffee shop. With Marian off work, she was going to have to step up her game. There would be no more lie-ins. No more nipping off for a break when she felt like it. Amy would help her for a few hours, but then Natalie would have to run the shop by herself. If she'd ever wanted a chance to prove herself, this was it.

When Amy arrived, they avoided the topic of Damon's

death. She wasn't sure she was comfortable talking about it herself yet. It was still such a shock.

She and Amy got on well together, but there was none of the synchronicity she had with Marian. Twice, they collided with each other, trying to get at the till.

'Me and my two left feet!' Amy said, trying to make a joke of it.

'No, it's not you, it's me,' Natalie said. She needed to do better. She needed to think more like Marian.

Of course, it didn't help that she was still dying to know if Amy was her daughter. Amy never said anything to hint that she might be, and she couldn't imagine that Amy was the tempestuous young woman Esme had described, but it nagged at her all the same.

When the morning rush quietened down, she slipped outside for a breath of fresh air and tried calling Esme again but the phone rang and rang. She left a message, repeating her mobile number carefully before asking for a picture of Heather.

She didn't hear from Esme until she was manoeuvring through the rush hour traffic that evening. She heard her phone buzz and took a quick look, keeping one eye on the road. A new message from an unknown number flashed up on the screen. Her heart raced as she read its contents:

Here's the picture of Heather you asked for. Please let me know if you see her. Love Esme.

Natalie hesitated for a moment before tapping the attachment. The image loaded slowly, pixel by pixel. At first, all she saw was a mass of curly hair, but then slowly, more details came into focus until she was staring into a set of very familiar green eyes. Natalie covered her mouth with her hand. She was looking at a picture of Daisy.

She pulled into the petrol station and took another look.

There was no denying the woman she was looking at was Daisy. Was it even possible? She did a quick mental calculation. Daisy was a lot younger than her, but young enough to be Heather?

Daisy's last name was Smith, just about the most common surname she could think of. Almost the direct opposite of Kipling. Was that why she'd chosen it?

Her temples pounded as she tried to unpick the puzzle. What were the chances she'd stolen her own daughter's boyfriend away from her and ended up married to him? What were the chances she had known Daisy all this time and never suspected?

When she had lived in the old flat she would often see Daisy walking the dog or pedalling past on her bike. She had assumed Daisy enjoyed the fresh air but why was she always on her street? It seemed clear now that Daisy had been stalking her for some time.

She took an abrupt left turn and followed the road towards her old neighbourhood, parking across the street from Daisy's townhouse. The porch light was on, and through the window she saw the flicker of the TV. She took a deep, fortifying breath before she walked up the stone path and knocked sharply on the door.

The door opened slowly and there stood Ted, lips pressed into a tight smile.

'Oh, hi, Natalie. Are you here to see Daisy? She's still at work, I'm afraid.'

'Mind if I come in and wait?'

His dark green eyes glimmered in the light of the hallway.

'Course not, come on through.'

She followed him inside. The cramped kitchen was a tiny rectangle of faded wallpaper and cheap linoleum in contrast to the lavish formal dining room. The scent of warm vanilla filled the air as he gestured towards the small round table. She saw a plate of freshly baked cakes on the windowsill but Ted did not offer her one.

She took a seat and waited while he carefully folded himself onto the chair opposite, his legs tucked awkwardly beneath him.

'I'm glad you popped in because there was something I wanted to talk to you about,' he said, rolling up the fabric of his shirt sleeves.

She leaned forward. 'What is it?'

'Daisy and I have been arguing about this, actually. And maybe I'm making a mountain out of a molehill but it would be good to get your perspective.'

'Oh?'

Ted averted his eyes and drew a deep breath. 'Well, this is awkward, so I'm just going to come right out and say it. I think we all spend too much time together, and I'm not sure it's healthy.'

Natalie raised a brow.

'I mean, I've nothing against you, or Hayden or your sister, but the history of it all, don't you think it's weird that we all do so much together? I mean, it just makes me uncomfortable, that's what I'm saying.'

Natalie chewed her lip thoughtfully before she responded. 'I can't say it really bothers me. I mean, I like Daisy. Hayden does too.'

'But they've seen each other naked. That weirds me out, Natalie. I don't want him there on our wedding day, looking at my wife, thinking, "I've seen that." But Daisy says he's her best friend and she won't get married without him.'

'She said that?'

Ted rubbed the back of his head. 'She wants him to give her away.'

Natalie's senses sparked. 'Doesn't she have a dad to do that?'

'No, she's never known her dad.'

'What about her mum?'

'They're not close. I'm still hoping she'll come to the wedding.'

She thought fast. 'Does Daisy have any photo albums? Pictures of her as a child?'

Ted studied her carefully. 'What's going on, Natalie?'

She felt the heat rising in her cheeks and she averted her gaze.

'I just...' She couldn't come out with it. The whole thing suddenly seemed preposterous. Of course Daisy wasn't her daughter. It was impossible.

'It's nothing.' She tried to laugh it off.

'So, what do you think I should do, Nat?'

'I think you should do the wedding your way. Why don't you do yourself a favour and take Daisy off to some sun-soaked island somewhere? It'll be romantic and you can make the wedding all about the two of you.'

'I wish. Daisy wants all eyes on her. It's the wedding of the century or nothing. She won't settle for anything less than a three-day party.'

'Well then, maybe I can get Hayden to talk to her? He might be able to persuade her to pick someone else to give her away. What about Andy?'

'He's got a face on him like a wet weekend.'

'Sure, but he hasn't seen Daisy naked.'

'He'd better not have.'

She glanced up at the clock. 'Right, well I'd better be going.'

'Are you sure? Daisy will be home any minute.'

'No, sorry. I've just remembered something I have to do.'

She hurried out of the house and legged it to her car, keen to get away before Daisy arrived. She paused only to pull up the message on her phone again. She pinched the bridge of her nose, trying to make sense of it. It wasn't real. It couldn't be. She didn't need to look through Daisy's photograph album. She had come to her senses. Daisy could not be her daughter, that would be absolutely crazy. Which meant someone was lying to her.

She stared at the text message and photo. Even though it had been signed off with Esme's name, she couldn't be sure if it was really from her. She had only spoken to Esme on her work phone number. This number could belong to anyone.

She tried dialling it but nobody picked up. She wished she could speak to Esme but it was already gone five. School would be over for the day. A knot of dread formed in her stomach as she considered the implications. Only one person knew she had been in touch with Esme Kipling. The prank picture could only come from Liz. But why would she do such a thing?

FORTY-SIX

NATALIE

Natalie held her forehead in her hands. Her sister had a strange sense of humour, but surely she understood that this was no laughing matter? How could she play such a joke on her? It wasn't the least bit funny.

She ought to ring Liz and have it out with her but right now she was far too angry. She wished she had someone to talk to, but there was no one, not even Robin anymore.

She wiped an errant tear away from her face and realised that there was someone she could talk to after all. Her head was buzzing, full of confusion and pain. Before she knew what she was doing she was driving out of town, towards Mulberry House. She didn't know his schedule like Liz did, but she didn't care. She needed her father.

She parked outside the care home and ran to the door. The receptionist asked her to sign the book before she hurried through to the lounge. Her dad was sitting in an armchair, squinting at the TV. His face brightened when he noticed her, a wide smile spreading across his weathered cheeks.

'You're back!'

Natalie took a tentative step toward him, her arms

outstretched. She closed her eyes and breathed in the familiar scent of his old pipe tobacco.

'Of course I'm back.'

She pulled up a chair next to him, and they sat there in an easy, comfortable silence. She looked over at him and saw that his eyes were glossy with emotion. He shifted closer and reached for her hand, intertwining their fingers together.

'Dad, I need you to remember. Is there anything else you can tell me about Heather? Did Esme Kipling ever contact you? I thought there might have been a letter or a photo? Anything.'

She looked at her father expectantly but he didn't seem to hear her.

'Did Liz ever say anything to you about her?'

He turned and looked at her. 'About who?'

Natalie rubbed her eyes.

'Have you done your homework?' he asked.

'Yes,' she answered sadly.

'That's good. You're so clever, Natalie. You know you can do anything you put your mind to?'

She nodded and looked down at her hands. She felt bad now. She should be there to visit her father for his own sake, not just to leech information out of him.

'What have you been up to, Dad? Did you watch the *Antiques Roadshow*?'

His smile began at the corners of his lips and slowly unfurled like a blanket.

She recalled being twelve years old, sitting cross-legged on the floor with her sister beside her. Her dad had always loved antiques. They had giggled as he explained how an old wheel-barrow was worth hundreds because it was used in a famous film.

Liz was dismissive, but Natalie had felt a flutter in her chest. The thought of owning something so rare and valuable had seemed like magic. She planned to be rich one day. She hadn't worked out how, but she was adamant it would happen.

A nurse came in, ripping her from her reverie.

'I'm afraid it's time for your father's podiatry appointment.'

'I'd better get going,' she said, rising to her feet.

Her father looked sad.

'I can come again,' she offered. 'How about next week?'

'You could bring me some peppermint cremes,' he suggested hopefully.

'Bye, Dad,' she said, lips brushing the soft skin of his cheek. A warm feeling pulsed through her chest and she smiled as she turned away.

'Or grapes,' he called after her, as the nurse wheeled him away. 'She brought me grapes.'

'Liz did?'

'No, the other one.'

Her heart warmed at the thought of his carers being so kind to him. She smiled to herself and left him in their capable hands.

The receptionist was on the phone when she passed, but paused long enough to give her a wave. 'Make sure you sign out!'

Natalie fumbled for a pen. Outside, the wind picked up and the pages of the visitor's book fluttered open. She saw Liz's name from a previous visit printed on one of them. Then she saw the name written directly below it; Heather Kipling. A numbing realisation crept over her. Liz already knew who Heather was. She knew and she had deliberately kept the truth from her.

FORTY-SEVEN

NATALIE

Natalie pounded on Liz's door with such force that it echoed down the street. There was no response so she moved to the window and cupped her hands around her face to get a better look inside. Everything was still and silent; all the lights were off. Fury bubbled up in her chest as she pulled out her phone and dialled her sister's number.

'How could you do this?' she demanded. 'You found Heather and you didn't tell me.'

Liz was silent for a moment. Natalie heard her breathing down the line.

'I've been looking for her for years,' Liz whispered. 'I didn't want to drag you into it. I thought you weren't ready.'

'How did you find her?'

'She found me. She recognised your name from the newspapers and then she found the press conference online and watched it. I was wearing my sweatshirt, remember? With the nursery logo on it. She figured out where that was and turned up at my work.'

Natalie's throat felt dry.

'So, we went for a drink and talked things through. She's an amazing person. I just know you're going to love her. She wanted to know about you but I wasn't sure you were ready to meet her. You never showed any interest before, did you?'

The desperation was clear in her voice. 'I thought maybe if you weren't interested, then at least she could have an aunt. I wanted her so badly. I have no kids, Nat. No meaningful relationships. She might be grown up now, but she needs me.'

'You took her to see Dad!'

'He's an old man, who knows how much longer he has? And I know he's wondered about her too. In recent years, he'd been questioning what he did, making you give her up. He genuinely thought he was doing the right thing. You were so scatty back then and it was clear Robin would not support you.'

Tears stung Natalie's eyes and her heart dropped to her stomach as she thought about how Liz had lied. She didn't know how she was going to move past this.

'What about the doll in my pool?'

'Heather was hurt and angry. You won all that money and still didn't have room for her in your life.'

'Is that why you sent me that picture of Daisy?'

'Sorry about that. I was just in a funny mood. I mean, of course Daisy couldn't be Heather. You must have known that.'

Natalie bit her lip. She still found it a little strange. Was this the kind of influence Heather had over her?

'Heather desperately wants to meet you. All you have to do is say the word.'

Natalie shifted uncomfortably, tugging at her collar. 'I... I think I had an emotional block before but now I'm ready.'

'That's great, Nat. I'll set up a meeting. Just don't expect too much, okay? She's been through a lot.'

Natalie hung up her phone. She had an urge to break something, to scream – anything to release the anger swirling inside her. Whatever happened with Heather, she was disturbed by the part Liz had played, sneaking around behind her back. How could she ever trust her sister again?

She drove back home. Hayden was out and she was feeling agitated. She ran herself a bubble bath, sinking deep into the water. Her muscles relaxed as she breathed in the scent of lavender. Yet despite the soothing effects of the water, she couldn't get rid of the knot in her stomach.

Climbing out of the tub, she wrapped herself in a towel and grabbed her laptop from the nightstand. She began scouring the internet for information on Heather. She had had no luck the last time she'd tried, but perhaps she hadn't looked hard enough. What if she tweaked a few of the filters? What if she looked a little further back in time? She tapped a few keys and waited patiently as the search results appeared.

She found a Twitter account for someone called Heather Kipling but the picture was of a bird. There was no personal information on the account and no knowing if this was her Heather. She wondered if it was worth searching for Heather Butler. That was Heather's name on her original birth certificate, before the adoption went through. She found several, but none that were obviously her daughter. She kept looking, further and further back, and that was when she stumbled on an old forum. There was a new topic, posted around a year ago by a user called Catwoman99. She read the post in amazement:

I'm trying to find my niece Heather Butler who was given up for adoption at birth. Her mother's name is Natalie Peel, née Butler, and the father's name is Robin.

The poster had then listed the name of the hospital where Heather was born as well as Heather's date of birth.

A chill ran down Natalie's spine. This post could only have

been written by Liz. Not only that, but it could be seen by anyone looking for an easy mark. When the press announced Natalie had won the lottery, it wouldn't have been hard for anyone to find this. So this woman Liz had met, had even introduced to their father, could be anyone.

FORTY-EIGHT

NATALIE

She grabbed her phone from the bedside table and dialled Liz's number. It rang, but after a few moments, a robotic voice asked her to leave a message. She tried again, tapping her foot impatiently.

'Come on, Liz. Pick up.'

This time Liz answered on the third ring.

'Hi.'

'Liz, I hate to be the bearer of bad news, but I'm not sure the woman you've been meeting is the real Heather.'

'She is, Nat. She knows stuff about us no one else would know.'

'Like what?'

'Her date of birth fits and she knows her dad's called Robin.'

'No, Liz, wait. You gave out all that info on a forum a few years back, don't you remember? I just stumbled across it. If I could find it, anyone could.'

There was a long pause. 'Nat, it's definitely Heather.'

'How can you be so sure?'

'She has ID.'

'She could have faked it. Does she even look like me at all?'

'I'm not... kids don't always look like their parents. Maybe she looks like Robin?'

Natalie sighed. 'Maybe.'

'Look, Nat, I have to go and take a shower. We're meeting at Barley Hill later. Do you want to join us?'

'Well okay then.'

'Right. Let me speak to her first. I don't want to just spring it on her. If she's okay with it, we'll meet at six thirty.'

A few minutes later, Liz updated her with a text:

Heather says yes!

Natalie's stomach churned with a mixture of excitement and anxiety. She was almost certain that Liz's Heather would not be the real Heather, but a part of her still bubbled with anticipation. What if it was her? If so, she was about to meet her daughter.

At a quarter past six, she walked out of the house, intending to take the Audi. At the last minute, she glanced at the garage and changed her mind. The silver Ferrari had barely been used since they'd bought it. Why not take it out for a spin?

She grabbed the keys and plugged Barley Hill into the satnav. She had never understood Hayden's obsession with fast cars – until now. The engine purred to life.

The sun shone through the sparse tree canopy as she drove down the winding road. The car hugged each curve of the asphalt as if it were a roller coaster, and her fingers tightened on the steering wheel with each bend.

She hadn't been to Barley Hill since she was a kid, when her dad used to challenge her and Liz to race down the hill. She understood now that the plan was to burn off their excess energy and wear them out but at the time it had seemed all important. She remembered feeling invincible during those races; like she was fulfilling some noble mission. Being older and taller, she had beaten Liz nearly every time, and yet Liz had always demanded a rerun.

When she arrived at Barley Hill, she pulled into the car park and searched for a few minutes. Liz's car was easy to spot, its once-metallic paint now dulled with scratches, but she had tucked it away in the furthest corner of the car park, where the gravel was as thick as snow.

There was no sign of Liz, and Natalie couldn't shake off a growing sense of unease. Her trainers scuffed the dirt path as she walked towards the little café. The front door was boarded up and the windows were covered in dust. She shaded her eyes, scanning the hillside. The sun hung low in the sky, casting its last light over the rolling hills. She kept walking but she heard nothing but the tweeting of birds and the soughing of grass beneath her feet.

She tried ringing Liz again, but she couldn't get a signal so she drew a deep breath and cupped her hands around her mouth:

'Liz!' The sound reverberated through the trees and stirred a flock of birds from their perches. They took to the sky in a flurry of feathers and squawks.

She navigated the winding paths, careful to avoid tree roots and fallen branches. As she cleared a bend, the landscape opened up and she spotted Liz alone at the lookout. Liz turned towards her as she approached, and the wind played with the tendrils of her hair.

'Where's Heather?' Natalie asked. Liz's shoulders sagged.

'We were just sitting here talking, and then she got up all of a sudden and left. I guess she wasn't ready to meet you after all.'

Natalie sank down onto the bench beside her. 'This woman you've been meeting. Did she show you a birth certificate or anything?'

Liz's eyebrows furrowed. 'It's her. I just know.'

Natalie reached for her sister's hand. 'I'm a lottery winner.

People will do anything to get my money. Including pretending to be my long-lost daughter.'

'No, she's opened up to me and told me so much about her life. Did you know she used to wait on her doorstep every year, hoping you'd send a card or something for her birthday? She couldn't understand what she'd done to make you not want her. I've told her what happened but she really wants the chance to hear it from you. We can set up another meeting. Maybe at her house.'

Natalie nestled her face into the curve of her sister's shoulder. 'I'm not sure.'

'She is Heather,' Liz insisted, her voice quiet but resolute.

Natalie kept silent; she could feel tension radiating from Liz's body. If Heather turned out to be a fake, it would take time for her to accept that.

They sat for a while, watching the horizon. The sky was illuminated with streaks of orange, red and pink as the sun slowly descended from its highest point.

'Shall we?' Liz asked. 'For old times' sake?'

'Shall we what?' Natalie asked, but before she could finish her sentence, Liz was off, hurtling down the hill as if her life depended on it. Laughing at the absurdity of it, Natalie took off after her. Liz was already a metre in front of her, but Natalie was determined not to lose her record. She ran flat out, pumping her arms as she struggled to catch her sister. They finished in a dead heat, both panting and gasping for air.

'Again?' Liz said, once she'd got her breath back.

'No, I'm happy to share first place,' Natalie said and reached out to shake her sister's hand.

They trudged back up the hill. It was never as much fun as the downward sprint, and Natalie was tired by the time they reached the top. It was a shame the café wasn't open because she could have done with a cool glass of water.

'Where did you park?' Liz asked, looking out at the car park.

Natalie scanned the area for Hayden's beloved Ferrari, but it was nowhere to be seen. Her face flushed and her palms sweated. 'It was right there. That woman stole my car.'

'Heather would never...'

'That woman was not Heather,' Natalie stated. She was sure of it now. She could feel the heat rising in her cheeks. 'Liz, think about it. She knew I was on my way, and she knew I'd likely be driving a brand-new car. Maybe not a sports car, but an expensive car, all the same.'

'How did she even steal it? Didn't you lock it?'

'Of course I did.'

She watched as the light went on in Liz's eyes. 'Perhaps she used a signal jammer? I heard a bunch of cars were stolen from a supermarket car park using those things. They stop the cars from locking properly.'

'Maybe,' Natalie said. She didn't care how she'd done it, only that she had.

'I can't believe I was so gullible!' Liz's foot connected with a rock and sent it skittering down the hill. 'I just wanted so much for us to be a family.'

Natalie placed a hand on her shoulder and gave it a gentle squeeze.

'It's okay, Liz. She's probably a professional scammer. You couldn't have known.'

They headed towards Liz's hatchback. No one was going to steal that.

'What are you going to do about your car?'

'It was one of Hayden's, actually.' Natalie tried to keep her voice light but couldn't stop herself from wincing at the words.

'Ouch. Doesn't your insurance cover it?'

'Hey, I'm loaded, remember? I'll just buy him another one.' She forced a smile, as she remembered how long it had taken for the cars to be delivered.

'I still can't believe she scammed me like that. I mean, I even took her to meet Dad.'

'I know, Liz. I...'

She stopped dead.

'What?'

She swallowed hard. 'Has Oliver met her?'

Liz shifted uncomfortably. 'He turned up once when she was at my house. I didn't know what to do; I thought about lying but she seemed excited when I mentioned we were related.'

Natalie's throat felt dry. For a moment, she couldn't breathe.

'Nat? What is it?'

She shook her head, unable to believe this could be possible.

'For God's sake, Nat, you're scaring me.'

Natalie licked her lips. She had to force the words out. 'What if he told her Damon was her dad?'

Liz's mouth dropped open as her face went pale. 'You're kidding me! What about Robin? I thought...'

'Robin was Damon. It was a stupid code name.'

'Oh, Natalie! I thought he was some college boy!' Liz shook her head in disbelief. 'Damon was... Damon was so old and...'

'Wrong for me,' Natalie finished for her.

The two stared at each other for a moment before Liz spoke again. 'That disgusting old man! Jesus, we knew him since we were little, Natalie. You used to sleep over at their house. That's not right.'

Natalie waited a moment, while her sister wrapped her head around this revelation.

'For God's sake, why did you never say anything?'

'I just... even back then, I knew it wasn't right. He was too old for me. Too married. I wasn't proud of what we did, I just couldn't resist him, Liz. He gave me so much attention, in the beginning. I felt so damned special, and I liked it. He made me feel so grown up.'

'Stop it, you're making me feel sick. If I had known for one minute, I would have kicked him right in the balls. And I would have told Dad. No wonder he took the coward's way out.'

Natalie shook her head. 'Please, I really don't want to get into all that. He's dead now. The point is, did Heather know about him?'

Liz drew a breath. 'What would it matter if she did? If she was a fraudster, then it would be irrelevant.'

'She might have tried to scam him too. He'd done alright for himself, Damon. After all these years it would have been awful for him if the truth got out. He would have lost everything.'

They both fell silent. It was a horrible thought.

Liz looked at her directly. 'I still think he was a twat for having an affair with a teenage girl. I mean, you were what, seventeen at the time, and Mum had just died. But he had a family too, and they didn't deserve to lose him.'

Liz's car beeped twice as she unlocked it and slid into the driver's seat. Natalie got in beside her, tugging at her shirt uncomfortably. She looked out the window as they drove away, watching the trees sway in the breeze. She tried to make sense of her thoughts, but they were as fleeting as the leaves scattered in the wind.

A few miles from home, Natalie's phone pinged as an email arrived. She pulled it from her pocket, expecting it to be Hayden. Her heart raced as she took in the subject heading: *DNA results: confidential.*

FORTY-NINE

NATALIE

Natalie's hand trembled as she opened the attachment. She scanned through the text, barely registering any of the technical details until her eyes landed on two words: Positive Match.

'Amy is my daughter!'

She stared at Liz, momentarily lost for words. A wave of relief washed over her, followed by immense joy. She forgot about Hayden's car, and fake Heather. She was surprised at the strength of her own reaction. Nice, sweet Amy had been the real Heather all along.

'I want to meet her,' Liz said.

'I don't even know what I'm going to say to her myself yet,' Natalie said.

'Why don't you just close the café for the morning? Then when she arrives for work you can sit down and talk. Don't mention the DNA test though. You were taking a bit of a liberty.'

'Hey, it was your idea!'

'All the same. We need to make a good first impression here.'

Natalie's heart was pumping. She hadn't realised how much she wanted this.

'I'm scared,' she confessed. 'What if she hates me?'

'I doubt she would have kept working for you if that was true,' Liz said. 'But don't worry, I'll be there with you. You don't have to meet her alone.'

Natalie intertwined her fingers, pressing her palms together until her knuckles turned white. She blinked back tears, her voice quaking with emotion. 'I can't put into words how I feel right now, knowing that it's true.' A lump caught in her throat as she looked at Liz for support.

'Tell me about it,' Liz said.

Natalie leaned across and patted her shoulder. 'Hey, I really am sorry about fake Heather. It really sucks that she played you like that.'

Liz swallowed. 'I'm fine. It's not my car she stole.'

Early the following morning, Natalie sat at one of the little tables with a cup of coffee and peered out the window, waiting for Amy to arrive. She wasn't expecting Marian to return until after Damon's funeral. She'd told her to take all the time she needed, and she put the 'closed' sign on the door so that she wouldn't have to deal with any customers while they were having their reunion.

She still hadn't worked out what she wanted to say. Should she apologise for giving her up? Or should she just let Amy talk? She must have questions of her own.

She remembered now that she had promised Esme she would let her know when she found her daughter. She would do so after she had spoken to Amy, just to let her know she was safe.

She glanced at the clock, a little annoyed that Amy was late, today of all days.

'Perhaps she's got cold feet,' Liz said.

Natalie shook her head. 'She doesn't know I've figured it out, and she's always been very reliable.' She went to the door and peered out. 'Ah, there she is now.'

Liz stared out the window. 'That's fake Heather.'

'But it can't be!'

'It is. Fake Heather was real Heather.'

Natalie didn't know what to do. Amy came strolling into the coffee shop with her usual cheery smile.

'Isn't it quiet today?' she said, looking around. Then she spotted Liz. 'Oh!'

'Oh, indeed.'

Amy's face drained of colour and she stumbled backwards, nearly tripping in her haste to get away. But Liz had already blocked the door, her arms crossed defiantly across her chest.

Natalie spoke in a calm voice. 'We're not angry. At least, I'm not.'

She looked at Amy and noted the way her jaw clenched and her hands bunched into fists.

'I know who you are now,' she continued. 'I just want to know why you did it. Why all the sneaking around, putting the doll in my pool and stealing the car?'

Amy met Natalie's gaze head-on. Her eyes glowed with an intensity that seemed unnatural.

'You threw me away like rubbish.' Tears welled in her eyes as she spoke.

'I wanted you to have a good home,' Natalie said.

'So you let me be adopted by a fucking head teacher who had no idea how to raise a child? Do you think she made a good mum?'

'I—'

'No, everything I did was wrong in her eyes. She didn't want a child, she wanted a model student she could show off to all her friends. And if that wasn't bad enough, she's absolutely clueless about men. She brought home the most vile, disgusting specimens and expected me to be nice to them, I don't know where she finds them. And that last one, that Kyle. He attacked me the moment her back was turned and when I told her, she took his side. What sort of a mother is that?'

'I'm so sorry that happened to you,' Natalie said. 'But I was just a teenager when you were born. I wasn't ready to be a mother. I thought I was doing the right thing.'

'The right thing for you, maybe. You ruined my life. I might have been able to forgive you if you had been willing to make up for your mistakes. Do you know how I spent my eighteenth birthday? At the adoption agency, trying to convince them to contact you, to let you know I needed you. And they did. They sent you that letter. It was sent by recorded delivery, *Mum*. So don't go telling me you didn't receive it.'

Natalie cleared her throat. 'It wasn't that I didn't want to. I was worried about digging up the past. I thought it might do more harm than good.'

Amy stepped towards her, closing the space between them until they were standing nose to nose. Her breath felt hot on her face. She leaned in and spoke through gritted teeth.

'You took the easy way out. You always take the easy way out.'

Natalie glanced at Liz but her sister seemed frozen, unable to utter a single word.

'Amy, I know I've screwed up really badly, but please. Give me a chance to make it up to you.'

'Well I'm glad you've finally remembered you had a daughter, but it's too late.'

Amy squared her shoulders and took a step towards the door. Liz tried to reach for her arm but she dodged the attempt and pushed past. She yanked the door open so hard it crashed against the wall before swinging shut behind her.

FIFTY

HAYDEN

Hayden lay in bed, tracing circles on the ceiling with his eyes. He thought of Damon Goodwin and wished he could get his mangled body out of his mind. He heard it again, that sickening crack. He shuddered violently and pulled the covers up around his neck. He felt claustrophobic, trapped in an endless loop of remembering.

His phone buzzed and he glanced at it – Lexi again. He owed her interest, she said. His stomach tightened as he thought about how much money he had already paid her.

He sat up and looked out at the river, feeling suddenly resolute. He would not give up. He was going to find that woman and make her wish she'd never messed with him.

Fury rushed through his veins as he marched outside, slamming the door behind him. He got into the red Ferrari and glanced at the petrol gauge. It was close to empty. Perhaps he should drive the other car today but this one was his favourite. He liked the way he felt when he got behind the wheel. Besides, the pub was only a couple of miles away. He'd fill up at the nearest petrol station.

He arrived at the pub and looked around the car park in

disappointment. There were a few cars parked there but none of them were the white Fiesta.

He pushed open the door and went inside. The only customer was an elderly man in a wheelchair, feeding coins into one of the slot machines. Hayden fought the urge to warn him off the machines and headed to the bar instead. The barman looked familiar.

'Hey, you were in here last week, weren't you? Do you remember the woman I was with?'

The barman shrugged. 'The girl with the freckles?'

'Yes, that's her! Is she a regular?'

'No, not a regular but I saw her in here once before with another woman. Might have been her sister, might have been her mum.'

'Can you describe her?'

'Tall, slim. Not very talkative. They got one of the games out.' He gestured towards the table by the window, and Hayden saw a stack of books, games and puzzles.

'Do you remember which one?'

'I think it was the Game of Life. They were messing around with it, playing with the fake money.'

'I bet they were.'

He scribbled his number down on a piece of paper. 'If either of them come in again, can you call me? I'll make it worth your while.'

The barman raised an eyebrow. 'What are you going to do? Take me out on a date?'

Hayden laughed. 'I was thinking money but whatever floats your boat.'

He wandered back out to the car park. He bet they were in it together, the two women. Had she been there that night, watching? Now he thought about it, Lexi had gone to the loo a few times. Perhaps they'd been conferring, discussing her next move?

He returned to his car and sat there for a few minutes, deep in thought. If only he had a picture of Lexi, he could show it to the shopkeepers on the street, see if anyone else recognised her. As it was, he had reached a dead end. The only other lead he had was the Regent Hotel, but Daisy would be there and he hadn't spoken to her since she had lured him into that hotel room. He was still annoyed about that. She was supposed to be his friend. Why didn't she understand how important it was that he found Lexi? It was almost as if she was trying to distract him, but no – that was crazy. There was no way Daisy was in on this. He was being paranoid.

He started the car and was about to head out of the car park when a battered white Fiesta drove past. He couldn't be a hundred per cent certain, but he was pretty sure he'd just seen Lexi at the wheel. He pulled out onto the street, ignoring the honking of horns as he merged with the traffic.

He kept the white Fiesta in his sights as he drove towards the dual carriageway. He was desperate to pull up alongside her but there were too many cars blocking his way. He tried to keep up an even pace, but he had to contend with the teenage learner in front of him. He was speeding up, slowing down and wobbling all over the road. Hayden would have honked his horn, but that would have only startled the guy.

The learner turned off just before the road merged with the dual carriageway. Hayden took his chance and moved into the fast lane, staying there while he overtook the two cars between him and the Fiesta. He could see the driver clearly now, and yes, that was definitely her. She'd clocked him too. There was a determined look in her eye as she pushed her car to the limit.

The Ferrari's fuel gauge plunged lower with every passing mile as he tailed Lexi into the Blackwall Tunnel. Sweat formed on his brow as the headlights illuminated the entrance and a wave of fear crashed over him – what if he ran out of petrol in there? He took a deep breath and drove into the depths of the tunnel. Instantly, the walls seemed to close in around him and lights flickered in his peripheral vision.

He pressed down on the accelerator, his heart racing with anxiety. His hands were slippery on the wheel but he didn't dare slow down. His car flew round the tunnel. He was losing control now, his eyes barely registering each turn. His mind kept sending him unwanted images, of the mangled body of Damon Goodwin.

He burst out of the tunnel, adrenaline coursing through his veins. Lexi's Fiesta sputtered ahead, but her car was no match for his Ferrari. He wove around other cars and squeezed into small gaps between them. He revved the engine, gaining ground on Lexi until he finally manoeuvred in front of her.

In the mirror, he saw her face contort with fear, then at the last minute, he pulled back into the outer lane. He raised a clenched fist into the air and roared with feral delight.

The other cars fell behind in the dust cloud the Ferrari left in its wake, leaving just the two of them on the open road. She pushed her tiny hatchback to its limits, but it was no match for his car. With one last hard left, he aimed straight for Lexi's car, his wheels screaming as they skidded across the asphalt. Then a faint sputtering sound began under the bonnet. He swore in frustration, but it was no use, he couldn't keep running the car on empty. He was forced to pull off to the side of the road. He turned and watched in utter disbelief as Lexi's little Fiesta disappeared into the distance.

FIFTY-ONE

HAYDEN

Hayden stood on the side of the road with his arms crossed, glaring at the cars that zoomed by. One driver even honked and stuck out her tongue. It seemed like hours since he'd called for help, but he was still here, waiting under the sun's glare.

He ignored the amused looks from other drivers. He got little sympathy from any of them. No one had any time for the rich bloke, he had learned that by now. Money bought privilege but rarely respect. Finally, a tow truck pulled up with a gentle beep of its horn and he breathed a sigh of relief. The interior of the cab was air-conditioned and almost too cold for comfort.

'Having a bad day?' the driver asked as he drove Hayden to the garage.

Hayden sighed and leaned against the window. 'I wish it was just a day,' he muttered.

The driver didn't press him for more details, for which he was thankful.

At the garage, Hayden had just finished filling his car with petrol when his phone buzzed in his pocket. He pulled it out, hoping to see a message from Natalie, but it was from Lexi:

Looks like I won this race. Better luck next time!

She had added a string of laughing emojis.

He deleted the message without responding, his jaw tight with anger. He had to get his own back.

He glanced at the dashboard clock as he pulled out of the garage and made his way home. Natalie should have finished work by now. She was probably wondering where he'd got to.

He drove in through the open gates and parked next to Natalie's Audi. He peered at the Glass House. The windows were tinted so he couldn't see inside. He unlocked the door with his phone. The hallway was filled with a stillness he hadn't noticed before. He set foot into the living room and saw Lexi, reclining seductively on his sofa. Her hair was tousled, and her lips set in a sultry pout. His stomach churned as he realised Natalie was nowhere to be seen.

'What are you doing here? Where's Natalie?'

Lexi laughed. 'That wife of yours is so absent-minded. She doesn't remember to lock the door half the time. You should really have a word with her.'

He cupped his hands around his mouth and bellowed, 'Natalie!' His voice reverberated through the airy living area.

Lexi remained unmoved. He stared at her accusingly. 'What did you do with her?'

When she didn't reply, his eyes wandered the room as he considered various weapons. Should he stab her with the poker from the fire or should he just shove her to the ground and stamp on her like the bloodsucking insect she was? Yet his hands felt like stones; their grip on reality was too strong to allow him to act out his dark fantasies.

'I don't have a clue where your wife is but you need to pay me the rest of what you owe me, or I'll tell her everything.'

'I already told you about the banking limits, you greedy bitch.'

She snorted and crossed her arms. 'Please, you must have some cash stashed away. Your kind always do.'

The words cut through the air like shards of glass.

'My... kind?'

'You know, weedy, airheaded, weak...'

His nostrils flared and his jaw clenched as he tried to suppress his emotions. He met her icy gaze. 'Why are you doing this? Do you hate all men or is it me in particular?'

Lexi lifted her chin. Her smirk betrayed a wickedness that made him shudder. 'How sweet! You think this is about you.'

'Well, isn't it?' he asked, desperation creeping into his voice. Everyone had something they were afraid of; what was she afraid of? Certainly not him.

'How well do you know your wife?' she asked.

'Very well,' he said with confidence.

Lexi stared at him, waiting for him to change his answer. 'A long time ago, she did something very, very bad,' she said. 'And I've been paying for her mistake all my life.'

'What are you talking about?' he said nervously. 'This has nothing to do with Nat. This is between you and me.'

Lexi smiled broadly. 'Then it might interest you to know that, technically, you're my stepdad.'

'Your...' He was about to laugh, when something clicked into place. Because there was something about Lexi that reminded him of Natalie. Something about the way she held herself. Some unidentifiable quality.

'My wife doesn't have any children.'

'Your wife is a lying bitch.' Lexi spat back. 'What's wrong? Didn't you know she was a teenage slut? She had me when she was seventeen and tossed me aside like a heap of rubbish. I was having trouble locating her. The adoption agency's annoying like that. They knew where she was, but they wouldn't tell me. I was about to take matters into my own hands when you conveniently won the lottery. That made it so much easier to flush her out, and that's exactly what I intend to do.'

'No. You must be thinking of someone else.'

Lexi laughed. 'Why else would a young woman be interested in you? It would kill Natalie if she ever finds out. She will never ever forgive you.'

Hayden's teeth chattered together. He didn't know why exactly. It must have been the shock. It was all lies; it couldn't possibly be true. *Could it?*

Before he had time to process what she'd said, she grabbed the collar of his shirt and yanked him close. Her eyes shimmered with menace, her teeth clenched so tight they might break. 'Last chance. I want my money. Now.'

He stumbled backwards, tripping over his own feet as he moved away from her. He scrambled to the sanctuary of his office, slamming the door shut behind him but he couldn't stay there forever. He had to get Lexi out before Natalie came back, wherever she was. For all he knew, she was upstairs taking a nap.

His heart raced as he unlocked the safe. The heavy metal door creaked open. He thrust his arm inside, feeling around for the thick stacks of cash he'd hoarded. He grabbed them, one by one, and stuffed them into a Waitrose bag. He dashed back to the living room but Lexi was not there.

'Lexi!' he called. 'Lexi?'

His voice echoed, mocking him. He spun around, eyes darting from one corner to the next. He flew to the nearest window and peered out. His eyes widened as he spotted her out on the driveway. Her eyes had a ravenous glint as she slowly circled his Ferrari, admiring the sleek curves. She ran her hand along the side, tracing its lines as if she could absorb its power through her fingers.

He hurried outside and handed her the money.

'This is all I have right now.'

She peered into the bag and gawked at the pile of crisp notes inside.

'What did you do, raid the piggy bank?'

'I want my ring back.'

She couldn't contain her amusement. 'No chance.'

She threw the bag onto the back seat of the Ferrari, obviously intending to take that too. His temples pulsed. He felt like all the veins in his head were pumping white-hot lava through him. He pictured himself grabbing the axe from the tool shed and driving it through her skull but he stood motionless, unable to do anything but watch as she glided her pale fingers across his beloved convertible.

A bitter taste rose in the back of his throat.

'You can't have my car.'

'I don't think you have a choice.'

His throat hurt. 'Why are you like this? What did I ever do to you?'

Her gaze travelled slowly from his expensive trainers to his dishevelled blond hair. 'You're everything that's wrong with the world. Rich, useless men like you. But your biggest mistake was marrying Natalie.'

'I'm calling the police.'

She smiled sweetly. 'Good luck with that. If you do, I'll expose you. I'll go to the papers and tell them exactly what you've been up to since you won that money. Everyone will know – your wife, your mum, your dad. Your life will be over.'

He heard a rustling sound. What was that? In a flash of movement, Daisy leapt out of the bushes with a feral howl, slamming straight into Lexi's side and taking her to the ground. He watched agog as she wrapped her strong hands around Lexi's neck and smashed her head against the concrete. Blood oozed through the cracks in the ground like a river. Daisy still had her by the neck, squeezing tight. She was like an attack dog.

He knew he ought to call her off. Instead, he watched in morbid fascination.

When Lexi became still, he pulled Daisy away.

Daisy stood motionless, her eyes glazed over in disbelief. Hayden's mouth hung agape, an incredulous mixture of shock and awe throwing him into a stunned silence. Daisy took a deep breath and wiped her forehead with her wrist, smudging a streak of blood from the corner of her eye to the edge of her jawbone.

'I'd do anything for you, you know I would,' she said quietly.

She leaned in closer, her eyes locking onto his, and the intensity of her gaze made him ache. Without warning, she leaned forward and pressed her lips to his. He felt the warmth of her skin against his own, and the intensity of her emotions. He was too stunned to resist.

Lexi lay at their feet, her body twisted and broken. Her chest heaved as she tried to take shallow breaths. Her eyes locked onto Hayden's, pleading for remorse. Tears streaked her cheeks, then her lids drifted shut, her head lolled to one side and she became still.

He cast a look around, but there was still no sign of Natalie. Wherever she was, he needed to move fast.

'What are we going to do with her?' he asked.

Daisy's hands shook and her legs buckled as she backed away from the situation. 'I... I hadn't thought that far ahead.'

He kicked Lexi with his foot. There was no response.

'Right, help me get her into the car. We need to make it look like an accident.'

Hayden wrapped his arms around Lexi's torso and heaved her limp body against him, feeling the strain in his legs as he struggled to carry her weight. Daisy grabbed her feet and together they shuffled forward, pushing her into the driver's seat of the car and fastening the seatbelt. She was motionless, her face pressed against the steering wheel. Hayden paused for a moment, panting with exertion.

'Now what?' Daisy asked.

He noticed Daisy's hands trembling as he spoke. He was worried she would collapse on him, so he grabbed her shoulders firmly and looked into her wide eyes. 'I'll take it from here, you have to go. Please,' he said softly. She gave a slow, imperceptible nod. Her lips were pursed in a thin line. Her face was ashen.

'Where did you park?'

'Next to the farmer's field, round the corner,' she said, her voice barely a whisper.

'Okay, go now, before someone spots your car. Please be careful.'

She took a step forward.

'Hey, you should mess the place up a bit,' she said. 'Make it look like a home invasion gone wrong.'

'Good thinking.'

Hayden watched as she staggered off up the driveway. The gate swung shut with a metallic clank, leaving Hayden rooted to the spot in shock. He was shaking, his eyes glazed over as he attempted to process what he had just seen.

He turned and looked fondly at his beloved car. He hadn't known her long, but they had had some good times together, with the top down and the wind in his hair. He ran a hand along the bonnet. Then he leaned over Lexi and started the engine. Her body was blocking the pedals so he walked round to the back and pushed it along the path between the house and the patio.

The Ferrari scraped the fence, but he kept going. It was harder than it looked. He gasped for air, wondering if he should call Daisy back but one more heave and the car gained momentum. There must have been a slight slope, leading downwards towards the pool. He reached into the backseat and retrieved the bag of money, tossing it onto one of the sunloungers.

He looked at the shimmering black depths of the pool and a chill ran through him, knowing what he was about to do. All at once, Lexi jerked in her seat and drew in a sharp intake of air. He shifted his gaze towards her. He'd been so certain she was dead.

He leaned in closer until there was barely an inch of air between them. She was still so young. Her life had only just begun.

His lips barely moved when he spoke, but his words were filled with a lifetime of rage. 'You brought this on yourself.'

His eyes darted around, scanning the river for any sign of movement, a solitary kayaker or jogger who could witness what was about to take place. He found nothing but stillness – now was his chance. He had to make his move quickly because he knew only too well that it could all change in an instant.

He felt like he was going to burst as he pushed against the heavy car with all his might. Ropes of sweat dripped from his brow, and the muscles in his arms bulged from the effort. One. Two. Three. With a guttural roar, the car shuddered and rolled towards its watery resting place, breaking through the pool's surface with an almighty splash that sent waves of cold water crashing around him.

He watched Lexi flounder in the murky water, tangled in her seatbelt, frantically trying to keep her head above the surface. Doubt flashed through his mind like a shadow. Should he help her? But then what? If he let her escape, she'd go straight to the police. At the very least, she'd take the rest of his money.

He recalled his terror at the doll in the pool. How he would have done anything to save that doll, when he thought it was an innocent child. But Lexi was anything but innocent. As he watched her pathetic attempts to stay alive, he felt only revulsion.

FIFTY-TWO

HAYDEN

His phone buzzed in his pocket. He pulled it out and squinted at it in incomprehension. Daisy had just sent him a meme. It had no significance to the crime she'd just committed, and from the looks of it, she'd sent it from her home computer. Which was impossible, considering she'd only left a few minutes before. She must have asked Ted to send it, to create an alibi for herself. That was pretty quick thinking. It was scary how her mind worked.

Lexi had stopped her desperate thrashing. He wondered how much time he had before some passer-by noticed the half-submerged car in the pool. Or perhaps Natalie would be the one to discover the carnage? He would spare her that if he could.

He walked back round to the front of the house and noticed a red smear on the ground. No, this wouldn't do. He steadied his breathing and rushed towards the shed. Where was the bleach? He found it and connected the hose to the outdoor tap, trying not to think too hard about why he needed it. He sprayed the stain with precision, scrubbing away the evidence until there was nothing left but a wet patch on the concrete. With luck, that too would soon be gone.

He strolled into the house and swept a few books off the coffee table, onto the floor. In the kitchen, he grabbed a delicate porcelain mug from a cupboard and hurled it against the wall. He watched in fascination as it bounced off and shattered. He stepped over the pieces and trudged upstairs.

'Natalie! Where are you?'

He checked the bedroom. Natalie was nowhere to be seen but he caught the scent of her perfume.

'Natalie?'

No answer. Maybe she had gone out with Liz.

He yanked out the drawers with enough force to send them crashing to the ground, sending contents in all directions. His eyes narrowed as he marched back into his office and grabbed a chair and upturned it. He kicked the safe with a satisfying thud and left the door hanging open. He picked up a framed picture and hurled it at the window, shocked when the glass panel shattered. They had been led to believe the glass was unbreakable, but it seemed he had found a weak spot. He grabbed the heavy crystal paperweight from his desk and hurled it at another section of the window, relishing the explosion of glass. It was strangely liberating and he looked around for another object, fuelled by a mad impulse to destroy it all.

Afterwards, he went back to the patio and retrieved the bag of money. He didn't really want to lose any more of it, but the home invasion story would be more plausible if Lexi had cash on her.

He grabbed some of the wads of cash and pulled off the elastic bands with a satisfying snap. He tossed the money in the air, letting it scatter into the wind.

He still couldn't shake the fear that no one would believe

him. He needed to be seen as the victim, not the perpetrator. He hurried into the shed and grabbed a pair of rusted scissors. The blades glinted in the dim light. No, the rust would give him an infection. He set them down and picked up a small knife instead. He walked outside, ready to do whatever it took.

He stared down at the blade in his hands, trembling. He glanced around, then quickly pressed the cold steel against his hip. He gritted his teeth and took a deep breath as he moved it up towards his arm. With a sharp intake of air, he felt the blade slice through skin, muscle and tissue. Sweat beaded on his forehead as he fought the urge to scream out in pain.

He looked down at the damage. It wasn't deep enough. Maybe he should try his stomach? But then he'd need to take care to avoid any major organs. He heard a car rumbling up the road. He panicked and drove the knife into his thigh.

White-hot agony ripped through him and he screamed, loud enough to shake the trees around him. He felt as if his body had been injected with acid. His legs wobbled as he reached for the wound and saw that it was already swollen and soaked in thick rivulets of blood. The scent of iron filled his nostrils, and he realised he had nicked an artery. Gasping for air, he ripped off his belt and tied a makeshift tourniquet, attempting to staunch the flow, but it was too late. He was losing too much blood. His vision swirled. He stumbled around in a haze before collapsing into the bushes, the world spinning around him.

FIFTY-THREE

NATALIE

'Nat? Are you listening to me?'

Natalie snapped her attention back to Liz. 'Yes. Yes, of course.'

Liz fixed her with a long look. Her sister always knew when her mind had wandered.

'So, what's happening with you and Andy?'

'Nothing's happening. It never did,' Liz said. 'Some men are off limits.'

'You'll meet someone better.'

Liz shrugged her shoulders. 'I'm perfectly okay on my own, Nat. I don't think I'd want to settle down with someone anyway. I'd hate to share my space.'

'You already share your space with your cats.'

'That's different. They don't drain my energy the way people do. No offence.'

'None taken.'

They approached the tunnel of trees that led towards Natalie's house. It was eerie, how quickly it got dark out here in the evenings, with no lamp light to guide the way.

Hayden's car was not in the driveway. She glanced up at the

house and saw that the lights were on. Something didn't feel right. As Liz pulled the car to a stop, something fluttered onto the windscreen.

It was a Scottish hundred-pound note. Another one whirled towards Natalie as she opened the door.

'What the hell? Hayden? Hayden! What's going on?'

Liz followed her up the path. The door was wide open. She peered inside. The place was a mess but there was no sign of Hayden.

'Perhaps he's round the back,' Liz said. She hastened up the path towards the patio. As she rounded the corner, she let out an almighty shriek.

'What? What is it?'

Natalie hurried after her and glimpsed the Ferrari, poking out of the pool.

'Hayden!'

Her ears buzzed like an old radio and she had a sensation like she was hovering above her own body, before she collapsed to the ground.

She woke up to the sound of sirens.

'You're okay, take your time,' Liz said, leaning over her. 'You've had a shock.'

Natalie looked at the pool and quickly averted her eyes.

'He's not in the pool.' Liz said quietly. She was horribly pale and her breath smelt like vomit.

'Are you okay?' Natalie asked.

Liz swallowed hard. 'Yeah. There are just some things you can't unsee.'

Slowly, Natalie clambered to her feet and they walked round to the side of the house.

She shielded her eyes from the bright lights. Urgent voices spoke in staccato tones. She squinted through the glare, making out the figures in blue and green at the edges of her vision –

paramedics buzzing around. Police officers watching over the scene.

The air around her felt thick and stifling as she forced the words from her throat. 'Where's Hayden?'

A policewoman walked over to her, the fabric of her uniform shifting with each breath. Her voice was gentle when she spoke. 'We are still looking for your husband but someone else has been found in your pool – a woman.'

The shock of the words reverberated through her. 'What... what woman?'

The policewoman gave an almost imperceptible shake of her head. 'We don't know yet. She hasn't been identified.'

'But where's Hayden? That's his car in the pool. He must be here somewhere.'

The policewoman conferred with her colleague. 'We don't know.'

'So he's... missing?' Natalie glanced at her sister for answers but saw the same bewilderment in her eyes.

'Over here!' someone shouted.

Natalie strained to see, watching as the lights of their torches bobbed and weaved among the bushes.

The paramedic had already headed over to where they were clustered, and Natalie watched as they lifted Hayden out of the undergrowth. His face was completely ashen, and his trousers were soaked with blood. She staggered forwards, her head spinning with vertigo and nausea. She held onto Liz's arm for support, swallowing hard against the lump in her throat. 'Oh God, what's happened to him?'

A bloody trail marked the path from the bushes to the place where Hayden now lay on a stretcher. A paramedic knelt over him while another hovered next to them with a med kit at the ready, tools gleaming in the fading light. Natalie stood back, her heart pounding as time seemed to still around her.

'We need to get him to the hospital,' shouted one of the paramedics. 'He's losing a lot of blood!'

Natalie was hysterical, tears streaming down her face. She shuffled towards him and begged to be allowed to go with him, but nobody listened. The paramedics kept on working as they loaded his limp body onto a stretcher and rushed him into the back of the waiting ambulance. It screeched out of the driveway, its siren blaring through the night sky.

Liz put her arm around Natalie. 'Come on. We'll follow in my car.'

FIFTY-FOUR

HAYDEN

Hayden reclined in the comfortable hospital bed, surrounded by crisp white linen. His mind felt foggy and his stitches were sore. Yesterday seemed like a dream now. He wondered if it had really happened at all. When the doctor told him he had nearly bled out, he felt like he must be talking about someone else.

Natalie was at his bedside. She'd nipped out to get him his favourite roast beef sandwich and some grapes. She insisted he eat the grapes. They had magical healing qualities, apparently.

There was a knock at the door and a nurse appeared. 'Hayden, the police are here to speak to you. Are you feeling up to it?'

He felt his throat tighten as he tried to reply. Natalie looked at him with worry evident in her eyes. 'Do you want me to stay?' she asked, hope edging out the concern in her voice.

He shook his head. 'No. Why don't you go home and get some rest?'

She looked dissatisfied. She wanted the full story but he was still formulating it in his head. He reached for the glass of iced water on the table and chugged it down. He needed to ease the tightness in his throat. He needed to maintain his composure.

Natalie pressed her lips to his cheek, lingering for just a moment before reluctantly turning to go. Just then, the door opened and two plain clothes police officers stepped into the room.

The taller of the two – a woman with short dark hair and an austere expression – took the chair that Natalie had just vacated.

'Hi, Mr Peel, I'm DI Sarah McDuff and this is my colleague, DI Fredrick White,' she said in a cool, unemotional tone.

There was a second empty chair in front of White but he remained standing, gripping his pen and notebook tightly.

Hayden's mouth twitched as he attempted a smile. 'I think I spoke to some of your colleagues yesterday,' he forced out, his words thin and trembling despite the effort to keep them steady.

McDuff nodded curtly. 'Right, so we need to go over your statement. Start at the beginning. Tell us exactly what happened from the moment you arrived at your home yesterday evening.'

Hayden swallowed hard, feeling a wave of nausea roll through him as he tried to recall what he'd said before. He'd been careful not to give too much away.

'I drove into the driveway and saw that the front door was wide open. I assumed it was Natalie, so I went inside. The first thing I noticed was that there were clothes and books and stuff scattered across the floor. I bent down to clean up when a strange woman stepped out of the shadows.'

'Who was it?'

'A woman.'

'Can you describe her for me?'

'I only got a brief look at her. She had reddish-brown hair. Really thin. Looked like she might be on drugs.'

'And you'd never seen her before?'

He got a flash of Lexi's naked body. Her long nails running down his back. The sensation of her lips on his.

'Never.'

'So what happened?' the detective asked.

'She came up behind me, knocked me to the floor.'

White looked surprised. 'She must have been strong, this woman?'

He shook his head. 'I wasn't expecting it, that was all. She shoved me and I fell. When I got to my feet, she was already out of my house. She'd stolen a bag of money and she was heading for my car, clearly planning to take it.'

The detective's gaze sharpened and he leaned forward. 'Where were the keys?'

He made eye contact again, his Adam's apple bobbing as he swallowed hard. 'I'd left the top down and the keys were still in the car.'

McDuff arched one brow, an unspoken challenge. 'Are you in the habit of leaving the keys in the car?'

'No. I did it because I was in a hurry to get into the house. Because I had a feeling something was wrong. I didn't know where Natalie was. I was worried.'

McDuff glanced around the room, her eyes narrowed in thought. 'There were no signs of forced entry. How do you think she got in?'

He swallowed hard, wracking his brain for an answer. 'Natalie can be a little absent-minded. It's possible she left it unlocked.'

McDuff nodded slowly, eyes piercing through him. 'So, what happened next?'

'She was trying to steal my car. I opened the car door to try and stop her when she stabbed me. I didn't even realise what had happened at first. I just felt this searing pain in my thigh. I was disorientated. I staggered backwards. I think that's how I ended up in the bushes.'

'And the woman? How did she end up in the pool?'

'I honestly don't know,' he mumbled, scratching the back of his head. 'I thought she'd driven off.'

MacDuff nodded, her breath heavy with resignation. 'Right, well, I think we're going to need you to come down the station and make a formal statement to that effect.'

He bit his lip. 'Okay then. I'm still waiting to be released.'

'Don't worry about that. I'll have a word with the doctor and see if we can speed that up.'

Hayden swallowed. 'How long should it take?'

'If all goes well, we can wrap this up quickly. It's just a matter of repeating what you said and getting it in writing. In the meantime, we'll be viewing the CCTV to see if there are any further clues there.'

'Our CCTV is broken. It doesn't work.'

'The front camera is broken. The back one seems to work fine.'

'The... the back one?'

White raised a brow. 'Maybe you weren't aware of it, but there is a concealed camera that overlooks the back garden. With any luck, we should be able to see exactly how that car ended up in the pool.'

Hayden's stomach heaved. 'Just the back garden?' he asked.

'I believe so.'

He swallowed hard. If there was no CCTV out the front, they would not see Daisy attacking Lexi. It would all be on him.

'You alright?' White asked him.

'Yes, yes, fine thanks.'

He ducked his chin and swallowed hard. He had been so certain there were no witnesses.

'We'd also like to talk to you about some financial irregularities in your bank account. Your wife has kindly given us access and it looks as though you've spent over a million in the last week, divided between cryptocurrency, and a Swiss bank account Natalie knows nothing about. Can you tell me what that was for?'

Hayden's brow furrowed and he shifted uneasily. His heart raced as his mind tried to come up with an answer that would save him. 'I'm not... sure.'

'Okay, well, perhaps your wife can shed some light on that.'

Hayden struggled to breathe. He knew that once Natalie found out the truth, she'd never forgive him. If there really was CCTV, then all his efforts had been in vain. He had stabbed himself for nothing.

FIFTY-FIVE

NATALIE

One Month Later

Natalie stared at her phone. The tension set her teeth on edge as she took in a deep breath and answered.

'Hello?'

'Natalie?'

Hearing his voice, a knot tightened in her chest and tears stung her eyes.

'Happy birthday,' he said softly.

Natalie swallowed, unable to speak.

'I love you,' he added quickly, sending a wave of emotion through her body.

I love you too, she thought. But she couldn't tell him, not after everything he had done.

He couldn't have known about Heather, but ultimately, he had cheated on her, and he had killed her daughter. She could have forgiven him for almost anything else.

'I hope someone made you a birthday cake,' he said.

Oliver had made her a cake but she couldn't bring herself to eat it.

'Hey, did you make a wish?'

She hadn't.

'If I could make one wish, I would give anything to go back in time,' he said. 'Anything to go back to the way we used to be. We were so happy, in our little flat. We had no money but there were no complications. It was just you and me against the rest of the world.'

Natalie clung to her phone. Part of her wished that too. If only they hadn't found that lottery ticket. If only it had stayed in the teapot until it expired. How different would their lives be then?

'Nat?'

'I'm still here.'

'It creates a sort of madness, the money,' he said. 'It takes you over. You're not in control any more, the money is. You can buy anything you want, drive any car. It goes to your head, Nat. It went to my head.'

She nodded, wishing more than anything that there was a way to get a reset.

Today she was forty. She had outlived her mum. But she had lost so much more.

FIFTY-SIX

NATALIE

Two Months Later

Natalie moved Liz's briefcase off the sofa and settled down, cradling a warm mug of coffee. Liz's flat was almost unrecognisable these days. In the two months since Heather died, Liz seemed to have had an epiphany. There were no longer tufts of cat hair everywhere, and only two small cats remained to rule the home. Magnus was draped over a chair while Cookie lay curled in a patch of sun near the window. The air was lightly perfumed with Liz's lemon-scented laundry powder, so much more inviting than the lingering smell of cat pee.

She and Oliver both reached for a custard cream from the packet on the table. She let him have it.

'I saw Hayden's mum in the Co-op this morning,' Liz said.

'Yeah, she rang me,' Natalie said.

Both of Hayden's parents seemed to be in serious denial about what their son had done. His mum in particular kept saying that it was all a big misunderstanding and asking did Natalie think he'd be out by Christmas? It was hard to comfort the mother of the man who had murdered her daughter, but Hayden's mother didn't understand any of that.

'If he's found guilty, he'll get fifteen to life,' Natalie had told her honestly. 'At least, that's what his lawyer believes.'

It felt brutal, dashing her hopes this way, but better she understood what was at stake.

'It's so unfair! I'm never going to be a grandmother!' she'd wailed.

'I saw the Glass House on Rightmove,' Oliver said.

Natalie nodded. 'I was never there anyway. It just didn't feel like home after...'

She had moved into the little flat above the café. It suited her well, and as a bonus, it meant she was never late for work.

Besides, Hayden had squandered over a million before he went to jail, and his legal fees were going to eat up another size-able chunk of the money. She didn't know how much would be left by the time the trial was over. With Hayden refusing to admit his guilt, it was going to be a long one.

She got up to get some sugar from the kitchen and noticed an invitation pinned to the fridge. She squinted at the delicate gold lettering.

'Are you going?' she asked Liz.

'To the wedding of the century? Do I have a choice?'

'I haven't been invited,' Natalie admitted.

Liz raised a brow. 'Seriously?'

Natalie nodded. After what had transpired at the Glass House, Daisy had dropped her like a hot crumpet. It was rather hurtful, actually. She had really thought she and Daisy were friends.

'Well, there's no way Hayden will be able to go, so I bet Ted's pleased about that.' She tapped the date with a polished nail. 'They're getting married at the end of November! Isn't that a bit... strange?'

'Daisy *is* strange,' said Oliver.

'I mean, it might rain.'

'It'll be colder than a witch's tit,' Liz agreed.

'I would have thought they'd wait till the spring,' Natalie said.

Liz shrugged. 'I spoke to Ted at Damon's funeral. He said they wanted to get married as soon as possible and November was the first date they could get with the registry office.'

Natalie had not gone to Damon's funeral. It hadn't felt right. Gail was so consumed by her own grief that she hadn't seemed to notice. Besides, with Hayden's court case coming up, Natalie had every excuse to avoid people.

'You know what I think? I reckon Marian killed Damon,' Oliver said.

Liz and Natalie exchanged a glance.

'What?' Natalie said.

His gaze shifted around the room as if he were piecing together a puzzle. 'Think about it. She could have found out about Heather. In fact, for all we know, Heather told her who her dad was. Then Marian arranges to meet him at the Canary Grand for a drink. He thinks he's going on a lunch date, but Marian has something more sinister in mind. She suggests they go onto the balcony so they can look at the view over the city and the next thing you know, she's shoved him off. He doesn't even see it coming.'

'I think you're talking bollocks,' Natalie said, breaking the heavy silence. 'Besides, Marian was at work the day it happened. I mean, I suppose she could have killed him in her lunch break, but that would be quite some feat. I can't see it myself.'

'Me either,' Liz agreed.

Oliver crossed his arms and huffed. 'I still say she did it.'

'It wasn't Mum. It was me,' said a voice from the doorway.

They all turned and looked. Gail stepped forward. A single tear trailed down her cheek, glinting in the harsh light of the living room. She held a sleeping Scarlett against her chest like a lifeline.

Oliver's jaw dropped open. 'What do you mean?'

Gail took a deep breath before continuing. 'I was at Mum and Dad's when Heather turned up. Dad was outside, painting the fence, and I was pegging out the washing, so I heard everything. She told him she was his daughter, his and Natalie's. He told her she'd got it wrong and that he only had one daughter. She looked at him and told him he was going to be sorry. He backtracked and started apologising, begging her not to tell Mum. It was pathetic. They started talking in hushed voices and I got the impression he promised her something to make her leave. I never let on to Dad that I heard, but I had to sit through Sunday dinner, pretending everything was... pretending everything was normal.'

'I'm so sorry!'

Natalie tried to catch her eye but Gail ignored her.

'I didn't know what to say so I kept quiet, but it was eating away at me, keeping your dirty little secret.'

Oliver stood up from the table. 'Come on now, she was just a kid when all this kicked off. I really don't think you can blame Nat.'

'She knew what she was doing,' Gail said. There was a fierceness to her tone that Natalie had never heard before.

'I decided to speak to Dad in private, somewhere we wouldn't be interrupted. That's how he ended up at the Canary Grand. I invited him to have lunch with me there. I made it sound like a spur of the moment thing because I didn't want him to say anything to Mum. So I met him there, up on the terrace. As soon as he arrived, I told him I knew. He denied it, but I'm not an idiot. It fitted with what I remember, how you disappeared that summer. You were away for months, Natalie, and never really explained.'

'I went to my grandmother's, so no one would know I was pregnant.'

Gail's nostrils flared slightly. 'I told Dad I knew. I told him I wouldn't back down until he finally came clean. He needed to face up to what he had done. Make it right. I wanted him to tell Mum the truth. I wasn't going to let him make a fool of her anymore. She deserved to know. I left as soon as I'd said my piece. I just wanted him to face up to what he'd done but he didn't rise to the challenge. He jumped, rather than own up. He was a bloody coward.'

Natalie hung her head. Tears welled in the corners of her eyes. 'Oh God, Gail. If I could take it back, I would.'

Gail met her eye. 'So would I.'

'It wasn't your fault, either of you,' Oliver said. 'Nobody pushed him. He chose his fate.'

Natalie gulped down air. 'Are you going to tell Marian?'

Gail thought about it for a moment. 'No,' she finally said. 'She's been through enough.'

FIFTY-SEVEN

NATALIE

Six Months Later

Natalie clutched the bag tightly as she walked along the pavement. She was meeting Phillip for a drink later, something she never would have imagined months ago. It was an unlikely friendship, but the events at the Glass House had really shown her who her friends were. After Hayden was arrested, Phillip had been there for her every step of the way. He visited her often at the café, and he was always ready with a sympathetic ear or an encouraging smile – even if his jokes weren't always funny.

From the way Hayden talked, she never would have guessed they were so close, but Phillip really seemed to care. He always asked for updates on Hayden and seemed genuinely concerned about how Natalie was coping on her own. In reality, Natalie wasn't best placed to give him updates on Hayden. She had visited him once, but she'd been warned by his legal team not to discuss the case and there was little else she wanted to know about. Although a part of Natalie still loved him, she couldn't get over the fact he'd cheated and killed Heather, and that wasn't something they could work on.

She pulled out her phone and glanced at her street map. She strolled along the riverside until she came upon an imposing warehouse building. It was made from huge metal panels and had a flag draped across its entrance that displayed the words 'Greenwich Home for Cats'.

Natalie stared at it for a moment, then pushed open the metal doors and stepped inside. The reception area was clean, if a bit neglected. There was a woman with dark hair bent over a pile of boxes in the hallway.

'Hi,' Natalie said. 'Is it okay if I take a look around? I'm thinking of adopting a cat.'

The woman gave her a suspicious once-over, eyes lingering on her high heels and polished nails. Her lips pressed into a thin line. 'Have you owned a cat before?'

'No. This would be my first time.'

'Do you have a garden?'

'No, I'm looking for an indoor cat.'

'Hmm, well feel free to have a look around and someone will come out to talk to you in a bit.'

'Okay, thanks.'

She wandered up the corridor and saw a number of little cabins with runs. There were several black cats, a few tabbies, a white cat and one that looked like the last cat made for the day, with patches of different colours that didn't seem to go together at all.

Her favourite was a black and white cat that appeared to be wearing a tuxedo. She peered into his cabin and he rubbed his head against the bars and mewed at her. He probably wanted to be fed, Natalie thought, but if she didn't know better, she'd have said he was trying to communicate with her. She watched, mesmerised, as the cat tried to poke his paw through the bar.

His bright green eyes begged her to take him home, and Natalie felt a tug on her heartstrings.

She looked around. She'd been here a while and still no staff member had come out to speak to her. They must all be busy. She wandered a little further and found a wall adorned with photographs of staff members. She scanned the corporate chart, her eyes browsing the various names and faces until they rested on one picture – a candid shot of Liz, beaming at the camera and cuddling a kitten. She inhaled sharply and brought a hand to her mouth. Beneath Liz's picture were the words: Liz Butler, CEO.

She marched down the corridor and located her sister's office. She pushed the door open without knocking and immediately spotted her sister sitting in a tall, black swivel chair. Liz's eyes grew wide as she crossed the room in long, determined strides.

'Natalie!'

'When were you going to tell me about all this?' Natalie demanded, setting the briefcase down on the desk. 'You left this in my car. It came open when I went to get it out.'

Liz shrugged, but Natalie spotted a slight tremor in her hands.

'I saw the headers on your paperwork.'

'Yes, I got a great new job,' Liz said, doing her best to sound nonchalant while she adjusted the cuffs of her shirt. 'Aren't you happy for me?'

Natalie took a step closer. 'You've been carrying that bag around for months now. It's not paperwork for the nursery. You don't even work there anymore.'

Liz put out a hand. 'Alright, Nancy Drew!'

'So, I thought to myself, why would you get a new job and not tell me?'

Liz sat there, waiting for her to guess.

'Because you funded this place, didn't you? All that money Hayden sent to Heather. This is what you did with it, isn't it? You set up your own cat charity.'

'Natalie, you're being ridiculous.'

'You were in on it, weren't you? So, when Heather died, it all went to you.'

Liz shook her head. 'You're overworked, Natalie. It's making you sound paranoid. You should take a holiday. Marian won't mind. She can run that café of yours single-handedly.'

Natalie banged her fist down on the table. 'Tell me the truth, goddammit. You owe me that much.'

Liz slowly raised her chin and paused, her lips parted. A moment of tense apprehension hung between them before Natalie realised that Liz was not going to deny what she had said.

'That and Dad's care home expenses,' Liz said.

Natalie's brow furrowed, unsure of what she was referring to. Liz continued, the frustration boiling within her.

'Do you have any idea how much it costs to pay for Dad's care?'

Natalie shook her head in confusion. 'Of course I do. I've contributed every month.'

Liz snorted. 'You "contributed" a hundred quid a month. That didn't even cover one week, and when I asked for more you always made excuses.'

'I was broke! That was literally all I could spare.'

'So where did you think the rest of the money was coming from for all that time, Nat? Was I just supposed to keep putting it on my credit card?'

Natalie leaned forward, her hands on the table between them, and narrowed her eyes slightly. 'If things were that bad, you should have spelled it out to me. Why didn't you explain it to me, Liz?'

Liz heaved a sigh. 'Because it's exhausting, Natalie. It's only recently that you've even deigned to visit the man. He might have made mistakes in the past, but don't forget he was also grieving for Mum. It was a lot for him to deal with, but you wouldn't know, would you? You were never there.'

Natalie hung her head, feeling a rush of shame. She opened her mouth to speak but no words came out. Her throat felt tight, her body tense.

'When I realised Heather was planning to rip you and Hayden off, I wanted in on it. She told me Hayden had offered to pay in crypto and she wasn't sure how to handle it so I offered to help. I was the one who set up her crypto wallet. And when she died, I took it over. I never used a penny for anything frivolous. I never bought any fancy cars or expensive footwear. I didn't buy myself a café so I could play shops.'

'Hey! My coffee shop is doing really well.'

'Only because you hired Marian. Meanwhile, I invested in this place, so I'd finally have room for all the rescue cats people bring me. And I paid off the debts on Dad's care home, and not a week too soon. They were going to move him out of his nice comfy room, into a run-down council facility where he would be living with ex cons and drug addicts.'

'I would have paid! You never asked me.'

'I shouldn't have to,' Liz spat back. 'He's your dad too. Your responsibility. Even if you don't care about him, you should have done the right thing. You didn't even give him a portion of your winnings.'

'I asked him if he needed money and he said no. I didn't think he had a use for it.'

Liz's eyes darkened. 'You didn't ask me. I deal with Dad's finances. He isn't well enough to handle it all himself. I told him he had plenty of money because I didn't want him to worry.'

Natalie leaned against the table, all the fight gone out of her.

'So, what now?' she asked in a small voice.

Liz clenched her jaw and her eyes blazed. 'Go to the police if you want, but if you do, you won't have a sister anymore.'

Natalie held her gaze, her stomach churning as she realised there was no way out of the corner she had been backed into. 'Then I don't have a sister anymore.'

A LETTER FROM LORNA

Dear reader,

As you close the pages of *The Wife's Mistake*, I want to take the opportunity to thank you for reading. I hope you enjoyed spending time in the lives and crimes of Natalie and Hayden.

At its heart, *The Wife's Mistake* is about a couple who are deeply in love but are unwilling to reveal their true selves due to fear and insecurity, which ultimately leads to chaos and heartache; not to mention the loss of their millions.

If this book resonated with you, I'd be immensely grateful if you could leave a short review. Reviews serve as invaluable encouragement for readers who may be considering reading my work for the first time.

To stay informed about new books as soon as they're released, simply click on the link below to join my email list. I won't bombard you with emails or share your address with any third party – I promise!

www.bookouture.com/lorna-dounaeva

If you ever want to catch up with me online, you can get in touch through social media or my website. Thank you once again for reading, and I hope to see you again soon!

Lorna

KEEP IN TOUCH WITH LORNA

www.lornadounaeva.com

facebook.com/LornaDounaevaAuthor

x.com/LornaDounaeva

instagram.com/lorna_dounaeva

goodreads.com/lornadounaeva

PUBLISHING TEAM

Turning a manuscript into a book requires the efforts of many people. The publishing team at Bookouture would like to acknowledge everyone who contributed to this publication.

Audio
Alba Proko
Sinead O'Connor
Melissa Tran

Commercial
Lauren Morrissette
Jil Thielen
Imogen Allport

Data and analysis
Mark Alder
Mohamed Bussuri

Cover design
The Brewster Project

Editorial
Billi-Dee Jones
Nadia Michael

Copyeditor
Laura Gerrard

Proofreader
Liz Hatherell

Marketing
Alex Crow
Melanie Price
Occy Carr
Cíara Rosney

Operations and distribution
Marina Valles
Stephanie Straub

Production
Hannah Snetsinger
Mandy Kullar
Jen Shannon

Publicity
Kim Nash
Noelle Holten
Myrto Kalavrezou
Jess Readett
Sarah Hardy

Rights and contracts
Peta Nightingale
Richard King
Saidah Graham

Milton Keynes UK
Ingram Content Group UK Ltd.
UKHW040837120224
437701UK00004B/208